# ADVANCE PRAISE

"In *Every Man for Himself,* Buffalo has a new hero in Pat Brogan. In Mark Hannon's well-told tale, Brogan works tirelessly to keep the ethnic streets of 1950s Buffalo safe from the bad guys. Readers will enjoy the colorful characters and recognize the places they inhabit."

—Tim Bohen, author of *Against the Grain: The History of Buffalo's First Ward*


"Mark Hannon has written a crime novel that summons a vanished city. Precise, authentic and alive."

—Stephan Talty, author of *Black Irish*


"Mark Hannon's new crime novel about illegal pinball gambling is a fun, full tilt read that will keep you on your toes!"

— Matthew Hobson, Ph.D, author of "The Audubon Guide to North American Suicides," published by the *Baltimore Review.*

# EVERY MAN FOR HIMSELF

*To Kathleen,*
*Enjoy the story!*

*Mark*
*11/10/22*

# EVERY MAN FOR HIMSELF

## Mark J. Hannon

Apprentice House
Loyola University Maryland
Baltimore, Maryland

First Edition

Printed in the United States of America

Paperback ISBN: 978-1-62720-094-3
E-book ISBN: 978-1-62720-095-0

Design: Mary Del Plato
Editorial Development: Alexandra Chouinard
Edited by Elizabeth Leik & Alexandra Chouinard
Author photo: Oleg Panczenko

Published by Apprentice House

Apprentice House
Loyola University Maryland
4501 N. Charles Street
Baltimore, MD 21210
410.617.5265 • 410.617.2198 (fax)
www.ApprenticeHouse.com
info@ApprenticeHouse.com

*To Jerry, Dorothy and Barry*

"Before the destruction of Carthage, the People and the Senate of Rome together governed the Republic peacefully and with moderation. But when the minds of the people were relieved of that dread, wantonness and arrogance naturally arose, vices which are fostered by prosperity. Thus the peace for which they had longed in time of adversity, after they had gained it proved to be more cruel and bitter than adversity itself. For the nobles began to abuse their position and the people their liberty and every man for himself robbed, pillaged, and plundered."

—Sallust, *The War with Jugurtha*

# CHAPTER 1

## THE WEST SIDE, BUFFALO, 1950

Pat Brogan lay back into the worn leather passenger seat of the patrol car and stretched his legs as far as he could, figuring his partner, Ray Zeoli, was squared away to drive. They were rolling over the ice down Niagara Street; the speedometer read twenty-five, and he had just settled his hat forward when the radio crackled. "Units respond to the armed robbery . . ." Ray slammed both feet down, one on the accelerator, the other on the siren switch.

"Take it easy, rookie!" Pat shouted over the siren. "What's the address, how many are there?" He grabbed the door handle as the big Plymouth went around the corner onto Delevan, fishtailing within six inches of a parked car. Pat tried to break in on the radio, but now everyone in the Fifth Precinct was calling in and responding.

"I think he said two suspects at Delevan and Grant," Ray said, slamming on the brakes to avoid a car stopped at a red light and skidding sideways. This time, Ray quickly regained control and roared off around the stopped traffic.

Pat was unbuttoning his long coat to get at his weapon when he spotted a guy with dark hair and a green jacket jogging down the sidewalk. *He's got a gun in his hand,* Pat thought, then shouted, "Stop the car!" Pat popped the door open as the car banged into the curb. Jumping out, he told the wide-eyed rookie, "Keep going to the scene. Get the other guy!"

The guy in the green jacket bolted up Congress, and Pat was glad he had done what the old timers had told him—turn your gun belt around so the holster is in the front and you can get your weapon out quickly from under the reefer coat. He drew the long barreled Colt and went around the back of the car, hesitated, and looked around the corner down Congress for the gunman, whom he thought was toting a .45 automatic in his right hand.

There he was, trying to sprint up the icy sidewalk about fifty feet away. Pat ran after him along the edge of the shoveled part of the sidewalk, getting better traction in the snow. At thirty feet away, the guy slipped, regained his balance, and kept going.

"Stop! Police!" Pat shouted as two women carrying shopping bags full of groceries jumped out of Green Jacket's way at twenty feet. At ten feet, Pat thought, *I've got him*, and then the guy turned and started to raise his pistol. Pat tried to raise his, but collided with Green Jacket just as Green Jacket's .45 went off. Pat grabbed the gunman's wrist and squeezed it as hard as he could as they crashed down on the ice. *I'm stronger than this bum*, Pat thought, as he tried to shake the gun loose, but the guy wouldn't let go. Pat looked into the gunman's red-eyed face and head-butted him just above the nose. He heard a cracking sound as skull met ice, but the guy still wouldn't let go. Pat slammed his head against him again, harder. This time Green Jacket moaned and dropped the gun.

Pushing his knee into Green Jacket's chest, Pat swept the .45 out of his reach. Grabbing the crook's gun arm with both hands, he lifted his knee and turned him over. Reaching under his coat, he fumbled for his handcuffs. *Oh shit*, he thought, *I turned the belt all around. Where are they?* A crowd was starting to gather.

"What's he done?"

"Did he shoot him?"

"What are all the sirens about?"

Finally, Pat grabbed both wrists and yanked Green Jacket up to his feet. The man was bleeding from the front and back of his head.

Pushing the hood around, Pat started leading him back down Congress towards Delevan but realized he'd lost his hat and stopped. Looking around, he saw his hat in one place, handcuffs in another, and the .45 in a third. Dragging the gunman, he scooped up the pistol and dropped it in a coat pocket. He picked up the handcuffs and exhaled while he slapped them on the groaning suspect. A kid ran up and handed him his hat. "Thanks," Pat said to the beaming kid as he put it back on and hoped it was halfway straight. When they got close to Delevan and Grant, five police cars were parked at the scene, lights flashing. Captain Sturniolo was there, standing in the doorway of his car, giving directions over the radio microphone. He spotted Pat and the suspect approaching and waved to Lieutenant Bremer, who turned.

"Emerling, Harrigan, give Brogan a hand with that suspect!"

As they took Green Jacket away, Bremer came up. "You okay, Pat?"

Pat nodded and looked around. Surrounded by police cars was a blue pickup truck with both doors open. On the sidewalk next to it was a fat guy in green work pants and a plaid coat with blood pooling out from under him. Pat felt bile rising in his throat.

"Siddown here on the bumper, Pat," Bremer told him. "You're turning green."

*I'm not gonna throw up*, Pat thought, choking back the puke.

"Holy shit, Brogan, look at this," Bremer said, holding the big collar on Pat's overcoat. There was a hole in it the size of a quarter, all burned around the edges. *Not again*, Pat thought, and retched into the street. Bremer jumped out of the way.

The captain spoke into the radio, "Very well," then to Bremer, "They got the other guy. The rookie chased him right into the hands of the D & D boys over on Lafayette."

Pat looked around again. *What was that noise?* He heard a rolling, clicking metallic sound as policemen walked about the scene. There were several metal boxes and nickels everywhere. Hundreds, maybe thousands of them. *That's what this is about?* he thought, dropping his head to spit out more bile.

# CHAPTER 2

## NORTH PARK, 1950

Father Crotty stood in the sacristy, behind the screen before the entrance to the altar, and listened to the people in the pews. It was where Monsignor Gunderman used to stand just before Mass and listen to the whispers of his parishioners before starting a service. While the Bishop, priests from the Cathedral, seminarians, and acolytes all rushed about preparing for the big ceremony, the parish priest relaxed and watched the people in the pews for a few moments as he adjusted his stole and tied his cincture.

Between the panels of the screen, Crotty could see the front pew where white-haired Joe Brogan sat with his family, straight as an arrow, eyes ever forward, in a three-piece, pinstriped blue suit he must have had since way before the war. Today must be the proudest day of his life, getting made a Knight of St. Gregory. Next to him sat his oldest son, Charley, wearing a brown suit with padded shoulders and lapels as wide as the characters in gangster movies, turning around again and again to see who was there, nodding to those he knew and wishing he could wave to them without his father's growling. To Charley's left was the next oldest, Pat, tall and dark haired, wearing a blue suit not much different from his police uniform. Charley's constant moving was clearly getting on Pat's nerves, probably aggravating a hangover, if Crotty's judgment of Pat's eyes were correct. *I don't know what happened to the boy over there during the war, but it's wearing on him now,* the priest thought. Next to Pat sat Tim, the youngest boy, the failed seminarian. Ever since his earliest childhood, he had sought to please his mother, following her around to all the church functions. He later tried to become a priest, which was her heart's desire. *A bad time of it when his mother died,* Crotty recalled, and then more in the seminary, for the poor boy couldn't grasp the studies and completely collapsed when they told him he had to leave. He still lived at home, taking the bus to his job as a printer's helper at the *Courier-Express* downtown, where his father got him hired after he got out of the sanitarium. Next to Tim was Mary Agnes, slender and blonde in a felt tilt hat, pushing her little brother's hair into place, just as she did when they were children. Her adoring husband, Peter, was there, smiling as always, and he treated Tim as a little child, too, taking him to ball games and such. *Time those two had children,* thought the priest.

His Excellency was ready to begin. A short man with glasses, the ceremonial mitre made him seem bigger. Now he stood at the door to the sanctuary, cross and candle bearing acolytes before him, and when one of the seminarians pulled the bell rope, he led them to the foot of the altar, where, after making the sign of the cross, he began to sing the Mass in Latin, "Introibo ad altari Dei . . ." to which the congregation, and Joe Brogan, with eyes closed, answered, "ad Deum qui laetificat meum juventum . . ."

The pews were filled on this Saturday afternoon, lined with family, friends, neighbors, business associates of Joe Brogan and those who wanted to be. Father Crotty noticed that Joe was smiling now, walking slowly up to the altar rail where he knelt before the Bishop, who would induct him into the Papal Order of St. Gregory instead of giving a sermon. At Joe's request—and Joe was probably the only layman to have this influence on the Bishop—the induction would be brief. *That's Joe for you,* Crotty thought. *No big dinners at the Statler downtown or a High Mass at the Cathedral, but a solemn ceremony, sung in chant at his own parish.*

"After decades of service to his Church . . . including the building of schools, the establishment of new parishes here in the Diocese of Buffalo . . . a lifetime ceaselessly dedicated to alleviating the suffering of the poor and the sick through his mighty works in Catholic Charities . . ."

Crotty remembered Joe's discussions downtown about the big red sash and large cross medallion that came with the award. It was over hamburgers at George's Lunch of all places, where

George did all the grilling on a stove that looked out the front window and waved his spatula at passersby.

"I don't want a bunch of guys in plumed hats banging around with swords, sashes, and all that nonsense," Joe had said, surprising the Monsignor, who planned the diocese's ceremonies. "Just Mass and the pin for my lapel will be fine."

So, now, instead of hanging the grand sash on the man, the bishop was pinning a red and gold pin to his lapel, so small that the audience could barely see it, saying, "Accept this cross and the apostolic service which it signifies . . ." after which Joe stood and faced the congregation, a few tears running down his ruddy Irish face that got the Connelly sisters reaching for their handkerchiefs. Never missed a service, those girls, and like Joe, had moved here to St. Mark's Parish from the West Side, oh, twenty years ago, Crotty reckoned.

Afterwards, when everyone was on the church steps, lighting cigarettes and taking a few pictures, Joe proudly crouched down and showed his new pin to a little boy, his nephew Michael, who seemed baffled by the entire enterprise. "It's an award from the Pope, Mikie. He's made me a knight, you see."

"But where's your armor, Uncle Joe?" the confused boy asked. Those around the child laughed, none louder than Joe Brogan.

Straightening up, Joe spotted a big man with gray curly hair in a dark suit limping down the church steps and went through the well wishers to greet him. When Joe caught him by the elbow, the man stopped and turned, then smiled at Joe. They shook hands, the man bowed his head a little, then went back down the steps and away in a waiting car.

"Wasn't that Monteduro?" Mary Agnes whispered to her husband behind her hand.

"Yeah, I think it was," Peter replied, but all the speculation ceased when Joe returned.

Even Charley, the man about town, looked confused at that last gesture, thinking, *How the hell does the old man know il Zoppo?*

# CHAPTER 3

## THE WEST SIDE, 1902

Joseph Brogan stood in the stable leaning on a shovel, listening to the men load the wagons with milk outside.

"Fookin' heavy today," his cousin Johnny said, swinging the milk can up towards the wagon. "Shite!" he exclaimed, as the big metal can collided with the wagon's gate, falling out of Johnny's grasp, tumbling noisily to the pavement and spilling its contents within moments. The last of the milk was splashing onto the paving stones when the foreman, Mr. Jones, strode down the alley to investigate the commotion. When he saw the gurgle onto the cobblestones, Johnny spotted him and threw himself against the wagon, grasping his lower back with both hands and sliding down the wheel to sit. "Oh, me back," he cried, his eyes clenched shut and his cap falling off.

Jones got up close to him and, smelling the whiskey over the odor of dung from the stable, waved his hand in front of his face and roared, "Whew! You drunken idiot! I thought you were soused when you came in! Just went from the bar straight to work again, eh? Well, this is the last time," he said, as Johnny scrambled to his feet. "Get the hell out of here, you drunken Mick! You've spilled your last can of milk here! Get out!" Jones shouted, as Johnny trotted down the alley, pulling his cap down tightly on his head in the pre-dawn cold. The rest of the men turned back to loading their wagons, some checking that their whiskey bottles were carefully stashed and shaking their heads for poor Johnny as he went past.

The veins in his neck still straining, Jones looked around at the line of wagons being loaded and then back at the stable where

Joe stood with the shovel. "You! Brogan!" he hollered, making the boy jump and wonder what to do with the shovel in his hands. "You know his route, boy?" he said, pointing to the horse at the head of Johnny's wagon.

"Yea, yes," Joe stammered.

"Well, it's your route now," Jones proclaimed. "Get it done right and you might keep it," he said, stomping back towards the office.

Joe thought about what had just happened. One second, he's shoveling shit in a stable, then, the route's his for the taking. Johnny was a drunk, no doubt about it. He wouldn't have made it to work many a time except for Joe, and this wasn't the first job he'd lost from the drink. Joe then realized that he had school that morning after stable work. *No time for that now*, he thought, being a twelve-year-old crammed into a desk meant for six-year-olds. He knew how to read and do his figures already, and he could learn the rest on his own, no need for the embarrassment of going to school with children, no matter what his mother would say. Da would understand; he went to work as a boy younger than Joe.

He finished loading up the wagon with the heavy cans of milk. At first, he tried to swing the cans up onto the wagon bed by the handles like the bigger men did, but after two of them, his strength failed, and the cans banged against the tailboard a few inches from clearing. Not asking for help, and fearing a fate like Johnny's, he began wrapping his arms around the cans near the bottom, squeezing them with all his might. Holding his breath, he lifted them up to the wagon bed with his legs. After three or four, he would climb up in the bed and drag the cans toward the front of the wagon, then hop down to load a few more. The other drivers went about their own work, leaving the boy to fail or succeed on his own. The last to finish loading, Joe hopped up on the seat and stirred the big Belgian to lumber forward, following the other drivers down the alley to Niagara Street, still breathing heavily and fearful of looking over at the office door where Jones stood watching. When the wagon reached Niagara, the drivers would split up and head for their various routes on the city's West Side. The horse pulling Johnny's wagon was named Bismarck, and he was an old horse, but the streets were flat and Joe was his friend. On their way up Niagara, Joe stopped just past a produce stand that was opening up, bought some carrots, and stashed them in the back of the wagon for later.

When they approached Forrest Avenue, Joe didn't even have to turn Bismarck at the corner; the horse knew his job by heart. *I can do this!* Joe thought, doling out the milk to the regular customers and collecting the bills like clockwork from people who were Irish, like Joe; Germans, who gave Bismarck sugar; and Italians, some of whom spoke no English. They met him out on the street with their pitchers for him to ladle the milk, giving Joe four pennies for each dipperful.

Towards the end of his route, Joe turned onto Bidwell Parkway and his stomach got tight. On the right hand side was one of his last stops, the Worths, who lived in a blue house with white columns in front. They had a green lawn, and Joe had seen a black man trimming their hedges. Joe had heard Mr. Jones telling Johnny to get the money the Worths owed the dairy many times, but the first time he knocked on the door, they told him he was to go around back, where Johnny would talk to the cook or the maid and never come back with any money. "They say they'll be sending a man around with a check," Johnny would say. "Very grand people, you see."

Every time Johnny came back with nothing, holding his cap in his hands before Jones, Jones would fume.

"What?! Send a man with a check? Rubbish! Next time, tell them we want the cash and don't take no for an answer!"

This time, Joe had an idea, one he had gotten from reading the newspapers to the old ones on the front porch of his house. He parked the wagon right in front of the house, went directly up to the front door, and, leaving his cap on, pounded loudly on the door, ignoring the twistable doorbell and knocker. A maid answered, a girl with a round, open face with pale, acne-ridden skin; thick legs; and big bright blue eyes, who whispered in an Irish accent for him to pipe down and come around to the back door.

"I'll not," he said. "I've come to talk about business to the Worths."

In the background, he could hear a woman say in a high tone, "Eileen, tell the young man the tradesmen must all go to the back door."

"I did, Missus," Eileen said, "But he says he has business with you," at which point the door flew open and a skinny, silver-haired lady wearing a starched white blouse and pearls around her neck came up. She saw the wagon in front and Joe on the step.

She turned to the maid and said, "Take Harold to the nursery, Eileen," who then pushed a little boy, who was watching, up a wooden staircase.

Then, turning to Joe, she said, "Young man, if Cooper's Dairy wishes to continue having our business, you will pull that wagon away from the front of our residence, and you will go to the back door."

Taking a deep breath, Joe spoke, "Mrs. Worth, if you don't pay the Cooper Dairy seven dollars and eighteen cents right now, Mr. Jones is going to have your name printed in the newspaper with the other people who don't pay their bills."

Mrs. Worth clenched her fists at her side and tried to stare the boy down, but he only looked her back in the eye. After a few seconds of this, she spun on her heel and stomped off, ordering Eileen to come with her, which she did, smiling behind her hand.

Joe waited on the doorstep for what seemed an eternity, worrying that he had to get the wagon back, but the door was still ajar. Finally, Eileen came back with the money, which she carefully counted out and left on the table by the door, insisting, almost as haughtily as the mistress, that he write out a receipt before getting it. He wrote the receipt, and after counting the money himself, shoved it in his coat pocket, thinking he caught a glimpse of a smile on Eileen's face at the last moment. He tripped back to the wagon, where Bismarck was nodding his head, impatient to get home.

Whistling on his way back to the dairy, Joe sat straight so all the people on the West Side could see him. He was glad he could read, and even gladder that the old folks would have him read all the newspaper to them, from the news of the war in the Philippines, to the column where they listed the bad creditors, for there was no better amusement than to read where some important person had fallen and had gotten embarrassed publicly, especially if he had an English name.

On the way down Niagara Street, Joe remembered the carrots and stopped by the firehouse. He asked a fireman named Herman, who was sitting at the watch desk sporting a mustache that a walrus would envy, for some water. There were horses in wire cage stalls along the inside walls of the firehouse, munching on their hay.

Joe fed his horse the carrots, and when Herman came out with a bucket of water, he said, "Bismarck, old friend. We used to work downtown together, at Hook and Ladder One. Now, we work on the West Side, but for different companies, no? You take good care of my old comrade, young Joe. He's old, but a good worker."

Joe and his partner returned to the dairy, Joe sitting tall in the seat, *a mighty man, indeed,* as Da would say.

# CHAPTER 4

## THE WEST SIDE, 1905

Teresa Monteduro finished washing her little boy, Torreo, scrubbing his legs thoroughly, and helped him get dressed in clean clothes. Happy at the attention, the five-year-old boy looked up at her and hugged his mother. She hugged him back, asking the Blessed Mother to please make her little boy well. The exertion had tired her, and she was wheezing when she got to the front door. She steadied herself by holding onto the frame as she tried to call out for her other boy, Rafaele. Nothing but a rasp came out. She snatched her handkerchief from her dress pocket to dry up the blood-tinged sputum on her lips. Struggling to draw a breath, she waved over to her friend Melissa sitting on the porch next-door, who was happily bouncing her infant daughter Katarina on her knee. When Melissa saw her wave, she came down the steps and over to the front yard, keeping a distance between the sick woman and Katarina.

"What is it Teresa?"

Teresa filled her lungs once, then again, and tried to speak.

"Rafaele . . ."

"You need Rafaele, Teresa?"

The sick woman nodded, still holding herself up in the door frame. Her friend began bellowing out the older boy's name, in one direction and then the other.

A few moments later, the gangling teenager appeared from between the houses down the street, and approached with an unsteady gait. *Drinking again*, Melissa thought. *Everything happens to poor Teresa.*

"Rafaele, come over here. Your mother needs you."

When he walked by, Melissa shook her head, smelling the wine on his breath. He went up the steps and into the house, knowing his duty. His mother got into a chair and nodded.

Torreo smiled at him when he came in and latched his arms around his neck when he bent over to pick him up.

"Oh, you're getting to be a big boy, Torreo," Raefaele said. "We're going to see Dr. Rodems today, Torreo. He's over on Richmond."

Carrying his little brother outside, Rafaele carefully placed him into the wagon in the backyard and pulled him between the houses to the sidewalk in front of the house. They began their journey down the street from the cramped, wooden two-story houses on Connecticut over to the spacious brick residences on Richmond. Rafaele pulled the handle silently, turning around occasionally to see his little brother smile at him. They stopped for Mr. Anzalone's fruit wagon at the corner of Normal and Connecticut, and Rafaele picked up the boy to let him stroke the horse's mane as Mr. Anzalone held the bridle steady.

Rafaele pulled the wagon down Connecticut Street. As they crossed 15th, a boy with torn coveralls saw them coming and ran back down the alley in his bare feet, where he found his older brother and two other boys, who had taken all his marbles a few minutes before.

"Hey! It's the Cripple and Staggers! They're comin' down the street right now!"

The three shooters snatched up their marbles and ran gleefully with the barefoot boy to the street. When Torreo saw them, his limbs stiffened and he cried out, "Ahhn," getting Rafaele's attention. The elder brother looked up from his trudging to hear the four starting to shout.

"Crip, crip, cripple! Crip, crip, cripple!"

"Get outta here, you little bastards," Rafaele shouted, waving his free hand and trying to speed up.

The four kept shouting, "Crip, crip, cripple!" and then the two older boys ran into the street. Picking up horseballs, they proceeded to heave them at Torreo and his brother. While the older brother shielded his face with his arm and caught the first clump on his sleeve, a second splattered on Torreo's ear, its wet center clinging to his curly hair and dripping down onto his freshly scrubbed neck and clean shirt.

Ladling milk into a pitcher, Joe Brogan spotted the one kid scoot between the wagon and Bismarck and scoop up some fresh horse dung. Following him with his eyes, Joe saw the boys dancing around the little wagon with the crippled boy and his brother, flinging shit at them.

"Hey!" he shouted at the bullies while the housewife he was serving started screaming at them, as well.

"Merdosos monstros!" she screamed, as Joe went after the kids, who were continuing to run about the wagon. Catching one, Joe grabbed him by the collar and kicked him in the behind as hard as he could swing his leg, driving the boy head over heels across the pavement. The housewife charged as well, screaming obscenities and swinging her fists to drive them away from the helpless brothers.

The four bullies scampered away, laughing. Torreo's face was wet with tears and feces, clods of horseshit on him and the wagon. Rafaele cried, too, and tried to wipe away the dirt from the little boy's sobbing face with his hands.

"Bring him inside, we'll wash the baby," the housewife said, and Joe picked up the little fellow, who clung to him, crying. Rafaele followed, still pulling the wagon. Inside, Joe put Torreo on the sink board, and the woman took his soiled shirt off him and washed the shit away.

"I'll go find him a clean shirt. You watch him, Joe." "You okay now, little guy?"

Stifling his sobs, Torreo nodded.

"They aren't going to bother you any more, the dirty little bastards."

Coming back with a clean shirt, Mrs. Lano said, "Those boys are no good. Always stealing stuff, wrecking things. No good." She continued in Italian, drying Torreo off with a towel and pulling the clean shirt over his head.

Carrying Torreo outside, Joe saw Rafaele tilting the wagon sideways, sweeping the horse dung out with his hand.

"Hey, Mrs. Lano, do you have a rag we can clean this with?" Joe asked.

She nodded, and when she came outside with a wet rag, she started jabbering rapidly in Italian at Rafaele, who kept his head down while he wiped out the wagon. When he was finished, Rafaele nodded as Mrs. Lano continued her lecture, wagging her finger at him. When they finally went on their way, Torreo turned himself around in the wagon and waved at Joe and Mrs. Lano, who shook her head.

"It's a shame. That baby's got no one to look out for him, Joe."

"That little fella's going to have a rough time of it, Mrs. L."

# CHAPTER 5

## THE WEST SIDE, 1912

From the stable where Cooper's Dairy kept the horses, Joe liked to look out the back door at the canals and the river at the end of the day. He loved the way the mighty Niagara flowed—strong, swift, and ceaseless as it rushed northward from Lake Erie to the Falls, uncontrolled by any man. In contrast, the new Barge Canal seemed almost sedentary, protected from the River with a break wall. Tugs pulled barges there, steaming up and down carrying coal, hay, and ore. Further inland, parallel to the Barge Canal and forgotten by modern commerce, the original canal was green with algae in parts, but perfect for fishermen and boaters, who built shacks along the towpath. On the land farther in still, just off Niagara Street, the modern age took hold once again, as locomotives' whistles screamed and their stacks spewed black smoke along the tracks of the New York Central, occasionally stopping at Ferry Street to drop off passengers for the boats going over to Fort Erie in Canada.

Joe noticed that, in the last hours of sunlight, a group of young guys had been gathering on Bird Island between the canals and were building a house there made of old lumber hauled to the site by the wagonload. By the middle of the summer, the "clubhouse," as they called it, was built, and the same men were showing up with skinny boats with long oars attached, pulling up and down the canal. The clubhouse had a fancy gray and maroon sign advertising it as "The West Side Rowing Club."

On a Saturday afternoon in August, Joe stopped by to see if the horses were fed and watered properly, and noticed a crowd of people gathering by the clubhouse: girls in white dresses with parasols; and boisterous young men, some in colorful tank suits and others in white shirts, wearing bowler and straw hats. The athletes were carrying boats and oars to the canal, and the men in street clothes were drinking beer and shouting encouragement to the rowers in green, blue, and maroon uniforms as they prepared for their races.

His stable inspection completed, Joe walked over to the foot-bridge to Bird Island and watched. The rowers were getting into their boats, and some of them were pulling short distances up and down the canal.

"They're still warming up, we're not too late," Joe heard from behind, as a group of people hustled over the bridge to the Island, festooned with blankets and baskets. One of them, a girl wearing a white dress with a big black belt, was holding the dress up at her wide hips, showing thick white ankles, hurrying along. A breeze caught her purple hat, and as she turned to catch it, Joe recognized the Worth's maid, Eileen. She cried out "Oh!" as she snatched it, and smiled as he said, "Hello," and touched the brim of his cloth cap. She nodded, then turned and hurried to catch up with her friends.

Joe walked the rest of the way across the bridge and stood at the edge of the crowd. The men were gallused and cigar chomp-ing, talking of the several clubs' prospects in what they called the "regatta," just like the rich men's sail boat races on the lake. They also spoke of their prospects with the women, who gathered on the blankets with the picnic baskets nearer to the water. In the crowd, Joe spotted Pete Gilhooly, a plumber, who had a shop with Joe's brother, Mike, on Niagara.

"Hello, Pete, what kind of show are you putting on here?"

"Why, Joe, how are you lad?" he said, pumping his hand. "We finally got the club together enough for some racing on the canal, boyo. Crews from the Celtic and Mutual from the First Ward are here to see if we can keep up with them. Say," he said, tapping the back of his hand against Joe's chest, "you're in right good condi-tion. You ought to think about joining."

"I dunno, Pete, awful busy with work these days. I'm foreman over at the dairy, y'know."

"Aw, c'mon. I know you boys at the dairy start early and you lay off work about midday. It'd be perfect for you, lad."

"Well, I got to think on it, Pete. Are those your boys in the dark red there?"

"It is. The Celtic lads are in green, and the Mutuals—you don't have to be Irish with them, but it helps," he winked, "are in green and black. They've been at this a lot longer than us," he said, hooking his thumbs in his suspenders and nodding, "but I think our boys will give them a good showing today, I do."

"So," Joe smiled, "how is it you're not out there this fine day, Peter?"

Leaning slightly forward at the waist, Pete answered, "Didn't make Crew Number One this time. Some Dago named Torreo Monteduro beat me out, gimp and all. C'mon, I'll get you a beer," he finished, leading Joe over to the clubhouse.

*Huh*, Joe thought, *could it be the same kid?* Looking over to where the West Side crew was assembling, he spotted a youth with dark curly hair, a powerful upper body, and one emaciated leg from the knee down among them. *Damned if it isn't*, he thought. *The kid made it.*

He walked into the clubhouse with Pete, who brought him a beer from the long table that was a makeshift bar. The windows were all open, and the light streamed in onto the mostly bare, dark wood walls. On one side, there were a number of long oars hanging on the wall, and on the other, a lone boat.

"Like I said, we're just getting started, so we don't have much in here in the way of furniture and trophies and the like."

"I was gonna say, it looks like you've got a good start, Pete. Where'd you get all this nice wood?" Joe asked, running his palm over the stained oak wall.

"Ahh, that. You know All Saints Church over on Henrietta? Well, when they built the new one, they tore down the old one and donated the lumber to us to build this place. It seems Mitch Peterson's da is big over there, and his company got the contract for the demolition of the old building. Mitch is captain of our eight-man crew and quite the sculler, ya see. We all pitched in to help tear it down after work in the evening. That brought the price down to Mitch's da, who discounted the job to the church, and we get the wood—one hand-washing the other, as it were."

"Very nice. You lads are here every evening, then?"

"During the week, after work. Saturday mornings at dawn." Pete added, "Only one dollar for initiation fees, then fifty cents a year dues. Meetings second Friday night of the month, and we

usually get a barrel of beer and some food."

"Lemme think about it, Pete," he said as they went back outside into the blazing sunshine. Walking towards the old canal, Pete spotted another prospect and hailed him, and Joe ambled over towards the blanket where Eileen and her friends sat. Spotting him approach, she nodded her brown curly head to him and continued talking to her friends. Walking to about a yard away on her right, Joe crouched down to watch the race just beginning. Looking out at the boats, he commented, "I hear all these lads on the other teams are from the First Ward."

"Yes, that's them," said the friend to Eileen's left, "and every one of them on the Celtics an Irishman."

"The Mutuals have many Irish, too, Bridy. Their captain, Bob

Cotter, for one."

"So where are you girls from?"

The two girls looked at each other then took up the challenge.

"Over here or back home?" Bridy answered. "Well, both, if it's your pleasure to tell me."

"She," indicating Eileen with her parasol, "is from Crusheen in Clare. I'm from Limerick City," she said, tossing back her blonde hair. "Now, we both live in St. Brigid Parish here in Buffalo."

"Ah, I see," he replied. "I'm from Cork City, myself."

The girls both looked at each other again, and then Bridy pulled her head and neck backwards like a swan and said, "No, it couldn't be. You talk like an American, sure."

"No, it's true," Joe said smiling. "I was born in Cork. I came over when I was nine, so everyone thinks I'm from here."

"Ohh, I see," continued Bridy. "Many's the one sailed out from Cork, or just heard of the place, and said it was their home."

"No, it's true. We lived in the Commons Road in Cork City. The da worked there, doing stonework. When he had the readies saved, he booked us passage here. We sailed on the *Majestic* out of Cobh Harbor, an iron ship with great canvas sails . . ." he hesitated, remembering bad food and sickness.

"Well, where do you live now, great sailor that you are?"

"Oh, over here," he said, indicating with a stick the neighborhood beyond Niagara Street, "on the West Side. In Holy Angels Parish."

The girls' friends were now passing out sandwiches among the picnickers, and Eileen finally looked up and said, "Would you care to have one, Joe?" which caused Bridy to look at her in amazement.

"Joe, is it?"

"Yes," he answered, touching his cap. "Joe Brogan. And I'd love one, thank you, Eileen," at which Bridy sat back on her haunches, looked at one, then the other, and wondered what else she had missed.

The bills to Cooper's Dairy had been promptly paid by the Worths since Joe's confrontation with the Mistress (as Eileen called her) years before, and Joe tried to run that route as often as possible in addition to his foreman duties. He frequently saw Eileen, who made sure she snatched the pitcher from the kitchen to get the household's milk. They didn't talk much, almost all business during the transactions (especially if some busybody like the boy Harold should be listening), but Joe finally figured out that she took the Elmwood streetcar to get home, and she left work around seven at night.

Rushing away from dinner several nights, he made it a point to be walking along Elmwood where she'd have to pass to catch the car at Bidwell a few minutes after seven, until one night he saw her rushing up the street to catch the car. She had just missed the clanging streetcar as it made its way south, and he walked up and said, "Heading south?"

Startled, she answered, "Oh, it's you. You gave me a fright."

"Sorry, Eileen. If it's okay, I'll wait here with you until the next one comes."

"Yes, well, that would be all right I suppose. It's starting to get dark earlier."

"Yes, it is," he answered, and both of them looked around.

"Does it take a long time to get home from here?" he finally asked.

"Oh, no, you'd be amazed at how soon I get downtown and change to the Elk and South Park car at Washington and Seneca, and then it's a hop, skip, and a jump home. If I catch the streetcars right, you see."

"Oh."

"Some nights, though, I stay at the Worths', if they have a late affair with guests and all. They put us up in the maids' quarters in the attic. You've seen her then. Anna? The Polish girl?"

"Yes, yes, I have. She is very . . . tall."

"She is. And fine blonde hair, like my friend Bridy."

"Uh, yes, she does." After a moment, he said, "Do you like working for the Worths?"

"It's a good position. The Mistress likes to act very high and mighty, but you get used to that in service. There's many a girl who's done worse, I can tell you that."

Hearing the clanging of a streetcar, Joe looked up the street as her car approached.

"Well, I walk this way quite often in the evening about this time. Do you suppose we might walk a block or two to the next stop some time?"

As she climbed aboard, Eileen answered, "Yes, but don't come by the house anymore if you can. The old lady hates you and gets in a lather every time she sees you. Goodbye, Joe!"

"Goodbye, Eileen," he waved, "I'll be back here again tomorrow night." The other passengers looked at them and smiled.

# CHAPTER 6

## THE WEST SIDE, 1917

When the wagons were all out on their routes, and Joe had finished the books, he took a break and walked over to the Rowing Club. He hadn't gone to the Friday night function last night. *Those guys will stay there until they get the last drop of beer out of the keg*, he thought. *Too much for me nowadays*, as he thought of his wife at home.

When he approached the clubhouse, he heard someone inside dragging furniture, and was surprised by the sight of broken glass and shattered windows. The inside of the club was a shambles—chairs busted up, tables knocked over, bottles and glasses all over the place. Pete Gilhooly was in the process of turning one of the tables upright and, as he did, Joe noticed the bruise around his left eye that seemed to be turning blue, green, and yellow as he looked at him.

"Jaysus, Pete, what the hell happened here?"

"Ah for fook's sake, Joe, you missed it last night," he said, straightening up and stretching his back, pulling up the suspenders over his long johns shirt.

"What's the other guy look like?" Joe jibed, jerking his chin at Pete's face.

"Which one?" Pete smiled back. "It was a regular Donnybrook, that's for sure. Those boys from down in your wife's old neighborhood, down in the Ward, came by, knowing we have a good feed and beer Friday nights. A few of the Mutuals, but mostly the Celtics, and they'd been drinkin' on their way here as well."

"Oh boy . . ."

Rubbing his chin, Pete organized the details of the conflict in his mind and continued. "Well, they're all welcome as good sports-men and all, and we're having a good time with the beer flow-ing and some real good beefsteaks and sausages and salami that we'd got, and naturally, there's some talk as rivals do, no problems there. Then, one of the Celtic lads, I think his name was Gerry, said something about our having Dagos in the club, and as you might expect, the gimp gets upset at this and tells Gerry, I think that was his name, anyway . . . to shut his Pig Irish trap, and that's about all it took for those two. Well, Gerry gets up and throws a punch at the gimp, and the gimp doesn't even feel it, he's so mad. Grabs your man Gerry by the neck and the crotch and tosses him, hmm . . .," looking around, he finally pointed to one of the shat-tered windows on the river side of the clubhouse, "through that window, I think.

"Well, their boys all jump up at that one and rush the gimp. He bein' a member in good standing and all, we jump up and the battle's on." Pulling his right fist back to his chin, he continued, "I had the one guy by the collar with my left, you see, and was just about to give him the right when someone threw a great heavy mug and got me where you see here," touching his swollen face proudly. "The room spun, I saw stars and just started swinging for me life. After a few minutes, everyone tumbles outside and the lads get wrestling on the ground." Shaking his head, Pete went on. "I think our more judicious use of the gargle then paid off, as their boys started getting winded and eventually retreated back to the mainland, as it were. We held our own, we did," but looking at the damaged clubhouse, even Gilhooly thought the damage may have outweighed the glory. "Next time," he vowed, "we'll go down there and give them a what for."

"I dunno if that's such a good idea, General," Joe commented.

"What? And let those guys think we're cowards? We'll bring the whole club, every one of us man and boy. We'll show 'em."

"Ahhh, Pete. If you bring twenty guys down there, they'll have fifty. You bring fifty and they'll get every Mick from Exchange Street to the Buffalo River, all of 'em with clubs and bottles wait-ing for you."

Pete considered this possibility, and Joe finished, "Look, lemme go back to work. When I get off, I'll come back and give you a hand cleaning up this place. Anyone else coming by to help?"

"Uh, yeah, I got hold of a few people who said they'd be by shortly."

"Well, look, I'm the treasurer this year, so take a few dollars and go over to Winegar's Hardware and get some glass panes, some putty, and a box of glazier's points so we can fix these windows. At least they didn't smash the sashes up."

Joe left, thinking how he used to drink when he was single like Gilhooly, but he'd never been as much of a boozer or a brawler like these guys. The gimp, he thought, was a pretty tough customer these days. A lot different from the crippled little boy he used to be. Joe also thought about how much having a wife had changed him as he went back to work, and how much happier he was with his life that way. He chuckled, thinking, *yeah, much better having a wife than having a three-colored shiner as a trophy like Gilhooly.*

# CHAPTER 7

## BUFFALO, 1918

Torreo balanced on his spindly right leg and pushed with his left foot to roll the two-hundred-pound beer barrel up the ramp onto the wagon, then gripped the top and tilted the oak keg upright against the others. *Last one today*, he thought, the middle kegs stacked straight, the outside row of barrels tilted inward for balance, as the old Germans had taught him.

He hopped down from the wagon and watched a boy lead the team of horses slowly to the front of the great, heavy, wooden vehicle. Torreo mopped his brow with a big, red kerchief, thinking, *Better you than me* to the lumbering Percherons as they were readied to drag the heavy, oak wagon and the barrels of beer out to Buffalo's countless saloons.

A small, blond-haired boy came running up to Torreo with a tankard of cool water. The boy, a grandson of the brew master, found the horses; the immense vats of frothing beer; and the incredibly strong men who would lift and move the wooden kegs of beer all day fascinating. Torreo was his favorite of all of them—the exotic dark Italian amongst the fair Germans, the one who seemed to be busting out of his shirt when he flexed, and whose one leg was as strong as most men's two. He had seen him do tricks at company outings when the men would try feats of strength, balancing picnic tables while standing on one leg, or seeing how many people they could lift off the ground hanging from their mighty arms. "Being big is good," Torreo would whisper to him as they watched the other competitors, "but the one that can balance the weight is the strongest."

Torreo took the water and tousled the boy's hair, and the two of them followed the other men into the beer garden, where they relaxed over the free beer the owner supplied at the end of the day. Torreo always drank a couple of pints of water first, especially in the summertime, or his head would spin on the walk home. The boy, Phillip, ran up to the serving table, refilled Torreo's water tankard, and grabbed one of the beers, which he carefully carried over to the long tables where the men sat. Running back to the serving table, his cousin Marta tried to give him a tumbler of birch beer, which he hesitated to take.

"No, no," one of the other bartenders said, "put it in a tankard, girl, like the men have!"

Marta complied, worrying how long it would be before the boy started drinking beer, like the men. Returning to the table, Phillip squeezed in between Torreo and Hans, a special place at a special time of day for him, when he was among the strong men he hoped to become.

After a few minutes of work talk, the subject turned to sports, with arguments bolstered by quotations from the newspapers. Some men liked baseball, some horses, and some boxing, but the favorite sports in this crowd were wrestling and bowling, by far. The company had several bowling teams. They played on the grass in summer and indoors in the winter. The wrestling matches were arranged with workers from other breweries, and rivalries between their individual champions were the talk of the town.

"So, Torreo, what do you think of Steinegar's chances against Getman next week?"

"I hope he's learned to go for the legs, or Getman will twist him into a pretzel."

Hearing this, several others expressed surprise and guffawed, as young Steinegar was the one among them who would hold up a corner of a wagon as they changed a wheel and was thought to be invincible.

"Awf, that's silly. When Heinz Steinegar gets hold of Getman's wrist, even, the match will be over!"

"Charge, get him around the waist, throw him, and it'll be over, I say," another said through a gathering cloud of cigar smoke.

"He'd better watch out for Getman's dodges, because I've seen him do it to lots of stronger men," Torreo continued to Phillip's rapt attention. "He'll feint you and keep escaping until you get tired, then sneak around behind, grab a leg and an arm, and tip you over like a turtle."

The discussions went on like this for some time, the beer flowing and the smoke filling the place. Phillip ate it all up, tilting the tankard of fresh birch beer back until its effervescence got in his nose. When the men started moving the tables off to the side to practice the moves they spoke of, Torreo finished his beer and slipped out of the place quietly. He had tried wrestling with them, but the others had learned that his gimpy leg would sooner or later betray him, despite the might in his other three limbs. As he walked down Niagara towards his house, he went past the Rowing Club. He hadn't been back there since the battle with the South Buffalo boys. *Silly Irishmen with their rowing. Silly Germans with their wrestling.* He had too much to do to waste time on games. The sun was still strong in the summer sky as he walked, and he paused to wipe his brow again with his kerchief, when he thought he would stop by the café, where his brother worked, and get a glass of wine. He smiled that Rafaele was working and wasn't drinking as much.

As he turned the corner on Jersey, his joy turned to concern, for Raffie had been from job to job, and he wondered if his older brother would ever be able to take care of himself. His pace quickened as he walked under the canopy of maple leaves that covered the street, and when he saw the café's glass front window, he stopped and looked in from an angle where he wouldn't be observed. The front door was open, and the voices inside were boisterous and laughing. He saw two men sitting at a small round table in the corner. They were wearing black suits with white shirts buttoned up to the neck and no neckties. One was young with slicked-back hair and darting eyes. The other was older, with a big mustache and a wide-brimmed fedora. Rafaele stood in front of them, his back to Torreo, who quietly entered the plank-floored shop and stood in the doorway. The younger man stared at Rafaele, then swept the small coffee cups in front of him to the floor. Rafaele tried to step back, but stumbled off balance and crashed into the table behind, knocking the cups there all about as the occupants jumped out of the way.

"This isn't café," the younger man said with a thick accent from the old country, "It's mierda! Can't you damned Americans make decent espresso?"

Rafaele sat on the floor and started to push himself up as the older man laughed.

"I'm sorry . . .," Rafaele began, and the young man's black eyes danced. He grabbed a sugar bowl off another table and threw it at Rafaele, who sat back down and crossed his arms before himself and started to weep. No one else in the cafe moved or said anything, and the older man continued to laugh.

"Damned drunk, clean up this mierda and get us some real café," the young man screamed, his face reddening.

Torreo couldn't move at first. He couldn't believe what he saw. He took a deep breath, and then the raging man with the slicked back hair saw him.

"What do you want, you stumbling fool?" he said as he reached into his pocket. The older man looked up and his laughter slowed. Torreo leapt across the floor just in time to backhand the young man's knife across the room with his left arm as he slammed his right fist against the man's face, driving it into the wall behind him, where it ripped the wallpaper. He then seized the man's face with his callused hand, covering it from jaw to eyes, and slammed the sputtering man's head against the wall three, four, five times as the crumbling plaster fell to the floor. The people in the cafe started to scream, and the older man struggled to get out of his seat, reaching into his jacket pocket. Torreo caught this out of the corner of his eye and let the wounded man slide down the wall, unconscious and bleeding. He grabbed the older man's arm at the wrist and the elbow, and twisted his arm ninety degrees until it snapped, and a revolver fell to the floor. As the mustachioed man crumpled to the floor, moaning, Torreo punched his face as hard as he could, cracking his jaw.

The aproned cafe owner ran over and threw his arms around Torreo. "No, Torreo, stop! You must stop or you'll kill them!" Torreo threw him off; looked at the battered men; the shocked customers bailing out in all directions; and his brother, sobbing on the floor.

"I'm sorry, Torreo. I'm sorry. I failed again," he wept.

Torreo stopped, and then helped his brother to his feet. Brushing him off with his hands, Torreo put his arms around him and led him out, saying, "It's ok, it's ok. I'll take care of it," as they went home to the flat where they were raised.

Twenty minutes later, the owner of the cafe came through the Monteduros' backyard, hustled up the back steps, and knocked rapidly on the kitchen door. Rafaele sat at the kitchen table, a glass of water in front of him. Torreo stood at the sink, massaging his hands silently.

"Torreo, it's me, Frankie, from the cafe."

"C'mon in."

"Torreo, we gotta talk about this. Those two guys, they're bad men. They're mano negro. The young guy, he's still out. They took him to the hospital; he may not live. The other guy, he's Pietro Sciandra; everyone knows him."

"Shit on them; they're garbage," Torreo said, getting mad again.

"In that case, here," Frankie said, and, opening a towel, dumped the knife and the gun from the cafe onto the kitchen table. "You, cazzo motto, are going to need them."

Rafaele stared at the heavy weapons on the table, and Torreo came over and picked up the big revolver, looking it over. Frankie stepped back, edging towards the door.

"Don't worry, Frankie. Those bums aren't going to bother you, or us, anymore."

# CHAPTER 8

## BUFFALO, 1918

When the police got called to Columbus Hospital, they recognized the battered, young hoodlum immediately, but he never recovered consciousness, and died that night. There was another guy there, an older guy, getting his arm set who one of the detectives, Packy Mulhern, recognized.

While the other officers gathered information about the dying man, Packy walked over to the older man and asked, "What happened to your pal Sciandra?"

His eyes danced in pain but none of the hairs in his handlebar mustache moved.

Packy leaned over close and smelled the spilt coffee.

"Jersey Street Cafe, huh?"

The older man's eyes blinked, but he said nothing.

Packy nodded and went to the other detectives, who were writing notes. "You guys get the rest of the information here. I'll see you at the station house later," he said, tugging his derby down tight.

When Packy walked into the cafe, everyone started speaking Italian. The place was clean, but the plaster on the wall was still busted. Frankie came over to him, and Packy pointed to the wall and said, "Who busted up Sciandra and his boy Frankie?"

"Huh? I don't know what you're talking about, detective. That wall is old. I just gotta find time to fix it. Ask anybody."

"Uh, huh." Packy asked the rest of the staff if they'd seen anything, but all he got were shaken heads and a lot of muttered Italian behind him.

As he walked up the steps at the Tenth Precinct, he ran into a patrolman named Dave Barone, who was getting off duty. "Hello, Dave, gotta minute?"

"Sure, Packy, whatcha need?"

"What does 'zoppo' mean in Italian?"

"Zoppo? It means cripple, or gimp."

"How about 'barcollante'?"

"That means staggering."

"And 'ubriconte, ubricone,' something like that . . . "

"Oh, you probably mean 'ubriacone.' That means a drunk; a sot."

Packy snapped his fingers, tucked a cigar in Dave's pocket, and went inside. *I find this gimp and a drunk waiter and I've got it solved,* he thought to himself.

It took Packy another week of asking around to find the Monteduros, as they weren't on any policeman's list of suspects for anything, but find them, he did. He had them both locked up. They never said anything, not even the one going through "the horrors," convulsing and screaming as the alcohol left his system. Without anyone talking, the police let them go: the waiter first, and then, a week later, the gimp.

When he got home, Torreo went into the house and found Rafaele lying on his bed, mouth and eyes open, bottles scattered around the floor. Torreo put his hands on his brother's shoulders to shake him, but he was cold to the touch. When Torreo pulled the body close to him to warm him, Rafaele's head dropped back, and Torreo held him there for a long time, crying the last tears of his life.

# CHAPTER 9

## BUFFALO, 1920

After getting locked up, Torreo lost the job in the brewery. It took a lot of his savings to bury his brother. Many a day he would sit on the front porch, or in the cafe, drinking coffee and eating only when Frankie or the others urged him. Nobody bothered him, and the outlaws stayed away from the cafe. Frankie found him a job loading trucks at a fruit and vegetable company on Niagara, and when an opening came up for a driver, he got it, the boss figuring the big man could load and unload himself, saving him money on a helper. Nobody would ever try to pilfer anything with this guy around.

One day, in winter, Torreo sat in the cafe on Jersey Street thinking of his family. It was quiet, and there was only one other customer. Torreo saw the burly man in a black suit with a round head and short bristles of hair, looking at Torreo and smiling. He was short, with no neck and no necktie, smoking a cigarette. He nodded at Torreo, and he nodded back.

"You're the truck driver, aren't you?" the man said.

Torreo nodded.

"I have a small business myself and could use a man who can drive a truck."

"I already have a job," he answered, looking out the window.

"This wouldn't interfere. The work is at night, and not very often right now." Looking at Torreo's arms, he said, "You can lift a barrel, no problem, yes?"

Torreo breathed and said nothing.

"You used to work for the Tedeschi, in the brewery, before this Prohibition foolishness started. You still know these people, yes?"

"You are a bootlegger?"

The burly man tilted his head to the side and crushed out his cigarette. "I am trying to make my way in this country as a businessman, trying to get enough money to go someplace warmer than Buffalo."

They both gazed out the window at the snow piling up. The only sound was the scraping of Frankie's shovel on the pavement, pushing the snow off the sidewalk.

"My name is Torreo Monteduro."

The burly man rose, went over to his table, and shook hands. "Vincente Tutulomundo."

# CHAPTER 10

## BUFFALO, 1923

Eileen Brogan was sitting at her dressing table, crying. It was the third time that she had made a Novena to Our Lady, but every month, the bleeding came and went as usual. She looked up at the statue of Mary with the rosary draped over her shoulders, and at the blotchy, red face that stared back in the mirror. *I look horrible*, she thought, sniffling and wiping her face with a handkerchief. *At least the pimples have gone away*, she thought, grabbing the fine lacquered hairbrush that Bridy had given her for her wedding, and brushing her hair back, now parted in the middle and trimmed to the bottom of her ears in the popular shorter style. With a final sniffle, she stood up and tugged her dress farther down her hips, wondering if she should lose some more weight. She looked at the cover of the *McClure's* magazine on her dresser, and saw the picture of the two girls in bathing suits at Atlantic City. *Why, those wee slips of a thing, how could they ever carry a child?* Yet, it seemed to be the way all the women in the advertisements looked nowadays, and the girls who all the young boys stared after. *Not my Joe, though*, she reassured herself. *He's my true love, and faithful as the day is long.* Maybe Gibson Girls aren't on the Coca-Cola ads anymore, their hair wound in elaborate designs on top, or in the Grecian style at the back of her head, like she had had it until Joe got back from the Army, but what of it?

Walking back to the kitchen, she spied the calendar, which silently kept track of her childlessness. Next to it, hanging on the wall, was the telephone. It was how she stayed in touch with Bridy and the other girls she had known in the First Ward since moving to their flat on the West Side. She thought of calling one of them, but left the phone alone. She thought of having one of the oatmeal cookies she had made, but smoothed down her dress and vowed to lose more weight. She looked at the phone again and picked it up, this time to call the doctor she had gone to in South Buffalo, Dr. Ryan on McKinley Parkway. Maybe he could help. She blushed and smiled, thinking God knows she and Joe were doing everything they knew. The priest had said to pray and trust in God, and the Lord would bring children if it was His will. It couldn't be wrong, though, to lend Him a hand. Mrs. Santora over on Garner had gotten pregnant again, and she was a woman in her late thirties with children ten and twelve years old. She thought it was some pills the doctor had given her.

Eileen picked up the receiver and dialed Seneca 4611, a number she knew by heart. *Marvelous, this direct dial they now had,* she thought, wondering if the old ones back home would ever be able to get a telephone.

"Yes, hello. I'd like to make an appointment with Dr. Ryan. Yes, I've been seen by him before. The day after tomorrow? Can it be early? Yes, nine o'clock would be grand," she answered, thinking she'd leave early after Joe went to work, and get there and back before he came home for lunch. "Yes, I'll have the two dollars," and she wondered how much the pills cost that Mrs. Santora had bought. Hanging up, she exhaled with relief and wondered if she'd have time to see Bridy or some of the other girls along Fulton Street after her visit to the doctor.

# CHAPTER 11

## BUFFALO, 1925

Joe had noticed. Eileen had lost a good eight pounds, and he slid his hands up and down her, twice sometimes, after a hug and a kiss before he went to work. With that, she cut out even having a glass of beer when they went out and stayed with the seltzer water. She lost another five pounds when she began taking walks in the morning after he left. Where Joe said, "You look like the girls in the movies," Bridy said, "You're fallin' away to nothing," and Eileen smiled, then walked a few more blocks before she caught the streetcar back from her visits to the Ward.

After making the ninth Saturday Novena on a spring day, she checked the calendar. *Could it be?* she thought. *I haven't bled in . . . yes, thirty-two days. Joe's out there with the rowers, no telephone about. I've got to call Bridy.* So excited that it took her twice to get the number right, Eileen told her friend the news.

"You've got to see the doctor to be sure, Eileen."

"It's Saturday, do you think he'd see me today?"

"I dunno, can he tell if you're pregnant this early?"

The sound of the word *pregnant* sent thrills through Eileen. "I don't know, I don't know," she said, desperate to be sure.

When she hung up with Bridy, she called Dr. Ryan's house, but he wasn't home. She left a message with his wife, saying it was very important. She waited ten minutes by the phone and couldn't stand it. She ran upstairs to her room and looked at herself in the dresser mirror. *Do I look pregnant?* she asked herself. Then, she spotting the rosary hanging over the statue of Mary before her; she seized it and ran to the church, where burning candles in the alcove gave most of the light at this quiet time of the day. She added a candle to the bunch, knelt down at the kneeler, blessed herself, gripping the rosary's cross, and began reciting.

# CHAPTER 12

## KENSINGTON, 1930

Johnny Walenty lay in bed next to his little brother, Edju, and shuddered when he heard the front door slam. He could hear his father breathing heavily all the way from the room in the addition, where he and his brother slept at the back of the house. His father stumbled in the dark and crashed through the door to where he slept with his wife in the front bedroom.

"Maja," he said, "I'm hungry. What is there to eat?"

"Stepan," the wife said, "Not again. You're drunk. Did you spend all the money?"

"Arragh! Don't you tell me what to do, too," Stepan roared, and when Johnny heard the first slap, he jumped out of bed and pulled his overalls on over his union suit. Edju grabbed a pillow and dove under the bed. His older two brothers and his sister all jumped out of their beds like an alarm had gone off and rushed to the front of the house to try and restrain their father. When Johnny heard his siblings' pleas, his father's curses, and his mother's screams, he opened a back window and climbed out while his two older brothers tried to wrestle their father down, and his sister helped his mother out of the way. Once in the backyard, Johnny ran through their yard and the neighbor's behind them to the street. He ran towards Grider Street with the bright streetlights, running until he was there and couldn't hear the fighting back at his house.

Once on Grider, he walked to catch his breath and saw a black panel truck glide quietly down the street to the hospital. He followed the black truck and watched as it went down a driveway and stopped. From the street, he saw two big men get out of the front and come to the rear of the wagon. There, they swung the rear door open and were joined by a man in a white coat and pants, pushing a gurney. The two big men pulled what had to be a body wrapped in blankets out of the back, and flopped it onto the gurney.

Pushing his fedora back on his head, one of the big men said, "Yeah, somebody knifed this poor bastard good, down on Busti. Cops were asking around, but nobody saw nothing."

Just then, Johnny heard a noise and looked down the street. He wasn't the only one watching the body get unloaded. There was a man with a cannonball for a head set on wide shoulders, dressed in a white shirt and a dark suit standing next to a tree, staring with unblinking black eyes. Johnny heard him crush out a cigarette on the sidewalk. As the body was wheeled into the hospital, the man walked away as silently as he came, and Johnny heard the man in the white coat say, "Shit, now I gotta wait for an autopsy before I get paid. You guys got any more jobs out there tonight?"

"Dunno, yet."

"Ah, cripes. The kid who washes the bodies hasn't shown up for a couple of days, either. You'd think he'd be grateful for the job, the little bum."

"Huh, how much you payin', Harry? I might send my kid over here if there's an opening."

"Ten cents a body, an' I don't take any backtalk about 'Ohhh, he stinks,' or anything like that either."

"Hell, this depression keeps up, I might just take the job myself, pal. I'll send my kid over tomorrow after school, okay?"

"All right by me, Mac. The job's gotta get done, one way or another."

When he heard "ten cents a body," Johnny forgot all about the man with the cannonball head. He walked back up Grider towards Delevan, considering his prospects. *Can't go home for awhile until they get Poppa calmed down*, which made him shudder again. Last time he went on a tear, the cops showed up; his Moms got in the middle and got clobbered by Pops again for her trouble. Slowing his walk, he heard a wagon clanging around the corner. *What good luck*, he thought. *One of the old milk wagons still rattling on with a horse. Perfect*, he thought, sliding up behind. When the driver stopped, the man with the white-peaked hat quickly grabbed his steel bottle carrier filled with glass bottles of milk, and headed towards a house. Johnny reached over, snatched a bottle, and was gone in a flash, the horse barely stirring. Trotting down the street, Johnny popped the cardboard cap off the bottle and sucked down the sweet cream on top. *That's the best*, he thought, and he didn't have to share it with anyone. Putting the cap back on the bottle, he slowly approached Delevan Street. Listening for signs of life, he looked up at the corner. The nearest streetcar stop was almost empty, just a few old babushkas there, heading home from cleaning jobs. Too early for the guys at the axle plant to be switching shifts yet. *Just about right*, he thought, moving into a barbershop doorway in the dark where he could watch the street, particularly the delicatessen. Slowly sipping the milk, Johnny waited, and after about fifteen minutes, a green delivery truck pulled up and a guy jumped out of the big open door on the passenger side carrying two bundles of newspapers. He dropped one batch bundled in wire on a green wooden stand and clipped the wires. Then, he clipped the second bundle; placed it on top of the first; clipped that, as well; counted off a number of newspapers; and returned to the truck with the remnant. Johnny waited until they pulled away, then, after looking both ways, jogged across the street and helped himself to a paper, before returning to the darkened doorway.

Breakfast was next. When a bakery truck pulled away from the deli, Johnny slid across the street again, this time snatching a couple of hard rolls out of the tall brown paper bags left on the deli steps. He took his haul back down the side street until he came to an empty lot with a pine tree growing in the back. Waiting for a moment to make sure no hobos were around, he went under the tree where he had slashed away the lower branches a few weeks ago, when the weather started to get warm. Sitting on a bed of soft needles and leaning against the trunk, he inhaled the pine scent and thought for a moment of Christmas, when he was little and Poppa wasn't drunk so much. *Mean drunk, anyway*. He shook his head and returned to the present, thinking about where he could clean up a little before heading back over to the hospital, while he munched on the crusty rolls and sipped the sweet milk.

*Hafta read the paper later, when the sun comes up,* he thought, antici-pating stories about bootleggers and bank robbers, fast horses and comics, like *Mutt and Jeff* and *Gasoline Alley.*

He woke with the sun coming up and kids trotting down the street, calling one another's names as they gathered along the route to school. He rubbed his eyes and spotted ants crawling on the ends of the rolls and in the remnants of the milk, which had tipped over while he slept. Dusting the crumbs and the bugs off his overalls, he stood up and stretched out, then walked around the corner. He looked up the street towards his house, and seeing no sign of commotion, thought about returning. *Nah, too much to clean up, probably. Too many questions.* Then they'd try to get him to go to school. *The hell with that,* to borrow his Pop's phrase, and with that, he turned around and went over to Fillmore, then down Fillmore, past the park, and onto C Street, where his grand-mother lived. She didn't have a phone and wouldn't know what was going on yet, unless momma and the others had fled there. He went in the back door and stamped his feet in the hallway, but got no response. The whole place smelled like cabbage cooking; the wallpaper permeated with the fart like odor. *When I've made money,* Johnny vowed, *I'll never live in a place that smells like cabbage.*

"Babka?" he said, walking into the kitchen and looking around. The soup pot was on the stove, but it wasn't cooking. "Babka?" he called again. Getting no response, he went into the pantry, found a bar of lye soap, and vigorously washed his hands, face and neck. Carefully combing his straight brown hair, he guessed his grandmother had gone out to Mass. Going out the back door and through the yard to the next block, he figured he'd dodge her return route from St. Adalbert.

Walking up Fillmore, he smiled at all the kids going to school. *Once I get this job, no more of that for me,* he thought. Farther up, he saw two men straining to carry a roll top desk down a ramp, off a truck. *The suckers. I'm not going to break my back like Pops so some doctor can write up his bills on some huge desk,* he thought.

By the time he had covered the distance walking to the Meyer Memorial Hospital, where the morgue was, Johnny had figured out what he was going to tell them. His Pops was out of work (maybe true); Father Zaprazal was recommending him for the job (Father Zap didn't speak much English); he had four brothers and sisters to take care of (well, his two brothers worked some, but why not); he'd finished eighth grade (rounding up from seventh); and he was sixteen years old (maybe he'd smoke a cigarette to look older than his stunted thirteen). Since they didn't have a phone at home, he doubted they'd check there, and he looked clean, he figured, so, working in a hospital was just right.

When he got there, one of the men from the night before was sitting out front, smoking a cigar. Johnny took a deep breath, straightening himself up to full five-foot-two height. He walked up to him and looking right in the man's reddened eyes, and said, "I'm here about the job washing the bodies."

Without a word, the man stood up, turned, and waved him to follow. Johnny caught the door as it was swinging closed and followed the man down a white-tiled hallway to a room where the label on the frosted glass of the door read *Morgue.* Opening the door, Johnny was hit by the smells: the sweet odor of the dead, a penetrating antifreeze—like the smell that he later found out was formaldehyde and the stench of feces— that made him stop.

The older man looked back and said, "C'mon, you want the job, doncha?"

Johnny followed, at first holding his breath, and then taking as shallow breaths as he could.

Pulling an apron off a rack, the man tossed it to Johnny and said, "Put this on."

Johnny barely caught it because his eyes were transfixed on one of the four zinc-covered tables, where a body lay. The abdomen was open and smelled like hamburger gone bad. The purple liver lay like a soft eggplant next to the chalk-white woman's corpse, oozing blood that drained into the gutter at the edge of the table. Her breasts sagged to the side, and the nipples were almost the same color as the mushy organ next to her. Her eyes stared upward, and the only sign of remaining humanity, that Johnny could see, was her hair, which was curly and brown.

"Hey, kid, c'mon. That one's already washed," the man said as he pulled a metal drawer open, revealing a bundle of dark gray blankets over another body, maybe the one he saw getting hauled in here last night, the guy who had been knifed. The man reached inside the blankets and grabbed a wrist, shaking the arm.

"Okay, this one's ready," he said, convinced that the rigor mortis had time to fade. "Gimme a hand with the gurney," he instructed, whereupon he pointed to a corner, where one was pushed up against a wall. Silently, Johnny forced himself to move his feet, thinking, *Ten cents a body, ten cents a body.* He rolled the gurney next to the drawer, and, at the man's signal, walked over to the other side of the drawer, where the man was.

"Okay, get his feet," the man said, and, following his cue, Johnny and the man pulled the blanket-covered body onto the gurney. "Next, roll it over here, and get it on one of the tables."

The man stood back and pointed to the table next to the dead woman with the curly hair. When Johnny hesitated, the man folded his arms and stood back. Johnny pushed the gurney snug up against the table, then dragged the body, first the head and shoulders, then the feet, over onto the dissecting table.

"This guy's little, kid. If you get a really big guy, and you're afraid you might drop him on the floor, go out and find an orderly to help you. They'll expect a nickel to give you a hand, so's better not do it often if you want to make money. Okay, now, take the blankets off and toss them in the hamper over in that corner," he indicated to an oversized canvas bag held open in a black, metal rack.

Johnny started pulling the blankets off and had to grab a waxy arm to keep it from rolling off the table. Tugging the blankets from the top of the table, he kept the corpse from rolling, and revealed an old man in pajamas and a waft of sour old man crap, which had saturated his pants. Feeling bile rising in his throat, Johnny's face turned green. The morgue attendant shoved him over to a slop sink, where the boy vomited curdled bread and milk in one, then two violent heaves. Grasping the sides of the sink and gasping for fresh air, he looked up and felt vomit dripping down his face. The attendant held him firmly by the arm in case he fainted, but Johnny kept his legs underneath him and splashed water on his face with his free hand.

"You gonna make it, kid?"

Johnny nodded, shut off the running water, and turned back to the reeking stiff on the table, noticing that the tables were all tilted slightly and the gutters on the sides and bottom emptied into a pipe that went down into a drain in the floor. The attendant released his grip but kept his hand near Johnny's arm as they approached the body again.

"All right, then. If you're ok, take these," the man said, handing him a pair of large shears. "Usually, the family wants the clothes back, but it was just him, and I don't figure even the St. Vincent DePaul wants some shit stained, worn out pjs. So, now, you take the scissors and cut the clothes off him and toss them in there," he said, pointing to a ribbed metal trash can. "Make sure you empty that out when you're done, and hose it out, too, or we'll get this place full of bugs."

Returning again to shallow breaths, Johnny sliced and tugged the threadbare pajamas off the old man, smearing wet feces on the table as he removed the bottoms. Holding the clothes at arm's length, he dropped the rags into the garbage and returned to the table, where the attendant had stretched a heavy rubber garden hose with an adjustable nozzle.

"Okay, sometimes you gotta use a brush to get 'em clean, but this guy ain't bad. Just hose him down, turn him over, hose down his backside, and then clean the table. The doc'll come in, take a look at it, and see if he's gotta cut into him. If he doesn't, we wrap him up in one of the sheets over there," he said, pointing to shelves filled with linen sheets. "And put him back in the drawer for the guys from the potter's field, or the medical students to pick up. Think you can handle this, kid?"

Clearing his throat, Johnny answered, "Yes," and held his hand out for the dime he was due.

# CHAPTER 13

## KENSINGTON, 1930

As Johnny trotted down the front steps that morning, he saw some big footprints in the freshly fallen snow and froze, looking up and down the street for his father. Not seeing him, he looked at the footprints, which showed someone had approached the house, then turned away and went on, their steps lost amongst the others on the sidewalk. *Phew,* he thought, that's all he needed now, was his old man to come back, screaming drunk, tearing up the house, and knocking them around.

Johnny walked quickly, north on Fillmore to Ferry, keeping his eyes peeled in case his father was in the neighborhood. He'd heard that Pops had been at Babka's a couple of times, but she chased him out for being a no-good, who didn't care about his family. He'd heard he'd been hanging out in the bars on Broadway, doing odd jobs loading and unloading at the market there, then drinking it right up. Nobody seemed to know where he was staying, he just heard about him being spotted around the East Side from neighbors who shut up until he was out of earshot, shaking their heads and saying what a shame it was, what a shame it was.

Well, Johnny was working at the hospital, as he always called it, and it was true. The morgue was just part of the Myer Memorial Hospital, and when he wasn't washing bodies, he was filling in as an orderly sometimes, mopping floors, cleaning beds, emptying bedpans, and just about any other dirty job no one wanted to do. A few more bucks a month and he might be able to get his own place, away from the cabbage smells of home, the fear of his father's return, and his family's ceaseless rounds of worry, prayer, and work.

When he walked into the basement entrance to the hospital, the coroner's wagon men were there, looking at a watch. They paid no attention as Johnny slipped by and went to the water fountain to get a drink and listen to them.

"Gotta be worth five bucks. We should split it."

"No, no, no, no, no, Herb, you get the ring, I get the watch this time. The luck of the draw, my friend."

"Yeah, but this one's different. It's expensive."

Herb raised his voice, nearly shouting, "Look, that's what we agreed, Lunkhead . . .," and then, they saw the boy looking at them.

"C'mon, dummy, outside with this," Herb said, whereupon they hurriedly went through the heavy metal doors, out onto the lot where the morgue wagon was parked.

Johnny had noticed that the bodies didn't have money or jewelry on them, and he had heard that the cops sometimes didn't inventory the personal possessions too carefully. He figured that they split up the stuff with the wagon men, or if the police were either sloppy or honest, the wagon men got all of it. If the body had family, the body usually went to a funeral home, but if it came to the morgue, it was pretty much fair game.

The only time Johnny got a shot at any of the swag was when a ring or something was stuck and he had enough time to work it off when no one was watching. He had a small box of stuff—a few rings, a bracelet or two, and a necklace—that the wagon men had missed, stashed at Babka's house in the coal bin, where no one would ever find it. The problem was turning it into cash. The pawn shops could figure out it was stolen and would give you next to nothing for it. Somehow, he had to find a fence that would give him some value for the stuff.

# CHAPTER 14

## BUFFALO, 1931

Johnny smelled the next body way before he came into the dissecting room and saw it— the unmistakable sweet odor of the dead, this one reeking of urine and alcohol, as well. The wagon men said he'd been found in a rooming house full of old drunks on Carolina Street on the West Side, lying in bed, a church key bottle opener tied to a lanyard switch hanging from a naked light bulb. He'd been there for a few days, the tenants oblivious, but the land-lord noticing. He not only stank, but there were maggots crawling under his clothes like a moving bed of rice. The medical examiner came in, took a look around the body, read the report, wrote a few notes, and told Johnny to go ahead. Between the maggots and the smell, Johnny was still a little queasy around this body, and delayed the medical examiner by striking up a conversation so he wouldn't be alone with the corpse.

"Say Doc, see these maggots on him," as he cut away the stained sport coat and shirts that were layered and stuck to the body. "What happens with them?"

"Well, most of them turn into flies and go on to bigger and better garbage. If they're not disturbed, the flies'll come back and plant more eggs there, and they'll turn into maggots that keep eating the body until there's not much left. If there's nothing left, and they get real hungry," he added, "I guess they start eating each other." Then he left, and Johnny hurried, dumping the clothes that smelled of booze and old piss, and hosing the bugs and dirt off the old man who, in his last days, looked like Johnny's father.

# CHAPTER 15

## BUFFALO, 1933

Johnny sat in the hallway around the corner from the morgue, far enough away so he wouldn't smell the bodies or the formaldehyde during his break. He reached into his shirt pocket, found his pack of Chesterfields, and ripped off the remainder of the top to get at the last of the smokes. Finding nothing but a few flakes of tobacco, he looked up at the cigarette machine farther down the hallway and thought about buying a pack, even if they were more expensive here than at the store. He sat back and put his hand into his pants pocket where he kept his change. Shaking the coins around in his hand, he came up with two nickels. *Shit. Where to get a nickel fast?* he thought. The last body. The man had some change in his pocket when they took the clothes off him. He'd tossed it into the big envelope where they put all the rest of the dead man's effects. The clerk hadn't inventoried it yet. Perfect. As he jumped up and hurried back into the morgue, he thought, *Hell, the wagon guys who pick up the body snatch stuff off these stiffs all the time. You just gotta be smart about it and not grab stuff the family's going to be looking for later.* Kind of an advance on his pay, he chuckled to himself as he picked out a nickel and a dime from the envelope.

When he came back out, a guy had the machine open and was stuffing packs of cigarettes into the slots. Johnny watched him as he quickly filled the machine, and then pulled out the metal box where the coins accumulated. He poured the coins into a canvas bag and knotted the top.

"Hey," Johnny said, as the vendor went to pick up a cardboard box on the floor. "Can I get a pack from you before you lock it up?"

"Sure, kid, what flavor?"

"Chesterfields."

"This is your lucky day, kid." He pulled a loose pack out of the cardboard box. "I got one left over that wouldn't fit in the machine. Just gimme a dime and they're yours."

"Thanks," Johnny replied, eyeing the canvas bag of change. "You makin' any money these days at this?" he asked, indicating the cigarette machine with a match before he lit up.

"Ahh, not like before the crash, but juke boxes and cigarettes are still doin' all right."

"Say, you need any help? I can count, fix stuff, load machines up, if you need a hand."

"Ah, I handle all that stuff, pal. Tell you what though. I need someone sometimes to help move the machines around, if you think you can handle it. It's not real regular, but if you got a phone . . ."

"Sure, I got a phone." The old couple that ran the deli downstairs from his room took messages for him on the pay phone as long as he helped unload deliveries.

The vendor pulled a pencil from behind his ear, and Johnny found a scrap of paper in his pocket. He wrote down John W, and the number on it, then wrote *Helper* and underlined that.

"This is me," he said. "If I don't answer, just leave a message and I'll call you right back. You pay in cash?"

"That's the way this business operates, kid. Strictly cash. I avoid a lot of paperwork that way; keeps things simple." Putting the pencil back behind his ear, the vendor looked at Johnny and put out his hand. "I'm Walter, kid. I'll give you a holler if I need you."

"John Walenty. I'm available any time I'm not here, just give me a call," Johnny said, hoping Walter would. He liked the idea of cash money with no taxes taken out, and wondered how close an eye this Walter guy kept on his inventory.

# CHAPTER 16

## BUFFALO, 1935

"I know it should be here. He always carried his pocket watch with him." *Shit,* Johnny thought, *the guy didn't look like he had any family, as shabby as he dressed, or I wouldn't have copped the watch.* He put his hands in his pockets and tried to slide down the hall to the exit like he was going for a smoke when he spotted Doc Woldman standing in front of him, arms crossed in front of his white coat.

"Johnny, come over into my office for a moment, please."

*The bald headed bastard knew. He'd been watching me lately. Shit.*

Once inside the office, Doc quietly said, "Close the door, Johnny." When Johnny did, the pathologist said, "You know why you're here, Johnny. Empty your pockets, please. Inside out." Johnny dumped a couple of dimes, a few pennies, a half pack of cigarettes, a box of matches, keys to his building, and a couple of toothpicks. He tried to palm the watch, but the doctor spotted the chain between his fingers and shook his head.

"Johnny, it isn't just that you're stealing. That watch might be the only thing that woman has to remember her father by when he's buried. Doesn't that mean anything to you? You're not going hungry. You haven't got a family to support. How could you do such a thing?"

Johnny shrugged. *The hell with this,* he thought, *just get it over with.*

"Have you got anything to say, son?"

Johnny stared at his shoes.

The doctor shook his head again, and said, "You're fired, Johnny. Give me the watch and get your stuff off my desk. I'm going to have one of the orderlies go with you to your locker and check it for other things you might have there that've been stolen. Consider yourself lucky I don't call the police."

He met the orderly at the office door. *Hmm, I dunno this guy, but I'll bet he'd steal plenty if he had the chance. Well, there's nothing in my locker, I know that. Anyway, the vending's going pretty good now. Time to unload this chemical, stinking funeral parlor,* Johnny thought.

# CHAPTER 17

## THE EAST SIDE, 1937

Walt Schneider took one last drag on his smoke and flicked it away. "Okay, kid, this machine ain't gonna load itself."

Johnny looked at the four-foot-high cigarette machine on the ground and the tailgate on the truck, and wished he were taller.

"Lemme know when you're ready, Johnny."

The both of them crouched down and gripped the heavy metal box at the bottom. When he had his hands firmly in place, Johnny squeezed, "Okay," out of his chest and they began to straighten their legs. Just before they got it level with the tailgate, all the weight shifted forward and the cigarette machine fell away from Johnny.

"Jesus, Walter!" Johnny shouted as he tumbled away from the truck and the machine crashed onto the pavement. Rolling away from the machine, Johnny avoided getting hit, as it first fell on its side, then forward off Walter onto the concrete, shattering the glass on the front and scattering packs of cigarettes everywhere.

"What the hell happened?" Johnny shouted as he stood up. Walter lay there silently with the machine across his legs. Johnny grabbed the bottom of the machine and started to drag it off Walter. It took him three heaves to get it off.

"Walter, are you okay?" Johnny gasped.

Walter was still, his eyes open and looking around. His mouth was moving, but he wasn't saying anything. He raised his one arm, but the other one just quivered.

Johnny got up close. "Walter, what's the matter?"

Walter's eyes stared at Johnny, then danced around. His mouth kept moving, but he couldn't talk.

A passerby shouted, "Call a doctor for that man!"

Soon, there was a small crowd there.

"Somebody call a doctor!"

"Get a cop!"

"Run down to the firehouse and tell them!"

Johnny didn't know what to do. He tried shaking Walter, who just lay there quivering. Finally, two police officers arrived, and Johnny helped them load Walter into their car.

"We're taking him to Deaconess, buddy," the one policeman said, as they slammed the doors and drove off. Johnny looked around at the smashed machine and the cigarettes in the street, and hesitated. Finally, he jumped in the front seat of the truck and followed the police car to the hospital.

# CHAPTER 18

## DOWNTOWN, 1939

Johnny trotted up the steps into City Hall just before noon, and headed directly for the Licensing Department on the third floor with a manila envelope. Inside, he nodded to Ed Rybeck, one of the clerks, who glanced at the two other people behind the counter. Johnny stood off to the side, letting three other guys go ahead of him with their requests. When the room cleared out and the other two clerks left for lunch, Johnny went up to the counter and presented his applications for licenses.

"New machines?" Rybeck asked.

"New machines," Johnny answered, "Plus, I want to switch the name on the other licenses to my name."

"John Walenty?"

"John Walters. Name of the company stays the same. *Walters Vending.*"

"How's Walter doing?"

"Not good. Docs say he'll never walk or talk again, and another stroke'll kill him. I give the wife thirty dollars a week."

"That'll keep them going, John. Your fees are twelve dollars," and in a low voice added, "Fifteen dollars for the other."

Johnny put a ten and two ones on top of the applications and a ten under them. "Like I said, I'm giving Walter's family thirty dollars a week."

Another clerk walked into the office, munching on an apple. Rybeck shrugged. "Times are tough all over," he said, and slid the money and the paperwork off the counter.

# CHAPTER 19

## NORTH PARK, 1942

After Timothy was born in 1930, Eileen was exhausted. The three others were no bother; they practically took care of themselves they were so good; but little Timmy always seemed to need her. He was smaller than the rest, and she was always urging him to eat. She always ate everything, to be an example for the skinny, little man. She thought it would help get her energy back, but it didn't. She tried Geritol, but that didn't do any good, either. Everything she drank seemed to come right back out. Then, she started losing weight no matter what she ate, which the neighbors thought amazing for a woman who had given birth to four children.

Bingo, Ladies Sodality, Cub Scouts—she and the boy went to them all, and she always said a Rosary on Saturdays at St. Mark's, to continue thanking God for the gift of her children. The most fun was bingo in the church hall. Timmy had started getting multiple cards and keeping track of each one of them. One time, Timmy was hollering, "Say Bingo, Mommy!"

Chatting with Rosalie Roaldi, she hadn't paid attention, so she said, "Which one, which one, Timmy?"

He handed it to her and she shouted "Bingo!" even though she could barely make out the letters and numbers on their card. *Ah, me, I must be getting old,* she thought, *but Joe, and now the older boys, do all the driving, so there's no need to get glasses just yet.*

# CHAPTER 20

## THE EAST SIDE, 1942

Captain Ed Falk picked up the newspaper on the table in the reserve room and read, "More Draft Notices Issued This Week."

*It won't be long now*, he thought, looking at the snow piling up outside. His brother, Tom, had just written from basic training in Fort Dix. Fifty dollars a month as a buck private. He'd get more as a married officer, but it was still peanuts. The desk lieutenant opened the door and looked around to make sure they were alone.

"We got another one, Cap."

"How many?"

"Three that we found, so far. The new ones, too. Gottliebs with the 'multiplier' features."

"What's his name?"

"John Walenty. Calls himself Walters, now. He's running Walter Schneider's vending route."

# CHAPTER 21

## NORTH BUFFALO, 1944

Eileen turned up the aisle where the canned fruit was. It was winter, and decent fresh peaches and pears were not to be had. She had waited until school was out so Timmy could come with her, over to the A&P market on Hertel. The boy would've insisted on coming, anyway. He kept a hand on her shopping cart, just like he did when she first took him out of the baby's seat, but now, the teenager would occasionally pull or push the cart to avoid a stack of boxes, or another cart she hadn't noticed. Charley and Pat called him a momma's boy, but he was a great comfort to her and very helpful, especially when it came to reading labels she couldn't seem to make out anymore.

Stopping the cart and reaching for a can of Ann Page pears, she suddenly felt dizzy and spun around the cart, her left hand holding on. Crashing into the stacked cans on the shelves, she collapsed onto the floor between the cart and the shelves, cans tumbling about her. She heard the metal cans rolling around, Timmy yelling, "Mom!" and other shoppers saying, "Oh my goodness!" and "What's wrong with her?" But it seemed like she was watching a movie and wasn't really there at all.

She laid her head down on the floor, thinking a wee nap was all she needed, and then reached out for the boy she could barely see when she heard him crying. She remembered hearing Tim reciting Joe's phone number at work to someone, and that was all, until she woke up at St. Francis.

There was a doctor in a white coat with a stethoscope around his neck and Dr. Butler, who had taken over Dr. Ryan's practice, on one side of the bed. Dr. Butler was in a nice tweed coat and striped tie. Joe was there with them. *My, but Joe has red eyes today,* she thought, *I wonder if he slept well last night.*

On the other side of the bed, all the children were lined up, staring at her, except for Charley, who was drumming his fingers on the bed rail and tapping his feet. She reached up to touch his hand and said, "Don't fidget so, son," which got sighs of relief from all around.

The doctor in the white coat called for a nurse and said, "The medicine's taking effect now. We'll sit her up in a minute and see how she's feeling." When the nurse came in, she and Dr. Butler helped Eileen sit up and propped some fine, fluffy pillows that smelled of bleach behind her.

"My, but that's a fine jacket, Doctor. We'll have to be calling you 'squire' now with such clothes."

Chuckles went around the bed, and the white-coated doctor shined a light in her eyes, then stood back and spoke.

"Mrs. Brogan, I'm afraid you have diabetes. You've no doubt had it for some time, but now it has become acute."

Confused, Eileen shook her head and blinked several times.

Joe stepped between the doctor and his wife, and took her hand in both his. "It's going to be all right," and with a glance at Dr. Butler, "We're going to take care of you."

# CHAPTER 22

## NORTH PARK, 1944

Joe sat at the kitchen table, having finished his breakfast, and read about the allied attacks on the Gustav Line in Italy. The map on the front page showed two swooping arrows representing the maneuvers of the British and American armies, as they drove the Germans northward. The articles told of the tanks, planes, and units in the struggle; and Ernie Pyle's column told of the soldiers pushing trucks in knee-deep mud, and boys about Pat and Charley's age being crippled by mines, and blinded by shrapnel.

As those two scraped the last of the rationed eggs and bacon onto their forks, Joe looked up from his *Courier Express* at them and imagined them in the war. *Good God*, he thought, *It might happen any time now.*

Charley seemed to have read his father's mind. The nineteen-year-old belched behind his hand, said "Excuse me," and folded his hands on the table before himself, as he had done in the past, when he was ready to advance his latest great idea to the family. Pat, meanwhile, was taking his plate and silverware over to the sink.

"Dad, I've been meaning to talk to you about something," Charley said.

"What's that, Charley?"

"I've been thinking," Charley replied, which set his father slightly on edge, for it usually meant he was ready to launch some risky scheme, if he hadn't already.

"I'm nineteen, almost twenty now, and signed up for the draft. They might call me up any time, so I figured I'd just go and join the branch I wanted to get into first, rather than wait for them to come get me."

"And?" Joe said, adjusting his rimless glasses.

"I figured I'd join the Navy," Charley told him, thinking of palm trees and hula dancers in the Pacific.

"Well," Joe began slowly, thinking of the picture in the *Courier* of the battleship *West Virginia* exploding in Pearl Harbor. "I think that wherever you might go, boys, it's bound to be dangerous. There's names printed in church bulletins all over town every Sunday of soldiers, sailors, and Marines dying, and being wounded, all over the world. Perhaps it might be better to wait and see where your duty to your country lies, and let the draft board make the decision that's best for the country." Joe looked at the two boys.

Pat knitted his brows in silent dissatisfaction and Charley squeezed his lips together and gave a little shake of his head.

They were silent for a moment, then Charley spoke.

"I already signed up, Pop. Went downtown and checked up on things. The guy there said I'll be shipping out for the Pacific for sure. And Pat . . ."

Joe had expected something like this brash foolishness from Charley, but he stared at his ever-steady Pat in disbelief.

"I joined the Army same day, Pop. They need us, Dad. They're talking about invading France. We're liable to miss the whole thing if we don't get through basic soon . . ."

Joe shook his head, stood up, and looked out the window, a single tear coming down his cheek.

"I know you've got to do your duty, boys, but it'll kill your mother, the way she worries about you."

"What's that?" Eileen said, coming down the back stairs in her bathrobe.

"The boys, mother," Joe said, holding his palm out to keep the youth seated, "have been talking about joining up."

"It's okay, Ma," Charley said, hurriedly. "I'm sure I'll be in basic for weeks, then traveling all the way out west, then on a slow boat to some quiet island in the Navy."

Joe locked eyes with Eileen, who clutched the folds of her robe together over her chest. *She looks so pale*, he thought.

Pat stared down at his plate and said quietly, "It's our duty to our country, Mom. We've already signed up."

"Ah, ya damn, young fools," Joe exclaimed. "You couldn't wait, could you? You couldn't wait for the draft! You couldn't even wait for me to break it to your mother that gave you life! If something . . ." He stopped, being on the edge of saying something he'd regret forever. Nobody moved, and the room went silent, except for Eileen's quiet sobbing.

# CHAPTER 23

## NORTH PARK, 1945

Eileen and Joe learned to give the injections of insulin, and made the adjustments in diet, but the blurred vision continued. She always had a terrible thirst, and used the bathroom frequently. When asked, she said she felt better, but her condition deteriorated. Her circulation to her legs and feet gave her pain, and kept her from walking very far. Gangrene set in to her toes, then her feet, one of which was amputated. Her faith in God never wavered, and Tim was her constant companion. Finally, she took to her bed, refusing to go to the hospital. Dr. Butler said her heart was giving out.

When she lost consciousness one evening, as Joe read to her, he called the doctor and sent Tim for Father Crotty. The doctor stayed while Father Crotty recited the last rites, and when he had kissed his purple stole and folded it up, they both spoke with Joe.

"The boys are away, and Mary Agnes is strong, Joe," the priest said, "But . . ."

Joe held up a hand, then opened the bedroom door and found Tim hovering in the hallway.

"Timmy, go downstairs and fetch Dr. Butler a glass of water."

When he had gone, the priest continued. "We'll all keep an eye on the boy, Joe. You know he's not as strong as the others, and this will hurt him terribly,"

The doctor nodded. "He's liable to take this very hard, Joe. If need be, I will prescribe something."

The two remained at the Brogan house until Eileen had passed away that night. They helped Joe break the news to Tim and Mary Agnes, and make arrangements with the funeral home. When the body was taken to the funeral parlor for preparation, Tim broke down and Mary Agnes helped him to his room, and stayed with him all night. For the three days Eileen was in the open casket in the front room of the house, the youngest boy was silent, and ate nothing. Those who came to the wake did their best to console him; after the services, it seemed half of him was buried in the Lackawanna graveyard by the Basilica.

# CHAPTER 24

## THE WEST SIDE, 1947

Joe Brogan entered the school through the heavy wooden doors reinforced with black iron bands, and thought, as he always did, of a castle in the movie *Robin Hood*. Smiling to himself, as he went into the foyer, he looked around the huge room, and marveled at the spotless black tile floor with the hourglass brass inlays, and the walls, which were polished black marble from the floor to waist level, and then admired the white limestone that went up another twenty feet to the vaulted ceiling trimmed in blue and gold. Going between the black marble columns on his left, Joe entered a part of the building that was all gray limestone, and walked up a circular stairway where Basil Rathbone could have tumbled down, dead from a thrust of Errol Flynn's sword. Walking down an arched hallway on creaking, but highly-polished, wood floors, he reflected on how his father had been one of the stonemasons who built this mansion for one of Buffalo's Delaware Avenue millionaires, who left it to the Masons. The Jesuits later bought it at a tax sale for their high school. After the meeting, he reminded himself that he should stop by the hallway where the graduation pictures were, and take a look at Charley's and Pat's class photos. He loved to look at those pictures, their young faces so full of joy and promise, dressed in white formal coats and black bow ties. Opening a thick, oak door, he was greeted by the waves and nods of a group of men gathered around a big mahogany table, the elder ones with cigars or pipes burning strong, the younger ones with cigarettes between their fingers, poised over glass ashtrays.

At the end of the table was the rector of the school, a heavy man dressed in the old-fashioned soutane, with curly white hair and thick glasses, reveling in the respect of these successful citizens, some of whom he had instructed in math and physics in his younger days. The most fawning among them were the men who hadn't gone to school there, but whose children had made the cut, and gotten into the academically elite boys' high school. They, the Jesuits knew, were the most likely to make contributions and serve on boards like this one, which set the financial course for the school, and helped decide scholarships and admissions.

"Father Schaus," Joe said, taking his place at the table.

"Ah, Joseph. Good to have you here to leaven our amiable brain trust."

The meeting began, on time, as always; the priest said a prayer and then turned the affair over to the board's president, who read the brief agenda—the sorting out of bids for the paving of a new parking lot, the acceptance of two new scholarship funds, and the settling of the last few spots for the incoming freshman class. The first two issues were settled quickly, with the paving contract going to an alumnus who gave the school a deep discount, and the scholarships, having trusts established for minimal fees at a bank, managed by another member. The final matter was settling which of three boys would get the last spot in the upcoming freshman class.

"Well," began the board's president, an alumnus who was a lawyer with a prominent local firm, "the last item on our agenda tonight requires a little more scrutiny than the first two matters—which of the three best-qualified boys gets the last open spot in next year's freshman class? All three have excellent academic records, all three did very well on the entrance exam, and none of the three will require any financial assistance.

"The first is James O'Toole, graduating from St. Joseph's on Main Street this year. He has a ninety-three percent average at that school, scored a ninety-two percent on the entrance exam here, has a paper route, plays baseball, and is an altar boy at St. Joseph's. His father is a vice principal in the city public schools, and his mother was a nurse before they had children. No immediate family in the school at this time, nor is his father an alumnus.

"The second boy is Andrew Maraschiello, who will be

graduating from Public School 83 this year, with an average of ninety-three percent there; scored ninety-two percent on the entrance exam here; plays the trumpet and drums; and is a patrol leader with the Boy Scouts. His father is a shirt salesman, president of the K of C at St. Margaret's, and a member of the Class of 1940. His mother taught at St. Margaret's for several years.

"The last candidate is Phillip Monteduro, who is graduating from Annunciation on Lafayette this year, with an average of ninety-six; he scored ninety-three percent on our entrance exam; is an altar boy; plays basketball and baseball; and is active in the Catholic Youth Organization at Annunciation. His mother is a member of the Women's Sodality, and is an active volunteer at Children's Hospital. His father is Torreo Monteduro."

The mention of the racketeer's name caused the previously silent group to begin talking amongst themselves, except for Joe and the priest, who kept silent. Joe smiled, thinking about how he and Torreo's paths kept crossing.

The president spoke up a little louder, saying, "All these boys scored almost the same on the entrance exam, are nearly equal in their grades at schools, have excellent extracurricular activities, and their families are active contributors to their parishes. I think any of them are qualified for Canisius' next class of freshmen."

"I think you're right, John, but we don't want il Zoppo's kid here," said a board member. "Who knows what sort of trouble these people might try to make?" He turned to the man sitting next to him, a doctor on the West Side—where Monteduro's rackets were centered—and asked, "What do you think, Vito?"

Thinking of the victims who were beat—whom he had treated—as a result of Monteduro's mob, Vito spread his hands wide and said, "I'm staying out of it."

Voices were raised, and Joe spoke up, cutting through all of them.

"It seems to me, gentlemen, that the Monteduro boy is the best-qualified scholar among them, and stands with the rest in the other ways." Looking right into the eyes of the man who wanted to keep young Phillip out—a contractor Joe knew, who benefited greatly from city contracts obtained through political connections—he continued, "I wouldn't throw stones at the boy's house, gentlemen. There's plenty of windows that might get shattered all around here if we keep *that* up."

There was a moment's pause, and Father Schaus reflected, "Yes, we must consider the Pharisaical aspect of blaming the sons for the sins of the father, and, as Joe says, he does stand above the others academically. Now there's always a few boys who choose not to come here, though they're accepted, for whatever reason, and perhaps these other two boys might get another chance to join us, if that happens. In the meantime, I think we should agree with Joe that young Monteduro is the best-qualified candidate, and notify his family that he will be welcomed into

Canisius' freshman class next fall."

# CHAPTER 25

## DOWNTOWN, 1950

Pat wore his brown suit for his first day as a detective, having put a good polish to his shoes the night before; only tipping two beers back while he listened to the Bison's hockey game on the radio. The Gambling Squad was on the third floor of headquarters, and, as he went to report to the inspector's office, he had to go through the bullpen, where the Gambling and other headquarters squads were. He could see all eyes on him. He rapped on the wood part of the frosted glass door, where a brass plate read, *Martin L. Wachter, Inspector-Headquarters.*

"Come in," came a resonant voice from beyond the door, and Pat pushed his curly, black hair back as he turned the knob.

"Patrick Brogan," the inspector stated upon seeing Brogan.

"Yes, sir. Reporting, as assigned."

The inspector was a tall man; taller than Pat's six-foot-one; with a prominent nose and receding blonde hair, slicked back. He wore a starched, white shirt with plain, black cuff links; a narrow black tie; and sharply-pressed, brown pleated pants. Worry lines were just appearing in the pale skin beneath gray eyes. He did not stand up, but stared at Pat.

"I need good men, Brogan. Ones who don't whine when I get 'em out of bed on cold nights. Ones who are never, I repeat, *never*, late. You went to Canisius, right?"

"Yes, sir."

"You know Father Gewitter, Prefect of Discipline, there?"

"Yes, sir."

"Ever get jug from him? Ever get cracked a good one against the lockers by him?"

"Yes, sir."

"Well, he's nothing compared to me. I'm not going to treat you like a kid, cuff you on the ear, and tell you to wise up. You screw up once and you're out, back on patrol, watching the trains go by on Walden in the snow. Screw up real good and I'll get you fired. The last guy got the heave ho, the one you're replacing, for ignoring a bookie's operation that was run by a guy he went to school with. I'm having him fired and charged with willful neglect by the DA. Do you have any friends you wouldn't arrest?"

"No, sir."

"Good. Go out there and see Lieutenant Constantino. He's your new boss; he'll break you in right. I run a tight ship, Brogan, and we're crushing them out there. If you work hard, got smarts, and stay as clean as a hound's tooth, you stay. Got it?"

"Yes, sir."

"Now get to work and do what the lieutenant tells you."

Pat spun on his heel military fashion, and left the room. Closing the door quietly, he looked around the room for Constantino. A beefy, short man, he was sitting at his desk, looking at Brogan, his brown eyes boring holes into him. The plate on his desk read, *Detective Lieutenant Louis Constantino* in smaller-than-usual letters, so it would all fit.

Constantino half-rose from his chair and shook hands with Brogan, then sat back down and pointed to a corner over Brogan's shoulder. "That's your desk, over there, Brogan, but you won't get much of a chance to sit at it. Those two desks belong to Dudek and Dowd, the other two guys on this squad. They were out working last night, raided a crap game going on in a hotel room on Michigan. Nabbed ten players, money, dice, the whole bit. By themselves.

"This morning, we're gonna pay a visit to see if a bar owner is still following the law like he said he would. You know the Golden Dollar, down by the Courier? Well, that's where we're going, see if he's rigged his pinball machines." The lieutenant quickly pulled on a black suit coat and fixed a buff-colored fedora with a black band on his head, shaping the brim, back up, front down over one eye, with a quick motion of both hands.

For a short guy, Constantino moved pretty quickly, like a bowling ball picking up speed going down the alley, always moving forward, even when he had to turn his broad shoulders to get past people. Brogan followed him down to the basement garage, where they hopped into an old Ford that had been painted from a patrol car. The marks where the decals had been still showed through the maroon paint. He waved to the guard at the door and accelerated up Franklin.

"Not using Main?" Pat asked, wondering why they weren't taking the most direct route.

"Nah, old habit. Everybody spots this car a mile away. We'll park it on Edward and walk up. Good drill for both of us. You know Sullivan, guy who owns this joint?"

"My pop does pretty good. He helped get my brother a job at the *Courier*. I met him a few times," Pat said, remembering the kitchen conferences between his dad and others, including an old friend named Sullivan, to find a place for Tim when he'd gotten out of the sanitarium.

Out of the car, Constantino picked up even more speed so that even the much taller Brogan had a hard time keeping up. He pushed through the silver metal art deco door, and Pat recognized several of Timmy's co-workers at the bar—printers, ink stained men, some with paper hats still on, who went to the bar for breakfast and booze at the end of their night shift. Constantino went right to the back room and spotted the machines—a jukebox, a cigarette machine, and two pinball games, the latter with players on them, and a couple of others watching and waiting to get on, too.

"Police inspection. Lemme see these games, boys," Constantino said, loud enough for everyone in the place to hear. Pushing past the pinball players, Lou flexed his knees slightly and pulled the solid wood and metal machine away from the wall. Taking a screwdriver out of his pocket, he removed the wooden back to the pinball game and placed it against the wall. He then pulled out a flashlight and looked into the inner mechanism of the game, inside the backboard.

"Good," he said, as Sullivan, an older man in a brown, buttoned sweater and glasses came up. "Nothing in this game to rig it, Mr. Sullivan. Now, let's check the other one," Constantino said. He went on to repeat what he did to the first machine, leaving the first one disassembled, as Brogan stood back where he could watch everyone in the place.

"Lou," Sullivan said quietly, "Why are you doing this? You know I don't go for that gambling horseshit," he pleaded, looking from one policeman to the next, showing surprise at seeing Joe Brogan's son there.

"If you've got nothing to hide, Sullivan, then you shouldn't mind me checking. Okay, this one looks okay, too," he said, putting the screwdriver back in his pocket and leaving the machines taken apart.

The old man stood there, hands in his pockets, and watched the detectives go back into the barroom, where Constantino looked over the men at the bar, all but one of whom were watching him. His eyes narrowing, he walked up to the man hunched over his shot and draft beer and said, "Eddie Sanderson, out on parole. You supposed to be drinking when you're on parole, Eddie?"

"Yeah, it's okay. As long as I don't get drunk, my parole officer says I can drink."

"Well, you look drunk to me Eddie," pulling him off the stool and shoving him towards Brogan, who grabbed the printer and spun him around, holding him tightly by the biceps.

"I didn't do nothing, Louie," Eddie pleaded while everyone muttered and started to shift in place.

"Well, we'll find out about that, Eddie, and it's Lieutenant Constantino to you, shitbird."

Sullivan watched, gritting his teeth. Before he could say anything to protest, Constantino ordered, "Put the cuffs on him, Brogan. He might think he's a tough guy."

Brogan hesitated, but thinking about the inspector's words, and seeing a nod from Constantino, he pulled out his cuffs and put them on Sanderson's wrists.

"If you didn't do anything, Eddie, you've got nothing to be afraid of, and you'll be back out in time to make your shift tonight."

"Pat, what the hell is this?" Sullivan demanded.

"Police business, Mr. Sullivan. If he's okay, he'll get back out soon. I'll see to that."

They went out quickly with the handcuffed man, to the mutters and stares of the barroom and Sullivan, who went right to the telephone as they left.

They marched up the street to their car, and Sanderson started to cry, saying, "The bosses better not see me, I can't lose this job."

In the car, roaring back down Main Street to the station, Constantino asked Sanderson about three different men whose names Pat recognized from gambling circles downtown.

Sanderson spoke about one, then another, but only where he had seen them, not what they were doing.

Looking in the rearview mirror, Constantino glanced at Brogan, then focused on Sanderson. "You could be in for a while, Eddie. Might miss your shift tonight if you're not telling the truth."

"Look, Lou . . . Lieutenant, I been staying away from those guys . . . Look, I heard about a couple of guys stashing stolen stuff with a guy. I can find out about that. Would that help?"

"Who?"

"Some guy who works at the zoo, that's all I know, now."

"How soon will you know?"

"Tomorrow, next day at the latest."

"We'll have to see, Eddie. Got to check and see if you've been a good boy while you're out. Call your parole officer, see if you've been seeing him regular. Probably wouldn't be good if I told him you were drunk at . . . hmmmm," he said, glancing at his watch, "a little before ten in the morning."

"I'll find out, I promise. If I lose this job . . ."

"It all depends on you, Eddie," said Constantino, as they pulled into the basement of the headquarters building.

As they led Eddie up the stairs, Constantino said to Pat, "Put him in a holding cell, tell the turnkey we're holding him for a possible parole violation, and I'll meet you upstairs in the office." He went out of the stairwell, leaving Pat to get the frightened parolee to a holding cell. While Brogan took Eddie to the cages, the lieutenant went to the inspector's office.

"Well?" the commander inquired.

"He did it. I don't think he liked it much, but he did it, right in front of his dad's buddy. We picked up a guy there, Eddie Sanderson. Small time burglar a ways back. He might have something. I figure we'll let him sit a couple of hours, then let him out to see what he can turn up. He's plenty scared, boss."

"A little bonus there, good. Keep Brogan working hard, show him the ropes. If you think we can trust him after a couple of weeks, we'll use him."

# CHAPTER 26

## THE EAST SIDE, 1950

Johnny had the glass top off, one of the bumpers replaced and the rubber bands back on, but couldn't get the pinball machine bumper to respond. "Shit," he muttered, thinking he was going to have to find the broken connection and solder it. There were about seven people at the bar, and five of them were watching him at the table as he tried to get the pinball to work. Every minute he took to fix the damn thing was costing him money.

Johnny stopped, lit a cigarette, and took a moment to regroup. "I'll have it goin' pronto, guys, don't worry," he assured the players.

One of the two guys not watching him was an old fella looking out the window, and the other was a big guy with a beard, talking to the bartender in a foreign accent. The bartender kept wiping down glasses, saying, "Uh, huh," every so often while the foreign guy emphasized his points by jabbing his finger on the bar.

*Hmm*, Johnny thought, *sounds kind of like a Polish accent, but it's not. Russian, maybe.* Then, taking a deep drag of his cigarette, he flicked the ashes into the ashtray, tucked the cigarette in the corner of his mouth, where the smoke wouldn't drift into his eyes, and went back to work, looking for the short with his voltmeter.

The bartender picked up the tray of glasses, said a final "Uh, huh" to the foreigner, and walked down the bar to put them away. His audience lost, the bearded man turned towards the old fella at the window, but found himself looking at his back. Spinning on his stool, he looked down the bar and saw everyone else watching Johnny work on the pinball machine. Getting up, he put his hands in his pockets and walked the length of the bar, looking down at Johnny and smiling.

*Oh, no*, thought Johnny, *another know-it-all sidewalk supervisor.*

"American electronics are the second best in the world," the big man said, raising his index finger.

"I suppose they make it better in Moscow there, eh, Ivan?"

The beard shook firmly in disagreement. "No. Certainly not. The Russians make garbage. But the Germans, now, they make the best . . ."

"Hey," Johnny said to the bar, "Am I mistaken or didn't we just kick the Nazis' ass?"

Nods of assent and muttered confirmations came from the bar.

Looking up at the big man, Johnny continued, "Now, you're gonna tell me how to find the short in this machine, right, Ivan?"

The big man removed his glasses and leaned over to peer closely at the opened pinball machine. "Hmmm, this is very interesting," he said, looking it over. "I would check there first," pointing where the wires were attached to the thumper bumper coil where Johnny was about to apply the tester's prong.

He did, and it was bad. Taking out the iron and a roll of solder, Johnny put a couple of drops on the end of the iron when it got hot, then put more on the wires, fusing it to the coil. That got the bumper working again, and the big guy was practically dancing with joy.

"Whaddya, playing pocket pool, there, Ivan?" Johnny said, sliding the glass into place and watching the foreigner bounce on his toes with his hands in his pockets.

"I know about electricity and machines," he replied, then spreading his hands out wide, "I can fix radios. Sometimes I even fix Mr. Ciminelli's jukebox here."

Johnny looked over at the bartender, who shrugged and nodded. "Yeah, one time it broke, we couldn't find you, so Mickey gave him the keys. He opened it up and had it runnin' in no time," the bartender said.

"Huh," Johnny said. "Where'd you learn all this, Ivan?"

In a low voice, he replied, "In the army."

"Whose army? Joe Stalin's?"

Quieter still, "Yes, 138th Signal Battalion. I was a radioman. The Russian radios were shit, and I had to fix them every day."

Looking him up and down, Johnny said, "Well, ain't that some-thin', Ivan."

"My name, sir, is not Ivan. It is Stepan Mikhailovitch Tovsenko. My family is from near Kharkov, in the Ukraine, not Russia."

The mention of the Ukraine immediately made Johnny think of a Ukie girl named Luba, from a high school dance at Burgard. Long, dark hair, body like Venus, and wanted absolutely nothing to do with him.

"So, anyhoo, Ukie, how'd you like to learn how to do this repair work for me?" Johnny said. He plugged in the pinball machine and the players started getting off their bar stools and pulling out their nickels.

# CHAPTER 27

## NORTH PARK, 1950

Tim was lying in bed and had turned off the Lone Ranger radio that sounded so loud in the dark, no matter how low he turned it. He had owned the little red box since childhood and kept the wire antenna strung up to the curtain rod, so he could pick up stations from Rochester and sometimes even Syracuse.

Not sleepy, he watched the shadows of the tree branches swaying on the ceiling in the breeze. When the wind blew harder, the leaves would shake and their images danced to and fro. The windows were open, and he could hear the leaves rustle. The cicadas buzzed like a high-pitched saw in the summer heat, and the crickets chirped constantly until threatened by the approach of a bird or a cat. Sometimes a bug would bang up against the screens.

Pat was snoring, a sure sign he'd been drinking. Dad was across the hall in his and Mom's room and always closed the thick wooden door when he went to bed. Pat stopped snoring after awhile and started mumbling. Nightmares again. Tim didn't like that. Whenever he'd drink a lot, Pat snored, then tossed and turned, then started talking in his sleep. After just a few moments, he'd jump up with a cry of surprise, sit there for a minute or two, then, go to the bathroom, piss, and wash his face. Sometimes he'd do that two or three times a night.

Tim remembered Pat belting Bobby May and chasing the other bad kids away on the playground at 81 when they'd kicked Timmy and his friends away from the wall, where they were playing strikeout. Pat had been in the Army and fought at the Battle of the Bulge against the Nazis. It disturbed Tim to know Pat could be frightened, and he pulled the covers up and ducked his head under the pillow.

Pat was jolted awake by the dream and found himself sweaty, thirsty, and out of breath. Looking at the luminous, round dial of the ticking Westclox alarm clock, he saw he'd been in bed only twenty minutes. *How did it happen so fast?* he wondered. *What was the dream this time? Father Kessler again, pacing the wooden floors with his hands clasped behind his back, calling me "squire," a term he used for guys he thought were spoiled and rich:*

"So, Squire Brogan, you were skylarking on a simple assignment the Sergeant gave you?" He spun suddenly on his heel and was now staring at Pat, who wanted to crawl under the desk. "'Skylarking' is the proper term in the military, is it not, Brogan?" he said, raising his voice to assure attention.

"Yes, Father."

"You were given some easy responsibilities? Keeping an eye on some young soldiers, taking prisoners back to the rear?"

*How did he know all this, how did they always know?*

"You even saw Captain, later Colonel, Urban go by, returning to the front lines, even though he had been badly wounded?"

The priest then addressed the entire class. "Lieutenant Colonel Matthew Urbanowicz should be an example to us all. A native of this city, he won numerous medals during the war, amongst them, the Medal of Honor. Never shirking his responsibilities, never failing in them," Father Kessler said, then looking right at Pat, he added, "He was wounded several times and kept returning to battle to lead his men for God and country. This is the kind of behavior we had hoped we taught you here at Canisius."

Then, Pat heard his mother crying in the back of the classroom. He looked around, and Mom and Dad were there, and Dad was dressed like a Doughboy from World War I, his campaign hat on his knee, shaking his head.

*What the hell is this? It can't be real*, he thought, and that was what woke him up. It always did.

# CHAPTER 28

## BUFFALO, 1951

Pat had finished the last beer in the refrigerator, and was worrying that his father would notice he'd knocked off three bottles since dinner, when the phone rang. Picking it up, he looked at his watch. 7:15.

"Brogan! Lieutenant Constantino here. Get yourself dressed for work. We're gonna pay someone a visit downtown. I'll swing by your house in ten minutes."

"Now?" Pat responded, looking again at his watch, as if it would change.

"Nine minutes from now. We work any time on this detail, just like the inspector said. You're not sauced or something, are you?"

"No, not at all," he answered quickly, thinking where he'd hung his holster, and if he had a clean shirt.

"Good, I'll be there in eight." Click.

Brogan ran up the stairs, rushing to beat whoever might want to use the bathroom, and brushed his teeth thoroughly. Flying into his room, he jumped out of his gabardine pants and sports shirt and rushed to put on his brown suit and a white shirt, strap on his shoulder holster, and yank a black tie off the rack. He had just finished putting a Windsor in the skinny necktie and was reaching for the coat when the doorbell rang. He was hurrying down the stairs as his father answered it, *Buffalo Evening News* ("the Republicans' paper," as he put it, grunting derisively) in hand.

"Yes?" Joe said, checking out Constantino, nattily dressed in a chocolate-colored, wide-brim fedora, with a small yellow feather in the black hatband, and a tan overcoat, tied in front.

"Pat Brogan here?"

". . . and you would be?" Joe replied, tilting his chin up and looking down through wireless spectacles at the shorter man.

"Detective Lieutenant Louis Constantino, Gambling Squad," he answered, putting out his hand. "I'm Bro . . . Pat's new boss."

"Joe Brogan," the old man replied, giving the detective a firm shake. "Come in, Lieutenant. Are you here on business?"

Chuckling, Constantino eased up. "No, I don't figure your house for slots, Mr. Brogan. We can work any hours. We go when my boss says jump."

"That would be Inspector Wachter, I believe, or is Chief Mahaney running this?"

"Ah, yeah, Inspector Wachter's the head honcho. Mike Mahaney's moved over to Narcotics."

"A fine man, Martin Wachter, and his father before him. Know them both from the Rowing Club. He'll teach you lads well."

At this, Pat reached the bottom of the stairs, hair slicked down, breath camouflaged, and necktie tight.

"Ready?" Constantino asked, glad to see Pat sharp.

"Ready for action. Dad, you met . . . Lou here? We've got some work tonight."

"I have," his father replied. "Well, go and do your duty, lads," he said, as the two policemen went out the door.

Returning to his chair, he turned the radio down and said a prayer to St. Michael the Archangel, asking him to protect these cocky young men, and then he thanked God for getting Pat out to work, and away from the drink tonight.

Lou Constantino pulled away from the curb with a squeal, accelerating down Woodward towards Amherst as Pat tossed a newspaper into the back seat.

"Your old man knows a lot of people."

"Yeah, he's been in business, church stuff, politics for a long time."

"He use any pull to get you this plainclothes job?"

"No, he stays out of my job. Didn't want me in it to begin with. Wants me to finish college, settle down in some office job, make money, get married, have kids."

"Huh. Anyway, we got a tip that they've got a couple of slot machines down in the basement of the Talon Inn, down on Pearl. You know the place?"

Pat remembered. He had been working overtime downtown when the beat man on Chippewa called for help on a stabbing. By the time he'd gotten there, an Indian was sitting on the floor, holding his stomach, trying to stanch the blood, and breathing hard. The patrolman had his stick out, keeping four guys up against the bar. Nobody else was there except the bartender, who reluctantly was calling an ambulance.

"Pat, Joe," the first patrolman, a wiry guy named Vicigliano, said to Pat and another patrolman named McAvoy, who arrived with him. "Look around for the knife," he said, never taking his eyes off the four men, keeping them against the bar at arm's length with his nightstick. "I got these guys trying to leave the back way. The rest of their pals disappeared out the front."

They searched the four men, no knife. They searched the bar, no knife. Nobody, including the Indian, saw anything. They asked the people on the street, including a couple of hookers plying the area. Nothing. After the Indian went to the hospital, the detectives asked him again. Nothing. They took the four men downtown, and the detectives interrogated them separately. Still nothing.

The three patrolmen stopped in the precinct locker room for a short break before they went back to their beats. The two older patrolmen lit up while Pat sat back and listened to what the veteran police had to say.

Vicigliano slapped Pat on the shin, saying, "Thanks there, young buck, it coulda got ugly in there without your help."

"And let me tell you something too, lad," McAvoy said, pointing with his hat at the young patrolman. "If you ever find yourself surrounded in a joint like that, throw something through the window to get somebody's attention. Somebody'll hear the commotion and get the cavalry."

Taking his hat off and running his fingers through his wiry black hair, Vicigliano nodded and gave his take on it. "All those guys are friends of Stretch Buscarino, who owns the bar. He gets somebody in there he doesn't like, like this Indian, he calls these guys to get rid of 'em and convince him not to come back."

"Yeah, that Wahoo'll do his drinking at The Quarry House or someplace on East Chippewa, like the Red Rose from now on, I'd say," McAvoy added.

The veteran policemen crushed out their smokes, put their hats back on, and exited the locker room, not dwelling on a crime they'd never solve.

In the car, Constantino said that, in addition to the tip about the slots, he had learned there were two guys at the back door, one outside, one inside at the top of the stairs to the basement. To get the guy inside to let you in, you used a password, "Just like during prohibition," the lieutenant said, "And I got a snitch who gave me the password."

Brogan remembered the layout of the place. "There's a stairway by the back door, pretty narrow, I think. Goes down to the cellar."

"Right. The back door goes out onto an alley, and the alley leads out onto Chippewa one way, Tupper the other."

When they got downtown, they drove around the block, watching for the lookouts. The people on the streets seemed like they were changing shifts. Hundreds of shoppers and business people were walking down the streets, pausing to look at the lit up displays in the department store windows, hauling packages onto orange and green streetcars and heading for their neighborhoods. Theatergoers, diners, drinkers, dancers, and bowlers were rolling in, looking to have fun under the neon lights. In the alley behind the bar, there was a guy with a pork pie hat on, leaning against the wall by the back door. They drove around some more, until a parking spot opened up on Tupper where they could see down the alley, at what the lookout was doing.

They sat for a while and watched a couple of middle-aged men exchange a few words and greetings with the doorkeeper, then pass inside.

"Where's your newspaper?" Pat asked, grabbing the paper from the back seat.

"I was checking out the movies downtown. What, you think you can sneak up on 'em, pretend you're reading the paper? That's nuts . . ."

Brogan rifled through the paper's sections until he got to the entertainment section and started reading.

"What the . . ."

"Here it is, just right," he said, looking at his watch. "The Palace Burlesque. Around the corner. They've got a show that lets out in ten minutes. The Paramount's got one letting out five minutes after that, and Shea's . . . is just letting out now. There'll be a crowd coming outta there onto Pearl, and we can slide through these streets with nobody noticing. Should we call Patrol and get a few more guys down here? These guys aren't gonna be happy when we crash their party, el-tee."

Constantino sat for a few seconds, looked at his watch, and thought. "Outstanding idea Brogan, but we don't call anybody outside the squad until we make the pinch. Boss's orders. There were a few parties we tried to crash like this; word got out once a call went in, real fast. Too many leaks at the precinct, too many leaks downtown. He says, 'The only guys we trust is ourselves,' so until we close the bag, we do it alone. Don't worry, though, Paddy boy, the D and D boys, Dudek and Dowd, should be on their way. Know why we call 'em the D and D boys?"

"Because their names begin with D."

"Nope. It stands for 'death and destruction.' They'll be all the help we need for this clambake."

"Okay, boss. How do we handle this?"

"I go to the back door and use the password. I may be a flatfoot, but I don't dress like one," he said, looking at Brogan's clothes, "And I'm a paisan. That, and the password should fool 'em long enough for me to get through the door and into the basement. Dudek will follow me in and collar the lookouts at the door and the top of the stairs. You and Dowd come in the front, nice and easy, and work your way through the bar to the back; making sure nobody escapes that way. You two guys'll go first, and I'll give you about three minutes to get around front and inside. Then, I'll slide down the alley with Dudek following."

"Okay. Looks like it's getting busy in there," Pat said. A couple more men were passed by pork pie hat through the back door.

The lieutenant, looking at his watch, said "It's almost eight;

where the hell are those guys?"

They sat a few minutes, waiting for the crowd to exit the theaters. Brogan could feel his heart speed up and his mouth started to get dry, like before the shooting started over in Europe. What the hell was the name of that lieutenant who always lost his voice, couldn't get a word out once the bullets flew? After trying to choke the words out, he'd just point, wave with his carbine, and run forward. It broke the tension, made the guys crack up a little the second or third time it happened, even when shells were going off.

Glancing over at Constantino, Brogan saw the thick overcoat over his chest rising up and down faster, too.

The show crowd started to come down the street, laughing and talking about the comics, gesturing about the shapes of the strippers, and firing up smokes.

"Shit!" Lou said, watching three more men enter, one slapping the lookout on the back. "We wait any longer and they'll lock the door and not let anyone else in. Let's go now. The D & D boys'll be here any minute and know what to do. Go!"

Brogan went out the door, going upstream against the crowd and around the corner, to the front of the building.

Constantino waited a few moments, his foot tapping the car floor, then slid out the driver's door, tugged his overcoat on tight by the belt, and went across the street to the mouth of the alley, slipping through the show crowd. The lookout was glancing back and forth to both ends of the alley, and Constantino approached the back door, a disarming smile for the lookout. Constantino moved towards him, then saw two guys come up the alley from the other direction on Chippewa, also headed for the back door. The lookout turned and gave a look of recognition to the two men, both in overcoats with the collars turned up, both taller than Lou. One glanced down the alley, spotting Lou's natty attire then knitted his brow in recognition. *Cop!* The lookout had already opened the door and looked inside, nodded, and was ready to let the two guys go in, when Constantino put his head down and charged the three of them like a lineman breaking up a kickoff wedge. Arms outstretched, he grabbed the lookout with one hand, and with his head between the bodies of the other two, took them all down to the pavement, knocking his hat off onto the dirty cement. Jumping up, he spun around and saw a pair of hands pulling the door closed from the inside. Charging the door and yanking it wide open, Lou pulled the hands loose from it. He turned to see the bared teeth of the doorman, his face flushed with anger and growling, extended hands reaching for him.

Lou knocked his attacker's right arm to the side with his left and threw the hardest punch he could with his right, connecting solidly with the man's big teeth. Stunning him, Lou grabbed the doorman's right shoulder with his left hand, pulling the man behind him onto the three guys in the alley, who were trying to get him from behind as he jumped inside. He saw the cellar stairway to his left, and there was heat, cigarette smoke, and noise coming at him from down there. Right in front of him was the barstool where the doorman with the big teeth had sat, up against a plaster wall with the wood lath exposed in spots and stacks of beer cases filled with empty bottles. To his right he looked into the bar, and despite the dimmed lights, he could see a lot of people, standing and sitting at the bar and at tables. Most of them were turned to him with *What the hell is this?* looks on their faces.

*Ah shit, I better announce myself, before this gets real ugly,* he thought, *But I don't know if we're gonna make this work myself, Paddy Boy, and just where the hell are you, anyway?* He heard glass shattering from the front.

Brogan moved easily through the show crowd, turning his shoulder and avoiding eye contact, and got right in front of the bar: a brick-faced front painted red, two big picture windows with beer signs, specials written on cardboard, and a neon one advertising cocktails in red and a stemmed glass in white. There was a stainless steel door with glass, and the foyer floor was set with tiny, black and white, octagonal tiles spelling out the address. Keeping his head down, Brogan pushed through the door and stood right in front of it inside, blocking the way out. He looked up, and slowly let out a breath as he sized up the place. Lights dimmed, red neon light framed the bar's mirror on his left. *Crowded, must be twenty, maybe thirty people,* he thought. There were wooden tables on his right, people two deep at the bar in some places.

Two guys he spotted, right off, at the bar. They were two of the four guys who had knifed the Indian. One was talking to the bartender, and the other faced him, squinting at him in vague recollection through the cigarette smoke that came from the long Pall Mall that dangled from his mouth. He nudged the other guy. The other guy turned and the bartender looked up at Pat, as well.

*This ain't good*, Brogan thought, reaching with his left hand for his badge, and feeling for his sap in the right overcoat pocket.

Just then the uproar caused by Constantino's entrance started at the rear, and Brogan could dimly see several bodies in violent motion a good thirty feet away from him there.

*Oh shit, he's in trouble*, he thought, *I gotta get to him. To hell with that not needing help crap*, he thought.

The guys at the bar slid off their stools with their hands reaching into their pockets. *Gotta get a patrolman's attention the old fashioned way.* He looked to his right and saw a petite woman with silver-blonde hair piled up high, a strand of fake pearls hanging down on an oversized bosom, and glitter on her eyelids. She was sitting on a barstool with her legs crossed, smoking a cigarette in a holder. *Stripper.* There were three guys standing around her with their hands in their pockets, jolted from their reverie by the sudden violence. There was a midget with a big smile sitting on a stool next to the girl. Dressed in a white Union suit, he was smoking a cigar and enjoying a martini.

*No empty chairs, gotta go with the dwarf 's*, Pat thought. He took his hands clear of his overcoat pockets and grabbed the little man's stool. The midget's eyes went wide, and he grabbed onto the seat with a death grip as Pat pitched him and the stool through the front window, onto the street. Pat then turned to the stunned crowd, pulled out his sap, and slugged the guy with the Pall Mall, as the thug pulled out a switchblade. Swinging back, he caught the other thug across the face and drove him back, raising an arm to shield his face.

Patrolman Joe McAvoy rubbed his eyes as he stood outside the back of the Palace Theater on Pearl and adjusted his hat securely forward on his head, having finished a nap in the back row of the theater. He was there ostensibly checking for overcrowding, pick-pockets, and perverts, as he would report, if anyone asked. The manager was swell with this deal, and if there was any trouble in the theater, he'd wake Big Joe. Joe looked at his watch and hoped the rest of the shift would go quietly. He planned to take the wife out on the town to Ma Broderick's Club Deluxe on Seneca after he got off. Then, he heard a crash and saw a kid in his pajamas rolling on the street and moaning.

The crowd on the street stopped in their tracks. *What the...*, McAvoy thought. He pulled out his nightstick and ran to the front of the bar, where he spotted Scotty, the midget acrobat from the Palace, on the ground, the front window of the Talon Inn smashed out, and all hell breaking loose inside. He ran in and recognized Brogan, in civilian clothes, ready to swing his sap at two guys with knives, the toughs having rallied from the sap's first blows. Before they could react to their new opponent, McAvoy grabbed his stick top and bottom and rammed it into Knife One's stomach, and when he bent over from that blow, McAvoy slammed it over his head, swinging the billy club with both hands as hard as he could. When Knife Two hesitated, Brogan stepped in with the sap, and this time belted his target across the ear, sending him to the floor.

McAvoy swung his stick back and jabbed a man in the chest who was headed for the door and shouted, "Nobody move, or by God, I'll give the lot of you an all mighty crack!"

Brogan rushed to the rear, scattering tables, bottles, and glasses to the sound of women's shrieks, and spotted two guys holding Lou's arms from behind.

Lou furiously kicked his powerful legs at a third guy com-ing at him from the front, and had another sprawled before him. "Goddamitt! I'm the police! You fuck up my clothes and I'll kill you bastards, every one of you!"

Brogan grabbed the guy in front of Lou by the collar and yanked him backwards, slamming him down with his sap. Getting his feet beneath himself, Constantino swung the guy on his right arm forward towards Brogan, who backhanded him with the sap across the jaw, then got hold of the guy on his left and threw him at the cellar stairs, where people were scampering towards the back door.

As McAvoy pushed the would-be escapee back into the barroom with his stick, he stepped towards the front door to block it, then heard feet crunching on glass and saw motion behind his left shoulder. Ducking instinctively, he felt a beer bottle come down, catching his hat and just missing his head from behind. Crouching lower, McAvoy swung his stick around, catching his assailant right across both shins. Letting out a yelp, the bartender dropped backward into a sitting position and wrapped his arms around his legs moaning, "Oh shit, oh shit, oh shit," and rocking back and forth.

McAvoy stood up, pulled out his long barreled revolver, and holding it at port arms, yelled, "All right, that's enough!" Pointing his nightstick towards the back, he said "Everybody get back where I can see you!"

The stunned, the injured, and the frightened stepped away from the door, except for the blonde on the barstool, who hadn't moved through the entire fracas and kept her smoldering cigarette, with holder, held high.

At the rear of the bar, Brogan and Constantino had also pulled out their revolvers and, trying to catch their breath, ordered the people coming up the stairs, back down. Kicking the guys they had wrestled and sapped, they forced them back into the bar while the sound of sirens approached, none too soon for the exhausted policemen.

The next policeman on the scene was Vicigliano, who slid on the broken glass through the front door. Once he saw the wreckage of the bar, three guys busted up on the floor and McAvoy with his gun out, he pushed his hat back on his head and said, "Forget making the late show at Broderick's, Mac. Judge Chimera's not gonna like this . . ."

As police car after police car pulled up to the scene, plainclothesmen and foot patrolmen ran up, the plainclothesmen gravitating towards the rear, and the uniformed men to the front of the bar. With the reinforcements having taken control of the situation, Brogan went to the front of the bar to identify his two assailants while Constantino went down into the cellar with Dudek, who had just arrived, while Dowd was throwing the three men in the alley against the wall, faces first.

It was hot, smoky, and crowded, with eleven men in their shirtsleeves in the cellar, and cases of beer and liquor stashed up against the stone walls everywhere. The only exit besides the stairs at the rear was a metal trap door at the front for bringing down cases and kegs.

Constantino could see a padlock hanging down from it. He grabbed Dudek's shoulder and told him, "Search up front, we're looking for slot machines, and maybe pinballs they got down here," which got a quizzical glance from the blonde-haired policeman, who looked around the crowded cellar and saw nothing.

The shirt-sleeved men mumbled to each other quietly while Lou pulled cases away, rolled beer barrels, and pushed people out of his way, but found nothing.

Finally, Dudek came forward, saying, "Hey, Lieutenant, look at this," holding a bundled up olive drab blanket. Disappointment showed on Constantino's face when he first saw Dudek hadn't found a machine, but he shoved a couple of the cellar's occupants back while Dudek laid the blanket on the floor, opening it up to reveal playing cards and money.

"Hey, looks like we gotta game goin' on here," the lieutenant said in triumph, crouching down to examine the blanket's contents. "Must be a couple of hundred bucks here. Big game, eh boys? We're gonna have to run all you guys in," he said, standing up. "The judge is not gonna like this at all." Then, he made eye contact with one of the gamblers in the back of the crowd. *Oh Jesus,* he thought, *it's Uncle George. The family's going to kill me if he gets arrested,* and the elderly man stared right at him.

"Dudek, keep an eye on this a second," he ordered, walking towards the stairs to consider his dilemma. When he got to the steps, Brogan was there, asking, "Whadja find?"

"Card game, Ziginat, bunch of old guys having big time fun. No machines, though."

"Well, we gotta have something after we set off the atom bomb in here. How many guys we got?"

"Uh, look Pat, there's a guy down here, my Uncle George, and, uh. . ."

"Lieutenant? Remember what Inspector Wachter said about 'willful neglect?'" Pat was enjoying the turnabout with his supervisor. "He's out front right now and wants to talk to us."

Lou trotted up the stairs, where a patrolman silently handed Constantino his crumpled fedora, soiled and featherless. He cursed and tried to knock some of the dirt off of it. He said to Brogan, "I just got this hat the other day, around the corner," nodding towards Court Street, "a brand new top of the line Peller & Mure hat." He headed for the front with Brogan, contemplating what to say to his boss.

*The rough stuff, okay, we can handle it,* he thought, *They started it. No slots, not yet anyway, maybe they're upstairs.* he gave himself a jolt of hope, thinking, *And there's the Ziginat game. Ah, shit, Ma's gonna kill me for running Uncle George in.*

As they got outside, they saw the bartender being loaded into the wagon and Vicigliano pulling McAvoy aside. "Mac, you might not want to do this," the wiry patrolman advised.

"Bullshit," the red faced McAvoy exclaimed. "He takes a swing at me, he's in. Period."

"Joe," Vicigliano whispered, "This guy's the judge's cousin, and his favorite bartender besides. He's just gonna turn him loose."

"I don't give a rat's knuckle who this son of a bitch thinks he is, he's goin' in. And if I gotta stay in court after the end of watch, and miss going to Broderick's, all these bastards can keep me company, no matter who they know," McAvoy said, at which his cooler partner shook his head.

"Okay, I'll call the wives and tell them the bad news," Vicigliano said.

# CHAPTER 29

## DOWNTOWN, 1951

After the midget acrobat was taken to the hospital, and as the paddy wagons loaded up the gamblers and thugs, the owner of the bar arrived and stood screaming on the sidewalk at the shift lieutenant from the Third Precinct, the deputy commissioner, and Inspector Wachter, all of whom had gotten phone calls from both the commissioner and the mayor "to find out what the hell was going on down there on Pearl Street." They all listened to the business owner's complaints, politely for awhile, for he was a known financial supporter of the mayor, then, quieted him down when Inspector Wachter started asking about gambling going on in the basement, mentioning that such things could cause trouble with the liquor board, and that newspapers would have a field day hearing about a police raid on the business of a prominent local businessman. In the end, the bar owner went inside to tally up the damages and get his people to clean up, vowing over his shoulder that "the city would pay for everything, down to the last busted shot glass."

Pulling up his two raiders, Wachter said, "You guys and the D and D boys get the people in the fight booked properly, sweat the card players for a couple of hours and see what you can get out of them, then, cut them loose. Then, when that's all done, I want to talk to you in my office."

Brogan and Constantino got in the car and headed downtown in silence, but after they turned on Pearl, both men burst out laughing so hard, Lou had to pull the car over.

"What the hell made you think of tossing the midget?" Constantino roared, gasping.

"Seemed . . . seemed like a good idea to get patrol's attention, at the time," Brogan laughed back. "Those two guys with the knives couldn't move when they saw that . . . And you should've seen the stripper . . . She froze up like a statue," he bellowed, "And hey, where's your friggin' hat, Beau Brummel?"

"Well maybe," Lou panted, "Maybe I should check their lost and found tomorrow for a new one," he said, laughing harder.

The two of them, trying to catch their breath, looked at each other and cracked up again.

"Great plan boss," Brogan chuckled, "Ought to teach it at the academy," he said, going into another laugh spasm. "Write it up and send it to Quantico, so the F.B.I. can learn it . . ."

"What . . . what the hell are you supposed to do if they don't have a midget handy?" Lou added, sending them back into fits of laughter.

When they finally caught their breath and wiped their eyes with their handkerchiefs, Lou pulled back out into traffic, and they continued downtown.

Brogan gave a low chuckle, and muttered,

"Zahar."

"Huh?"

"Lieutenant Zahar. I was trying to think of his name a while ago."

"Who the hell is he, a midget?"

They cracked up again, but Pat calmed sooner, remembering the lieutenant who couldn't get the words out in combat and was blasted by artillery that showered his men with clothes, blood, and entrails.

"Wachter's," Constantino said, still laughing a little, "Gonna kick our asses."

"Not for a while. We still gotta get all those bums booked. Maybe the brass'll calm down by then."

"Hey, speaking of which, you gotta do a favor for me."

"Oh, no, I ain't getting your uncle out of this one . . ."

"Nah, I know we can't do that. But how about this: you call my cousin, Pete; tell him what happened, and he'll come and get his dad out when we're done with them. Just leave my name out of it. I'm still gonna have to pay hell with my family, but I can buy a little time this way, at least until he gets out and tells his sister what a no good ratfink cop her son is. Jesus, Mary, and Joseph, I'm gonna have to go into hiding after this."

After the card players were parked in the drunk tank, the two thugs, the doormen, the guys from the alley, and the bartender were booked; and the knives and a bottle (any one would do) were put in evidence; Lou and Pat went up to the inspector's office; the only one with lights burning. The smell of coffee came through the door. They both took a deep breath as Lou knocked.

"Come in."

Entering, they saw the inspector reading a report, tie still neatly knotted. Two paper cups of coffee were on his desk and a chair beside it, for someone who had just left. He looked at them over his wire-rimmed glasses. "Sit down."

When they had, Wachter stood up and leaned on his desk.

"No more Wild West stuff, do you understand?" he demanded. "You could've gotten killed there, you pair of hot dogs! You need help, wait for the rest of the squad! Got that?"

In unison, they answered, "Yessir," both standing at attention.

"The midget's boss at the Palace is going nuts. He's got some cuts and bruises, but they say he's going to file assault charges, or, his boss is for him, anyway. What are we going to do about that?"

"He wouldn't let go of the chair, Inspector," Pat said, and both detectives covered their mouths to stifle the laughter.

Wachter stared until they calmed down.

"No machines found, and that was the point of the whole raid, was it not? Were you smart enough to get the warrant to read 'gambling paraphernalia' there, Lieutenant?"

"Yessir," Constantino replied. "I mentioned verbally to the judge about slots and oneballs, but we put 'gambling devices and paraphernalia' in the warrant to cover all the bases."

"Good. Score one for Gott's boy," Wachter said, referring to Constantino's old principal at Lafayette High School. "All right. Here's what we're going to do now. Get one of these cups of coffee and get out to your desks and write the reports. I'm going to check them before you turn them in. One thing that's on our side is that you didn't shoot anybody. Make sure you put in the reports that it was crowded, and you didn't think it was safe, even though the perpetrators who assaulted you had knives and menaced you with bottles, were engaged in criminal behavior, and out-numbered you. It shows restraint. Got that?"

"Yessir," they both said together.

"All right. I'd heard that bozo had a game going in that joint for years, and you crushed it. No machines, but gambling's gambling, and that's what we're after. It may not have worked as planned, but Constantino, Brogan, good job. Now, get your coffee and get out of here. I've got to do some thinking."

When they'd closed the door, Lou put a finger to his lips and motioned Pat over to his desk. There, he hurriedly wrote down Fillmore 0717, and the name Peter Lalle.

Whispering, he said, "Quick, call this number and get hold of this guy. He's my cousin, my Uncle George's son. Tell him what happened and to go and get his dad out. He knows his dad likes to play cards, so he'll keep it quiet, too. Maybe they won't find out I did it. Whatever you do, keep me out of it!"

Brogan went to his desk and waited until Lou had rolled the report, carbon paper and copies into the typewriter and begun to type, before he picked up the phone and dialed. Looking at his watch, he saw that it was now almost midnight.

After four rings, a woman answered, "Hello?"

"May I speak to Peter Lalle, please?"

"Who's this? Peter's asleep, gotta work in the morning. You drunk or something?"

"No, Ma'am. This is . . . Mr. Able with the I.R.C. We believe we found Mr. Lalle's wallet on a bus today."

"His wallet? Wait a minute, there, Able. Hey, Peter. Peter, wake up. You lose your wallet?"

"Huh?"

"You lose your wallet? There's a man on the telephone from the bus company, says he found your wallet."

"No, I don't think so, I think I still got it. Who's on the phone?"

"Mr. Able, from the bus company. Go talk to him, I'm going

back to bed. It's late."

"Hello?"

"Pete Lalle?"

"Yes?"

"Listen up. Your dad, George Lalle's in jail, downtown. Picked up for gambling. He needs you to get down to Police Headquarters and get him out." Click.

Pete looked at the phone for a few seconds, then hung up and started hustling into his clothes. As he was going out the door, he said, "Hey, Ma, I'm goin' to get my wallet, I'll need it for work tomorrow. Don't wait up."

As he closed the door, he could hear his mother saying, "Hey, your Papa's not come to bed all night! What's goin' on here?"

Looking over at Brogan, Constantino got a small smile.

"That was quick thinking, Pat," Constantino said. "If this works out, Pete will get Uncle George out, and they'll both keep quiet about it. Then, I'll just have to talk to Uncle George and Pete. That won't be too bad. I owe you big time on this one, partner."

And with that, they went to work on their reports, hoping that the inspector would cover for them about the midget and the other rough stuff; Lou hoping his family wouldn't find out about Uncle George's pinch; and Brogan smiling to himself that he had made the team.

As dawn came up over downtown Buffalo, cleaning crews were leaving the office buildings and early Mass-goers were entering St. Joseph's Cathedral across the street from Police Headquarters. Several sleepy policemen were headed for Sunrise Court at the City Court Building at 42 Delaware Avenue. Also coming out were the accused, chained together, and loaded onto sheriff's wagons to meet their accusers again before a judge.

The City's Attorney and the police filed in on one side of the courtroom, the accused mumbling and clanking into the benches on the other side. The judge entered briskly from his chambers, and the bailiff began, "Oyez, oyez, oyez. All those having business in this Court of the City of Buffalo in the State of New York now come forward and be heard. The Honorable Francis Chimera now presiding." Once in the court, the judge, a younger man with wavy, dark hair, a pencil mustache, and a perpetual smile, looked out over the courtroom and beamed as he sat down at the elevated bench.

"Well, it looks like we had a busy night last night here in Buffalo."

Recently elected to the City Court, the up and coming lawyer was known for his sense of humor and was amused by the big crowd at the early session, finding it more entertaining than the usual few sad prostitutes, thieves, and vagrants he usually had before him. "Bailiff, call the cases, if you please."

"The Court calls Thomas Agro and John Cofrancesco. Accused of the following: On March 3rd of this year, at approximately 8:30 P.M., Misters Agro and Cofrancesco did assault with deadly weapons, Patrolman Patrick Brogan while he was in pursuit of his duties in the premises of 462 Pearl Street in this city. They are further accused of attempted murder, as they did arm themselves with knives in their attack on Patrolman Brogan; possession of illegal weapons; interfering with the actions of a police officer; refusing the reasonable requests of a police officer; affray; public disorder; drunk and disorderly conduct; attempted mayhem; and resisting arrest."

The prosecutor stood up. "Your Honor," he began, "This was a dastardly assault on a policeman of this city who was in the course of carrying out his duties, to wit, conducting a raid on a premises used for gambling purposes, when these two men attacked him with knives and without provocation. Showing admirable restraint in a crowded public place, Patrolman Brogan used his sap rather than his pistol to defend himself, and, with the assistance of Patrolmen McAvoy and Vicigliano, took these two assailants into custody after a considerable struggle. The State asks these individuals be held over for trial."

Eagerly awaiting the defendants' replies, the judge looked over at the defense table and asked, "Are the defendants represented by counsel?"

"Yes, Your Honor, Ross Oberpfalz for the defense," replied a law school classmate of the judge, from a row behind the defendants.

"I have been engaged to represent these two men, Your Honor, and they plead innocent. They are both natives of this city, with gainful employment and considerable family here. At the time that they were on the premises in question, they witnessed Mr. Brogan, out of uniform and failing to announce his presence as a police officer, attack a Mr. Scott McClive, a resident of this city, employed by a local theater who was seated in the premises at 462 Pearl Street having a drink. Mr. Brogan first assaulted Mr. McClive without provocation, throwing him through the front window of the establishment, and my clients went to his defense."

Looking up from the charging documents, the judge interrupted, "With eight-inch switchblade knives?"

"We'll dispute that, Your Honor. Those weapons were planted on the defendants when the police realized their most numerous and grievous errors of conduct."

"This should be interesting. I'm sorry I can't be the trial judge for this one. According to the ever efficient Court Clerk Mr. McCann, the trial date for this case is set for 10:00 a.m. on Thursday, March 15th, and I set bail for both of these men at one hundred dollars apiece," the judge said. With a slam of the gavel, the court moved on to the next case; the assault on Patrolman McAvoy.

Waiting outside for his lieutenant, Brogan saw the bartender skip down the steps and into a cab. When Constantino came out, he was talking to a bailiff who was telling him where his uncle and cousin Pete had gone.

"Hey, Brogan, hungry?" Constantino asked.

"Hell, yeah, want to go over to Bowles, maybe catch some more court side gossip?"

"Outstanding," he replied, and as they went down the steps, they heard McAvoy and Vicigliano coming down behind them.

"The lousy son-of-a-bitch. The guy takes a shot at me and gets away with it. To hell with him and his cousin."

"Joe, I tried to tell you," Lou said. "You could've saved yourself a lot of aggravation by just forgetting it, but no, you had to push it and watch the guy walk."

"You wait. He'll foul up again, and I'll be right there waiting."

"Sure, Joe. In the meantime, let's get out of these uniforms, and go get a drink and some breakfast. We gotta be back for roll call at four tonight."

Lou said to Pat, "I called the inspector when you were before the judge with the prosecutor. He says to go home and get some sleep. I'll give you a call around noon and let you know what's doing. That's one of the advantages of this assignment, Paddy. If we do good, we set our own hours."

"Hey, boss, I got a question. What game were they playing down there in the basement? Blackjack?"

"Oh, that game, that's called Ziginat. It came from the old country. You play it with a forty-card deck; no eights, nines, or tens. One guy's the dealer, working for the bar here. He deals out two cards for the players, one for himself. Everybody but the dealer bets on one or both of the players' cards, whatever the house's limits. Then he deals another card. If that card matches one of the players' cards, the dealer collects those bets, and gives the house a cut. If the card matches the dealer's, he pays off everyone's bet, and the house backs him. No matches, bet again, and keep dealing. Gets real expensive sometimes. Once it gets started, it can go on for days, and once you're in, you don't want to leave. Hopefully, Uncle George wasn't making money, will keep his mouth shut, and I'll still have a family."

During breakfast, they regaled each other by recapping the barroom battle, and glowed when someone recognized them. Someone gave them the final edition of the morning paper, but when they found the article, Lou's face fell.

"Police raid gambling den in downtown nightclub," Pat read. When he saw the picture, he knew why Lou was frowning, for it showed Uncle George being shoved into the paddy wagon and Lou in the background.

"I'm doomed," he said, dropping his fork on his plate.

# CHAPTER 30

## THE WEST SIDE, 1951

The car stopped half a block from the bar on the corner, and the passenger and driver watched the street, and the adjoining parking lot. The passenger was just about to get out of the car's back seat when the bar's front door opened, and the light and noise of the revelers poured out into the winter night. The couple closed the door, checked the weather for snow, tugged on their gloves, and walked towards Elmwood. When the sound of their feet crunching in the snow faded from the idling Cadillac, the man in the back seat waited a few moments; then, stepped out of the car.

"Plan on coming back around three, Stormy, I'm feeling lucky tonight, but call around two on official business anyway, in case I'm not," the mayor said, winking at the plainclothes officer behind the wheel.

Pulling out a key, Mayor Joseph Jezerowski walked quickly to a side door of the bar, went inside, and then relocked it behind him. He slowly went up the narrow staircase to the second floor, careful to make as little noise as possible. At the top of the steps, he stopped and listened just before the door. Along with the clinking chips and glasses sounding from within, there were several men's voices.

*Hmm,* he thought, *Ed's here, talking about walking a beat years ago in the snow, means he's probably losing . . . Ah, Richard's here; I heard his judicial throat clearing, perhaps to place a bet on a bluff like he always does. There's Ocky, always keeping track of the cards. Seems happy, everything must be okay in there.* The fourth voice he didn't recognize right off: a younger one. *Of course, the young lawyer,*

*Verrone, what is it? Begins with a C. Carl, that's it. New to the DA's office; ambitious. Well, kid, let's see how you play your cards . . .*

Opening the door abruptly, the mayor's best electoral smile beamed on the four men around the card table. His large, brown eyes lit up as he went around, smiling at each, gripping their hands firmly, welcoming young Carl to the game, and telling him to keep his seat as they shook. He whisked off his black wool overcoat and gray scarf, carefully hanging them in a closet, and came back to sit down at the large round table covered in green felt with poker chips, cards, and tumbler glasses stationed at each man's place. A tall, broad-shouldered man, with his dark brown hair in a side part, just going gray at the sides, Mayor Joseph "Jazz" Jezerowski took off his double-breasted, blue, pinstriped suit coat, and hung it over a chair set aside for himself, then shot his hands forward out of the French cuffs of his laundered, white shirt as he sat down.

"Well, boys, how are we doing tonight?" the mayor inquired, grinning around the table. "Ah, I see Ocky seems to have a lot of chips. Don't let his incessant patter distract you, Carl, he may talk a lot, but his mind is always on the cards. That's why he's my right hand man in politics. Your Honor, how about you give me twenty dollars' worth of chips? I plan to be here for awhile tonight and enjoy myself with you good friends, unless duty calls."

The chips out, the cards were dealt; dealer's choice. Judge Richard Dickerson, a florid heavyset man, preferred variants of seven-card stud, especially roll your own, which could postpone the finish to a dramatic last card. As yet unsure of his place in the game, Carl stuck to five-card stud and tried to read his fellow players. Ed Falk, the deputy police commissioner, started with draw poker, jacks or better to open, but as he became slightly glassy-eyed with gin, reduced his choices to the simpler games, and still lost steadily. Ocky, the mayor's campaign manager, and a saloon-keeper by trade, changed games every time he dealt, and rarely the games chosen by his fellow card players. The mayor favored progressive draw poker, where jacks or better were required to open, and if no one could, it progressed through queens, kings, and aces, with antes required for each failure to get the minimum hand to begin.

Behind the judge, a table held a bucket of ice; glasses; and a variety of liquors and mixers in front of a window still covered with wartime blackout curtains that looked out on the street in front of the bar. The judge drank little, taking small sips of his scotch and soda, while Ed put the gin and tonics away in quantity, despite the fact he was technically the on-duty supervisor for the police department after eight o'clock. Ocky drank his Canadian whiskey straight, and chased it with water. The mayor made a great show of fixing a drink, pouring precisely two ounces of whiskey into the glass, then blasting it with soda from the charged seltzer dispenser. Ocky kept track of how much His Honor drank, and it wasn't a little, but not a real lot, either, and he hadn't seen it faze him yet, which he found to be a useful skill amongst successful politicians. When one of their number got up to fix a drink or use the bathroom, each of the others nonchalantly put his cards down, for, although they all considered themselves gentlemen and friends (though Carl knew he was still working on achieving this latter status, no matter what the others said), there was money involved, and business was business.

After the mayor had sat in a few hands, Ed was slowly dealing a hand of straight up seven-card stud, and the mayor asked, "Well, Carl, how's your career going on over at the DA's office? I presume District Attorney Stone is keeping you jumping nowadays?"

Looking from the cards coming out, to the others who were watching him, Carl answered, "Very busy in some bureaus, but fairly routine in City Court. Mostly petty thefts, prostitutes, a few frauds these days. The guys who handle the bank robbery and other felony cases seem to be doing the most interesting work."

"Had any experience over there, yet? You've been in the office about three years, now, isn't it?" the mayor asked, to which Ocky thought to himself, *two years, eight months exactly, just like I told you earlier, Jazz.*

"Uh, yeah, I've been there about that, Your Honor. So far, I've just been in City Court."

"Well, that's interesting. Do you like it there?"

"It's fine, but at some point I would like to broaden my experience."

"I think that's a fine thing, too. Too many of our young lawyers in public service get tied down with the same job for years, and then what happens, I ask you? They look elsewhere, find a position in private practice, and that's the end of a potentially great career with government. Don't you agree, Judge?"

"Certainly. I stayed in public service, worked my way up through the prosecutor's office, and earned my robe, but there's many a young attorney who gets bored and thinks private practice is where his future lies. Now, some do well there, but others, without connections in the right law firms, wind up doing wills and notary, never going anywhere, and regretting they left government service."

"And government service is not going to shrink, Carl. Ever since the New Deal, whether the Democrats or the Republicans are running things, federal, state, and city governments are getting bigger all the time. There should be some opportunities in all branches for a sharp young man like you."

Carl thought about the future and what he had just heard.

"It's to you, Carl," Ed said after looking over the cards he had dealt. "You've got a jack showing."

"Oh," he said, pulling back from the reverie of his own judge's chambers. He glanced at the dealt cards and said, "I'm in, for . . . fifty cents."

"Okay, Judge, how about you?"

Often, the hands would come down to head-to-head battles between Ocky and the mayor, jacking the pots up with large bets, trying to out-bluff each other occasionally, and keeping the others as spectators while they played with the other players' losses.

Half an hour later, Carl realized he had dropped more than he had planned on spending. Passing the deal, he stood up, saying, "With your permission, gentlemen, I think I'd better go home now, and get some shut-eye. I've got a case to present before Judge Kenna tomorrow, and he'll expect me to be ready."

"Just so," joined the mayor, as the four others watched Carl straighten his tie and put on his coat. "Keep in touch, Carl. Give some thought about what we said here tonight, and I'll talk to District Attorney Stone and a few others to see what opportunities are out there."

"I think the next game'll be a week from tonight, Carl," Ocky added, his eyes now fixed on the cards the judge was dealing. "I'll give you a scream where and when."

"Okay," Carl replied as he went out the door, his mind trying to figure an excuse for not making the game next week. *Can't afford these stakes too often*, he thought.

After Carl left, Ed tried to focus on his watch.

"Tired, Ed?" the mayor inquired.

"Yeah, can't keep the hours I used to. Better call it a night. Technically, I'm still working—the nighttime duty officer, you know," he chuckled.

"I'm about done-in as well, gentlemen," added the judge. "How about if I give you a ride home, Ed?"

"That'd be fine, Judge."

Getting into his hat and coat, the judge headed for the stairs, knowing the mayor wanted a few words with Ed. "Take your time, Ed. I'll bring the car around the side."

"Okay, Judge. I'll be right down," he said, yawning.

After he heard the door at the bottom of the stairs close, the mayor looked up from his cards and asked, "What's Wachter up to now, Ed? I heard a couple of his men tried to demolish the Talon Inn the other night, threw some poor midget through a window, bludgeoned a couple of Stretch's comrades at the bar."

Pushing his glasses back up on his nose, Ed nodded, smiling. "Sure did. One came in the back, one in the front. A couple of guys pulled knives on Joe Brogan's son, Pat. He throws the midget out the window to get patrol's attention, and he kicks both their asses. Meantime, Lou Constantino's wrestling three guys at the back door, keeping the lads from escaping the basement until the cavalry arrives. Musta had a tip, they had a game goin' in the basement. Caught all of 'em. Hell of a job they did."

"Ed, there are some serious complaints about their violent ways, and the city will have to deal with them, perhaps in court. It could be very expensive for the taxpayers when the police are riding roughshod on the citizens. Doesn't Wachter get the warrants for these raids?"

Ed shook his head. "No, he hand-picks his men, introduces them to the hows and whys of warrants, then turns 'em loose.

Sharp guys who can handle snitches and get the warrants themselves. Raids, too, mostly. No, Wachter runs a tight ship. You want him outta the way, it's not going to be for screwing up. Tough cookie, good copper."

"Well, I certainly don't think his firing would be in order in the midst of such a splendid career," the mayor said. "Perhaps, however, he might be moved to a less sensitive position to avoid future citizens' complaints, he being under constant public scrutiny in his current post. Yes, Ed, I'd like you and the commissioner to give that serious consideration, very serious consideration—where Inspector Wachter might fit into the department in the future."

Ed nodded, putting on navy blue earmuffs, and a brown fedora. *Keep your ears warm, no matter how it looks,* he thought, a habit learned years before walking beats on cold nights. He waved goodnight, then went down the stairs, tapping his hip under the thick wool overcoat to make sure his weapon was secure. *I'm still a policeman,* he thought, reassuring himself of his status. *Yup,* he thought, *Just two, maybe three more years. Retire, move to Florida, no more mayors to keep happy anymore. Just got to keep squirreling away more bucks to pay for it all, and Mary and I are gone, out of this freezing city.*

The mayor parted the curtains and watched. "What do you think about this violent raid on Pearl Street, Cornelius?" he asked, calling his political adviser by his seldom-used first name.

"Transferring him now won't be good. I can see the papers now: *Crusading Cop Given Heave-Ho. Mayor Stooge of Gambling Syndicates.* Wouldn't be good at all. You just appointed a new commissioner when you got elected, now you're not happy that the cops are doing their job? Looks real bad. The Republican big shots in County Hall and Albany might not like it, either."

"Hmmm, absolutely correct, as always, Ock. We'll have to find a better spot for Inspector Wachter on the force. But, not just now, I think. We'll let him continue on his crusade for awhile longer, and make sure we have the attention of the bon vivants who run the games. Then, if they find it in their hearts to support our campaign fund to a greater extent, Sir Wachter's crusade could be neutralized any number of ways. For example, don't you have a number of friends with Western Union and the phone company?"

"Yeah," Ocky drawled. "There's always a few guys I can ask for a favor or two."

"Inspector Wachter has built quite a staff for himself, isolated from the rest of the department, which he considers somewhat unreliable, and not at all closed-mouthed about his various squads' activities, does he not?"

"They're loyal and closed-mouthed, that's for sure. Getting gutsier all the time, too."

"Well, although we may not have access to his plans through normal channels, perhaps one of your friends could arrange to overhear a few conversations between his office and his men and their informants. This information could be quite valuable to the men of chance, who might consider some greater financial support for future elections in their best interest. Then, when Inspector Wachter's crusades have waned and the newspapers move on to something else, we can have the good inspector moved to a more suitable position."

After a pause, Ocky said, "The money would come in handy, that's for sure. Give us some independence from the boys in the County, and Albany. Make a run on our own even." Thinking of the mayor's last overwhelming showing amongst his fellow Poles, he continued, "With the East Side solidly behind you, and a little work in the county, we could be going even bigger places, or at least, the big boys would have to deal with us if they wanted anything around here. Hmm. Bugging phones, though, could be dangerous. Maybe get the feds involved if someone gets caught."

"If," the mayor said, raising his index finger, and smiling. "If the conversation is not between two states, it isn't a federal matter, and the state laws are very vague on the subject, very vague, indeed. Besides, if it is discovered, they'll just think the bookmakers did it themselves. After all, they are the ones setting up the wired horse rooms and telephones, aren't they?"

"Yeah," Ocky said, running through the names of potential candidates for the job.

"Speaking of the East Side," the mayor continued, "Don't we have a dinner engagement at the Polish Falcons tomorrow night?"

"Yep, sure do. Give about a five-minute speech about the Falcons, have dinner, hand out awards that their basketball teams earned this year. All set."

"Excellent. Now, let's play some cards," the mayor finished, and they did, going head-to-head until shortly before dawn, back and forth, with Ocky slowly but surely getting ahead, his concentration never flagging. To the mayor, it seemed the only thing that moved on Ocky were his hands, dealing and holding cards, and his eyes, which His Honor sometimes suspected could see through the cards.

Around five-thirty, the mayor got up, washed his face in the bathroom, and then peeking out onto the street, said, "Ach, it'll be dawn soon." Looking at his dwindling pile of chips, he went on, "Big day ahead, my man, and you have a business to run. We should call it a night." Wagging a finger at his friend, he cautioned, "I figure you're up about twenty-three dollars on me tonight, Ock. I made a few bucks on the other guys, but I'll get mine back from you next time." Finishing his drink, he went to the closet and pulled on his coat, carefully wrapping the scarf across his chest.

"Need a ride, boss?" Ocky asked, cashing in their respective chips.

"Nah, Stormy's got the car just around the corner. I will take a ride from you tonight though, when we go to the Falcons dinner." Going down the stairs, he called back, "Give me a call around four in my office."

Taking a deep breath of the crisp winter air, the mayor stepped carefully on the icy sidewalk as he approached the car, where Stormy was nodding off. Opening the door, a hot booze-and-perfume smell rushed at him. Stormy straightened up and adjusted his wide-brimmed fedora.

"Jeez, Stormy, where the hell did you get warm last night?"

"I, uh, got some coffee at a friend's house, Mr. Mayor."

"Do they serve coffee over at Big Gray, now?" the mayor asked, referring to a whore house known by its paint job.

"Naw, not me, Your Honor," he said, as he pulled out of the

parking spot without his lights. A block later, the lights were still off.

"Stormy, are you okay?"

"Sure, boss, you're goin' home to clean up, right?"

"Stormy, turn the lights on, it's not dawn just yet. We don't want to hit any paperboys, even if the *Courier* didn't endorse me."

Pulling up to the mayor's house, Stormy licked his lips and said, "You want me to wait here, Mr. Mayor?"

Standing next to the driver's door, the mayor spun his index finger in a circle and Stormy rolled the window down.

"Stormy, here's what I want you to do. Roll *all* the windows down," he added, shaking his head, "I don't care how cold it is. Drive the car to your flat. Take a bath, change your clothes. Then go see Rick at the bakery on Sycamore and get a bunch of rolls and doughnuts for the people in the office. Sit there and drink coffee until eight, then come back and get me, and maybe, if the car doesn't stink, you'll have a job when you get here. Got it?"

Wide-eyed, Stormy muttered, "Yessir," as he rolled the windows down and pulled away from the curb.

Watching him go, the mayor regretted it, but he'd have to call Ed and tell him to get him a new driver. Stormy was a good man to have around when he was sober, but that wasn't very often these days, and he was bound to get into trouble again. *A nice long beat? No, let Ed handle it, that's his job. Ah, now for a bath and some bacon and eggs. Like I told Ocky, big day today . . .*

# CHAPTER 31

## NORTH PARK, 1951

Pat belched loudly, muttering the beer company's slogan about having no artificial bubbles, and urinated, holding himself at an angle with his left hand on the tile wall behind the toilet. Usually, he tried to keep such noises as quiet as possible to keep his father from hearing, but he didn't care about hiding his drinking from his father tonight; it just didn't seem to matter. Sliding across the ceramic tile floor in front of the medicine cabinet, he straightened up and looked at his red, unfocused eyes and slight weaving, and thought, *What a mess I am. Better brush my teeth good tonight, that'll help.* He bared his teeth. *Shit. What time is it?* he thought, checking his watch and winding it. *21:40. Hmm, still early. Maybe get another shot of whiskey and listen to the radio a little more.*

He opened the bathroom door quietly and looked for signs of his father or brother in the hall. *The coast is clear*, he thought, as he went down the back stairs to the kitchen. Nobody there either. He opened the liquor cabinet, took out the bottle of rye, and got himself a glass. He poured himself about an ounce, then sighed and poured himself about twice more that. He tossed that back, poured himself another ounce, then put the bottle back, making sure it was behind some other bottles.

He turned on the radio and fiddled with the dial until he found some music, stopping at a station that was playing "Mood Indigo." *Yeah, Linda Telford. Straight black hair, tiniest waist. Danced with her to this tune at a Holy Angels dance, junior year. The band did it pretty good, too.* She never made eye contact, and kept moving away every time he tried to get close to her. When the song ended, she went back to her friends from school, no second dance, no phone number. The song ended on the radio and an ad jingle told people they didn't want that balogna, they wanted Wardynski's.

He glanced over at the refrigerator, where Tim had taped up an article from the newspaper. The title read, "Police Nab Coin Crooks After Fatal Robbery". *Yep, that got me the detective's job*, he thought. He started reading the article.

"Buffalo police arrested two men who have been robbing vending machine operators after the gunmen shot and killed Thomas Gauner in an attempted hold up on the city's West Side . . . Patrolman Patrick Brogan, a four-year veteran of the force . . . pursued the pistol wielding . . . undaunted by the bullet that passed through his collar (*more like scared shitless*, Pat thought) struggled with the gunman . . ."

*Yeah, that's me*, he thought.

"The police recovered over $1,200 in cash, most of it in coins . . ."

*This guy, Gauner, one of the small-time vendors, making a haul for one week of over twelve-hundred bucks. Shit, that's, ah, I dunno, something like fifty-five, fifty-six grand a year, cash money, and I'm making just under four a year, before taxes?*
A big yawn interrupted his reading. Figuring he had enough in him to get to sleep, Pat turned off the radio and slipped back up the stairs. Tim was in the bathroom, so he went to his room and got into his pajamas, set his alarm for six o'clock, and double-checked his shirt, underwear, socks, shoes, and suit for work. *No time to fart around tomorrow*, he thought. He passed Tim coming out of the bathroom, and his younger brother averted his eyes and went right to his own room. *Must know I'm high*, he thought. *He always avoids me when I've got a load on.*
After another long piss and a thorough teeth scrubbing, Pat wished his brother and his father good night from the hallway and got into bed with a last long belch. He looked at the clock, *10:05, good and early for a work night*, he thought, *regardless of the booze.*

A few minutes later, his brother, reading a comic book in his room, could hear the noisy snoring, a sure sign that Pat was real drunk. When Tim heard him talking in his sleep, he knew the nightmares were coming. He quickly turned off the radio and the light, covering his head with his pillow.

It was really dark in the classroom, and Pat could hear Father Kessler's feet hitting the wooden floor with his deliberate approach to his desk. Pat's hands tightened on the books on his desk, and he wanted the bell to ring, ending the class before Kessler could get to him, but it never did, no matter how many times he had had the dream. Clutching the desktop, the priest leaned over. Pat could smell his cigarette breath, and looked at the top of his books as the priest's weight made the desk top creak.

"You knew it was wrong, didn't you, Squire Brogan?"

"I didn't . . .," Pat choked out, the bespectacled blue eyes of the Jesuit boring into him. "They were Nazis, Father," Pat stammered.

"They were soldiers, just like you, Brogan. They had surrendered, Brogan. They were unarmed, Brogan."

"I thought . . ."

"No, Brogan, when you left here, Canisius diploma in hand, you knew right from wrong. Are you saying now you didn't do it?"

"No, Father," Pat said, and his mind went blank, unable to defeat the old priest and his logic.

"So, you admit you did it?"

"Yes, Father," he got out, knowing what was coming again.

"So, knowing it was wrong, you gave into your sinful impulses and committed a terrible crime, didn't you, Brogan?"

All he could do was nod, and somehow, the classroom was filled with students who heard this confession. From the back of the room he heard his mother crying. *That's not possible*, he thought, *Mom died before any of this happened; she couldn't know.*

The priest continued, "There are no secrets before God in Heaven, Brogan. He sees everything we do, everything that's in our hearts."

"Noooo," Pat cried out, both in his dream, and in his bed. His father heard his anguish and wondered what he could do and what had happened over there to cause these nightmares to his once happy boy.

# CHAPTER 32

## NORTH PARK, 1951

Pat sat on a stool at the diner on Colvin, and felt too whipped to take off his overcoat. He had walked there from home on a snowy Saturday morning, figuring the cold air would help clear the cobwebs out of his head that the whiskey had installed. He wanted to get out of the house before his dad gave him a talk on the evils of drink.

"Coffee?" the Greek offered, pot and cup at the ready.

Pat silently nodded, adding, "Water, too, please."

The Greek nodded and smiled.

Half an hour later, Pat was still negotiating the eggs and toast, water, and coffee while trying to concentrate on the morning paper over the noise of the pinball game bells going off. Two patrolmen came in dressed in double-breasted blanket overcoats, shaking the snow off their hats and stomping it off their galoshes. Pat struggled to think of their names. *One's McDermott, went to the academy with him, and the other guy's Al something, been on this beat for years. Seen McDermott hanging around headquarters a lot, probably kissing ass to make detective,* he thought, as the two policemen looked at him and nodded, then at each other, and walked to a booth at the other end of the restaurant. The Greek hustled coffee over to them, spoke a few words. *Did he pass something to them?* The Greek went back into the kitchen; then, the two patrolmen got up, coffee untouched, and went back out to their car and drove off.

When the Greek came out of the kitchen, he glanced where the police had been, and then walked down the length of the counter where Pat had given up on reading and eating. "Everything okay this morning?" he asked Pat, smiling and wiping his hands on a towel.

"Fine, Spiros, just not too hungry today. Everything okay with you?" Pat continued, nodding to where the police had been.

"Yeah, yeah. They come in to see if Anna works, they like her. Not stay if just the boys here." He hesitated as Pat stood up, the check pad in his pocket.

"How much I owe you, Spiros?"

"One ten. Hell, make it a dollar, my friend."

Pat left a dollar and a quarter and went outside, the cold air and snow finally reviving him. *So the guys up here are in on it, too,* he thought, *because everybody knows Anna always works nights.*

# CHAPTER 33

## THE EAST SIDE, 1951

Ocky went home after playing cards, arriving at his bar on Broadway just at closing time. There were three customers in the bar: shift workers from the Danahy Meat Packing plant, drinking beer and reading the Niagara Edition of the *Courier Express*, picking their horses for the upcoming day. The porter, Tommy, was at the front door. A retired guy from Chevy, he had three bars to clean before sun up and wanted to start right at four-thirty in the morning, when the last drink went off the bar.

"Mornin', Ock, howza Mayor?" Tommy asked.

"Okay, Tom. Goin' to the stag for Steelhead, Thursday?" Ocky asked, referring to a bachelor party being thrown for a vet who had a metal plate in his skull.

"Yeah, I'll play cards for a while."

"Okay, pal. You got all the supplies you need?"

"Just about, but can you order some more ammonia? We'll be out of that by the end of the week."

"Can do, Tommy. Morning, boys," he said to the three men at the bar. "Got any winners for me today?"

"I would," said one guy, "If I knew when that rat bastard Canuck jockey LeMonde was going to pull up," he said, drawing chuckles from the others.

Reaching the end of the bar at the same time as the bartender, Ocky lowered his voice, "How'd we do, Arch?"

"Okay. Fairly steady all night at the bar. I figure we'd double it, with the pins going, though."

"Not yet, keep the free plays off for now. Any strangers come in?"

"One couple around nine, and a couple of guys from the stock-yards. No cops snooping around though, at least, none not from around here."

"All right. Need any help closing up?"

"Nah, me and Tom got it. I'll bring the bag up when it's done."

Coming behind the bar, Ocky went up the stairs behind it to his apartment on the second floor, where his family slept. He made a pot of coffee, and when Archie brought the cash bag up, he gave him a cup as they counted out the money. When Archie had left, he counted out a bank for the day shift, remembered how much he had won at cards, put some of that in a sugar bowl for his wife's expenses, made a deposit slip for three quarters of the bar's take, and put it in a bank deposit envelope. The rest of the money, and the rest of his winnings at cards, he put in a tin box retrieved from beneath the floorboards. *Almost time to make another visit to Canada,* he thought, where he had a safety deposit box in a small bank on the other side of the river, his "you never know" fund. He looked in on his three children and went to bed.

Ocky slept until around two, had breakfast, and went down-stairs. He checked the invoices and orders, nodded to the custom-ers, and checked the register. When the kids came in from school, he scooted them upstairs to do their homework and told his wife he'd be back after dinner. He drove the Fleetline across town, parking in front of a saloon across the street from Forest Lawn.

In the wooden-walled barroom, the bartender dropped a coaster before him, shook his hand and said, "Long time, no see, Ocky. What brings you out of Polonia today?"

"Your world famous roast beef, Donny. Can I get one, medium rare, 'weck roll?"

"By all means. Whadya drinkin'?"

"You still got birch beer on tap? I'll take one of them."

"Sure," Donny replied, smiling. "Tough night last night?"

"Ahhh, playing cards, way too late."

Setting the bubbling birch beer in front of Ocky, Donny turned to the steam table and opened the lid, engulfing himself with steam. Picking up a razor-sharp knife with a flexible blade and a meat fork, he examined the top round of beef for a second, then cut off a chunk that was red, but not bleeding. Putting it on a cutting board, he swiftly cut the beef up into paper thin slices, which he piled on a bottom half of a roll. Then he took the fork and speared the top of the roll, which was covered in pretzel salt and caraway seeds; dipped the bottom of it in gravy; put it on the sandwich; sliced it in half; placed a slice of fresh pickle on the plate; and slid it in front of Ocky.

"All right?"

"Terrific."

Donny then looked out the large, plate glass front window and spotted a telephone company truck going by. Checking the clock, he saw it was five minutes to five.

"It's that time," he said, going to a cylindrical beer cooler behind him, pulling out two bottles of Simon Pure, one Utica Club, one Manru, and an Iroquois ale, and carrying them to the bar. Tossing five cardboard coasters in front of five stools next to Ocky, he popped the caps off each bottle with a church key, arranged the bottles on the bar, and put three small glasses in front of the bottles of the Manru, Simon Pure, and Utica Club. The front door swung open and five guys came in, wearing Bell Telephone jackets. They took their places at the bar and put their money down, which Donny scooped up and made change. One of them noticed Ocky.

"Hey, look who it is, Ocky Owczarczak, all the way from Bvawdvay." The boys turned, said hello, and shook hands, and then went back to talking about their upcoming contract. Ocky nudged one of them.

"Hello, Bill, how are you?"

"Okay, Ock, a little tight this close to pay day, you know."

"Hey, Donny," Ocky waved, "Get us a drink here, pal," he said, indicating the whole bar, "Something for yourself, too."

Donny walked down the length of the bar, holding the church key out so it rattled against the bottles. Pulling beer bottles out of the cooler, the barman started popping caps off, asking, "Another one of those, Ock?" nodding at the glass of soda pop.

"Nah, get me a draft Iri beer, pal."

When the customers were served, Donny put a shot glass on the bar and poured himself a measure of rye. Holding it up, he toasted Ocky, sighed, and said, "Unaccustomed as I am," threw down the whiskey, and went back to work. The bar was filling up with people heading home.

"Cheers, Ocky," they all wished him, for a bar owner was sure to buy at least one round, and always welcome.

"Yeah, thanks, Ocky," Billy said again.

"Bill, wanna bowl a game?" Ocky nodded towards a shuffle-board bowling game in the back of the bar.

"Sure," he replied, hopping off the barstool and grabbing his beer.

Ocky put the nickels in the machine and asked what game Bill wanted to play.

"Regulation, Ocky. Never was any good at the flashy games."

"Regulation it is, my man." Ocky pushed the selection buttons for two players as Billy sprinkled a little sawdust on the table.

"You first, Ock," Billy said, watching him take a position at the end of the table, sliding the puck back and forth and then shoving it swiftly at the pins. As the pins flew up and the bells signaled a strike, Billy said, "Good shot, Ock. You know this table?"

"Nah, just lots of practice," Ocky replied, as Billy threw, racking up nine pins on his first toss.

"So, Billy, how's the family?" Ocky asked, as Billy aimed carefully for the last corner pin standing.

"Mary Lou is still at her mother's with the kids. I hear she's looking for a job and talking about getting her own place," shoving the puck overly hard to take out the last pin.

"That's tough. Giving 'em any money?"

"Yeah, a little. The lawyer says it's going to be expensive."

"Getting any overtime?" he inquired, sweeping away a little of the sawdust and sliding the puck evenly at the pins.

"Uh, a little," he replied, watching the bells signal another strike, "But I'm still short all the time."

"Use a little side work?"

"Sure, Ock," he answered with enthusiasm.

"Good. Let's finish this game, have another beer, and I'll tell you all about it outside," Ocky replied as the pinball games in the room started to click and ring, surrounded by players.

# CHAPTER 34

## SOUTH BUFFALO, 1951

Rita waited for the Number 14 bus at the corner of Woodside and Abbott Road. She pulled her skirt down to make sure it extended four inches below the knee, as the nuns had taught her. She felt relieved when she heard the diesel engine of the bus gearing down, and looked up to see the usual driver, a fat guy, hat perched on the back of his head, sliding the bus to a gentle halt on the ice before her. The doors opened and she ascended the two steps, feeling the heat from inside the bus envelop her as she took the token from her glove and dropped it into the fare box. She looked around the bus while the driver glanced at her legs, whistling, "There Ain't Nothin' Like a Dame."

Looking for an open seat and friends, Rita saw a bunch of young workers headed for Republic Steel with plaid mackinaws and lunch boxes at the back of the bus, nudging one another when she got on. Quickly turning to her right, she wedged herself in the middle of the three front seats facing the center of the bus, between a big lady wearing a babushka, who was rummaging through her change purse; and a skinny lady with black hair, a baby on her lap, and a big shopping bag. The woman with the baby slid a couple of inches over, and, after glancing at Rita's chestnut hair done up in a Victory Roll, patted her own hair held back with bobby pins. Rita smiled at the baby, a chubby kid with straight blonde hair falling in his eyes, who held up a faded rubber Donald Duck to her with an "Eeee yaaa!"

"Is that Donald Duck?" Rita said to the preening baby.

"Eeeeyaa!" the baby returned, banging the toy on his mother's leg, which made it squeak, and him laugh.

The lady wearing the babushka looked up from her purse, glanced at Rita's nurse's cap, and asked her, "Hey, Sally, you work Mercy?"

"Yes," Rita answered, "I'm a nurse there."

"I go visit son Bogdan there now. He break noga at work Lackawanna. You help me find his room?"

"Yes, I can help you find him," wondering how all these people found their way to Buffalo after the war with no English.

"I'm old lady. Come here with Bogdan from Jarocin, get away from Roskis. Very bad there. How you say . . . Ksiadz-Priest, Swiety Stanislaus bring us here . . .," and for the rest of the ride, Rita listened to the woman's epic of German tanks smashing houses, Russian soldiers stealing hogs, escaping to America, and what a good boy Bogdan was.

She helped the old lady off the bus, who kept a death grip on her arm all the way to the hospital, babbling continuously. When she got to the front desk, her friend Louise smiled at Rita's new friend.

"Clean, clean," the old woman said, waving her free hand around. "Very nice. Bogdan break . . . ummm," and then she slapped her leg.

"His leg," Rita assisted, nodding, hoping the woman would just be quiet for a minute so she could get this sorted out.

"Tak, leg!" she chimed, learning the word.

"What is Bogdan's last name?" Rita said, using a louder voice, hoping the volume would overcome the language difference.

"Bogdan? He break leg Lackawanna."

"No," Rita tried. "His name. What is his name?" she asked, her voice almost rising to a shout, ignoring Louise's chuckling at her predicament.

"Bethlehem stil," the old lady guessed.

Taking a breath, Rita tried another tack. Placing her hand on her breast, she said, "I am Rita, Rita Crawford." Pointing to her friend, she said, "She is Louise. Louise Donnelly." Then, nodding at the old lady and opening her palms in front of herself, said, "Bogdan. Bogdan . . ."

"Ahhh. Bogdan. Bogdan Trzepkowski," she answered, and then

pointing to herself, she said, "I Elzbeta Trzepkowski. Maz, Jerzy Trzepkowski, dead. Nazis kill in war . . .," and on she went, as Rita led her to her son's ward, Louise laughing behind her hand.

"Tell them in the Accident Room that I'll be there in five minutes," she ordered Louise over her shoulder, trying to hurry Elzbeta along.

# CHAPTER 35

## KENSINGTON, 1951

Stormy woke up when he couldn't draw enough air through all the phlegm in his throat, sat up on the floor, and coughed a green blob into the opened refrigerator at his feet. He took a couple of breaths and looked around. *Ok, I'm in my own flat. Still got my clothes on, but one shoe's missing, gotta find that. Refrigerator door's open. Musta gone for a snack when I got home,* he hoped, until he smelled the stale beer and spotted the Blatz bottle tipped over on the floor.

Rubbing his face with his hand, he noticed the inside of his thumb and index finger were raw and had bled a little. *Ah shit,* he thought, *this one was a bad one. Twisted the cap off a bottle again.*

Stormy continued to sit, sucking in air to revive himself. Palms on the floor, he locked his elbows to keep his torso upright while trying to remember what had happened. *Oh, yeah, that's right, I got kicked out of the mayor's detail when I came back with the rolls and doughnuts. Jazz didn't even do it himself. D.C. Falk called me out into the hall to tell me I was out. That was . . . that was around eight a.m.* Looking out his kitchen window, he saw it was daytime. *Afternoon? Morning?* Looking at his watch, it read ten-thirty. *Okay, it's morning.* A wave of fear sweeping over him, he hoped it was only the next day. Looking around again, his senses revitalizing with more air, he smelled himself. *Not good,* he thought. *Sweat, booze, and even a little piss odor. Must have missed sometime. I smell like . . . like guys I wouldn't let in the back of a patrol car, for Chrissakes.*

The phone rang, the bells rattling against the inside of his skull. He scrambled up, hoping it wasn't someone mad at him for something he did, and then thought, *Oh, shit, it might be the department.*

"Snyder!" the voice roared, before he could say hello.

Stormy cleared his throat and got out, "Yes?"

"This is Nick Tibolo up in the Fourteenth Precinct. Listen, you drunken sot, this is the third time I've called you today. You got a clean uniform you can fit your fat keester into? You're gonna need it to start walking a beat if you don't get your ass in my office, cleaned up, and ready to work before noon, and not a minute after. And if you don't get here by twelve-thirty, you're not gonna need any badge, uniform or anything, because I'll tell Ed Falk just how AWOL you are, and get your ass fired! Got me, you lazy son of a bitch?"

"Yeah, I got it, Nick. I'm on my way," Stormy replied, figuring, *Call a cab, take a fast bath, and if I've got a clean suit and shirt, I can make it up to the Fourteenth Precinct in time.*

As he hung up, Lieutenant Tibolo looked across his desk at Deputy Commissioner Falk and smiled, shaking his head. "Thanks, boss, thanks a lot. They're gonna start calling me 'last chance Tibolo' with all the wash outs you send me."

"Ah, Father Tibolo," Falk replied, affecting an Irish accent, "You have a way of bringing the lost sheep back into the fold, you do."

"Oh, brother, and now, I've got Stormy Snyder to reform."

Turning serious, Falk continued, "Let's not forget, Mike, what he can do, when he's on the straight and narrow."

"Or, even when he's not," Tibolo replied, and then the rotund detective with a shock of brown hair stood up and looked the deputy commissioner in the eye. "Remember the Dixon guy, from over on Woltz Street?"

"Ho, ho, boy, do I? I was a detective then. We'd just found out he was holed up on the second floor in that place, and zoomed across town when Stormy crashed up there and shot the guy."

"Yeah, but a lot of guys don't know he was half in the bag when he did it. I was a blue suit then, assigned to the perimeter, keeping people away when this Ford rolls up, horn blowing, and practically runs me over on the sidewalk. Stormy and Bobby Becht jump out, all red-faced, and go running up to the house.

"The commissioner's loading up a Thompson gun, he's gonna lead the charge up the stairs where Dixon's got his girlfriend and her mother in the upper, trapped with him, screaming all kinds of shit about 'I'll kill all you bastards, I got three guns, and I got plenty of ammo for all of 'em.' Then, Stormy gets all upset, crashes through all the guys at the bottom of the stairs, and starts blazing away as he goes up."

Falk chuckled at the memory, saying, "Dixon got so rattled when he saw this big ape charging up the stairs roaring, 'You son of a bitch!' he turned around and started to run. Stormy fires off six shots with a .38 special, and hits Dixon with one in the ass. It goes into his guts and he dies on the operating table at Buffalo General."

"Yeah," Tibolo added, "And the other five bullets go flying everywhere, outta windows, everywhere. Cops were jumping all over the place to get outta the way."

"Don't forget Commissioner Rogan, either. He slams a magazine into the Tommy gun, then turns around and all hell's broken loose because some crazy plainclothesman's gone nuts. What could he do? Nobody but the bad guy got hurt, the photographers and reporters were all over the place, he had to make a hero out of the guy."

"And now, I get him, ten years later, and still drunk," Tibolo finished, shaking his head.

"Well, Nick," the deputy commissioner said, standing up, "It's your turn. Keep him out of trouble, straighten him out if you can, but above all, don't let him hurt anybody or shoot up any houses."

They shook hands, and the head of the Fourteenth Precinct's detectives rolled his eyes at the possibilities.

Stormy looked at his watch as he climbed into the back of the cab. The driver looked in the rear view mirror and waved his hand in front of his face to dissipate the cloud of aftershave Stormy had dragged in with him.

"Where to?" he inquired, wondering if this big guy was going to be a problem.

"Fourteenth Precinct," Stormy replied, then when he saw the cabbie hesitate, added, "The police station at Main and Mercer, right by Bennett High School, next to the firehouse."

The cabbie drove carefully out of Stormy's street on Langfield Drive, then picked up speed as he went up Bailey. *I'm going to make it*, Stormy thought. *Nick Tibolo's not going to put me back in uniform or get me fired*. He sat back in the leather cab seat, lit a Camel, and put his feet out on the seat folded onto the floor. *What a night*, he thought. *Let's see*, he tried to drag last night out of his alcohol-ravaged brain, *I left City Hall and headed over to Broadway. Stopped at the Broadway Market, had a couple of beers, trying to find out where the mayor's Polack cronies were, that's right. Then I went to Shadrack's, The Polish Village, and Kwiatkowski's; even busted into the card game there, trying to get Councilman Frankowski to get me back in good with the mayor. Oh, God, did I make an ass out of myself there?* Rubbing his forehead, he tried to recall the next stops, but all he could remember was stumbling into Ocky's. Ocky was behind the bar, and everyone was staring at him. Ocky called him a cab and told him to get out now if he wanted to keep his job. Some of the guys at the bar helped him out the door, not shoving, but making sure he went. With tears coming to his eyes, he thought, *Hell, in the old days, nobody'd try that with me, drunk or sober, or I'd have knocked all of them into next week. What a jackpot this is.* Looking up, he told the driver, "Take Amherst up to Main, it'll get us there quicker."

The driver sped up Amherst and over Main, but jammed on the brakes just before the police station as Engine 34 pulled out of the firehouse, siren wailing. The firemen, still shoving arms into rubber sleeved coats and pulling on boots, cursed the cab as the pumper swerved to avoid them. Stormy tossed some money over the front seat to the driver and bailed out the back door, straightening his tie and checking his watch. *Ten minutes to spare*, he thought, pushing through the front door of the station, and spying Tibolo, who was looking at his own watch.

# CHAPTER 36

## MAIN STREET, 1951

When Larry came into the office with a case of cold beer, the girls finished up what they were doing and put their coats on. That much beer was a sure sign that the Niagara Coin Machine Operators Association was having a meeting, and they didn't want any part of it. Johnny kicked back in his desk chair, put his feet up, and looked out the floor-to-ceiling windows while the snow fell on the Main Street traffic below. Johnny pulled a church key out of his desk drawer and tossed it to Larry, who popped open a couple of beers and stared after the women as they strutted out of the office.

"Ever get anywhere with them, Johnny?"

Johnny shrugged, tossed the toothpick into the wastebasket, and picked up his beer. Other members came in, hung up their coats, grabbed a beer, and made small talk while Johnny sized them up. *Weak*, he thought. *A little pressure from the cops and a lot of these guys will cave.*

Johnny called the meeting to order, and eleven other vendors grabbed chairs and sat down.

"I dunno where the hell Vice President Neufeld is—probably hiring an armored car to haul all his cash to the bank. Anyway, it looks like a quorum to me," Johnny said, "So, let's get down to business. First off, I got a note just typed up by Betty," Johnny said, which caused whistles around the room, "And she says we've got four thousand, eight hundred dollars in cash, on hand." He then tore the letter up and said, "I'm having Helen put down one thousand, one hundred dollars in the books," at which everybody laughed. "Our friends downtown will be appreciative."

"So, Johnny," said Pete, "They gonna get this Wachter guy off our backs?"

"They can't right away, Greek. It's too soon after the elections. It'd be too obvious."

"Who says so, Johnny? Who do you talk to?"

"Better you guys didn't know. You trust me, don't you?" he said, to several "yeahs" and a few grumbles. "I been letting you know when the heat's coming down so far, right? Just let me handle it, that way, if there's any trouble, you don't have to worry about it." He paused for a moment as they considered his words, then added, "Speaking of which, I got the word they've been scouting around in North Buffalo, and are getting ready to raid some places where they say winners have been getting payoffs."

A small, balding man shifted in his chair, making it squeak. "Hey, Johnny, you know if it's any of my locations?"

Chewing on another toothpick, Johnny shrugged. "Dunno, Benny. The word I got just said North Buffalo, and the hammer's gonna be coming down soon."

"But Johnny, I got a family. I can't be getting arrested," Benny said, and several others nodded with him.

Another guy said, "Shit, this is just part time for me. I get arrested, I might lose my contractor's license."

"Look, fellas. We all knew there was risk involved when we got into the pinball game, and if you don't want the money, somebody else will. Give our friends a little time, and they'll get the cops causing trouble moved around."

Benny wiped his brow with his handkerchief and shook his head. A few others stared at the floor. After a moment of silence, Johnny said, "If it worries you that much, there is something I can do, meanwhile."

"Like what, Johnny?" Benny said.

"Get the names on the pinball licenses changed."

There was a lot of muttering, then Pete said, "The names changed on my machines? To what? How? Why would I want to do that?"

Holding his hand up, Johnny went on. "I got friends in the licensing office. They'll change the names on the licenses for me, pronto. For some consideration."

"And whose name they gonna put on these licenses, eh?" Pete said.

"Mine," Johnny replied, to which there was a lot of muttering and a few "horseshits."

"Listen to me, guys. Here's the deal. We're all makin' a ton of money on these pinballs, right?" Johnny asked, to which there was general assenting. "We're all paying six bucks dues a month, per machine, me included, to our vendor's association here to take care of business, right?"

More nods, cigarettes crushed out, and heads shaken.

"If you're worried about getting pinched, I can provide the insurance with my name on the pinball games license. It's still your machine, and you split the money with the location, just like always, but I'll take the heat if the cops raid the joint and find out they're payin' off."

"What do you get out of this, Johnny?" Larry asked.

"Another dollar a machine a month. I take care of the name on the license, and I keep the change."

"What if you get arrested?" Lenny asked.

"In for a penny, in for a pound. I been in jail before, but they won't hold ya for this. It'll cost me in fines and lawyers' fees. I can handle it, so, if any of you guys want some get-out-of-jail-free insurance, lemme know."

When the rest of the meeting was taken care of, Benny and a few others came up to Johnny to buy his "insurance." After they all had left, Johnny started working the phones to call the absent vendors with his sales pitch.

# CHAPTER 37

## SOUTH BUFFALO, 1951

Dan Finnegan knew trouble. It was how he wound up in Buffalo in the first place.

Born in Belfast, he grew up on Lisbon Street in the South Strand. He went to sea at fifteen, first on the big four-masted barques, and then the steamships, growing strong and earning his pay as a deckhand. He remembered a few good times when he would come home from a voyage, turn over his pay, and share a pint with Da at one of the polished teakwood bars where the sailors gathered.

He was away when all hell broke loose after the Rising in 1916 and the weapons that came back from the Western Front that armed both camps in the segregated city. He had snatched a few pistols himself from the returning soldiers and turned them over to his brother Tom, who organized the locals to protect themselves for a civil war in Ulster that was bound to come if Ireland got free. Finnegan kept hoping it would all go away, or, looking back at his own fear, that if anything bad were to happen, it would happen when he was at sea.

It didn't, of course. The usual tensions turned violent when the Protestants feared they would lose their jobs and rights if there were a Catholic government in Dublin, and he had just come home from a voyage to Bombay when Declan, a neighbor boy he had brought toys to over the years, turned up floating among the piers in the Musgrave Channel with four bullets in him.

"Angus Coulter's gang did it. They knew he was moving the guns," Jackie Curtain said to him at the wake, looking Finnegan right in the eye. "We'll need your help, the night your ship sails."

It wasn't a question to the curly-haired youth. Jackie Curtain had come back from the trenches of France with a permanent rasp from a dose of mustard gas, and tales about flamethrowers roasting men alive, and bayonets pinning soldiers to trees. Curtain had quickly swept aside the men on the council who didn't want to believe they were at war there in the streets of Belfast, and had his men retaliate against the Orange gangs without hesitation.

Two nights later, Finnegan took deep breaths as he turned into the darkened brick alley where they met, Curtain clearing his throat to show his presence. A few moments passed, the slender girl walked by, her shoes rapping on the paving stones.

"Here, wait, girl, you dropped this," Coulter's Scottish burr sounded, and when he passed the alley, the three of them pounced. Curtain and the farmer grabbed Coulter's arms and dragged him into the alley, where Curtain pummeled him with punches and kicks, the Orangeman fighting back until Curtain clouted him with a pipe behind the ear. Breathing heavily, they dragged the unconscious body down the alley, where they sat him up against some ash cans.

"All right, quick now," Curtain rasped, pulling out a revolver and handing it to the farmer, who pointed the pistol and fired, saying "For Ireland's freedom," as the big pistol roared and the body jumped. He turned it ,grip first, to Finnegan, who hesitated.

"Now, boy, before we get caught here!"

"For Declan," Finnegan said, in tears, and Curtain snatched the gun and fired another shot into Coulter's throat. The other two grabbed Finnegan and pulled him down the alley.

Curtain said, "You, farmer, back to Sligo, and you, Finnegan, off to your ship. Never come back."

When Finnegan's ship docked in New York, word got to him about the killing in Belfast, and that his name was connected to it from a ship's chandler named Roach. The ship's next port of call was Liverpool, and Finnegan knew it was time to get off and get lost before it pulled out. There was help along the way, from the longshoremen in New York, who slipped him past the customs men, to the trainmen on the Lackawanna Railroad, who got him west to Buffalo. When he got there, he started with a job delivering milk for a man named Brogan who was from Cork, did well at that, and tended bar nights. Eventually, he bought his own place; a tavern with a fine, long, mahogany bar amongst the Irish in South Buffalo, never looking back or hearing from Ulster again.

Finnegan thought of this, as he sat at a table and the policeman, Tony Regan, walked in, wearing a fine, gray, wool overcoat and black fedora. *Hmmph, thinks himself one of the hard men,* Finnegan thought. He also thought of the Belfast constables, who looked the other way when the likes of Angus Coulter did their dirty work, and the thirty years work it had taken him to get to this place. Regan smiled as he walked up to the table and put out his hand.

"Mr. Finnegan, good to see you tonight," Regan said. Finnegan gave him his hand, but did not rise, thinking these young pups all talk a hundred miles an hour.

Looking around, Regan leaned forward and whispered, "We were wondering if your contribution was ready."

Now, standing up and looking down at the top of the officer's head, the gray-haired sailor said, "Look, you narrowback gobshite, I've seen your kind from Belfast to Singapore. I'm not payin' you, I'm not paying the vendors, I'm not payin' Rybeck at Licensing. I paid the fees for the licenses, and I bought the machines meself." His voice rose, causing the customers to look up. Regan put his hands in his overcoat pockets, looked at the floor, and took a step closer to the reddening Irishman.

"Look, Finnegan, if we're going to keep this thing going, everybody—," Reagan started when Finnegan seized the policeman's wrists, yanked them out of his pockets, and spun the wide-eyed cop around, and off balance. Getting Regan's gun arm twisted in a half-nelson, Finnegan reached under the overcoat and got hold of the man's crotch. Finnegan propelled him towards the front door, customers scattering. As Regan got out, "What the . . .," he crashed into the door frame, and then pitched out onto the pavement, tumbling and yelling, "Oh shit!" as he went.

Turning back into the bar, Finnegan shouted to the bartender, "Gimme the phone, Mike." When it arrived before him, he pulled a card out of his pocket and dialed while the customers muttered,

"Wasn't that guy a cop?" and "Tony Regan, yeah."

The deputy commissioner had barely gotten out, "Falk here," when Finnegan roared, "Ed, one of your peelers just tried to shake me down! I threw his arse out into the road where it belongs, and I'll do the same to any man who tries it!"

The slamming phone echoing in his ear, Falk shook his head and thought for a moment, then dialed the Fifteenth Precinct.

"Lieutenant, one of the boys, Tony Regan, got himself into some drunken foolishness off duty at the Mahogany. He's out in front of the bar now, on the street. Who's in plainclothes tonight? Good, get them over there now, take Regan back to the station, cleaned up, and brought home. Pronto. I don't want to hear any noise about this, understand? Call your captain at home and tell him when it's done."

Then, the deputy commissioner called up the Fifteenth Precinct's commander, Pete Siefert.

"Pete, Ed Falk. Dan Finnegan just tossed Tony Regan out of his bar on Abbott Road when he was off duty. They're taking care of it at your precinct, but I want you to talk to Tony tonight, and find out what the hell happened, and then you buy me a cup of coffee at Sobeck's joint. Got it? I don't want to see or hear of any reports about this, at all." He hung up and went to the closet for his coat, announcing that work had called, and he had to go out for a little while.

# CHAPTER 38

## LACKAWANNA, 1951

Bogdan Trzepkowski spent forty minutes on the bus from the East Side getting to the company doctor, getting off the Crosstown bus near Gate No. 1 at the Bethlehem Steel Plant. After showing his metal disc at the guard booth, he hobbled with his crutch to the clinic, and waited with four other guys with various injuries to see the doctor. When it was his turn, the white-coated doctor bent his knee back and forth, and had him push his foot against his hand.

"The cast comes off in two weeks," he said, writing notes furiously. "Another two weeks after that, you can come back to work. Here, take this to your foreman," he continued, putting his glasses back on top of his head.

Dismissed, Bogdan took the note and left the one-story, brick clinic, walking across the plant into the smell of rotten eggs, towards his workplace at the coke ovens. Coming to railroad tracks, he looked to his left at the mould yard and saw cranes working high in the blackened hundred-foot-tall building with a small, orange train before it. Going across the first set of narrow, gauge tracks, he heard the mighty, little, diesel engine blow its air horn, muscling a load of ingots out of the yard. *Can't dodge it with this crutch,* he thought, and stepped back. The locomotive coughed black smoke, but steadily pulled three buggie cars with the brown ingots towering over the locomotive down the line. Bogdan stepped back another foot as he watched the train approach, the ten high, six-foot-wide ingots wobbling. Oblivious to the motion on the cars behind him, the engineer, Coke Bottles Monaghan, blew the air horn again, as he approached Bogdan.

Squinting through his thick safety glasses, he smiled when he recognized him and shouted, "When ya coming back, ya gimp?"

Bogdan waved his paperwork and shouted, "One month, four eyes!" He watched and waited until the last car passed, then started across the four sets of tracks again. Another hundred yards down the drive, he went by the ship canal, where giant, yellow cranes were unloading taconite from a lake boat into forty-foot mountains of the tiny, orange, iron balls. When he got to the coke works, he waved to his pal Lidtop Jerry on one of the long, narrow ovens. Jerry had a kerchief wrapped across his face like a bandit, and his coveralls were sooted with black dust. Jerry waved back, then, stepped carefully on the red-hot oven in his wooden shoes, and pried open the oven's lid with a long wrecking bar. Instantly, scalding fumes poured out of the oven and enveloped Jerry and Bogdan. Inhaling at the wrong time, Bogdan felt a catch at the back of his throat and coughed out the burning feeling. He went on to the foreman's shed, but no one was in the office, so he left the note on Mr. Carmody's olive-green, metal desk, and began the half-mile trek back out to Fuhrmann Blvd.

When he got there, he checked the money in his pocket and figured his financial situation. *Let's see, I got the workman's comp check last week. Gave half to Matka. Paid the grocery bill and the rent to Mrs. Kirschgessner. Dime for the bus, a nickel for transfer. Leaves me with three dollars, eighty, eighty five cents.* The clock in the office said it was just ten-thirty, but it must have been about ten of eleven, now. Checking the schedule posted on the pole at the bus stop, he saw the next bus came by at 11:03, the one after that, 11:46. *What the hell,* he thought, *Get a beer and a sandwich at the bar, catch the second bus home,* he thought, grabbing the crutch by the middle handle, and going up the concrete steps into the saloon.

Once inside, the bartender smiled in recognition. "Hey, Treppy, good to see ya, pal. How are ya?"

"Oh, you know, Willy, okay, getting better. Had to see the company doctor today," Bogdan answered, slapping his leg. He noticed yellow, red, and black soot rising from the spot and thought, *My clothes are dirty after that short walk through the plant.*

"Whaddle it be, pal?" the barman asked as Bogdan signed himself in for the weekly drawing and sat down.

"How about a Simon Pure and a ham and cheese on rye?"

"Sounds good," Willy replied, starting to pour the beer. "Want to make that a Katie Weiss?"

"Sure, throw the onions on, clothes are dirty, no girl tonight. Say, when is your brother Dominik coming back to work at the plant?"

"Dominik? Dominik Pericak?" Willy said with a wave of his hand. "Maybe never. Ever since the Navy released him in San Diego, he stays there. Has a job selling insurance. No more steel plant, no more Lackawanna, no more Pericak family, not even Christmas."

As the bartender set the beer before Bogdan, the bells of the pinball machine in the back started clanging.

Seeing Bogdan turn, Willy said, "Yeah, we got a new pinball in, just the other day. Makes all kindsa noise when you make a big score, *and*," he said, "it's the new kind with the flippers that keeps the ball going."

After a sip of beer, Bogdan and Willy both approached the machine. Willy stopped to check the score, then pushed a button on the side. The free game meter on the backboard started clicking, the digits rolling back to zero. The bartender went back to the register, opened it, and gave the player a handful of nickels.

"This guy," Willy started, indicating the player who returned to the game after collecting his winnings, "has been on here all morning, once he found out we had a Humpty Dumpty machine."

The player, a young man just under twenty, with a varsity jacket and a blonde crew cut, fed four nickels into the game, adjusting the odds to four to one, watched the king and the girls in bathing suits on the backboard light up, and pulled back on the plunger.

"Now, I got it figured out, Willy. With these flippers," he said as he moved the buttons on the side and gave a slight jostle to the machine, "There's no stoppin' me."

Bogdan watched the first silver ball bounce, roll, and bang around the playing field, scoring 10,000 points off a triangle, then 10,000 more off a green, circular bumper farther down, finally rolling onto a lit, kick-out hole, before it ended its run and Humpty rolled off the wall, and down the backboard towards the babes as the score clattered up to 30,000.

"More free game time comin', Willy, now I gotcha," he said, whacking the left side of the machine with his palm as the second ball bounced and rang the scoring bells. The numbers kept clicking upward as the backboard flashed on the pictures of the king and the women.

"Whoa," the kid said, as the third ball rolled down the field towards the bottom rack, where it would move no more. He tried to pick up his end of the machine slightly to keep the ball from its demise, but suddenly the machine gave a cranky buzz and "Tilt" flashed across the upright back screen.

"Shit," exclaimed the youngster, yanking the plunger and sending another chromium ball back into play. That ball hit two of the top bumpers, ringing the score to eighty-thousand, just twenty-thousand points below another payoff. "Get a couple more rolls of nickels ready, Willy!" the boy shouted. As the ball rolled backwards, the youth tried to time hitting it until the last second, figuring if he hit it off the very end of the flipper, it would careen right into one of the yellow twenty-thousand-point bumpers. He missed, slapping the device and cursing it. Bogdan stood there watching, waiting to see what the kid would do. The last ball was sent careening upwards, and the young man manned the flipper buttons. As the silver missile rolled back towards the flipper, Bogdan thought *Now, hit it now*, but the kid hesitated an instant too long and missed it, ending the game. *I can do that*, Bogdan thought, as the kid deposited four more nickels into the machine.

"Your sandwich is here, Treppy," the bartender said, and Bogdan walked back to his barstool, watching the youth tickle, slap, and occasionally shake the pinball machine as it rang, buzzed, and clicked, the lights flashing as the score went up. Bogdan finished his lunch and ordered another beer, which he took to the back of the bar and watched the kid play.

"I wish I had a half dozen of these; everybody loves them," Willy exclaimed, as he watched the kid shove the last of his previous winnings into the machine. A minute later, that game was over, the kid looked up at the clock on the wall by the door, said, "I gotta go," and went out the back door to the alley behind the bar.

Bogdan gave the bartender a quarter, which he changed for five nickels, and he carefully slid one into the coin slot. The first three balls he played, he scored thirty-thousand points. The fourth one, he sent with the spring-loaded plunger all the way to the top of the playing field, intuitively shaking the game box sideways to try and get the ball's course over where he wanted it. The machine tilted, causing Bogdan to think, *I've got to be oh-so-gentle with this girl; she's sensitive.* The next ball flew up the field just where he wanted it, and using the flippers, he kept ringing up points to the flashing lights until the score reached one-hundred-thousand, assuring him of a free play, and then fell out of the reach of the flippers and his most gentle taps, scoring twenty-thousand more points on a star feature before going down the drain. The next ball, he flung exactly where the last one went, giving him the confidence he had the mark, and the ball bounced between the twenty-thousand and ten-thousand-point bumpers, then fell down the side where he caught it right at the end of the flipper, returning it to the top of the playing field, where it made the bells go off over and over. Between his slams on the flipper buttons and his gentle taps on the side, he kept the silver sphere up there for another thirty seconds before he lost control and the wanton ball dropped out of play. Behind him, the bartender looked at the score, opened the register, and took out eight nickels, putting it into Bogdan's palm, as he reset the free game meter with the knock off button on the underside.

"All that fun and money, too," Willy smiled. "You want another beer?"

Bogdan nodded, finishing his glass and handing it to the bartender.

Bogdan played until all his coins ran out, then went back to the bar to get the change from the dollar he had left for his meal. He looked up at the clock when the 33 bus roared by in front of the saloon. *Twelve-fifteen, ah shit, I gotta get outta here,* he thought. There was twenty cents on the bar, so he left a nickel on the bar for a tip, and went out the door with fifteen cents in his hand, enough for the bus fare and transfer that would get him back home.

# CHAPTER 39

## MERCY HOSPITAL, 1951

Rita checked the clipboard for the next patient. Laceration to the scalp. Fall in barroom, it said. *Oh great, another drunk who fell off a barstool.* Looking out into the waiting room, she saw two young men in suits, sitting alone, one holding a rag with ice to his head, the other wearing a yellow fedora with a wide brim. They both turned and smiled when they saw her. *Two more drunks with bad thoughts at two in the morning. Just what I need.*

"Patrick Brogan?" she asked formally.

Pat was the only injured person in the room, but both policemen stood up and approached the swinging doors.

Using the clipboard to hold Lou at arm's length, she said, "Patients only in here."

Lou shrugged and Pat smiled as he went through to the Accident Room.

Stepping away from him, Rita pointed to a chair next to a gurney and said, "Please sit over there and wait for the doctor," and went off to gather iodine, sutures, and instruments she thought the doctor would use, as Pat watched her long chestnut hair swing and her backside move beneath the white dress. *Wow. Ava Gardner,* he thought.

When she returned, Pat took the soggy bar towel with the melting ice off his head and brushed the hair off his forehead. Putting the chair's back between herself and the patient, Rita examined the wound, reflecting on Pat's curly, black hair for a moment before the smell of booze hit her.

"Whew! Where did you fall down, in a brewery?"

"No," Pat started, trying to turn to look at her, "We were Indian wrestling over at McFadden's. See, I beat Lou the first time, but he's strong and got me the second time . . ."

She turned his head forward, away from her.

"Pretty nasty gash," she said, as she wiped it with gauze and a liberal dose of alcohol. "Probably take three, four stitches."

He gritted his teeth but kept silent at the cleanser's

sting. "We went to McFadden's after work," he said between clenched teeth. "We just got off at midnight."

Noticing the holster under his opened coat, she said, "Are you a cop?"

He silently reached into his pocket and held out his badge, to which she sighed "Hmmm," dismayed that yet another drunk cop had to come to the emergency room for off-duty shenanigans.

The doctor, a short Greek with straight, black hair, and a pencil mustache, came in, and Rita told him, "Mr. Brogan, here, was wrestling with his policeman friends in a bar tonight and got a gash on his forehead. There was no apparent loss of consciousness. I've checked the wound; there's no foreign matter in it, and I have cleaned it. I have laid out several size needles and sutures on the table. Will you need any hypodermics, Doctor?"

Putting his hand firmly on Brogan's head and examining the cut from different angles, the physician spoke, "No, Mr. Brogan seems to be a pretty tough guy, I don't think we'll need any novocain, but you ought to get him a tetanus shot, Nurse Crawford." Then, looking at Brogan over the top of his glasses, he said, "You're not going to cry on me, are you?"

"No, sir," Brogan replied, thinking of wounded men getting stitched up by the medics on the battlefield.

As he sutured, the doctor spoke. "What is it about you Irish cops? Firemen, too. You spend all day calming people down, helping them out. 'Nah, you don't want to do that, buddy, I'll have to arrest you.' Or, 'Nah, don't do that, your house will catch on fire.' Then what do you do? You go out to the bars, drink like there's no tomorrow, smash your heads against the wall, and try to kill each other. I've been seeing it in this hospital for ten years, now, and you Micks have been doing it since there were stagecoaches going up and down Seneca Street."

Pat and Rita both chuckled as the doctor finished the stitches.

"Miss Crawford, put some iodine on this wound, and a bandage, so he won't look like Frankenstein when he goes to work and scare the citizenry. And you, Trelos!" the doctor said, wagging his finger at Pat, "Stay away from the whiskey."

When the doctor left, Rita took a small bottle marked with a skull and crossbones, unscrewed the lid, and daubed iodine on the applicator while Pat flexed the muscles in his forehead against the tightly stitched skin.

"Hold still, silly."

Pat smiled.

"I guess you get a lot of cuts and stuff this time of night."

"Yeah, we do. Car wrecks and drunks doing stupid things mostly." She sighed, not mentioning the sad cases of sick children and old folks having heart attacks.

"Hey, you get off work at midnight after a hard shift, sometimes you're still a little wound up, you know."

"Uh, huh," she replied, recapping the iodine. Then, not seeing any way else to do it, she stood in front of Pat, careful to keep her distance and bending over slightly, reached out to carefully apply the oversized Band-Aid to his head.

*Wow,* he thought as she leaned forward, *She's got some boobs,* and then quickly forced his glance up to her green eyes, so she wouldn't catch him staring at her chest. When she stood back and checked the bandage's position, their eyes met for a moment. He smiled, and she turned away before she did, too.

As he watched her muscled calves move, and her white shoes click away on the floor, she pointed to the door without looking back and said, "You can sign yourself out at the desk, Officer."

"Pat Brogan, Nurse . . ."

"Rita Crawford," she replied, and the swinging doors closed behind her.

When Pat went out into the waiting room, Lou jumped up and smiled, putting his hat on and adjusting it.

"Hey, it doesn't look bad at all, partner, turning Pat's face towards him in the light. You wanna go get some breakfast or try for best outta three?" he joked, making them both chuckle as

Pat gave the desk nurse five dollars for the hospital's fees. As they walked out, Lou asked, "You get anywhere with the nurse?"

"Got her name, but no phone number."

"Hey, it's a start. I'd definitely give her a tumble, she's a looker. Tall, too, just your size, pal."

"Yeah," he said, thinking about her leaning forward to put the bandage on him.

"Probably from down here in South Buffalo, but definitely worth the trip, I'd say, especially after all the shit you're gonna hear at work about this cut on your noggin."

Pat nodded, touching the bandage, and wondered if he'd saved enough money to put a down payment on a car yet

# CHAPTER 40

## THE EAST SIDE, SYCAMORE STREET, 1951

His last week using a crutch, Bogdan Trzepkowski, was doing any errand to get out of the house. *Another week of this, and two more before I go back to work*, he thought. His mother wanted some vegetables for soup, so, he pulled himself out of his chair in the living room where he had been listening to the radio, and hopped out the door to Groczyk's deli down the street. Adept at balancing on one leg, he pulled the door open and hopped up the concrete steps, into the store. Mrs. Groczyk smiled and nodded to him. At the end of the counter, Bogdan saw the jockey and horse framed by a horseshoe, and the flashing colored lights on the backboard of the new Jumbo Turf King game. *Well, alright*, Bogdan thought, *Maybe being homebound isn't going to be so boring, after all.* He pulled out the seventy-five cents he had brought and changed one of the quarters for nickels, got a bottle of Orange Crush, and tried his hand. When the nickels were gone, he put down the pop bottle and thought that the deli's old, wooden floor must be warped, or maybe the adjusting screws on the frame were set wrong. He bent over and looked at it from the side, but could see no obvious slope. *Hmm, I think maybe the frame's not screwed together tight enough, makes it tilt easier. Just gonna have to adjust to it.* When another quarter was gone, Bogdan noticed three boys hanging around, watching him at the machine.

"You watch, guys, now I got it figured out."

When the next silver ball slid down the gobble hole, he slapped the machine on the side, lighting up the tilt alarms to the boys' chuckling. "Shit," he said, digging for a quarter in his jeans pocket. Empty. *Damn, now I've got to go get more money, I'll lose my place at the machine. Oh, yeah, I'll have to get some dough for the vegetables, anyway,* he thought, hobbling out the door.

As the boys swarmed around the Turf King, Mrs. Groczyk invested a nickel in the pay phone to call Johnny Walters, to get another machine. *We'll get rid of the pickle barrel to make room for it,* she thought.

# CHAPTER 41

## DOWNTOWN, 1951

Rita gathered up her shopping bags full of linens as the orange Number 4 approached, and then pushed herself onto the down-town car with everyone else heading south from Sattler's white sale on Broadway. Looking for a seat, she spotted Elzbeta Trep . . . Zep . . . Jib . . ., whatever the old Polish lady's name was, and pretended not to notice.

"Hey, Sally. Nurse Sally from Mercy."

Rita smiled and nodded.

"Hey, Sally, my friend. Hey, Johnny," Elzbeta said, pushing on the young man seated next to her, "You go stand, make room for nice girl, my friend, Sally, here."

The guy looked up from his magazine, saw Rita, tipped his hat and stood up in the aisle.

"Nice, nice, my friend nurse," she said, patting the cushioned seat next to her.

*I'm doomed*, Rita thought, *I'm going to have to listen to her all the way downtown.* Nodding and smiling, she listened to Elzbeta's complaints about gamblers stealing Bogdan's money, some old crook named Groczyk, and how she, Elzbeta, was going to tell the police downtown about it because the police who came by in the car didn't care.

When Rita got off the car to transfer to the bus to South Buffalo, Elzbeta got up and, again, latched onto her arm with a death grip and cried.

"No money, no money anymore. Bogdan give it all to gambler. Sally, you help me. Help old lady."

Unhitching her arm, Rita pointed west and said, "The police

department is over on Franklin Street."

Elzbeta followed Rita's long arm towards the big buildings amongst the crowds, cars, and buses, and wiped her eyes, nodding. Rita watched as she hesitantly got across the streetcar tracks, and then jumped back as a car blared its horn at her. Rita sighed, adjusted her packages, and shook her head. She nimbly picked her way through the traffic, and, when Elzbeta grabbed her by the elbow, Rita led her over to police headquarters.

# CHAPTER 42

## FIRST PRECINCT,
## POLICE HEADQUARTERS, 1951

Lieutenant Frank Salterelli checked his tie and his hair while he dried his hands in the men's room, and then came back to his place behind the huge, oak desk in the First Precinct on the first floor of Buffalo Police Headquarters.

The patrolman hopped up from his seat and shook his head when Salterelli asked, "Anything?"

Salterelli glanced around the room and observed the same few idlers and lost souls sitting and waiting, but sat straight up when the slender brunette in the green raincoat walked in, helping an old lady with a black shawl and headscarf, through the revolving door.

"Can I help you?" he beamed, looking right into her green eyes.

"Well, not me, her," Rita said, indicating Elzbeta, who nodded and continued to babble in Polish.

"Uh, huh," he said. "What seems to be the problem?"

"I'm not sure. It's something about gamblers taking all her son's money. Somebody named Groczyk, I think."

"Is she your mother?"

"No, see, her son was a patient . . . never mind. She's a friend and she was lost downtown, looking for police headquarters, so, I helped her here. She doesn't speak much English."

"Polish, huh?" he said. Picking up the phone, he added, "Lemme get somebody here who speaks the lingo."

A couple of minutes later, Patrolman Kazmerczak was there,

trying to slow Elzbeta's torrent down.

"She's got a complaint about gambling on pinball machines in a deli on the East Side.

Seems her son's taken to blowing his workman's comp check on the Turf King game, Lieutenant."

Salterelli nodded and, picking up the phone, said, "Gambling's bailiwick. Lemme turn this over to them," as Pat and Lou came through the door.

"So, I figure the Bison tickets . . .," Lou said as they both spotted Rita and stopped in their tracks. Lou slapped Pat's chest with the back of his hand and nodded towards the desk. They nodded at each other. Lou winked and continued onward to the stairs. Pat approached slowly, then looking at Rita, said, "Is there something I can help with here?"

"Oh, it's you," Rita said, surprised at seeing Pat sober and well-groomed. He smiled, then said to Kazmerczak, "What's this about, Greg?"

"Another guy getting cleaned out playing pinball, Pat. Her son," he indicated to Elzbeta, and nodded towards Rita, "No relation. A little deli over on Sycamore called Groczyk's."

"Well, Miss Crawford, isn't it?" Pat asked Rita. He got a nod and a small smile in return. "That's exactly what my unit is investigating. I think I can take it from here, fellas," he said, as Salterelli hung up the phone and smiled.

# CHAPTER 43

## SYCAMORE STREET, THE EAST SIDE, 1951

Off-duty a day later, Pat spent one dollar, five cents to finally get a winner in Groczyk's Deli. Dressed in a flannel shirt and blue jeans, he led a weeping Mrs. Groczyk outside after he arrested her, mouthy teenage boys following, and bluecoats looking surprised, as they pulled the squad car up to transport them.

Before Judge Chimera, Pat ground his teeth and thought, *Rita had better say 'yes' to going out with me after this.*

The judge waxed gleefully about the fearless members of Inspector Wachter's crack investigative team crushing a crime wave that threatened to overwhelm the East Side. He fined Mrs. Groczyk twenty-five dollars, and ordered the confiscated machines held, pending future court decisions. Mrs. Groczyk shrugged, pulled the cash off a roll of bills, and signaled her nephew, seated in the back of the court, to drive her back to the store.

# CHAPTER 44

## ELLICOTT SQUARE BUILDING, DOWNTOWN, 1951

Richard Smith sat at his desk on the third floor of the Ellicott Square Building, and puzzled over the message he had just received from his secretary.

"Mr. Pfeiffer just called and said he'll be here in ten minutes, Mr. Smith, and he also said, 'Tell him don't go anywhere.'"

*Pfeiffer,* he thought. *What the hell was the chairman of the state Republican party doing here in town? When did he get in? Was I supposed to know this? What the hell is going . . .*

"Hello, Dick!" Bill Pfeiffer blew through the door and extended his hand. "You know Jim Mason, of course," nodding to a handsome, brown-haired man who came in with him. "We just flew in from Albany for a quick chat," he said as he dropped onto the couch by the door without taking off his coat. Mason stood by the door, smiling, his hands in his pockets, looking over the place as if he were getting ready to redecorate it.

As Smith slowly eased back in his chair, Pfeiffer started. "Our friend, the mayor, needs some sound advice, Dick." Holding his hat by the crown and pointing with it at a picture of the governor on the wall, he said, "The governor may be running for president again next year, we all know that. He made his reputation as a crime buster, and now his own Republican mayor up here in Buffalo is looking the other way while a bunch of hoods, dagos, and God knows who else, are making book, running slot machines and pinballs all over the place. We can't let that happen, Dick. The Democrats see it, too, and as long as Truman's president, the federal attorney's a Democrat, as well. It won't be long before they start making noise about 'upstate gambling havens,' and the IRS and the Feds have a field day at our expense. The governor's trying to shut down that Irish bastard, O'Connell, in Albany, and that's hard enough to deal with right there under our noses on State Street for Christ's sake. We don't need any trouble up here, as well. Talk to the guy, get him straightened out. Get him to ban pinballs, like they did down in the city a few years back," Pfeiffer finished, and with that, he stood up and put on his hat.

Mason opened the door and nodded to Smith as he went out.

Smith stood up, and said, "How long are you in town for?"

Pfeiffer, his hand on the door, stopped, and turned. "We're catching a train for Syracuse in an hour. Oh, and Dick, tell the guy if he's got any idea about raising his own campaign funds from these rackets and going it on his own; District Attorney Stone is a very good friend of the governor. Good night."

He closed the door, pushing Mason away from the secretary in the front office and into the hallway.

# CHAPTER 45

## CITY HALL, DOWNTOWN, 1951

Patrick Hruska sat in his office, thinking. When he did thatis, he took a new No. 2 pencil between his thumbs and forefingers, and tapped his front teeth while staring through his glasses with an intensity that nothing could disturb.

"You'd think he had Superman's X-ray eyes," his secretary, Julie, said. Sometimes she'd glance into his office and see him like that, wondering what the hell he was thinking about. If she spoke to him, she'd have to say it two or three times, and louder each time, to get his attention.

"Yeah, his eyes are weird," Julie's friend, Patty, would say over chicken salad sandwiches in the lunchroom. "And that hair, yeech. He must use a gallon of Wildroot, or something, every day on it," she would say, causing both of them to shiver momentarily at the man's blonde hair, which he was futilely trying to save with various hair tonics.

At that moment, Patrick was thinking about politics. Ever since the current mayor's election, more and more city jobs had been going to his loyal Republicans, and the Democrats who had coughed up five percent of their salary to demonstrate loyalty to their party in the previous administration, were getting the heave-ho. Patrick had heard the current job holders were pledging up to six percent for their jobs, with three percent going to the GOP, and three percent into the mayor's coffers to pay off his campaign debt.

He had heard this at Feiner's Sandwich Inn, the fast moving cafeteria on Washington Street, where the workers from City Hall, the county building, and various other government offices went and rushed through cheap lunches at close quarters, and incessant conversational noise. He had heard it on the 13 streetcar going home, heading back to his mother's house on Stockbridge, reading papers from work. He had heard it at the Olympic Democratic Club, where he was secretary and treasurer, keeping track of the dues, bankbooks, meeting minutes, and all the other papers in his own fashion, with everything regularly updated and ready at a moment's notice.

When his concentration finally broke, the outer offices were silent. A glance at the clock on the wall said 5:38. Everyone else had gone home. He had time to catch the 5:52 back to his neighborhood, get something to eat, and get to the club, which was holding a Board of Directors meeting tonight at seven. The councilman from the North District was supposed to be there. As he pulled on his buckle boots, he thought, *This idea will get their attention, and give them a weapon to use, for sure.*

He hurried to the bus and thought of where the records he would need were to be found. Instead of getting off near his house, he got off at Bailey, right by the club, getting there over an hour before the meeting started. A couple of members were there already, playing cards. They exchanged greetings as Patrick rushed upstairs to the rooms, where the file cabinets were. He carefully combed through the meticulous records of who was on the various boards of the city, the Health Board, the Safety Board, and especially the Liquor Board. By the time everyone was there, shook hands, and had a couple of drinks, he was ready.

Councilman Charley Merriweather sat back in his double-breasted pinstripe suit, flush with whiskey, and filled with a good turkey dinner that the club president had bought him at Pratt's, and listened politely as Pat read off the roll, the Treasurer's report, and the minutes of the last meeting. The president gave his report, speaking of new members enrolled, dues collected, and upcoming plans for dinners and dances to be held at local halls. The councilman was invited to all of them. The councilman was introduced and spoke of the setbacks the party had incurred because of the current Republican mayor's election, of the backward steps this had caused the city, and the efforts the party was taking to regain City Hall. He did not mention the matters discussed with the club president at dinner: the defections to the mayor amongst formerly loyal Democrats, particularly amongst the Polish population; the loss of city jobs to Republicans; and what the club was doing to undermine these advances by the opposition.

The next order of business was old business, and there was the usual bickering over who paid what bills, who got contracts to do repairs in the hall, and whether or not they should buy a new refrigerator. When new business came up, the councilman was paring his fingernails and contemplating bailing out because of another appointment, when Patrick was recognized. Just as he had done on the debate team, he stood up, looked around into all the faces about him, and spoke in a voice that could be heard at the back of the room. He could see the insiders give wee shakes of their head at his formality and look away when he began, "Councilman Merriweather (who nodded politely and smiled at the young man), Mr. President, and gentlemen of the Olympic Democratic Club: We all know that our great party has suffered serious reverses in the last election, that the progress that our party represents has been stymied," (Patrick loved an occasion to use that word), "and that many formerly dependable Democrats have become turncoats, and now follow the GOP standard of the mayor. It is also known that the mayor is gathering support to himself, and is getting a lot of financial resources from the pinball operators in this city, and the police don't seem to do anything about it." He paused. Looking down, saw he had Merriweather's attention. "I believe, however, the Democratic Party has the responsibility and the ability to step in where the police are unable, or unwilling to tread. I have here," he held up a list, "the names of loyal Democrats on various Boards and Commissions, particularly the Liquor Board, who oversee businesses where the pinball games are located, who surely would find it intolerable that gambling occurs at these sites throughout the city, and might find it necessary to take disciplinary action against these businesses that continue to tolerate these machines, where children are allowed to play these games of chance, and the workingman is fleeced of his hard-earned wages."

Sitting down, he found the room was abuzz and the president

was being quizzed by the councilman. Patrick reset his glasses and smiled at the way his hard work had paid off, and gotten him noticed, at last. Merriweather got up from his seat and walked over to where Patrick was sitting, and shook his hand, followed by the president.

"Young man, it's a pleasure to see the membership of this club get up to the plate and take a few swings at the ball," the councilman said, thinking, *Get this kid to a decent barber and a trip to the men's department, and we might be able to use him.* Moving around behind him and looking over his shoulder, Merriweather said, "What is it you've got here, lad?"

"It's a list of all the Boards and Commissions in the city, Mr. Merriweather. I've underlined all the Democratic members and looked up their phone numbers and addresses."

"That's our Patrick, Mr. Merriweather; keeps everything in apple pie order," piped in the president. "I don't know what we'd do without him."

"Let's see," Merriweather said, thumbing through the sheets of legal papers, "Yup, here's the Liquor Board, and as I remember, there haven't been any positions come open since the last administration. This is jim-dandy, boy." Then, in a lower voice, he added, "Tell you what, lad. After this meeting breaks up, Ralph and I'd like to buy you a drink down at Ray Keller's," then, touching Pat's shoulder with the papers, he whispered, "You haven't told anyone else about this yet, have you?"

"No, sir," he answered. It would be the first time he'd been to a bar since his brother-in-law had asked him out after cousin Jerome's wedding over a year ago.

When the meeting broke up, the rank and file went back to playing cards, the councilman and other officers immediately went to Keller's over on Bailey, and Patrick straightened up the office before he left to join them.

"I tell you, some of these machines around here bring in as much as a hundred dollars a week!" the club president said, trying to keep his voice down.

"The way I see it, Ralph, we have options about these pinball machines," the councilman said. "We can ban them, cutting everyone out of the money they bring in, which makes nobody happy, except a few headline-seeking policemen and some old biddies who haven't been happy since Prohibition ended. However, the city is collecting taxes and fees on these machines, which makes them about as legal as it gets, and that keeps taxes down." He poked Ralph in the chest for emphasis. "So, to my way of thinking, a better option would be to examine the locations with Liquor and Health Department licenses from the boards we control, like young Hruska mentioned, and persuade them it is in their interest to assist Democratic candidates in the next election cycle."

"Ah, here's young Hruska now. C'mon up here, son, have a drink and let's hear more about your idea."

While Patrick espoused his thoughts, Councilman Merriweather considered how much more he and a few other councilmen would charge for not siccing the Liquor Board on the bar owners with the machines, or banning pinball machines the next time he saw Johnny.

# CHAPTER 46

## ERIE COUNTY HALL, DOWNTOWN, 1951

Eric Neufeld stood up and pulled off his overcoat in the hallway outside the grand jury chambers, as the steam sweated through the radiators on the first floor of County Hall. As he tossed it on the dark, wood chair next to him, the summons from the grand jury fell on the floor. He picked it up and stuffed it back in his coat pocket. He sat down again, sliding around on the well-polished, wooden seat, and noticed the other guys looking at him. All the other officers of the Vending Association were there, all except Johnny. Ang Malatesta, this year's treasurer, sat across from him, biting his nails and saying nothing. Curly-haired Larry Dobbins sat next to Ang, leaning forward with his hands folded on his knees, staring at him.

*This is the first time I've ever seen him not try to crack a group of people up with jokes,* Eric thought.

Charley Brogan, the recording secretary, was looking at him too, holding the summons in one hand and slapping it into the other. Some recording secretary he was. Never took note one, just signed off on whatever Johnny told him after Johnny had the girls write up the meeting minutes.

A door handle two chairs away from Eric rattled and a skinny guy in a blue suit and glasses came out, looking at a yellow legal pad. He scanned the hallway and said, "Neufeld. Is Mr. Eric Neufeld here?"

Eric raised his hand halfway, and the guy in the blue suit came over and smiled at him. "Good morning, Mr. Neufeld, I'm Ken Roth, Assistant District Attorney for Erie County." Roth stuck his hand out.

Eric stood up, shook it slowly, cleared his throat and answered, "Eric Neufeld."

"Mr. Neufeld, if you'd come with me, please," Roth said and opened an unmarked door on the other side of the hall for him. Eric gathered up his coat, glanced at the other guys, and went in where he was bidden. It was a small room with a wooden table and a chair on either side of it. The lawyer put his arm out, palm up, and gestured Eric to be seated. Roth then sat down across from Eric and placed his legal pad between two white, official documents on the table. He picked up one of the documents, tapped it square, and laid them before Eric.

"Mr. Neufeld, before you testify before the grand jury, it is necessary that you sign one of the documents I have on this table. One is a waiver of immunity from any crimes that may be revealed before the impaneled jury. Should you choose to sign that document, you will be liable to prosecution for any high crimes and/ or misdemeanors which the jury may find evidence of in its inquiries. The other document, which I have placed in front of you, is a grant of limited immunity for any crimes revealed by your testimony here today, which may have been committed on behalf of the Niagara Coin Machine Operators' Association, so long as those actions have not caused bodily injury or death, between the dates of July the First of 1949 and the present date, in the Counties of Erie, Cattaraugus, and Niagara, in the State of New York. I believe you took the office of vice president of the Niagara Coin Machine Operators' Association on July One of 1949, did you not,

Mr. Neufeld?"

"Uh, yeah, that's right . . ."

"You may read these documents, before you choose, Mr. Neufeld."

Eric picked up the grant of immunity and tried to read, but couldn't concentrate. He stared at it, only comprehending a phrase here and there. *Scope of immunity . . . impeachment of testimony . . . prosecution for perjury . . . subsequent appearance(s) before the grand jury. What the hell is this all about?*

"Do you need a pen, Mr. Neufeld?" the lawyer asked, uncapping a black fountain pen.

Eric took the pen and signed the grant of limited immunity silently. The assistant DA did, as well, and, capping his pen and putting it in an inside pocket of his suit coat, gathered up the papers and opened the door, ushering Eric back into the hallway.

Keeping his eyes downward, Eric followed the assistant DA across the hall. Roth opened a solid, oak door marked with a brass plaque *Grand Jury Room-Admittance Restricted,* and waved him through. He shuffled into the room, and Roth guided him into another polished, wooden chair situated in the middle of the room all by itself. In front of him were two dozen similar chairs in two rows on a platform, one row elevated behind the other. About fifteen seats were filled by what looked like a group of grumpy old people. To his right was a long wooden oak table where three middle-aged people were seated, and they were all looking at him from their perches.

He had just sat down when Roth said, "Please stand and raise your right hand, Mr. Neufeld."

He did as he was told, and the lawyer then speedily said, "In this high inquisition of the People of the State of New York vs. John Walenty, also known as John Walters, et al., do you solemnly, sincerely, and truly declare and affirm that the statements you make are true and correct?"

"Yes . . ." Eric replied, and he tried to sit down, but the lawyer waved him back up again with his papers.

"In this high inquisition of the People of the State of New York vs. John Walenty, also known as John Walters, et al., do you solemnly swear not to divulge the proceedings of this grand jury, so help you God?"

"Yes," Eric said, collapsing in the witness chair.

The assistant DA then quickly walked over, just to the left side of the elevated jurors; tucked the papers under his arm; cleared his throat; and in a clear voice began:

"Mr. Neufeld, you have been duly sworn. Now, how long have you known Mr. John Walenty, also called John Walters?"

# CHAPTER 47

## TONAWANDA, 1951

Johnny and Stepan had the Pharaoh machine open, and were replacing the rubber bands on the playing field. Stepan, or Steve, as Johnny had started to call him, was concentrating on the machine and handing Johnny the right size bands after carefully checking their size. Johnny looked up and saw half a dozen guys at the bar. Three of them were watching him, anxious to play the machine again. Johnny smiled, "Just a few more minutes guys, and we'll have this re-rigged for action." Then, under his breath, added, "Suckers."

The barroom door opened with the rattle of loose glass in the frame, and Larry Dobbins entered. He waved at the bartender, calling for a split bottle of Old Ranger, and walked straight back to where Johnny and Steve were working. Glancing at Steve, then at Johnny, Larry remained silent. Johnny looked up at Steve and told him, "Hey, Steve, go out to the truck and get those new screwdrivers I bought. I wanna tighten up the whole machine while we're at it."

Slightly confused, the big Ukrainian shrugged and left, carefully placing four of the right sized rubber bands on a chair where Johnny could get them.

Larry stood there for a moment, took a glance around, and said, "I saw your truck outside, John, and I've got some news I figured you'd want to know."

Johnny sat back, and both men took swigs from their beers.

"I heard some indictments just got handed down by the grand jury."

"I talked to those lawyer SOBs two weeks ago. They didn't find out nothin' about the slush fund from me. The guys who bought my insurance oughta be covered for their machines."

"Well, they got possession of gambling devices for the ones who didn't, or for the machines they didn't cover, which the lawyer says is a misdemeanor. You and a coupla the distributors are getting charged with possession of gambling devices, leasing and selling gambling devices, and conspiracy to violate gambling laws."

"Shit."

"There's another one just for you, Johnny. Perjury. That one's a felony. That could mean some serious jail time out in Attica or someplace."

"Shit," Johnny said again, banging the beer bottle down on the table. Stepan returned, admiring the new screwdriver set in a wooden box.

"Steve, finish this job up, will ya? I gotta talk to this guy."

Steve nodded, happy for the responsibility. Johnny and Larry took their beers to an empty part of the bar.

"Gimme two shots of rye, Keith," Johnny said, to which the white-shirted bartender nodded and poured the amber liquor.

Waiting until the barman had receded, Larry continued. "The association's lawyer's gonna talk to you, but I thought I'd pass the word now."

Johnny threw the shot down and nodded.

"The lawyer figures the DA will slap all the vendors they've nailed lately—the ones who didn't buy your insurance, with the possession charge, and make them all run for cover and give up the business. A few of them, the guys nailed for conspiracy, he'll sweat and offer a deal for information."

Johnny shook his head. "I knew this was coming, Larry. Thanks," he added, sticking out his hand for a shake. "I know I can count on you to clam up, right?"

"My lips are sealed, Johnny. I'm no virgin. Fines come with the territory." He threw down his shot.

With a wave to the bartender, Larry left. Johnny stayed at the bar for a few minutes after indicating Larry's drinks were on him.

"All good, Johnny," Steve said proudly.

"Okay. Keith, you're all set here. How much I owe you for the cocktails?" Johnny said, pulling out his cash roll.

The big man behind the bar shook him off. "We're all set, my friend," he said, as the customers got up to play the pinball game. "I'll catch you next time." Johnny wondered when the hell that might be as he went out the door, leaving Steve to carry the tools.

Johnny and Steve made three more stops that afternoon, fixing machines and cashing some out. At each one, Johnny had at least one beer and a shot, sometimes more. He only muttered at Steve's talk, having him do most of the work, and when they returned to the shop, he had Steve put away all their tools and equipment while he took care of the cash, snatching a hundred dollars from their safe and putting all the canvas-bagged coins in their bank's night deposit on his way home.

When he came up the steps, Johnny's wife, Harriet, looked at him carefully and figured he was at least half in the bag. A little boy got up from the floor where he was roaring his cars around, and started to approach him with a smile.

"Aw, Johnny, you're drunk again," she began. The boy stopped in his tracks, and his smile disappeared.

"Dammit! Can't a guy have a glass of beer after work? I been busting my ass all day."

"Johnny, you knew we're supposed to go out for dinner with the Monsignor tonight."

Johnny noticed for the first time she was wearing her new green dress. "We got to talk to him about getting
Jimmy into St. Gerard's."

"Ah, hell, what's wrong with the school he goes to, anyway?" Johnny countered, and the boy stared at the floor.

"We've been over this and over this," she replied. "We've got the money to put him in Catholic school now, and you promised we would," she said, stomping a foot in frustration and tears beginning to form.

"Ahhh, cripes, stop whinin'," he spat and raised his hand. She stepped back and the boy rushed to her, clutching her waist. Johnny stopped, remembering his old man. Harriet and the boy rushed past him and through the screen door onto the porch, and Johnny could hear the boy saying, "Mom, are we gonna go see the Monsignor now?" as he walked back into the kitchen and got himself a beer.

# CHAPTER 48

## ALLENTOWN, 1951

Johnny and Steve were putting screws to the legs on a Citation pinball game when they heard the rap on the door in the outer room. Johnny nodded to Steve to get it while he gently shook the playfield to check the tightness of the machine. Steve hustled back through the curtained doorway wide-eyed, pointing behind him. "It's the police, Johnny, two of them."

Johnny nodded and handed his screwdriver to the mechanic. "Don't worry, I'll handle this," he said, as he swung his short legs in big steps to meet the patrolmen. Looking over the half-curtains in the display window, he saw two blue-uniformed police he didn't know, and a patrol car at the curb. Making eye contact with the bigger of the two, he said through the glass, "Yes?"

"Are you John Walters?"

"Yes."

"Open the door, Mr. Walters."

"If you insist," he said, unlocking the door.

"Mr. Walters, I have a warrant for your arrest, issued by the district attorney for Erie County. You are charged with perjury, conspiracy, possession of gambling devices, and trafficking in gambling devices."

After the police fingerprinted him, photographed him, and booked him at headquarters, the two officers took Johnny over to County Hall to be arraigned. They led him through the mosaic-floored foyer and into a brass-door elevator.

One cop said "Three," and the elevator operator stared at Johnny as he snapped his gum.

Johnny had hoped everyone would tell the story they had

agreed on, that the dues were a dollar a machine a month, but he thought, *I guess some of them didn't hold up.* As they got off on the third floor, a big brass handle on the door to the courtroom turned, and a guy in a gray suit opened it, letting Eric Neufield walk out. Wiping his face with a handkerchief, Eric pulled a brown, short-brimmed fedora onto bushy gray hair, and walked quickly to the elevator without making eye contact.

*We're in trouble now,* Johnny thought, as his vice president disappeared, and he was led into the courtroom by two policemen holding him firmly by the elbows. It was hot and crowded inside the big, dark, wood-paneled room, and everyone except the DA's numerous assistants had loosened their ties as the steam banged and hissed through the radiators. A crowd of vendors were being arraigned, and Marty Wells, the association's lawyer, was rushing around red-faced, sweat marks under his armpits, and sheaves of paper in both hands. One of the vendors, Angelo Malatesta, looked at Johnny and shook his head. Wells rushed up to Johnny and said hurriedly, "Don't worry. This is just an arraignment. We've got Veazey doing the bond work so you can go afterwards."

The lawyer in the gray suit looked at a legal pad, then straight at Johnny, then around the room and said, "Walenty. Is John Walenty here?"

"Yeah, right here," Johnny replied, raising his hand. *Nice, call me by my old name, you prick. You think you know exactly who I am. Let's see about that, wise guy,* Johnny thought, as he strode across towards the judge's bench. Just before he reached it, he stopped suddenly, and the lawyer walked right into him, dropping his papers. Johnny took another step and smiled at the judge, who narrowed his eyes at the little man.

When he had picked up his papers, Gray Suit gave the judge his name as John Walenty and started rattling off the charges. Johnny noticed the plaster walls above the oak paneling had painted pictures of Indians and pioneer farmers. Johnny picked one of three Indians just above the judge's head and concentrated his eyes there, following its outline from the upper right-hand corner across, then down, back across, and up again.

When the judge said, "How do you plead?" Johnny and Wells

said in unison "Not guilty," and Wells added, "Your Honor."

"Five thousand dollars bail," the judge proclaimed, slamming down his gavel.

As they turned from the judge, Wells sputtered, "Veazey's our bondsman. All you need to do is sign the papers and . . .," on he went, while Johnny looked around the courtroom.

*Hmmm,* he thought, *Charley Brogan's here.* Interrupting Wells, he asked, "What have they got Brogan for?"

"Uhhh," Wells leafed through his papers, "Conspiracy . . . some other stuff . . . it's got something to do with the fact he's the association's recording secretary . . . He's got his own lawyer." Johnny observed the bespectacled man pushing his hair back off his forehead while he whispered to Charley, who nodded and crossed his legs.

*Wonder if his dad got him this shyster? He's got connections. Gotta look into this guy.* He took Wells' black-and-white striped fountain pen and signed the bond papers. Wells was still babbling away while Johnny said to the bondsman, "Gimme the figure, and I'll get the cash to you later." The bondsman nodded and Johnny left the chaotic courtroom.

# CHAPTER 49

## NORTH PARK, 1951

Joe Brogan hung up the phone and couldn't understand. On the notepad in front of him, there were already three messages from "Bob Casserta—Army buddy" for Pat. One taken by Joe, two more by Tim, and now this one. Pat had been in and out of the house all weekend. He must have seen these; he always checks the messages.

The fella seemed like a friendly sort, happy, and eager to see Pat. Said he was in town for a few days on business. Staying at the Hotel Markeen, at Main and Utica. Lived in Pittsburgh these days, served with Pat over in Europe.

When Pat came in later for dinner, Joe asked him about it.

Holding his fork steady over the plate of meatloaf and mashed potatoes, Pat looked off in the distance and said, "Yeah, Bob Casserta. I was in the Army with him in the 60th Infantry. Good man, damn good man," and nothing more.

Tim, ever interested to hear about the war, asked, "Is he gonna come over, Pat?"

"Sure, Pat, if he's a friend of yours, no point in him staying in a hotel. We've got plenty of room here," Joe said.

"Naah, I . . . I won't have any time to see him. We've got a lotta work. He won't want to stay way out here, anyway. Too far from downtown."

# CHAPTER 50

## BELGIUM, 1945

Corporal Pat Brogan sat on the ground with his back up against the tank's wheels, and tried to suck the last few drops of water out of his canteen. Snow was falling and the muddy ground was wet underneath him. Steam was coming off of him and it didn't seem like he was ever going to get enough air. Bobby Casserta was still standing up, his arms folded over his rifle on the tank's fender, leaning his helmeted head against the steel wheel cover. He hadn't moved much since the shooting stopped; just laid his M-1 on the tank and leaned against it, listening.

Their squad had been advancing across a field towards the woods, closing in on the German mortars that had been tearing up the column. When they were almost within rifle range, the Germans opened fire with machine guns on their left flank and in front, dropping Sweeney and Thomas instantly. Everyone dove for whatever cover they could find and returned fire. The sergeant split the squad into an angle shape to keep up fire against both positions.

When they heard the Sherman tank rumbling up towards them, the German machine gunners snatched up their gear and trotted back into the woods, and the mortars stopped firing.

Then, Sergeant Dunaway shouted in his Kentucky twang, "Get up and after 'em boys, before they get a chance to set up again."

The squad rose and swept forward, firing at the gray-green-and-white, camouflaged figures retreating into the pine trees of the Belgian forest. One of the Germans had stopped at the edge of the woods to fire his automatic weapon at them from behind a tree: first, a few rounds at one group directly in front, striking Voessler in the chest and neck, splattering his 19-year-old blood on the snow. The German then re-aimed towards Dunaway, Tolliver, and Keller, to his left, and fired just over their heads as they dropped to the ground near the dead youth while blood pumped out of his neck. Casserta and Pat, approaching at a right angle to the gunner, raised their rifles, quickly aimed from their shoulders, and fired off two rounds each, splintering the pine tree and knocking the enemy soldier onto his side, dead. Once in the woods, they slowed down, looking and listening for the enemy. Behind them to their left, the Sherman clanked off, looking for a way through the trees.

Dunaway whispered to Keller on his right, "Get yourself ready with a rifle grenade, son," causing the recent arrival to scramble through his shoulder bag to find the deadly missile.

As they reached the edge of this copse and came to a farmer's field, they stopped and watched for signs in the next woods beyond, when they heard the telltale thump of a mortar round going airborne.

"Get down!" Dunaway yelled for the benefit of the two new guys, who didn't intuitively dive into the ground as the mortar shell whistled down through the branches and exploded, sending dirt and rocks flying behind them.

*Good,* Pat thought, *they're firing behind us.*

He moved up, crouching in front of as wide a tree trunk as he could find, when two Germans broke cover to his left. They were both dashing pell-mell through the woods. He and Casserta were taking aim, when suddenly, Pat spotted a third German out of the corner of his right eye, beneath the tree branches, just about to swing a stick grenade side arm towards them.

"Bobby, look out!" Pat choked out, rolling behind the tree and kicking behind him futilely to make a hole. Pat clung to the base of the tree, and Bob tried burrowing face-first into the snow, pine needles, and soft dirt, as they listened to tiny pine branches snap along the grenade's airborne path. In the interminable next second, Pat heard his teeth clack shut, and he curled up in a ball. The bomb exploded with a roar, the metal fragments cracking branches, shaking snow and pine needles on them. It had exploded far in front of them, having collided with a tree that kept it from its target. Blinking quickly to assure their living status, the two Americans then jumped up and began firing wildly into the area where the ambusher was last seen. They rushed forward and spotted the German hobbling at the edge of the woods, one leg dragging and both arms grasping at a tree to pull himself forward through the brush and branches. His head snapped back to spot his pursuers, and Pat saw a small man with sleepless, bloodshot eyes in a face filled with fear as he tried to jump back into the forest. Bob and Pat both squeezed off the remaining rounds in their magazines, some kicked up dirt, some splintered bark, but a few thudded into the fleeing soldier and sent him motionless to the earth.

The tank had busted out into the field from their left, and Dunaway rushed forward, getting directly behind it. There he snatched up the telephone receiver on the tank's rear to give the tankers instructions while he waved his men to come forward, advancing behind the steel vehicle. Pat and Bobby quickly reloaded, and as soon as the squad came out of the woods, the machine gun and small arms fire commenced again, whistling around them, pinging off the tank. As he ran forward across the open ground, Pat's mouth went dry and he felt like someone had reached up from the earth and yanked at the tail of his overcoat. When he reached the Sherman's steel hull and braced his shoulder against it, he looked down to see a hole ripped in the skirt of the long overcoat, still smoldering where the bullet had passed through.

"Okay, swing around," he heard Dunaway say. The sergeant hung up the phone and pushed the men to his right, just as the tank pivoted sideways and stopped. The soldiers moved behind the tank's side as its turret swung left to aim the 75 mm gun at the German position in the woods. After its first cannon round exploded in the trees, the sergeant leaped up on the tank and started firing the .50-caliber machine gun from the turret, its finger-sized bullets shattering wood and ripping whatever they hit to shreds. The other men then came out of their crouches and started firing their rifles around the tank's body, into the woods.

*Another explosion shook the woods, but it didn't come from our tank's gun*, Brogan thought. More small arms firing, then shouting in English and German, and the sergeant held his hand up to signal them to cease fire. Smoke still emanating from their M-1 muzzles, the men looked to the woods, and Dunaway said, "Hah! The boys from the Polack's section got 'em flanked. Sons-a-bitches musta given up."

After a few moments of relative quiet, Dunaway hopped down and spoke into the phone to the tankers again. The men stepped back. The tank swung around and began moving towards the woods, the soldiers loping behind it. When they reached the edge of the woods, Brogan saw the men from Sergeant Lewandowski's squad pointing their weapons at a number of Germans who were sitting on the ground, their hands clasped on top of their heads.

Dunaway ordered, "Tolliver, Keller, run back and see to Sweeney and Thomas." He added, "Get a medic if it'll help." Looking around at his squad, he said, "The rest of y'all okay? Take a break while this squad gets these Krauts searched."

The veteran sergeant's words proclaiming temporary safety, the troopers relaxed in near exhaustion after a fight that had lasted only minutes. Dunaway lit a cigarette with shaky hands and waited for Tolliver and Keller to return.

When they came back up, Tolliver, one of the newer men, was white as a sheet and kept repeating to Keller, "Are you sure it was Sweeney? That guy's face was gone. Are you sure it was him?"

Keller looked at the sergeant, shook his head, and said, "They're both gone, Sarge."

"Okay, boys," the Sergeant said quietly to the two new men, "Get me one of all of their dog tags—Sweeney's, Thomas's, and Voessler's," repeating their names with a momentary reverence, "And make sure the other one's on them good," refraining from telling them the prescribed method—jamming the flat dog tag between the dead man's teeth by holding his skull and slamming the jaw shut. "Bundle them up in their blankets and bayonet their rifles into the ground right next to them with the helmets on top so the body detail can find them. When you get done with that, check your weapons and meet us over by where that tank is now."

After the men had moved off mutely to see to the morbid

detail, Dunaway addressed the two veterans, who were now sitting by the tank, Casserta smoking a Lucky.

"You boys done good. Flanked that Kraut with the Tommy gun, or whatever he had, and took him out before he could jump us good. Nailed a couple more in the woods," he added, nodding at two German bodies tangled in the brush. "Check your weapons and ammo, and then take a break. There's a stream just up there if you need water. I'm goin' to go check with the lieutenant, see what else needs be done."

The two GIs sat silently, grateful to have survived another action. As the tension of combat wore off, they carried out their post-combat routine of checking weapons and ammunition, and then they ambled off towards the stream to fill their canteens. They came by where Sergeant Lewandowski's squad had stopped, finding half the section wolfing down canned fruit rations and the others watching the prisoners, who were sitting in a circle talking in low voices. The Germans' weapons, equipment belts, and helmets removed, they, too, had lit up cigarettes, careful not to make any sudden moves that might set off the nervous young Americans, who were still edgy after the deadly encounter with these more experienced Nazis, who were sitting calmly, just a few feet from them. As Pat and Bob walked by, Pat noticed one German seemed to be doing most of the talking, a slender guy with straight blonde hair that he brushed out of his eyes, while the rest of the bunch sat facing him and listening. Pat looked at his uniform and recognized the inverted chevrons of a sergeant on this one's sleeve, along with the lightning flashes of the SS on his collar.

*Well, whaddya know,* Pat thought, *we beat Hitler's varsity today.*

The Nazi sergeant noticed him looking and followed Pat with his eyes, as he kept talking to his men while Pat and Bob passed by. Pat couldn't make out what the sergeant was saying, but it sounded like instructions that non-coms give, the short emphatic phrases, while the others nodded and smoked.

Pat and Bob filled the canteens from the frigid stream, took big swigs, and topped them off again before returning. It never ceased to amaze Pat how thirsty he got during and after combat, no matter how cold it was. Sometimes there never seemed to be enough water in the world to slake his thirst. When they got back to where the sergeant told them to meet, the tank had moved off and the sergeant was spitting, his signal that he was ready to address his depleted squad.

"Well, boys, I guess you know that Voessler's dead, and Sweeney and Thomas didn't make it neither, but the new boys made it through their first action okay. Polack's section had three of their boys wounded, and since they were short, anyway, we're joining up with them. Over yonder there's sixteen Krauts gotta go to the rear where they're gathering POWs. Brogan, you and Casserta take our two rookies and two from the other squad, and march 'em back there. It'll be dark before you get there, so there's six of you to handle it. I'll show you on the map where to take them before you leave. Don't be doin' no dawdlin' in the rear, either. This third army's chasin' the Krauts hard, and General Patton's after their hides. Awright, let's get on over to them other boys and get organized."

As they walked over to meet up with their new unit, Bob noticed an unusual weapon, the muzzle slung down over Dunaway's shoulder, the sergeant's own issued carbine slung across his chest. "Hey Sarge," he asked, "Is that one of the Krauts' weapons you got there?"

"Sure is. The one they got Voessler with. Haven't seen this one before. Some new kind of automatic they got. Mean to check it out when I get the chance."

As the men joined together, talking of the deaths and injuries in the recent skirmish, their platoon commander, Lieutenant Gomps, pulled his sergeants aside and established the new order. A short, rotund man with a pointy mustache, he was a second generation Russian Jew from New York, and spoke rapidly.

"Okay, Dunaway, you're the new boss of this squad. Elevenski, you're goin' over and runnin' the mortar section now," he ordered, thumping the tall Pole's chest with a forefinger, adding, "And don't take any crap from those sodbuster pukes about the rounds being heavy, got it? I want those tubes movin' up fast and on the ground firin' immediately, if not sooner, when I call for 'em. Do you get the picture? You get the idea?"

"Got it."

"Well, move out, goy boy. Whaddya waiting for?" Then, looking at Dunaway and pointing at Brogan, he said, "Okay, get your corporal here squared away on the prisoner detail, and let's move out. The tanks are ready to roll and there's Nazis to kill." Turning to Brogan, he cocked his head to one side and said with a smile, "Are you back yet?" and everyone moved.

Dunaway pulled out a map and said, "Okay, Brogan, you and Casserta are taking our two new guys and two new guys from the other squad. The POW depot is just outside Monschau. Go up this road, here, two miles to the village we came through this morning, you know, then, take the road west and march 'em another six to the pen. Seems they flushed a few more quail out since the shootin' stopped, so, you'll be taking nineteen Krauts altogether. Your boys are over there," he said, pointing to the recently bloodied new men, "And the Krauts are over yonder. Deploy your sentries, two to a side, and send the men guarding 'em up now. We gotta get movin'."

Pat walked up slowly to the four men, three of them standing and one kneeling down, tying the laces on his boot. They all looked directly at him. He knew Keller and Tolliver for just over a week; the others, not at all. He exhaled and said to the first new man, a small boy in a big helmet askew on his head, "What's your name?"

"Trout, Sarge . . . I mean, Corporal."

*Perfect,* he thought with a smile. "Okay, Fish, swim upstream. Get the Krauts in two lines along the road over there, and then drop back to the middle, so you can keep half of them in front of you."

"Sir . . . I mean, Corporal . . . I don't know any German."

"That's okay, lad," Pat replied, suddenly sounding like his own father. "Just shout 'Raus!' to the blonde-haired guy with the stripes over there, hold up two fingers, and point to the road. They'll figure it out. Keller, you take the opposite side of the column, across from Fish, here. How about you, what's your name?" Pat asked to the other stranger.

"Ma name's Jenkins, Corporal," with a slow voice from the deep South, and a smile of pure sunshine.

"Okay, Jinx," he said, "You and Tolliver take the rear two corners of the column, and all of you fix bayonets to let them know you mean business. After about five miles, we'll take a break, let 'em take a leak, get some water if there's a creek nearby. Any of you guys speak German? All right, once we get them lined up, ask and see if any of them speak English. In the meantime, give any orders to the blonde-haired guy with the stripes; he's their sergeant. Okay, detail, take your posts, get them lined up, and let's get moving, so maybe we can get these guys to the POW depot before dark."

Pat watched little Fish go hesitantly over to the Germans, who were sitting or crouching together, watching him approach. He brought his M-1 up to port arms and Pat could see he was gripping it tightly. As he got farther away, the little fella seemed to get smaller and his rifle and helmet bigger. He approached the Nazi sergeant, almost formally, and waved his right arm with two fingers extended. The blonde Kraut with the stripes stood up, looked at him, and nodded. With a few words, he signaled his men, and they all stood up and started slinging their gear and lining up. Little Fish stepped back, and then looked over at Pat and smiled.

*This isn't going to be so bad, at all,* thought Pat. *I could use a break after that last shootout.* He looked down again at the bullet hole with the seared edges in his coat, and thought of the grenade bouncing off the branches in the woods. How many skirmishes had they seen like that since they got moved up there? Eight? Ten? Seemed like they were becoming more frequent since the Krauts were on the run. It'd only been a few weeks since they got to the front, but the lieutenant said they were learning fast, and acting like veterans. *Fire a few mortar rounds, throw a few grenades, some machine gun fire sometimes, or snipers, and then they run, just enough to slow us down a little. Thank God the only tanks they had encountered were smashed up,* he thought. Some guys they had talked to said when they were working, it didn't seem anything could stop the big tanks.

On their way up to the fighting, they'd stopped for a break and met up with a bunch of walking wounded that were headed for the rear, and ate around a campfire with them. There was one guy with a bandaged stump of an arm who described his first encounter with German armor.

"We were comin' up on this village, see. Our whole company was spread out and there were four Shermans with us. Everything was quiet until we hear those diesels roarin', and then they came bustin' out of that town like horses comin' out of the gate. The Shermans stopped and took aim, and we just watched. The first Tiger stops for about one second, fires, and a Sherman goes up like a Roman candle. Big orange flame, straight up, ya see. Another Sherman gets off a shot, but all his shell did was burn the paint on the Tiger's armor. The other Tiger fires a shot and blows up another Sherman, then, machine guns and snipers open up from the town and some of our guys start droppin'. Nobody had to say nothin'. We all started runnin' like hell. I heard another explosion, musta been the third Sherman blowin' up as I went past it. I could feel the blast, and it knocked me ass over tea cup. I'm not sure what happened next, but the Krauts blasted the last tank, cooked all those guys inside, and kept firing at our guys. Scattered us good. One of the bastards musta run over my hand," he said, holding his arm up and looking where the missing limb would be. "Then, they went back into the town." He hesitated, and then added, "The medics worked on me, but I wouldn't let 'em take me back. Our guys surrounded the town and then blasted the sonsabitches with anti-tank guns. They got the tanks and killed most of those damn Nazi assholes." The soldier finished, resting his head on his knees, while the rest of the men stayed silent, considering the deadly possibilities that lay ahead.

*This should be easy,* Pat thought. His guys and the Germans were forming up nicely and starting to move along. *I guess the war's over for these SS supermen, and the new guys are handling this just fine. Take this hike back to the rear, get some hot food, and catch up with the outfit later.*

Pat walked up to where Trout was and asked him, "Any of them speak English?"

The boy's face dropped. "Uh, I dunno. I didn't know how to ask 'em.'"

Pat smiled and, looking over at his prisoners, shouted, "Hey, any of you Krauts speak English?"

The Germans looked at one another, and the blonde guy looked back at one of them and nodded to him. He had a particularly dirty uniform, a crumpled *feldkappe*, and his face and hands were covered in soot. Pat waved him up to the front of the column and motioned him next to the sergeant as they walked.

"Tell him," Pat said, addressing the sergeant, "That we're going to walk five miles. Then, we're going to take a break. Water. Latrine. Then, walk some more. Understand?"

"Ja," he said, nodding, and he translated it to the sergeant, who looked straight at Pat and nodded as well. Pat faded back down the column and wondered how old the sergeant was. *Couldn't be more than twenty-one or two*, he thought, *But he acts a lot older.*

Looking over the rest of his prisoners, he noticed they all looked pretty young, up close. Awful dirty, too. Pretty squared away, though, and all of them had those SS tabs on their collars.

They set a good pace and stayed in their two lines, just like they were told. The only time they flinched was when a couple of American Jeeps and a truck came tearing up the road towards them, and the lead Jeep had a mounted fifty-caliber machine gun with a guy manning it. *The Germans didn't like that gun*, he thought. *Rip a guy's head or arm off like it was paper.*

The small column of vehicles screeched to a halt beside them, and a captain in the passenger seat of the lead Jeep stood up, his hands on the windshield. Pat saluted. The captain returned his salute and asked, "Second Battalion up ahead, soldier?"

These men all still had clean uniforms, except the captain, whose wrist and neck were bandaged. *Holy shit, that's Captain Urban*, Pat thought. *He was dying, last anyone had heard. The rest must be replacements.*

"Yes, sir," Pat replied, "About a mile ahead." *This guy's from Buffalo, too*, Pat thought. *Just got shot up and he's headed back to the front already, while I'm skylarking on this detail.*

"Have your men keep their eyes open, Corporal. We got word of infiltrators around here," the Captain said, and with that, they saluted each other again and Urban signaled the Jeep to get moving.

The four young privates looked at each other, and Pat noticed his new soldiers were, again, gripping their rifles tightly. The Germans had no reaction, and just started forward again, although at least the one guy must have understood, and they whispered amongst themselves.

Pat figured the chance of coming across Kraut commandoes was pretty small, and getting smaller the farther they got from the front. He walked at the rear of the double column with Casserta, feeling more relaxed. *Good God*, he thought, yawning, *I could take a nap right along the side of the road.*

"Don't start that," Casserta said smiling, "Or we'll wind up asleep like Dorothy in the poppy fields," at which they both laughed.

The Germans kept up a good pace, and the only one who ever looked back was their young sergeant, checking occasionally to see how his men were doing and observing the American guards. Whenever he did that, Fish, Tolliver, and Keller would cast a worried look back at Pat and Casserta. Jenkins kept up a steady patter of talk about the countryside, the weather, and animals he spotted darting in and out of the woods, wishing he could put his rifle to recreational use.

They kept along like that until almost dusk. Feeling winded, Pat turned to Casserta and said, "Feels like about five miles, Bob. Time for a break?"

"Phew, I'll say, five miles or not."

"Private Fish!" he shouted, smiling at Casserta.

The little soldier turned sideways and kept walking, trying to see his leader and watch the prisoners at the same time.

"Tell the guy who speaks English to stop. We're gonna take ten here."

"Yes, Corporal," he answered, and then trotted to the front of the line to pass the word.

The column stopped, and Pat waved them over to a clearing on the side of the road. When they had settled, canteens and cigarettes came out, and Pat and Casserta sat on a crumpled old wagon to catch their breath.

Taking his helmet off, Pat rubbed his head and said, "I'm gonna sleep for a year when this is over. A solid year."

Passing him half of a Hershey bar, Casserta adjusted his glasses and nodded at the Germans. "Look at these guys. One minute, they're trying to kill the whole world for Hitler, now they're as

relaxed as if they're headed home from work."

"Hell, Bob, war's over for them. Why fight it?"

"Ah, shit," Bob said, looking up. "It's just about dark, and now the snow starts to fall."

Pushing himself up on his rifle, Pat said, "Yeah, the sooner we get these guys behind the wire at Monschau, the sooner we can get some hot food," and, with that, he signaled the men to reform and get moving again.

They had walked another two miles when the snow started to come down hard, and the wind kicked up. After three miles, everyone was breathing hard. Pat felt his legs starting to cramp and called a halt where there was a ditch along the side of the road. "Fish, tell the guy who speaks English to tell his sergeant get these guys down in the ditch while we take five. You guys line up on the road side of the ditch and keep an eye on them from there."

Looking worried, Trout straightened his big helmet and gestured with his bayoneted rifle to the Germans, who calmly climbed into the ditch and huddled together. Pat went into the woods and took a leak. When he came back, he saw the new soldiers at the far end of the ditch shivering, and heard the Germans talking, a couple even chuckling, probably at the boy soldier nervously manning his post.

Pat went to the opposite end of the ditch and sat down on the edge of it, pulling his collar close around his neck and tucking it under his helmet in the back. He felt a snowflake hit his nose . . .

When the first rifle shot cracked, Pat leaped up from his sleep and pointed his rifle forward. He saw a German fall backwards with something in his hand, and Trout shouting, "He's got a grenade!"

The rest of his men must have been dozing as well, but now, jolted back to wakefulness by the gunshot, they raised their weapons and a couple more shots were fired. The Krauts started shouting and trying to get out of the way of the bullets, jumping every which way and running towards Pat's end of the ditch. The next thing Pat knew, the blonde sergeant was right in front of him, waving his arms, shouting, "Nicht schiessen! Nicht schiessen!"

Without thinking, Pat pulled the trigger twice and jammed his bayonet into the young man's chest. The boy coughed, his hair flopped into his face, and eyes went wide, staring at Pat with incredulity as he attempted to grasp the steel in his ribcage. Falling backwards, he pulled Pat forward until the American yanked the rifle back. Slumping into the snowy ditch, the German's eyes never left Pat's face, a look Pat would never forget, and then went blank as he died.

Casserta was yelling, "Stop firing! Stop firing!" and when the shooting stopped, he jumped into the ditch and flicked the "grenade" out of the first dead Kraut's hand with his bayonet. It was a canteen he had been waving, asking for water, and now there were four dead prisoners and one who was dying, moaning and choking on his own blood.

Pat ran forward, stumbling over the young sergeant's body whose blood was still dripping off Pat's bayonet. "What the hell, what the hell. . .," he said, trying to grasp what had happened.

Casserta looked at him, and they both recognized the results of panic.

"All right, all right!" Pat shouted, looking for the English speaker, who was lying dead at his feet. "Raus! Raus!" he hollered, pointing with his weapon to the road, and the Germans cautiously climbed out of the ditch and quietly formed back into two lines, fearful of making any sound that might cause any more of them to die.

"Back to your posts, men. Let's get this detail moving now and get the hell out of here!"

The men fell to their positions, all but Tolliver, who looked down into the ditch where the wounded German was still twisting and moaning.

"What about him, Corporal?" he said.

"Leave him! He's gonna die anyways! Now, let's get moving,

dammit!"

The column moved off and marched at a fast clip despite the snow and the wind, eager to get away from the scene. No one spoke, no one looked back, and soon the groans of the dying man were unheard. When they got close to the town of Monschau, Pat asked the MPs directing traffic where the POW depot was. When he found out, he practically ran the men to the wire enclosure.

"Yeah, yeah, fifteen prisoners," he told the officer of the guard. "My unit? Yeah. B-Company, Second Battalion, Sixtieth Infantry. Me? Brogan, Corporal Brogan," he tried to mumble, as the guard wrote it down. *Oh God*, he thought, *They'll find out I didn't get all the prisoners here. They'll go back and look, find the bodies, and then . . . What if these Krauts start complaining? Oh shit, oh shit, oh shit . . .*

Casserta, meanwhile, had found a truck carrying some replacements headed back to the front and their unit. "Good, good, Bob," Pat sputtered, not making eye contact with him or anyone.

Climbing into the deuce-and-a-half truck back to the front, nobody from Brogan's detail said a word, and it was so dark, they couldn't see anyone's face. The new guys spoke about the snow and the cold, and where they would catch up to their units. In the dark, Pat grasped at their accents to distract himself. *One of these guy's a Southerner*, he thought. *Funny, the way voices get clearer in the dark. I can't even see the guy's face, but I know he's from way out in the boondocks in Georgia or Alabama.* With the snow flying and the wind howling, they kept the canvas tarp pulled down across the back, but with no heat and just canvas covering the truck body, it was freezing in the back. The men stomped their feet and shivered in the cold. The only light came from the occasional flash from a match scraping against the metal deck floor and a few cigarettes glowing red. Butts were crushed out underfoot, except by the men at the back who would pull the tarp back just enough to toss a butt outside.

Glancing outside when one of the butts were tossed, Pat noticed that it was pitch black and still snowing. *Not much traffic tonight. The driver'll never see them down in that ditch, he's moving too fast. Yeah, that's it. Maybe they won't find the bodies until spring. They'll never figure out what happened. What if the Germans start talking?*

*Those guys are no dummies, they could find the bodies again, show them to the MPs. They've got some guys who speak German guarding them now. Ah, they're too busy to worry about what some Kraut POWs say anyway,* he hoped. *Those Nazi bastards would remember everything about us. Ah, nobody would believe them, they're all liars, always have been. SS sons of bitches, they're all murderers, deserve what they got. Maybe if they'd shot all . . . no, don't even think that way. It's bad enough as it is.*

One of the other guys tried to strike a match in the dark, but it snapped off and the light sputtered. "Ah, fer fook's sake. Let me see one a yer fags, there, Magoo, catch a light off it."

*English, no . . . Irish . . . just like Mom and Dad . . . .Oh, what have I done?* Pat thought, putting his head down and holding his helmet with both hands. *Home will never be the same again, after this.*

The driver was wasting no time at all, keeping his foot to the floor and only slowing a little to downshift and take a curve. Pat sat up as they bounced along, grateful that no one could see his face and afraid someone would speak to him and figure out what had happened. He didn't even dare to talk to the Mick and find out where he was from, like his parents always would, happily listening to the talk of the old country. They suddenly hit a big bump in the road, bouncing all of them up off their seats.

"Whoops," the Irishman said, "Another pedestrian done in by the Red Ball Express," getting a laugh from his detail. "Iya hope it was one of them Kraut infiltrators," the southerner added, getting a few more chuckles. Tolliver jumped up, and, rushing to the rear, pulled the canvas back and puked onto the road, holding onto the frame to keep from falling out. "Sheeit, boy," the southerner said, "Ma joke couldna been that bad," which kept the laughs rolling, except from the boys of Brogan's detail.

The driver slowed down a few miles later, and started asking sentries for unit locations as he cruised by them. The third time he slowed down, a man on guard duty said, "Yup, that's us, B Company," and the truck stopped. "B Company boys, get the hell out, you're home," the driver shouted, revving his engine. Brogan and his comrades eagerly scrambled out over the tailgate to the other men's shouts of "See you in Berlin!" and "Back home for opening day!"

As they pulled away, the Irishman said, "Fookin' lot of sad sacks, that bunch," to which the southerner quipped, "Couldn't take the MPs' food, I reckon," setting them on the way to their part of the front, laughing.

Pat asked the sentry where Sergeant Dunaway was, and his men followed him, heads down in a slow walk. Dunaway and three others were still awake, sitting in a foxhole, examining the weapon the sergeant had picked up earlier in the day by firelight.

"Hmm," said one man, pointing at the magazine. "Curved magazine, like some of our carbines got. How many rounds it hold, Sarge?"

"Looks like thirty, Ace. Got twenty left. Takes these short pistol rounds," he said, holding out a handful for all to see.

"Sarge?"

"Oh, hey, Brogan," he said, looking up at him. "You guys made it back. Good. Get some hot chow in the rear?"

"Uh, no, we caught a ride back right away."

"Alright. Guard duty's already set. You and your boys'll escape that tonight. Go get yourselves settled and get some sleep. We're back after the Krauts tomorrow."

Pat stood there for a moment, uneasy. He'd forgotten about the fact they were still in the war, that there were still enemies out there to kill or be killed by. *Wasn't today enough?* he thought. *Doesn't Dunaway know what happened? Sweeney and Thomas gone, just like that. Voessler's neck spewing blood out on the snow. The bullet burning through his coat. That fucking grenade bouncing around in the woods. The young Kraut sergeant staring at him . . .*

"Nice wooden stock," Dunaway said. "Little heavier than an M-1, I'd say, though."

Pat came out of his daze and walked over to where the bivouac was set up to dig a hole in the ground and get out of the wind. He tucked his coat beneath him, bundled up the blankets around him, and pulled in his knees. Sleeplessly, he watched the sky and wished he could make the last few hours go away.

When the rumors about reassignments came up, Pat asked around, hoping to get moved. None of the men ever said anything about that night on the road, nobody ever came around asking about the dead Germans, but every time he looked at one of the men from that detail, he thought their eyes averted him and talking seemed short and businesslike. *Nothing is ever going to be good again*, Pat thought. *Nothing is ever going to be clean, no matter what I do.*

# CHAPTER 51

## POLICE HEADQUARTERS DOWNTOWN, 1951

The D and D boys were getting ready to pay a social call on a newspaper stand that wrote numbers, and Pat was writing his weekly report. "Hey Dudek," Pat asked, "You know anything about a guy named Walters, runs a vending business outta Allentown?"

"Johnny Walters? You mean Johnny Walenty? Hell, I've known that runt since we were kids," he said with a wave of his hand. "Always had some scheme going. He'd make some money, put it on a number, and when he got older, put it on a horse. Always had some get-rich-quick idea. 'I'm gonna be rich, you'll see,' he was always saying." After a pause, he added, "When his old man was in the picture, he used to knock those kids around. Mrs. Walenty, too, something terrible. Well, Dowd," he said to his partner, who smiled as he slapped the cylinder of his revolver closed, "Let's go crush some crime."

Pat was checking the spelling on his weekly report when Lou came up and stood in front of his desk. "Hey, partner," he said, tugging on the coat of his gray pinstripe suit, "When you get done with the chicken shit, how about we knock off and head down to Dean's Cafe in Kaisertown for a cocktail and a little campaigning?"

Pat looked up at the big, round wall clock, and then over at the boss's office where the inspector was poring over reports like he did every Friday before he went home. Pat yanked his report out of the typewriter, tapped it on the desk to get the carbons and the copies straight, and then put it flat and signed it. One copy for the file, one for the DA's office got dropped into baskets, and the last one got put quietly into the inspector's In basket.

"Night, boss," he said as he slipped his suit coat on while

Wachter grabbed a buzzing telephone. He and Lou hurried out before another detail came their way, Lou tightening a new maroon tie. In the elevator, Pat got a whiff of aftershave.

"What's the plan for tonight there, Don Juan?"

"I saw two of the ripest tomatoes in the market over in the DA's office just before lunch today. One blonde, one redhead. The redhead was tall, just perfect for you. I think they were new hires as secretaries or something, and I figure we ought to advise them on working in the D.A's office before the lawyers do."

"Sounds like something fellow civil servants should do, but, uh, how do we know where they'll be?"

"Ah," said Lou, "As I carried some vitally important documents to the File Thirteen receptacle, I heard them mention Dean's place over on Clinton Street."

As Pat slid into the passenger seat, Lou looked over at him, taking in his dark gray suit.

Lou shook his head as they pulled away. "You know, pal, you're going to look good in that suit, when they lay you out."

"Well, hey there, Liberace, we can't all be fashion plates like you," Pat said, checking out Lou's attire. He had a new hat on, a buff-colored fedora with a maroon band that matched his tie.

"You gotta be the only guy over twenty-one who doesn't wear a hat these days, too. Why is that, Pat? You forget so many in bars, you just don't bother anymore?"

"Nah," Pat reflected, "All the time in the Army, I hadda wear something on my head. A helmet, a garrison hat, an overseas cap. Take it off whenever you go inside, put it back on when you go out. Keep 'em clean, get the right one from the orders of the day. What a pain in the ass. Now I just wear ear muffs when it gets real cold, or maybe a cap in the rain. Keeps it simple."

"Ahh, makes you look like you're lost or something, looking around for where you left it, you ask me," Lou said, turning the car onto Clinton Street.

Once they got to the bar, Lou and Pat looked around. Bar to the left, booths to the right, tables in the middle and in the back room. Lou hung his hat up by the front door and nodded to Pat, directing his attention to a table right in front of the bar. They sat down, and the waitress came over.

"What'll it be boys?"

"Corby's and water," Pat said.

"BV and water for me, Sandy."

She went to the bar to get the drinks.

Pat said, "You know everybody in this town?"

"Comes with the territory, partner. Young couple, Sandy and Dean own this place. They buy their meat from the place I worked cutting meat. Hey, did you hear Jim Backus on the radio last night? He was doing this old guy routine, Mr. Magoo, he called him, and . . ."

As Lou finished his story, Pat, seeing their glasses were nearly empty, looked towards the bar for the waitress when the family entrance door came open and two women entered. The blonde came in first, turning her head to the side as she said something to her companion behind her. Lou, still chuckling from the radio story, shut up and stared as she tilted her chin up to show a long, white neck leading up to a delicate chin; perfect, white teeth framed by bright red lips; and an aquiline nose. When she looked forward again, Pat noticed her tight blonde curls, one of which dangled over her deep-set brown eyes that sat under pencil-thin, black eyebrows. She scanned the room, and then came forward on high heels, waving to the bartender. Her eyes latched onto an empty booth. Lou looked down from the long, white neck to a brown turtleneck sweater that was stretched over what the guys called "torpedo tits," a wide, black belt that cinched a high waist and a long, tweed skirt that was so tight, it had to make climbing stairs almost impossible. He stepped on Pat's toes to make sure he saw her and started rocking the base of his glass back and forth.

Pat saw her, all right, but it was the friend who followed her who magnetized him. She was taller, had to be about five-ten or eleven, with long, red hair rolled forward on her forehead, over her ears on the side, and straight at the back, ending in waves that hit her shoulders. She had very pale skin with a hint of childhood freckles, and light blue eyes that matched her faceted earrings— did they meet his for just a second? Her dark pink lips were parted just enough to let you know she knew you were watching. A bright green dress set off her face and hair, and swung around long legs that moved straight forward. Watching as she walked past, Pat saw the legs move without bending inward at the knees, the motion being transferred to her hips that twisted and rose as her heels clacked on the barroom's wooden floor.

Pat looked over at Lou, who was staring forward and blinking, still tapping the bottom of his highball glass back and forth on the table, which is what he did when "thinking strategically," as Pat called it.

Pat waved the waitress over, glad to get her attention before any of the other guys in the place.

"Hey, Sandy, I'll take another Corby's and water, Lou'll take another BV and water, and see what . . . "

" . . . our fellow civil servants will have in the last booth," Lou interjected, strategy in place.

Sandy smiled, dropped her order book in the pocket of her rounded, white apron, and said, "If you don't, somebody else will, Tiger." Then, she walked back to the booth where the two women had settled in, purses at their sides, and legs tucked under the table. The redhead looked over at Lou and Pat in careful evaluation, and the blonde turned and gave a little wave of her fingers. A moment later, they were back to their conversation, the smitten men forgotten.

Sandy walked away, thinking, *This happens all the time to these two. Happened at the last place they went before they skedaddled on the last two suckers.* She sighed, remembering after-work Friday nights in years past of her own, then, walked up to the end of the bar and said to her husband, "Another round for the gendarmes and two whiskey sours for the gold diggers of 1951, Dino."

He set up the glasses as he looked over at the two policemen, leaning forward in their seats staring at the girls, who ignored the men completely. *I love this job,* he thought, as his wife shook her head and dropped coasters on the serving tray.

"Well, what's our next move, Julius Caesar?" Pat asked.

"Wait a minute or two, then I go over and offer to make introductions." Lou tapped his glass on the table for a few seconds more, then got up, tugged on his lapels, cleared his throat, and walked over.

Pat took a swig of whiskey and watched, trying to catch the conversation. Lou bowed slightly, then said, "Excuse me ladies, but, didn't I see you earlier today in Mr. Stone's office? My friend and I have a rare evening off from our duties. Perhaps we might. . ."

The blonde held her chin in her hand and kept smiling at Lou, but the redhead sat there stone-faced. She did glance over at Pat once, when Lou gestured in his direction and said something about "much decorated veteran."

*Oh jeez*, Pat thought, *What bullshit is he telling them?*

Finally, the blonde looked at the redhead, who nodded slightly. Lou waved Pat over, who picked up their drinks and went to the table.

"Pat, I want you to meet Helen Volker and Betty Harper."

"Pleased to meet you, ladies," Pat said as Lou took his drink and slid in next to blonde Betty. Helen hesitated, and then made room for Pat in the booth.

Standing at the service end of the bar, Sandy said to her husband, "Keep 'em coming, Dino, and I better tell the cook to get some steaks and the veal special ready."

"Well, what brings you two ladies to this cafe?" Lou opened.

"We heard they had a great veal special," Betty said.

Pat turned to Helen and, after staring a second, said, "What do you girls do? Lou seemed to think you might be getting jobs in the district attorney's office."

"No, Betty works as a secretary downtown, and I'm thinking about going back to school. We were just there to talk to one of the lawyers."

"Oh," Pat said. "A boyfriend?"

Taking a sip of her drink with closed eyes and smiling, Helen said, "Why, are you scared, war hero?"

"Uh, look, I'm not scared, and I'm not sure what Lou told you, but I'm not a war hero, either."

"Well, an honest one. Didn't drive the Germans out of Normandy single-handed?"

"Nope, wasn't even there."

"Well, how about that," she said, pulling out a cigarette and letting him light it.

"Hey," Lou said as Sandy came by with menus, "Let's see what the specials are."

After decimating salad, soup, blue plate specials, and a couple more drinks, Lou said, "Say, I see where the Al Williams is playing over at Frank's Casa Nova. Whaddya say we take a ride and go do some dancing?"

"Sounds great," said Betty as she pushed herself up from the seat.

They all piled into Lou's car, and as they rumbled over the New York Central tracks on Bailey, Pat felt Helen's leg bounce against his. *Wow, solid*, he thought, as she flexed her leg and moved just an inch away so he still felt her dress on his trousers. Inside the club, the smoke was banked down to their ears and the brass section in the band was letting loose. A table was just clearing out, and they snagged it before someone else did. Pat waited for a waitress to order drinks and Lou led Betty out on the dance floor. Stepping lightly, Lou spun her about, and she threw her head back and laughed with joy. After their drinks came, the band slowed the pace down to play "Near You," and Pat and Helen got up on the floor.

"Nice song," he said.

"Francis Craig," Helen said.

"Huh. I thought it was the Andrews Sisters who did it."

"Francis Craig and his orchestra did it first." "You follow music?"

"Love it," she said.

"Hey buddy, I'm cuttin' in," said a bleary-eyed guy, clapping a huge hand on Pat's shoulder.

"Nope, not tonight, pal," Pat said, tilting Helen away, then swinging her away around another couple.

"That was smooth," Helen said, as the big guy blinked, shrugged and went back to the bar.

"Let's sit down," Pat suggested, taking a seat where he could keep an eye on the guy at the bar.

"So, Helen. You like music and are going back to school. What are you going to study?"

"Oh, I don't know. Maybe accounting. I really haven't made up my mind. I don't know if I'm going to be around here long,"

Helen said.

"You mean Buffalo?" Pat asked.

"Yeah, I left my job, and I'm tired of the winters and all the roughnecks around here. Maybe go out west where it's warm."

"Like California?"

"Maybe," she said as he got her cigarette lit on the second pass.

On a second trip to the dance floor, Pat fended off another guy who wanted to cut in, this time telling him to shove off, and then both girls left the dance floor.

Heading over to the table, Lou whispered to Pat, "I'm gonna escort Betty home, partner."

When they had disappeared, Pat ordered another round of drinks. Helen took a sip of hers, and excused herself. Pat finished his, and wondered where she was. He ordered another drink, and kept an eye towards the ladies room. When he finished that one, he went over to the coatroom and asked the girl if she'd seen the tall redhead in a green dress.

"Big tall girl?"

"Yup. Green dress. Lonnng legs."

"Got a cab and left, ten minutes ago, at least. Where you been?"

He headed for the door, and the waitress snagged him by the elbow.

"Hey, you almost forgot the bill."

"Oh shit, I'm sorry. Let's see. Okay, here ya go, keep the change, sister."

"Thanks."

Checking his pockets outside, he saw he didn't have enough money for a cab home, so he walked over to the bus stop and waited for one headed up Ferry. *Shit,* he thought, *twenty-five years old and I'm still catching the bus home from the dance with no girl.*

The next morning, he went through his pockets. Matches, loose change, and some crumpled paper. *Hmm, what's this?* he thought, unfolding a cocktail napkin. On it, he read, "If you remember my name in the morning when you sober up, my number is Kensington 1125." Scratching his head, he thought, *Well, it wasn't a complete disaster after all . . .*

# CHAPTER 52

## ERIE COUNTY HALL, DOWNTOWN, 1951

Inspector Wachter entered the district attorney's office and observed Assistant DAs Roth and Lauria sitting to the side with stacks of files in their laps. DA Clifford Stone sat behind his desk in a khaki suit with his glasses on, examining a file, a cigarette smoldering untouched in an ashtray to his right.

Looking up from his papers, Stone said, "C'mon in, Martin. I think we've got a plan pretty well thought out for these characters."

"Good," Wachter replied, sitting down. "Have you got a list of witnesses complete yet?"

"Just about. The three main witnesses I want you to get in here as soon as possible to depose are these," he said, passing papers across the desk. Looking over his metal rimmed glasses at his assistants, he added, "There are others we've spoken to," getting nods from the seated lawyers, "But we'll leave them where they are, for the time being." Leaning back in his chair and chewing on the end of the glasses temple, he asked, "How much do you know about this racketeer they call 'the Gimp,' Martin?"

"Torreo Monteduro, also known as il Zoppo—Italian for gimp," Wachter said, reciting a familiar history. "Born of Sicilian parents on the West Side, suffered from polio as a kid. Father's gone, mom dies of TB, brother dies an alcoholic, pretty much raised himself. Took over from the Black Hand boys back in the old days, drove them right outta the business. Bootlegger during Prohibition. Arm breaking, maybe a couple of murders, too, but nobody ever testified, never even got arrested. He walks with a limp from the polio, but when he catches you, you're in a vice, I hear. Runs numbers, horse rooms, crap games, card games, and now, we think he's behind moving slot machines and pinball machines around town. He's got friends in Chicago who supply them. Slowing down, though. We hear now that some guys up in the Falls and from Cleveland are moving in, getting more aggressive, maybe pushing him out of the way."

"We believe that some of our witnesses can connect the pinballs to politicians in City Hall, Martin. Do you see any way we might be able to connect Monteduro to them?"

"He's way too slick for that, at least from what I've seen. He probably arranges the prices for the machines from the guys in Chicago to the distributors here in town and takes something off the top for that. He talks to some guys in the vending business, who talk to some guys in politics, who talk to guys in City Hall, but he doesn't get close to them. Now, if somebody gets out of line and starts wrecking a good deal, he'll get somebody to take care of it, but he's not around when it happens anymore like the old days. The best we can figure, a man named Ferraro was the last guy to get it from him. He was a bookie who takes a trip out west to Nevada. He comes back with some narcotics, which he's selling on the side for himself, and then disappears. Completely gone off the face of the earth. Some stories have him in Lake Erie using chains for ballast, but we've got nothing."

"Do you think they'd go after women who are witnesses?"

"You mean like these girls that worked for the Vending Association?" Wachter asked, holding up the files he had been handed. "I doubt it, but some of these new guys moving in, I'm not so sure."

The lawyers exchanged glances. "Perhaps," said Stone, "We should arrange for them to be kept in hotels before and during the hearings?"

"I think that's a very good idea." Shuffling through the papers, Wachter nodded. "We should pick up the two bookkeepers right away. We'd better find someplace to hide them, too, and carefully. These guys would try to scare them, maybe even kill them, and you certainly don't want them to wind up like Abe Reles."

At the reference to a witness who had been thrown out of a hotel window in New York while in police custody, Roth said,

"Perhaps we can arrange for the witnesses to stay at a hotel, and they can be watched by sheriff's deputies."

"Not a bad idea, young counselor, but everybody in Buffalo knows everybody. We might want to find someplace secure outside western New York to be safe."

"Yeah, but how are we going to have access to the witnesses regularly if they're in, say, Rochester?"

"Hmm, perhaps across the river in Canada?"

Wachter snapped his fingers. "That gives me an idea . . . Mr. Stone, I think I've got a solution to this problem."

The DA, the lawyers, and the policeman worked on the logistics of the inspector's plan for over an hour. When District Attorney Stone returned to his office, he put in a call to the state Republican party chairman. When his secretary buzzed that the call was going through, he picked up the phone.

"William, Clifford Stone, here. How are things in Albany?"

"The governor's enemies are alive and well up here, Cliff, thanks to the O'Connell brothers. Are you keeping the troops in line on the frontier there?"

"Well, I think I can say that proceedings here are advancing rapidly now, and we should be seeing substantive results over the next several weeks."

"Well, that's good news. The most important thing is that we get a handle on the issue before the opposition gets the federal attorney involved up there."

"We're way ahead of them there, Bill. Also, you needn't worry about the security of witnesses either, like they did in the city," Wachter said, a comment that made the chairman grind his teeth at the memory.

"I certainly hope not, Clifford. We'll keep our ears to the tracks and expect to hear good vibrations soon," the chairman said, and hung up.

The district attorney smiled. *Things are looking up, indeed*, he thought, *As long as Martin comes through and my boys keep the grand jury on course*. He buzzed his secretary to put another call through.

# CHAPTER 53

## POLICE HEADQUARTERS, DOWNTOWN, 1951

"How're you making out with the redhead?" Lou asked.

Pat mumbled, "Ahh, got her number, haven't called her yet."

In his best Claude Rains voice, Lou said, "How extravagant you are, Rick, throwing away women like that. Someday they may be scarce."

They both chuckled.

Wachter looked at the names and addresses he had gotten from the DA's office. The inspector called out through the open door, "Lou, Pat, c'mon in here," which Pat thought was unusually informal.

"I have got here," the inspector said, "A couple of subpoenas that need to be served by a couple of fine young men."

Lou nodded and Pat remained immobile, waiting for the inspector's description of the detail.

"These two, you young guys are going to like."

Lou and Pat exchanged glances and smiles.

"It seems the DA would like to have further words with two secretaries by the name of Betty Ann Harper and Helen Volker, who have worked for the Niagara Coin Machine Operators' Association."

Lou's eyes widened and he turned his head slowly to look over at Pat.

"Miss Harper currently works over at the vendor's association, in their office on Main Street, and lives in a building at 2819 Main Street, apartment 213. That ought to be at Main and Depew, if my memory is correct. Miss Volker no longer works at the vendor's association, but her home address is over in Kensington, at

53 Schreck Avenue, probably rents a flat there." As he prepared to hand the papers over, he looked up at his two detectives: first Lou, whose face had fallen, and then at Pat, whose hands were in his pockets as he stared at his shoes.

"What?" he demanded. "What's wrong?"

"Well, Inspector," Lou started, rubbing his chin, "I think we're already acquainted with these two . . . witnesses."

Knitting his brows and lowering his chin, the older man rose from his desk.

"Close . . . the . . . door . . . Detective . . . Brogan," Wachter forced out, his face turning red and his chest starting to heave. Pat quickly shut the door and returned to his spot, going into a military at ease position.

"Yeah, uh, Pat and I," Lou began, gesturing back and forth between Pat and himself, "Went out after work last Friday. Friday, right, Pat?"

"Yeah," Pat nodded, "Friday."

"Yeah, well, we went out to this restaurant, Dean's, over on Clinton, and we had a couple of drinks, see . . ."

"Lieutenant. . .," Wachter said between his teeth.

". . . And we met these girls there. Betty and Helen. Said they were secretaries, used to work at the same place. We didn't know they were witnesses!"

"Lieutenant . . ."

"Well, we had a couple of drinks, and Betty and I were getting along pretty good, and Pat and Helen seemed to be getting along pretty good . . ."

"Lieutenant . . ."

". . . So, Betty and I got up and left, so Pat and Helen could, uh, get better acquainted, and uh . . . "

"So, you two have been boffing two of our witnesses?"

"Well, see Inspector, I did take the one girl, Betty, back to her place, but I don't think Pat talked Helen, I mean . . ."

"You idiots! You top of the line morons! These women probably know as much about the inside of this vendor's operation as anybody! How could anybody be so . . . frigging stupid?"

"I swear to God, boss," Lou said, clapping his hand on his

heart, "I didn't know where she worked until just now," and holding his hand out like a lawyer indicating his client, "And Pat, here, didn't get past first base . . ."

"Every time. Every single time one of you guys gets into trouble, it's because you've got your dick where it doesn't belong. Remember Langmeyer who was in the unit before Brogan, Lieutenant? Remember how he got jammed up? He looked the other way because he was fooling around with his buddy the bookie's wife. Remember? Remember the 'accidental discharge' of the weapon in the park, the bullet that caught him in the ass but didn't tear his pants? Agggh! What the hell am I going to do with you . . . you . . ."

Leaning forward, his fists on his desk, Wachter's face slowly receded from crimson and his breathing slowed.

"All right. All right," Wachter said, trying to think. "If you didn't do her," pointing at Brogan, "Did you go to her place?"

"No, sir, I . . . I just got her phone number."

". . .And you, moron! Does she have roommates who saw you go to her place? Other people in the building? Does she know you work for . . . Ahh, what's the use? Just when I think I've got two squared-away men, they turn out to be just like every other guy on this job who thinks with his . . . All right, here's what we're going to do. I'm going to call over to the sheriff's office and have them pick up these witnesses, and I'm going to talk to them myself before the DA's office does again, and see if they'll keep quiet about you. Now, get out of here before I decide to replace the both of you!"

After Lou and Pat had fled his office, Wachter sat at his desk, pondering his next move. He could hear and see the activity in the bullpen outside his office, where Dudek and Dowd were sitting on the front of a desk, talking to a woman who had been beaten in a gambling club. They were examining her neck that was reddened with finger marks, and Wachter saw she had eyes blackened like a raccoon.

*What idiots!* Wachter thought. Seeing Dowd signal the woman to open another button of her blouse to check her for more damage, the Inspector cleared his throat loudly, causing the two policemen to stand up, and one to return to the seat behind his desk.

*Is getting laid all that these guys think about?* The message given, he got up and closed the door to his office. He sat down at his desk with a sheet of loose-leaf paper placed on the blotter and his fountain pen full of ink. There he sat, pulling the pen's cap off and pushing it back on until an idea came to him, which he then wrote down on the paper as he thought about what to do about the two female witnesses, what he should tell the prosecutors, and if he should hammer the two numbskulls who had just left. He wrote down a few ideas and scratched off a few. After about twenty minutes, he concluded he should speak to those two women first, before he called the district attorney. He carefully tore up the loose-leaf paper.

# CHAPTER 54

## KENSINGTON, 1951

Helen was sitting at her dressing table, winding her hair into a side reverse roll when the phone rang. Putting down a cigarette, she wondered if it was the tall guy whom she had dazzled the other night. *Nice looking, but kind of awkward.* On the second ring, she thought, *Or, maybe it's that crazy bartender, Paul, from the bar on Delaware, the one who used to play football at Canisius. Nothing I couldn't handle, there. He's nice looking, too, with blonde hair, sure to take me if I mention someplace nice.* The phone rang again. *Maybe it's the guy from the bank. If he asks me out, this would be the third date. He's got money, but he's married, and a third date would make me a home-wrecker. Nope, time to give him the breeze.*

She picked up the phone and answered "Hello," with her business voice.

"Helen!" Betty said, "Do you know who those guys were? The ones we met the other night at Dean's?"

"Lou and Pat? Sure, they're cops, silly."

"Yeah, but do you know where they work?"

"Pat's going to change his name to Bud and they're going to take over for Abbott and Costello. How should I know?" Wondering if anyone was listening on the party line, she added, "Did he drop you off after you guys left the club?"

"He came up for a while. He was something, but I'll tell you that later. Anyway, one of his cards fell out of his pockets. It turns out he works for the Gambling Squad, so I called Mary Pat Fahey, you know? She went to high school with me at Bennett and works in the DA's office now. She says she sees him all the time, and the guy, Pat, too. She says they're both working for this guy Wachter you read about in the paper who's after all the bookies and bars, where they're taking money for the pinball games. Mary Pat also says they've been bringing witnesses to the grand jury, asking about payoffs and stuff. Do you think they'll ask us about that, being the bookkeepers and everything?"

Like a train that suddenly shifted tracks in her head, Helen began working on the possibilities.

"Sure, they might ask us that stuff. Have you heard from that guy, Lou, since the other night?"

"No, but I figure he'll call. We were pulling up to the apartment house. . .," and on she went, describing their late evening at her apartment, while Helen figured the possibilities. She had seen Johnny hanging around with some guys, real hoods, and had no interest in getting caught in the middle of this mess. The money had been good, especially what Johnny was paying her under the table to adjust the books, but this could mean real trouble with the law, or maybe worse, with those bad guys who ogled her and tried to play Casanova every time they came into the office. She looked through her open closet door at the nice clothes she had accumulated over the last few months while Betty went on about Lou, and wondered how fast she could move the lot of it out, and where.

# CHAPTER 55

## LAYFAYETTE SQUARE, DOWNTOWN, 1951

After a fast visit to a travel agent in the Hotel Lafayette down-town, Helen picked a hotel out of the brochures about Miami and left, promising to call back. Then, she went down Main Street to Hengerer's and bought two suitcases and a trunk, and took a cab back home. She hauled all the baggage upstairs, packed her possessions, tied her red hair up in a bun, and covered it with a scarf. She waited until the family downstairs left for bingo, put on her raincoat and sunglasses, called a cab, and took everything to the DL&W train station. She had her trunk shipped by Railway Express, had a porter take her suitcases to the train, and tossed the voided passbook from her savings account in the trash. When the train pulled out for Pittsburgh and pointed south, she sighed in relief. It wasn't as bad as the time she left Billy in New York, and she hated leaving Betty like this, but it was every girl for herself these days.

# CHAPTER 56

## THE EAST SIDE, 1951

The mayor sat back in his shirtsleeves, watching Ocky release his ball down the lane from the right corner of the alley. Its black and white speckled surface spinning sideways as much as forward, it tumbled into the pins just to the left of the head pin and knocked them all down with a loud wooden clamor. *Damn, the guy's hot tonight*, the mayor thought. *Third strike in a row.* Taking a sip of beer, he marked an X on the score sheet and added up the score as Ocky walked back wiping his hands on the powder-blue towel he always used. The pin boy set up for the next frame.

"Should be, uhhh, one hundred eighty-six, Joe," Ocky figured, sliding into the bench and reaching for his own beer on the table.

Tapping the pencil on the sheet, the mayor looked up and smiled, "Right you are, Cornelius, right you are. You're having a hell of a night, I must say."

"Might just break my own record this time, Joe. One more strike, and fifteen points on the last frame any which way, and I score two hundred thirty-one, one point better than my best at two hundred thirty."

"Yes, but what about the team scores, Ocky?" the mayor asked. "I've got a respectable one-sixty going with two frames and Ed's got one-seventy-two. Carl's lagging behind with only a one-twenty. It'll be hard to catch us as a team."

As Ed got up to bowl, a shout went up from one of the other lanes and sang a campaign slogan.

"Hey, hey, hey, it's Jazz."

The mayor turned, illuminated his face with a smile, and waved to the bowlers unpacking their balls from canvas bags.

Ed Falk approached the pins from right of center, and tried to put a curve in his delivery. It hit the pins farther to the left than he wanted and left him with the seven-ten split.

"Damn," said Ed.

"Tough pick up," said Ocky.

"Jazz 'er up," said another bowler, quoting one more of the mayor's campaign slogans.

Raising both fists in the air, the mayor acknowledged them and said, "Ed'll get it. He's gotten us out of tighter spots before, eh, Ed?"

"Ever since high school, Your Honor," Ed commented, launching his ball down the lane, where it nicked the seven and sent it flying, just missing the ten.

"Ach, look at that, just missed. Looks like it'll be a close finish, gentlemen. You're up, Carl."

Feeling the pressure, Carl lined up just to right of center of the lane and rolled his ball just right of the headpin. The plain, black ball crashed into the pins, leaving the seven and eight pins standing.

"Easy pick up, Carl, easy pickup," Ocky assured him.

This time, the lawyer took a spot at the far side of the lane and angled his ball into the middle of the two pins, clipping them both.

"Good job, Carl. The spare gives him one-thirty-eight."

The mayor rose and picked up his highly-polished red and white flecked ball, sending it down the alley with enough body English, that it rolled along the front of the pins after it made initial contact, and gave him a strike.

Turning, he smiled at Ocky and Carl, saying, "We'll be tough to beat now, fellas."

Sitting down between Ed and Carl, the mayor signaled to the bartender, spinning his index finger in the air for another round of beers.

"So, counselor, how many cases have you had, now, over in the Felony Trial Bureau?"

"Well, just the one, so far. They've got me filling in for ADA Courtade while he's on vacation."

"Good, good, lad. I'm sure you'll do well there and get the next full time opening when one comes open. I also hear that they may be requesting some of my men from the police department for a special investigation. Isn't that right, Ed?"

"That's what we're hearing."

Ocky shattered the pins again and swung his fist uppercut style with a big "Yes!"

"Uh, yeah. We're hearing there's going to be two more lawyers and three cop . . . policemen and a commander requested for the pinball investigation."

"Well, Carl, that should leave some openings in other bureaus for you to move into, at least temporarily. How long do they figure this will take?"

Ed settled his glasses on his face and picked up his ball.

"Well, I've heard that the grand jury's going to be held over again, so, that means at least a month, maybe more."

"Ah, that's good for you, my boy. You'll probably be filling in several places, get a good look around, get some valuable experience and see what interests you."

Ed knocked down nine with his first roll and picked up the spare with his second. As he went forward with his last ball, the waitress brought over their beers.

"These are on the fellas on lane eight, guys," she said, putting the bottles on the table.

"Well, that's great!" the mayor said, as they held up their beers and looked to their benefactors a few lanes over.

"We're with you, Jazz," one exclaimed, as they held up their drinks, as well.

"Ah, I love midnight bowling now and then," the mayor said, settling back in his chair with his hands on top of his head as Ed knocked over nine with his last roll. "Not too crowded, not too loud, just go bowl with some friends, let your hair down and have some fun."

Carl got up to bowl, and as he approached the pins, Ed looked at the floor and remarked to the mayor quietly, "This is going to be hard."

Reaching out and shaking his shoulder, the mayor smiled and

said, "Don't worry, Ed, I'm going to put it out of reach."

Carl knocked down nine pins with his first delivery, spared it up, then dropped eight with his last roll.

"One-sixty-six, Carl. Not bad for a college boy," Ocky quipped.

The mayor got up and tried his English spin move again, and got nine pins with the first delivery. The others watched quietly to see what he would do next. He spared it up, and then scored nine more pins with his last roll.

Ocky got up, wiped his hands, and threw the delivery he had been using all night, but only scored eight pins. He spared it up then rolled a nine with his last ball.

"Well, Ocky, a mighty game," the mayor said, finishing up the scores. "You get your best game ever with a two-thirty-five, but . . . Edju and I still beat you guys for the game, four-twenty-six to four hundred and one, and the series . . . twelve-fifty-three to eleven-twenty-four."

"You gotta watch these guys, Carl, they're sharks," Ocky remarked.

"Teamwork, my boy, teamwork is what does it. Why, Ed and I have been kegling together since our days at East High School."

"You guys must play a lot together to score like that," the young lawyer surmised.

"A great way to unwind after a long day in the city's service, right, Ed?"

"Nothing like it, Jazz."

Pulling his coat on, the assistant DA said, "If it's not too personal, Mayor, where did the name Jazz come from, anyway? Those guys down there were calling you that, and it was all over the place last election."

The three comrades chuckled, looking at each other, remembering how people were always accusing the mayor of giving them the jazz until the name stuck.

"Well, my boy," the mayor said, clapping Carl on the shoulder, "I used to play trumpet in what we Polacks call a jazz band dance group, and . . . 'Jazz' is a hell of a lot easier for the voters to remember than Jezerowski, particularly with Republicans," which got them all laughing. "Well, lads, what do you say we belly up to the bar and have a night cap?"

Carl shook his head, grateful that bowling was a lot cheaper way than poker to make points. "Not tonight, fellas," he said, looking at his watch. "Gotta be sharp tomorrow for work."

At the bar, the three men settled into a quiet corner and ordered whiskey. Staring into the liquor as he swirled it in his glass, Ed was the first to speak. "This could be bad. You know they're going to want Wachter, and he's going to pick his best

bloodhounds for this pinball investigation."

"Yeah," added Ocky, "And except for one guy, and maybe Carl, we don't have the connections in the DA's office we do in the city court. Hell, it took everything we could pull to get the DA's chief assistant to move Carl over into the Felony Bureau temporarily, Jazz."

"Hmmm," the mayor thought, staring into the mirror behind the bar and sipping his whiskey. "Yes, it would seem that since Governor Dewey's man, Chairman Pfeiffer, paid his most recent visit to Mr. Smith, our relations with our fellow Republicans in the district attorney's office have been a good deal less cordial, and yes, they're sure to insist on the crusading Inspector Wachter to head up the investigation team."

At this, Ocky threw back his drink, and Ed shook his head.

"However, gentlemen, I think we can make this work to our advantage," Jazz continued, getting his two companions' immediate attention.

"We have been looking for another position for the good Inspector Wachter, have we not?" the mayor asked, smiling again. "Why, this is just the thing," he continued. "A reward for his years of service to the city."

"While he's being eased out of his current permanent job, running the investigative squads like gambling," said Ocky.

". . . And someone gets appointed off the list to fill his spot in the city while he's off in the DA's office," Ed added, continuing the line of thought. "So, even when he does come back, it'll be in another spot."

"You grasp my vision precisely, men. Now, about the officers to work with him . . ."

"Every time they have one of these big investigations, they always want the best guys, stripping them from the units that are already working on these types of cases."

"So, give them two of the inspector's best, Ed. It's the least we could do for this mighty effort to quash these 'gambling rings' as the papers call them."

"So, we pick the third guy . . . Who'd you have in mind, Jazz?"

Ed and the mayor looked at each other and said, in unison, "Stormy Snyder," which made Ocky grin broadly.

"Yes, I think Detective Snyder would be ideal for this job, Ocky. An experienced investigator with a distinguished and heroic record, currently languishing in . . . Where is he now, Ed?"

"Fourteenth Precinct. His boss, Nick Tibolo, has him processing prisoners in the station lockup and checking reports, keeping him out of trouble."

"Well, I'm certain that Stormy will appreciate his return from exile in the provinces, and perhaps, just perhaps, even keep us well informed of the activities of our auxiliaries in the service of Erie County. If Inspector Wachter complains, explain to him, Ed, that this is not Hollywood, and we have a police department to run."

Ed looked up, squared his shoulders, and nodded.

Putting his hands on the shoulders of his companions, the mayor continued, "They can't keep this grand jury in session forever, boys, and with a new one, they'll have to start over, have new jurors to break in, and new priorities. If things keep quiet now, we'll weather this storm, all right, and afterward, there will be more bowlers than ever, grateful to Jazz and his friends."

# CHAPTER 57

## RIVERSIDE, 1951

Dowd tossed his cigarette out the car window when he spotted the pickup truck pull up in front of the bar.

"That's him, Benny Gilbert," he said, watching the balding, little man hop out of the truck and head into the front door of the saloon with a large ring of keys, a cash drawer, and a canvas sack.

"Good," Dudek said, "We've got the vendor, and the owner's in the bar. Give them about three minutes and get them in the middle of cashing out."

Two days before, the D & D boys had sized up Dickie's Riverside Café, a workingman's bar that sold fast lunches and daily specials for dinners, cashed paychecks, and had four pinball machines that were in constant use by the three shifts of autoworkers that rotated through the place. After making sure he wouldn't be recognized by the staff, and not seeing anyone he knew go into the place in the afternoon, Dowd had donned coveralls, gone into the bar, and smiled when he spotted the Citation game, one of his favorites. With a handful of nickels, he waited with a bottle of beer until his game came free. He shoved eight nickels into it, advanced the odds to the one-sixty bonus, and launched the first silver ball. After ten minutes of tapping, cajoling, and gently nudging, the flashing clover leaves lit up around the horseshoe, the bells went off, and the counters clicked on and on for a high score. A couple of admirers walked over to see the score, and Dowd nodded to the owner who was behind the bar.

The barman walked over, smiled, and said, "Got a winner, eh?" He looked up at the flashing backboard, checked the score, paid Dowd his eight dollars—all in nickels—and reset the machine.

Dowd played a while longer, dropping fifty cents of his winnings, and then left, carefully checking the time for his report.

Benny Gilbert jangled as he walked. Between the keys, the rolls of change in the sack, and the metal cash drawer banging around while he walked through the barroom, his nervous disposition preceded him. "

Take it easy, Benny, I'll be right there," Dickie said. The beefy owner wiped his face with a napkin as he got up from his lunch. The two of them approached the row of pinball machines, waiting for a game to end before they began the weekly process of cashing out. The owner burped behind his hand, said "Excuse me," and the vendor tapped his foot and shook his keys. One of the players said "Shit!" when his ball went down the gobble hole and the vendor said, "Excuse me, please," inserted a key into the cash drawer, pulled it out with both hands, and slid an empty cash drawer back in its place.

Stepping out of any potential player's way, Dickie said, "Back in business on this one, boys," as Benny dumped the nickel-laden contents of the drawer he'd removed into the sturdy canvas sack. They repeated this process for the other three games, as well, limiting the down time on each game to a matter of seconds. The two then went to the kitchen, put the sack, a pile of nickel wrappers, and a receipt book on a small table in a corner and pulled up stools to split the money. The vendor was busily rolling nickels to the owner's comment, "We may have to cash out more often if this keeps up," when out in the barroom the bartender shouted "What the hell is this?" as Dudek and Dowd stormed into the place.

After Dudek had bounced the bartender's face off the bar to convince him he really did want to know where Benny and Dickie were, Dowd walked into the kitchen with a grin, looked at Dickie and said, "Hi, remember me? You're both under arrest."

Dickie sat back against the wall and said, "Well, I'll be damned."

Benny bounced up off the stool and Dudek's big hand slammed him back down, then twisted his hand behind his back to handcuff him.

"Look," Benny said, "I'm just cashing these machines out for a guy. I don't own them."

"Yeah, yeah," Dudek said as he pulled him up off the stool.

"No, I don't. Really. Check the licenses, officers. They've got Johnny Walters' name on them."

"Uh, huh."

After they got outside, past the bartender with a rag full of ice on his face, Dudek stopped. Cars slowed, the people in them staring at the two men in handcuffs.

"Shit," Dickie said. He turned his head and shouted into the open barroom door, "Tommy, call Phyllis and have her get the bail."

Benny dropped his head and tears began to well up in his eyes. "This can't happen to me. I've got kids . . ."

Dudek caught Dowd out of the corner of his eye and said, "Mr. D, why don't you call downtown for a wagon to haul the machines in, get a squad car, and take your prisoner down to booking that way. I'll take Mr. Gilbert here in our car so we can have a nice long chat on the way downtown in private."

Benny sat handcuffed in the detectives' car for a good half an hour, trying to hide as people walked by, watching the police load up the pinball machines into a truck while the D and D boys supervised. Then, Dowd put Dickie into the back of a patrol car and rode down to headquarters.

"There you are," Dudek said as got into the car, "All trussed up like a Christmas turkey for jail."

"No, no, you can't do this. My wife and kids . . ."

"Shoulda thought about that before you rigged the games to payoff there, foolish."

"I gotta pee, real bad."

"You better hold it, asshole, or I'll wipe the back seat up with your face if you make a mess back there."

"Ohh, this is terrible," the vendor said, shaking his head.

After a few minutes of silence, Dudek said, "You know, Benny, there may be a way out of this for you. Just maybe."

"Yes?"

"Yeah, just maybe."

"How?" he begged as they drove slowly towards downtown.

"Now, me, I think we should just toss you thieving bums in the klink and forget about you, see if a stretch in the pokey teaches you the error of your ways."

"Please, if there's a way out of this . . ."

"Well . . . It depends on you, see?"

"What do I have to do, officer?"

"Well, I might be able to talk to one of the lawyers in the DA's office, see?"

"Yes?"

"If you cooperate."

"How? I don't own those machines, I'm just . . ."

"Nah, I think I'm right. I'll just pull up at headquarters and get you booked at the desk . . ."

"No, look, wait. We pay a fee, some money that goes to the Vendor's Association for every machine. Johnny takes the money for a slush fund . . ."

"Lemme see, looks crowded over at the station, maybe they got more room parking by the County Hall . . ."

After Dudek rushed him to a bathroom on the first floor of County Hall, Assistant DA Roth couldn't get the paperwork for immunity in front of Gilbert fast enough.

# CHAPTER 58

## NEW YORK STATE SUPREME COURT, ERIE
## COUNTY HALL, DOWNTOWN, 1951

Jimmy Nolan stood at the defendant's table in his rumpled, blue suit, opened his worn, brown briefcase, and began pulling out papers that he put into three separate piles in front of him, quietly humming. His client, Charley Brogan, sat rigidly in his chair next to him, just like Jimmy had ordered him, not looking around at anybody as the courtroom filled. The judge, Justice Harold Worth, narrowed his eyes and thought, *The milkman's son, eh, and a night school graduate for a lawyer.* Jimmy pushed his hair back off his forehead.

What the judge didn't know, and wouldn't have cared if he did, was that Jimmy was the pride of Republic Street in South Buffalo's First Ward. The son of a South Buffalo Railroad brakeman, he had graduated from South Park High School and, as the judge suspected, gone to night school. Taking accounting at Canisius College, he was grateful for the leather cushions on the streetcar seats as he coughed grain dust, riding uptown after the long days of shoveling grain on the Lake Erie waterfront. Halfway through the University of Buffalo's law school in North Buffalo when the Army called, he was grateful that they looked the other way when he cheated on the eye exam, afraid he'd be the only one on his block rejected for service.

He feared he'd miss all the combat when, shortly after arriving in the Philippines, he came down with dengue fever. Three days of chills and sweating buckets. A skull that he wished would explode and get it over. Bones that felt like they were in a vice. Finally, the fever broke and he was sent back to his unit, just then, entering

Manila.

After two days of house-to-house fighting, the company's other officers were dead or wounded, and there were seventeen guys looking at Lieutenant Nolan to get them the hell out of there. At the top of the street there was a three-story stucco building, and the Japs had their Nambu machine guns blazing away at all the lower ground around them. Under orders to take the place at all costs, Jimmy had the men redistribute all the ammunition they had left to them, which turned out to be four rounds each. Remembering the story of San Juan Hill, he told his guys to fix bayonets. *Rough Riders, shit*, he thought. *Just let us kill these guys, Lord, and we'll be safe for awhile. Let us take this house, and we'll be closer to home.* Then, they drank the last of their water and waited for dusk.

When the light was just about gone, Jim thought to himself, *Please, God, don't let me screw up.* They rushed the building in silence. Once inside, they started screaming at the top of their lungs as they ran through the building, shooting, at first, then, bayoneting the Japanese, sometimes discovering them in the glow of their cigarettes in the darkening rooms. On the top floor, Jimmy and a tiny Texan named Youngblood kicked in a door, stood back for a second, then, scrambled in as a couple of hand grenades rolled out. Inside, the Texan let out a rebel whoop as the grenades went off behind the,m and rushed a Jap soldier with his bayonet. He ran the soldier through, and his momentum pushed the Japanese out a low sill window. Meanwhile, Jimmy proceeded to use his rifle butt to bash in the head of a squatting machine gunner, and then he kicked the body and the gun out the window. Turning around, he started sucking in air and saw the Texan standing at the window shaking his head.

"What?" Jimmy gasped.

"I'm sorry, Lieutenant," he drawled, crying. "I lost my rifle out the window. It fell out with the Jap."

Jimmy sat down on the floor and started laughing. "It's okay, kid, you can go out and get it out of his guts. He won't argue with you."

Jimmy felt the judge's eyes on him as he arranged his papers, and resisted the urge to say, "What are you looking at, numbnuts?"

Instead, he kept quietly humming and thinking, *This guy wouldn't have lasted five minutes in my outfit.*

"Well, counselor," the judge said to Jimmy Nolan, "Are we quite ready?"

Pushing his brow-line glasses back up on the bridge of his nose, Jimmy answered, "Yes, Your Honor."

"Then let us proceed . . . Mr. Roth," he smiled.

"Your Honor, after consulting with this defendant and his attorney, the state would like to accept a plea of guilty by Mr. Brogan to the charge of possession of gambling devices," Roth said, causing the judge to nod, "And drop the charges of conspiracy and perjury against him at this time," he said, driving the judge back against his high-backed chair.

Jimmy Nolan looked over at his colleague and waited until he had finished.

"The defense would also like to point out to His Honor, at this time, before he considers my client's sentence, that there has been a substantial deferment of punishment sought by the district attorney's office for numerous other cooperative defendants indicted and brought to trial for these same charges, who have pleaded guilty in the same manner, and uniformly sentenced to a five-hundred-dollar fine."

"The court will consider all the options open to it for sentencing the guilty party, Mr., Mr. . . . Nolan." As the judge slammed the gavel down to end the hearing, he spotted Joe Brogan, the milkman, sitting in the back row of his courtroom.

"Well," whispered Jimmy to Charley as he pushed him down the aisle towards the door, "The law professors said never go to trial if you don't have to." Outside in the hallway, Charley pumped Jimmy's hand enthusiastically. "Thank you, thank you, thank you."

"Yeah, well, anyway . . . ," Jimmy said. Then, they both turned to Joe Brogan, who came up and also shook the lawyer's hand. "A fine job, Seamus, a fine job." Then, turning to Charley, "Let's hope we've all been made wiser by the experience." Jimmy looked at Charley, who shrugged.

# CHAPTER 59

## NEW YORK STATE SUPREME COURT, ERIE COUNTY HALL DOWNTOWN, 1951

After the indictments were handed down, some of the vendors did what Johnny figured and ran for cover. Naming Johnny as the bag man, the district attorney slapped them with fines and dropped the conspiracy charges. Johnny kept to his story about collecting one dollar per machine per month dues to the association and kept silent about where it was going, so, they nailed him with perjury charges on top of conspiracy. When the jury came in for Johnny's trial, the clerk's office phoned Wachter. Stormy was out getting lunch, but Lou and Pat were at their desks, keeping one eye on the inspector's office. When Wachter hung up, they jumped up in unison. The inspector buttoned his suit coat as he came out of the office.

"They're coming in," he announced and headed for the stairs, as Lou and Pat snatched their coats and tried to keep up, swinging around the corner landings like kids at the playground. In the foyer, Wachter straightened his tie, Pat pushed his hair back into place, and Lou adjusted the wide brim on a new brown fedora with a yellow band he bought for the occasion.

"All right," the inspector said quietly as they approached the courtroom, "No matter what the verdict, keep a poker face on. If it's bad, we don't let them see any disappointment. If he gets convicted, it's just what we expected and he deserved."

The two detectives nodded and followed their boss into the foyer. Eyes were on them as they paved a path through the crowd of reporters, vendors, and lawyers. The bailiffs moved people out of the way, opened the heavy, wood doors into the courtroom, and the three policemen slid behind the last row of seats as the jury foreman handed the verdict to the bailiff. The judge read it, then, looking out over his glasses at the crowd, said without emotion, "Has the jury reached a verdict on the count of perjury?"

"We have, Your Honor," the foreman replied in a most serious way he had practiced the night before. The room was silent.

Then, the judge moved his eyes over at the foreman and said, " . . . and it is?"

The foreman said, "We, the jury, find John Walenty, also known as John Walters, guilty of perjury in the first degree."

A murmur came through the audience, the judge silenced them with his eyes, and said, "And, as to the verdict on the conspiracy charge, how do you find?"

"We find the defendant also guilty of conspiracy in the first degree, Your Honor."

" . . . and, as to the charge of possession of gambling devices?"

"We find the defendant guilty, Your Honor."

At the prosecutor's table, Ken Roth shook Lauria's shoulder. In the far corner, Gordon Stone stood, his arms crossed in front of his gray Hong Kong suit. *Everything was coming together. Time,* he thought, *to really clean house.* Checking his watch, he thought, *Just in time to make the city edition of the evening news.* He left through the door marked *Court Personnel Only.*

Johnny sat, unmoving, with a small smile on his face. *Never let 'em see you sweat,* he thought. *Don't do nothing until Lawyer Wells says so.* Feeling the counselor's hand on his shoulder, he thought, *What's he worried about? I ain't gonna panic.*

The judge then pronounced, "The defendant will remain free on bond until sentencing, and. . .," he said, looking over the schedule the clerk had handed up to him, "Sentencing will be scheduled for January Fifth, in this courtroom, at ten o'clock in the morning," adding, "Yes, Mr. Wells, the defendant will have Christmas and New Year's with his family," as he stood up.

"Your Honor," Wells said, rising rapidly from his seat, "The defendant has numerous business affairs to get in order, in addition to a family to look after . . ."

"January fifth, ten o'clock, Counselor," the judge said as he left the bench.

"Nice try, Marty," Johnny whispered as he stood up. "How about buying me lunch and giving me a ride to the bank so's I can get you your money?"

The three policemen remained standing against the back wall, stone-faced, holding their hands clasped in front of themselves, as the crowd filed out of the courtroom. When almost everyone had left, they walked out.

A reporter from the evening news, dressed in a suit that badly needed pressing, and an old gray fedora came up to them and said, "Do you think the city council will ban pinball games now, Inspector?"

Looking straight ahead, Wachter replied, "I have recommended that to the city council previously, asking that they repeal the existing ordinance licensing pinball machines. I have never received an answer to that request. This conviction is justice done, and hopefully will be followed through at sentencing. As there is a great deal more to be done about gambling in this city, my men and I will have no further comment."

"Inspector, do you expect any indictments of police officials or politicians to follow?" shouted a *Courier Express* writer.

"No comment," he said, walking down Franklin Street, away from their office, to the surprise of the two detectives who followed.

The *Courier* reporter smiled. "Relax, guys. He said a lot without words. We're gonna be on this story for quite a while, yet."

As they distanced themselves from the reporters, the two detectives broke into smiles and Lou said quietly, "We got 'em boss. Whaddya think the judge'll give 'em?"

Suddenly stopping by a phone booth, Wachter turned to his men and said, "You boys got anything pressing at the office that can't wait?"

Now, they were all smiling.

"Nope," Pat answered.

"Not a thing," said Lou, and with that, the hardest man in the department went into the phone booth, called the office, and told them that he and his men were taking the rest of the day off.

Coming out of the phone booth, Wachter pointed down Court Street towards Main and said, "Follow me," causing the two detectives to exchange glances. He led them across Main, to Washington, into the Hotel Buffalo's *Old English Grill*, and called for a table for three. Once seated, they all glanced around the place. Their eyes settled on four guys at the bar, each with a small stack of singles in front of them. Two of them, facing each other, were shaking their fists down low and suddenly threw out fingers of their right hands.

"Seven!" the one on the right said.

"Six!" the man facing him said at the same time.

The three policemen laughed. "We can't get away from it, boss," Lou said.

The waiter came up and handed them menus while the busboy set them up with tumblers of ice water. "Can I get you a cocktail, gentlemen?" he asked.

"Yes, I think so," the inspector began, "I'll have a Manhattan, standing up, with bitters, please."

Lou nodded at Pat, then, turning to the waiter said, "VO and water for me."

Pat ordered a bottle of Iroquois.

When their drinks arrived, the inspector looked around to see who might be listening and said, "You men have worked hard on this case, and the results just showed in that courtroom. Excellent, just excellent police work." He paused as the waiter came over to take their order.

"Let's see," Wachter said, looking at the specials listed on the blackboard behind the bar. "I'll take the roast spring chicken."

"And your two vegetables?"

"Mashed potatoes and green beans." "Sir?" the waiter asked, looking at Lou.

He put his thumb and index finger together in front of his face and said, "Sirloin steak. Medium rare. French fries and applesauce. My absolute favorite dinner."

"And you, sir?" the waiter asked Pat.

"Calf's liver and bacon. French fries and peas."

Lou winced.

Pat said, "Hey, I like liver."

The inspector cleared his throat, and picked up his cocktail glass. "To justice and good police work."

They all raised their glasses and repeated the toast.

Setting the cocktail glass carefully before him, the inspector said, "The good work goes on, men. I know the hours have been rough on you. Rough on me, too. Mrs. Wachter doesn't like it when I'm not around in the evenings or away much. We like to spend time at our place over in Canada when the weather's nice, and we haven't been able to do that while these cases have gone on."

They all drank again, and their leader continued.

"We're not done by a long shot, either. The city council, in their infinite wisdom, refuses to ban these pinballs, unlike they did in New York City, so we've got a lot more work to do, and the next step isn't going to be very pleasant." He paused for another sip and said, "We shook the tree this time, and a lot of rotten apples fell off the branches, but some of the branches still bear bad fruit, and might poison the whole tree. We're going to be working out of the DA's office for a time—got to cut the bad branches off and get rid of the whole rotten business, boys. That means going after some of our own who got paid to look the other way, and the politicians that profited from these arrangements. Then, maybe, they'll ban these damnable machines entirely."

Both of the younger policemen squirmed in their chairs a little. Wachter reached out with both hands and laid them on Lou and Pat's wrists.

"Are you men going to go with me on this task?"

They both nodded and said, "Yes, sir."

When the food arrived, the mood lightened up and they discussed the fines the vendors would get and how much time Johnny would serve.

"Well, the felony he was convicted of gets him a year, at least," the inspector said.

"Not on the farm in Wende, either," Lou gloated.

"No, he'll be bunking with the real bad guys in Attica for his time," Pat said with satisfaction.

"I gotta admit," Lou said, "He's a tough little weasel. He never gave anyone else up, never broke down through this whole thing."

"We'll be dealing with Mr. Walters again, lads. He isn't the kind to go back to the straight and narrow after this, if he ever was on it to begin with."

Pat and Lou kept ordering drinks through the meal, while the inspector switched to ginger ale. After the busboy cleared their dishes, they all ordered coffee, and when Wachter had a brandy with his, the two detectives, again, were surprised.

Swirling the liquor in the snifter, he stated, "Lou, I see the announcement for the captain's test just came out. You should already have the books and be hitting them by now."

"Uh, well, I've got most of them. Just started reading the first one, boss."

"Good, good. There should be some openings for the candidates on this list. I think you'll make a fine precinct commander, Louis."

Pat was looking down into his coffee cup when the inspector looked his way.

"Patrick Brogan, you've got a fine mind and you're a hard worker, but you've got no ambition."

Pat smiled and Lou smiled with him, two schoolboys before the teacher.

"You'll be a good, full-fledged detective sergeant, hunting down the bad guys, but you wouldn't like the responsibility of supervising people, I think. At least not for now."

They all fell silent for a moment, then Wachter called for the check. Both detectives reached for their wallets, but he waved them off. "I'll buy the victory dinner, lads."

They parted outside, with the inspector swiftly walking to his car. Lou and Pat walked slowly back to where Lou was parked, debating whether to carry on the celebration after Wachter's mention of "back to work tomorrow," as he set off for home.

# CHAPTER 60

## MAIN STREET, MASTEN PARK, 1951

Johnny didn't waste any time. He paid off the lawyer, went to the office, made some phone calls, and then went to the Checkerboard Lounge where he'd asked several of the other vendors to meet him. Sitting down in a booth against the wall, he thought about getting good and stiff, but figured he had business to do and ordered a beer instead.

Everybody in the joint had heard, came by, shook his hand and said, "Tough luck," "Hang in there," and "We're behind you all the way, buddy." They all bought him a drink and left.

Finally, some of the guys he'd called started showing up. Benny Gilbert was the first. He came in, looked around, and then quickly sat down in the booth, when Johnny waved him over.

Tossing him a chit for one of the drinks he was backed up, Johnny said, "Have a drink on me."

"Look, John, this is terrible, what happened to you. I didn't think . . ."

"Never mind, Benny. I'm going to take the heat and do my time. Don't worry. When I changed the names on all your pinball licenses to me, it was done. Nothing's going to come back on you. But," he paused to make sure Benny was paying attention, "Don't forget your part of the deal. When I get out, the locations we talked about are mine—cigarette machines, jukeboxes, pool tables, candy machines, the works. Got it?"

Benny nodded.

"Have a drink, Benny."

"Nah, not tonight, Johnny. I gotta go . . .," he said, and he slid out of the booth.

*Pissant,* Johnny thought. *Well, think of it as an investment, Johnny. An expensive one.* The last time he'd gotten locked up, it was for holding stolen goods. A couple of months on the farm in Alden. He chuckled as he finished his beer. *Another investment,* he thought. *That one kept me out of the Army.*

The front door swung open and another vendor showed up. "Hey, Burley, you four flusher, come over and have a drink!" Johnny said.

Driving down Main Street, Lou said, "Whaddya say we rub it in a little, Pat?"

"Rub it in? How?"

"Well, you know how the big shot vendors are always hanging in the Checkerboard. Hell, they say the distributors own the joint. Whaddya think, we go in there and show the colors tonight and have a drink?"

"Hah! I like it! Let's do it, el-tee."

Lou geared down as they approached the flashing neon sign featuring a chessman knight. He pulled around the corner on Glenwood and parked halfway down the block. They trotted to the club, and when Lou pulled the door open, he bowed to Pat, who returned the gesture and entered. Inside, they stood next to each other, making sure everyone saw them.

The band was playing, and Lou nudged Pat and said, "Look, there's Fred and Basil at the bar. Big time distributors. Hey, and there's the man of the hour himself . . . ," but Pat was already charging over to the table, where his brother Charley and a couple of women were toasting Johnny, and they were all smiling.

"You son of a bitch! Whaddya doin' drinkin' with this bastard?"

"Pat! What the hell? Johnny and I did a little business . . ."

"Get the hell out of here, flatfoot," Johnny said. "You come for a pound of flesh or somethin'?"

Pat yanked Johnny up by his shirt and hauled back to punch him when Lou grabbed him from behind.

"Whoa, partner, you're takin' fun a little too far," Lou said, pulling him away.

"Charley, when I get through with this asshole, I'm gonna kick your ass, too," Pat said.

The girls bailed out, and Charley and Johnny got out into the aisle, where Johnny punched Pat on the chin.

"Hey!" Lou yelled. "Okay, you asked for it," he said, turning Pat loose.

Pat threw a right that Johnny ducked, but caught him with a left uppercut that sent his eyes rolling back in his head. Another right sent him backwards into the booth and out. Pat turned, and he and Charley charged each other while the band's horn section picked up the volume. As they grappled on the floor, the manager and the bouncer rushed over to break it up. Seeing it was turning into a melee, the bartender reached under the bar for a baseball bat.

"Un-uh-uh," Lou told him, wagging his finger.

"Charley, I'm gonna kick your ass, and then dad's gonna kick your ass, you idiot!" Pat raged as they rolled around on the floor, banging into tables and spilling plates and drinks everywhere.

"Oh, now I get it!" Lou exclaimed with a laugh, "It's family!"

The bartender and the manager dove in on the tiring brothers, and Lou helped them get Pat and Charley separated, then pushed them all outside, where he started explaining to the manager.

"Police business can get a little personal sometimes . . ."

# CHAPTER 61

## UNIVERSITY HEIGHTS, 1951

After Lou talked their way out of the Checkerboard, Lou and Pat rode over "to another little joint I know," where, as Lou put it, "there might be some girls."

When Pat looked at him cross-eyed at the prospect of meeting women on a Tuesday night, Lou slapped him on the shoulder and replied, "Comin' home from bowling night, partner," and pointing to his head and winking, "Always thinkin' pal, always plannin' the possibilities."

Further up North on Main Street, Lou said, "It's just up here, past St. Joe's. Ahh, there it is," and pulled a U-turn without looking, parking the car right by a place with a sign picturing a frothy glass and the words "Bickerton's Lounge."

As they got out on the sidewalk, three teenagers came running out of the bar to shouts of ". . . and don't come back, you punks!" Looking back, one said to the others, "I oughta kick that old man's ass," while another said, "Forget it, Terry, Murph'll try his brother's ID down the street at the liquor store."

The three straightened up when they saw the two adults coming towards them and silently walked past.

Going into the bar, Lou said, "Remember that, Paddy Boy? Trying to sneak into saloons underage?"

"Sure do. I always got caught in North Park; somebody always knew my dad. Had to travel pretty far out of the neighborhood to get away with it." Shaking his head, he remembered going into a place that advertised "Dancing Nightly."

"McVan's," Pat said, "And we always got into fights there."

"Oh, jeez, that joint," Lou replied, and they both laughed.

Inside, there were two guys at the bar with draft beers going flat. The bartender, a fat guy with glasses and a white shirt, was complaining about underage kids always trying to sneak in.

"I could lose my license," he shouted, waving his arms up in the air.

Seeing no prospects there, Lou said, "Ah, well, it's been a long day, whaddya say we have a nightcap in this joint and call it a day?" After the wild U-turn and a look in his partner's red eyes, Pat nodded in agreement and wondered how cockeyed he, himself, looked.

"Whaddle ya have, partner?"

"Uh, how about a brandy," Pat said, squinting a look at the bar for a brand name he knew.

"Hey, good idea. Bartender, one brandy, and I'll have a stinger on the rocks."

Unaccustomed to the uptown order, the bartender started looking around for brandy snifters and the two beer-drinkers turned to see who had ordered. Pat and Lou sat down at a table. When the barman brought the drinks over, Lou paid him with a dollar and said with a flourish, "Keep the change, my man," to which the barman nodded and smiled.

Raising his glass, Lou said proudly, "Success."

"Success," Pat answered, raising his glass, as well.

Lou sipped his brandy, tempered with crème de menthe, and added, "Ahhh."

Pat, jolted by the straight brandy's punch, sat up suddenly.

"Yeah, partner, a big day for the good guys," Lou said and he leaned back in his chair, tipping his hat comfortably back on his head.

"What a job," Pat reflected. "All those hours to put away one no-good."

"Yeah, buddy, it's somethin', all right."

"How'd you get into this racket, anyway, Lou?"

Rubbing his chin, Lou leaned forward and said, "Well, before I went into the service, I was always havin' to look out for my little brothers and sisters. You know, keepin' kids from knockin' 'em around, keepin' the guys from gettin' fresh with the girls. In high school, the neighbors started expectin' me to look out for their kids, too. Somebody'd get into a fight, and they'd say 'Go get Lou, he'll get 'em out of it. He'll straighten 'em out.' My cousins, the same thing. Then, when I came outta the Navy, it starts over again, the same thing, only with a new, younger bunch of kids expectin' me to help 'em out of whatever jams they got into.

"Anyway, a couple of guys from the neighborhood tell me the PD's givin' the test, and did I want to sign up with 'em for it." Stretching his arms out wide, he continued, "I thought about it for a minute an' figured, 'Perfect. I gotta look out for all these kids anyways, I might as well get paid for it. Besides, I didn't much like bein' a cutter in the meat locker, bein' cold all the time, even in summer, bein' covered with blood and comin' home stinkin', no matter how much you wash. Nah, this is the life for me. I got a secure job, workin' with good people, made lieutenant, maybe even make captain someday. Yeah, this is for me, pal. How about you? Why'd a guy, family's got a little money and connections, went to Canisius, gotta a good war record and a little college, want to get on the force?"

Surprised, Pat realized Lou must have been through his file.

"Ah, shit," Pat said, waving his hand in front of his face as if to blow away the words Lou had spoken, "Not much to it, really. I got outta the Army and came home, and everything that was real important before the war seemed like so much horseshit—school, plans to go into business or law school, start a family, make money. None of it seemed to matter anymore. Anyway, I did start college, like you said, but I'm there with a bunch of kids. Bright, happy kids, having fun. They think stuff like *Dante's Inferno* is scary, and price rising with demand's important. They've never seen a whole city bombed into a pile of shattered bricks or people that look like skeletons so weak they can't even beg anymore, or guys bleedin' so fast there's nothin' you can do, or. . . Well, anyway, it just seemed like so much crap that, when I read about the test, I took it, passed it and went on the force. At least I felt alive again, somethin' I knew—wearin' a uniform, bein' part of a unit, bein' responsible for stuff. I told my old man that I could keep up my studies, but I didn't; I just didn't care anymore. I was walkin' a beat downtown, haulin' drunks out of bars, chasin' pickpockets and scam artists, chasin' the whores away sometimes. Kinda sad, when you think about it. Then an opening came up for this job in plainclothes, and that's," he added with a smile, "How I got hooked up with you guys."

Lou, surprised at the way Pat disregarded opportunity, smiled back and tossed down the rest of his drink. Affecting a Southern accent, he stood up saying, "Well, like Miss Scarlet said, 'Tomorrow is another day.'"

Pat, wishing to stay on until closing, reluctantly threw his brandy back as well. Almost gagging on the potent liquor, he slammed his chest with his fist and shook his head. "Yeah, that's good," he gasped and followed Lou to the car. He thought about making another stop after Lou dropped him off. When he saw his dad's bedroom light on, he reconsidered. *Too many explanations to make, too bad a hangover at work tomorrow, and I think I blew all my money anyway,* he thought, quietly opening the front door and heading up to his room.

# CHAPTER 62

## ELLICOTT STREET, 1951

Pat dropped into his chair after a third trip to the water fountain, hoping the inspector would stay in his meeting with the DA all day. Lou was out of the office most of the morning, getting a list of machines from the license office, and then matching it to the machines they had locked up in the city garage on East Ferry Street.

After comparing the two, he said to Pat, "Do you realize we've seized only about one-half of one percent of the pinballs licensed in this city, and they're probably gambling on nearly all of them? That's nothing, not to mention the ones that haven't got licenses, the ones in back rooms . . ." He looked up and saw Pat, with a vacant red-eyed stare, wasn't, at all, well that morning. Lou flipped the yellow pencil he had been using over his shoulder, and said, "Kraut food."

"Huh?"

"Kraut food. It's the answer to your hangover. Get your coat, my man, and let us head over to Virginia Street for lunch."

Wondering how Lou could feel so good this morning, Pat went along as Lou whistled, "I'm Looking Over a Four Leaf Clover."

When they walked into the front door of Erlich's Tavern, Lou immediately shook hands with a black-haired guy well over six-feet-tall behind the bar.

"Pat, this is the owner, Jimmy Delaney. Jimmy, meet Pat Brogan."

"Pleased to meet you, Jimmy."

"Say, aren't you the Pat Brogan who used to play basketball for Canisius?"

"I played at the high school in '41 and '42."

"Oh, yeah, you beat us for the Father Fornes Trophy in '41. I played center for Ryan."

"Oh, yeah, now I remember. I think I still got bruises from that game."

"Yeah, things got a little rough on our little court there, sometimes," he chuckled.

"What's good today, Jimmy?" Lou asked.

"Hasenpfeffer's good, sausage platter's got bratwurst, knockwurst, leberwurst, and we got pork loin today, too."

"Great. C'mon Pat, a dose of some of the pork loin, some red cabbage, and German potato salad will fix you right up."

After a glass of water and a small beer, Pat and Lou ate their lunch in the dining room, and Pat had to admit, he felt better.

Drinking coffee, Pat asked Lou, "How'd a Mick like Jimmy Delaney come to run a German place like this, I wonder?"

"Jimmy came back from the war speaking German and got a job here tending bar. Old man Erlich's daughter was working here, too; one thing led to another, and he winds up marrying the girl. Knows what he's doing, too. Hasn't changed a thing," Lou said.

Pat looked around the old fashioned dining room with tin walls and ceilings embossed with fleur-de-lis, and a piano in the corner, as they left. In the barroom where Jimmy was holding court, wooden beer coolers with glass windows and brass fittings behind him, Jimmy shook their hands again and told Pat it was a pleasure to meet him.

"Oh, hey, wait a minute, fellas," Jimmy said. "I got a cousin of the wife's here. Works in the kitchen now; he's a DP from over in Germany. Been here about six months. Loves basketball. Lemme introduce you. Hey, Greta, get Willy out here a second, will ya?"

Jimmy talked to Lou about how business was while Pat looked around the bar at the many years' accumulation of trophies and knickknacks, trying to make out the signatures on a couple of three-fingered baseball gloves, and leather football helmets.

"Ah, here he is. Willy, I want you to meet a real basketball player. Pat Brogan."

Pat turned, and when he saw the smiling kid's floppy blonde hair, he knew he was going to throw up. He grabbed the bar and lurched out the door as Jimmy looked at Lou and the kid blinked in incomprehension.

Lou said, "Bad hangover, that's all," and rushed out the door after his partner who was retching cabbage into the gutter on Ellicott Street.

"What the. . .," Lou asked as Pat heaved again.

Pat shook his head and leaned against a tree, clutching the Elm's rough bark.

"I just got a worse hangover than I thought . . ."

# CHAPTER 63

## ATTICA CORRECTIONAL FACILITY, 1952

Johnny Walters was processed under his real name, Walenty, and when he had his clothes taken away from him, it was only a pair of old, green work pants, and a flannel shirt.

"No point in wearing a good suit," the lawyer had said, "You're not going to see it for a while."

After that, he was led into a big shower room and hosed down by a guard, and then taken naked into a doctor's office and examined for disease by a doctor who smelled like whiskey, and had thick glasses that kept sliding down his nose. Johnny's issued prison clothes were gray, rough, and too big. He had to hold the pants up with his hand, and was told to find a sewing kit and fix them himself. First, naked in front of strangers, now, dressed like a clown in the prison uniform that didn't fit. His shoulder muscles tensed up as he was led by a guard through the gates, his number called out and checked off at each point, the barred gates slamming behind him, going ever inward into the prison, a fool in the oversized clothes, in a place where he had no friends, and it didn't look like he would find any. When they got into the halls with cells, it was like being in a fishbowl. The prisoners (*I'm one of them now*, he thought) would look out the bars at him, sizing him up, one rocking back and forth on the bars and muttering, "New man, new man, new man. . . ," another giving a low laugh and stroking himself, and another leaping across the cell and reaching through the bars to try to grab him, growling. Johnny jumped out of the way, tripped over the oversized pant legs and fell against the bars of the next cell. One of the inmates there sloshed piss from a tin cup on him. The guard whacked his billy club against the bars; the inmate jumped back; and the guard said to Johnny, "Get up, convict. They're just playing with you, for now."

When he got up, all the prisoners on this tier started to howl and laugh at him, which echoed through the three-story wing. He staggered to his feet and walked down the hallway, reeking of urine, carrying his blankets, and holding his pants up. At his assigned cell, there were three men staring at him from a very small room with four bunks, and he had to stop himself from saying "This is wrong, I don't belong here . . . "

*Time to suck it up*, he thought, holding his breath and throwing his gear on the empty upper bunk. The cell door slammed behind him, and Johnny Walenty felt like he was drowning.

He must have been staring at the ceiling, the solid cement ceiling. *Even an ocean*, he thought, *wasn't solid, no matter how deep you were in the water.* He was looking for a way to swim out of the deep, imagining that the ceiling was water and he was in a swimming pool, a pond, a lake, anything not solid, when the guy sitting on the lower bunk across from his said, "Hey piss boy, there's no escape hatch up there. You got any cigarettes?"

The others laughed, and Johnny came out of his daze and looked around at the three men in the tiny cage, where they all lived. The man who had addressed him was small with black hair like a helmet, bushy eyebrows over a big nose, and dark skin that was creased with many deep lines. He sat on a bed that was made as tight as a barracks bunk with his legs crossed, turning a gold lighter over and over on his knee.

"You deaf, too, pissbum?"

Johnny took a step back, trying to get some space between himself and the others, and backed up against the unmoving bars. He reached at the pocket where he normally kept his cigarettes, and then realized they'd been taken from him when he was processed into the jail, put in a box with his clothes and other stuff, and the men chuckled.

"No, they took them from me comin' in," he said, trying to sound tough, standing stiffly against the bars.

"Danny, let me have one of yours. Something's gotta kill the smell of this guy," one man said, at which the other two chuckled again, and the man on the upper bunk shook one out to him. He was a big man, filling the length of his bunk where he lay on his side, a brown flat top over slit-like blue eyes and a flat nose, a comic book before him.

He was grinning, but it wasn't at Superman on the pages.

The man with the gold cigarette lighter lit up and blew a cloud of blue smoke up into the cell. Johnny looked at his gear on the bunk, which included a clean uniform, and noticed the guy on the bunk below his. About the same size as Johnny, this one was bald and lay flat on his back with his hands clasped behind his head. The only thing that moved were his eyes, following everything Johnny did. Johnny reached for his spare uniform pants and hesitated. Changing here wasn't like a locker room, it was like the middle of a bus station. These guys might be queer. Three strangers could see everything he did in this cell, all the time, including using the toilet that was against the back wall in a corner. He thought, *How the hell do you get any privacy in this place*, and realized, *You don't.* This isn't like the prison farm out in Alden, at all. As he pulled the trousers off his bunk, he thought, *Suck it up*, and while he changed, the little man lying below his bunk said, "This is gonna stink until laundry day, Pissbum, and that ain't for another three days. You oughta keep us in smokes until then. Whaddya think, Carmine?"

"Sounds fair to me, Barry. Danny?"

The big man nodded and kept grinning at Johnny. Carmine had resumed turning the gold lighter on his knee, and Johnny noticed Carmine's uniform shirt and pants were pressed, and the cheap prison shoes were polished to a fare-thee-well.

"Like I said, fellas, they took mine from me when I came in, and I don't owe you nothin'," Johnny replied, at which Barry kicked the bottom of the springs on Johnny's bunk, and his blankets and clothes went flying into the air. Before Johnny could say anything, Danny had snatched a blanket out of the air and covered Johnny with it. Barry spun on his bunk and kicked Johnny with both feet in the stomach. Danny then shoved him forward, smashing his chin into the metal bunk. Johnny tried to turn and swing an elbow, but the big guy then landed a punch right on his ear, making him see stars and lose his balance. Barry's fists were working, too, catching him in the stomach and then on his head as he went to the floor. Johnny moaned and tried to get up. The big guy slammed another punch on Johnny's arched back, and his legs crumpled again. Moaning, Johnny got one hand under himself and pushed up, trying to throw the blanket off with the other. Barry kicked him again, this time in the side, driving him into Danny, who grabbed his wrist and yanked him up by the arm with one hand, nearly pulling it out of the socket, and hooked his other fist into the center of Johnny's chest. Johnny's vision was mostly white light and his head buzzed with a thousand bees, and when Danny dropped him and the blanket fell away from his face, he saw Carmine still sitting on his bunk, turning the lighter on his knee.

"Get up, Pissbum, and make your bunk. You can owe us the smokes. I figure three packs should cover it."

His head still buzzing, Johnny rolled over onto his hands and knees, pushed himself to his feet, and threw his bedding across his bunk. Then, he folded up the rest of his clothes and stowed all his possessions in the only empty cubicle-shelf in the corner opposite the toilet. He grabbed the upper end of the bedstead, holding on with both hands to keep himself upright in the back corner of the cell. The other three started talking like he wasn't even there. He stood there until lights out, taking shallow breaths to reduce the pain in his ribcage, and then crawled into his bunk, with his clothes and shoes on, listening throughout the night to snores, toilets flushing, and moans and cries throughout the darkened tier. Like a child, he thought about being in a dark jungle full of wild animals waiting to eat him.

# CHAPTER 64

## ATTICA CORRECTIONAL FACILITY, 1952

The rest of that first week, Johnny ran errands for his cell-mates, cleaned the cell while they read the paper, and paid them the three packs he owed, always being referred to as Pissbum. He sat with them at meals and they never talked to him unless they wanted something. The other cliques knew the system and left him alone. Johnny hardly said a word to anyone, except as spoken to, and in the laundry where he was assigned to work.

Going to the meal hall, the laundry, the yard, and back to the cell quickly became a routine, and time began to drag more and more, like the clocks were all moving at half speed. He would look up after loading the dryers a few times, but the clocks hands had hardly moved, and it seemed like he would be there forever. The cell was worse. He never knew what his cellmates would do, and although they never beat him up since the first day, they would wave a hand to threaten him, and he would jump back while they laughed. He was there three days before he ever slept, and a week before he took a dump. After the prisoners presented themselves at the front of the cell for the count and the lights went out at night, he would lie there and hear the noises: farting, snoring, grunting, and sometimes howling, when someone would crack up or get attacked.

Mealtime was the most normal time, as if anything was nor-mal in these cages within cages. The men would file out of their cells and march down to the dining hall. They would pick up a metal tray, usually still wet from the last washing, take a left, and go through the food line. The first ones in line got the food that was on the top of the massive pots, so their food might not be the tasteless, watery, shapeless vegetables that had been steamed into near mush. Coming from a family where competition for food was keen, Johnny adapted quickly, keeping his elbows out and his tray protected at all times, no matter what it was. While the food was shoveled in, messages were passed in low tones through mouths full of food. Carmine and his two compatriots often got messages from two tables over, acknowledging the muttered communiqués with nods to a jittery, sharp-faced man. The twitchy guy sat near an older Italian with a balding, round head who said and moved very little, but to whom a lot of the messages came and went. *There is a pecking order in this place,* Johnny thought, *and I'm at the bottom of it.* After ten days in prison, Johnny began to think how to work his way out of his silent, degrading situation.

During meals, Johnny noticed the guys who weren't part of any clique, or were on the fringes of one. Some were insane, constantly talking to themselves, others were outcasts from larger groups, weasels who failed to work within the convict society and became tools of the guards, and some were convicted of offenses against children. These were shaken down for cigarettes, candy and other items, and were sometimes slapped and punched if they held back. The weasels were in constant terror, bouncing back and forth between retributions by the convicts and threats and rewards of the guards, a perpetual state of hell from which there was no escape until release or death.

Johnny saw the prisoners who had harassed him when he came in the first day, the guy who threw the piss on him and the guy who was stroking himself, who was well known as a predatory queer who would ambush weaker prisoners when he got them alone, landing them at the bottom of the prison society. The latter was just about Johnny's height of five-six, wore his hair in a gray crew cut, had a barrel chest and short arms, and smoked constantly. *Well,* Johnny thought, *There are slobs even lower than me in this joint.*

One time, Barrel Chest slid into line behind Johnny coming back from dinner and pushed himself up against him. Johnny felt his hard on and threw his head back, the back of his skull cracking the guy's face. Then, he lifted his knee and slammed his foot into the guy's shin. The motion attracted a guard's attention, but by the time he got over there, everyone was marching upright, and Barrel Chest was cursing him under his breath.

A week later, Johnny looked at the clock and saw the day was finishing at last. He pushed the last cart into a corner and wondered if he could dally there until the end of the shift, where no one could see him. That was when Barrel Chest appeared, taking a quick glance to see if anyone was watching. He looked right at Johnny and smiled, tapping his breast pocket saying, "I've got smokes for us for after," chuckling as he approached.

*Shit,* Johnny thought, *It's too loud for anyone to hear; I got to stop him now,* and with that, he flipped a cart between them and they started jumping around the cart. Finally, Johnny feinted one way, fooled Barrel Chest, and ran back to the front of the shop, Barrel Chest shouting, "I'll keep these smokes for you. We'll have 'em later, heh, heh, heh."

Barrel Chest lived for his cigarettes. If he could get them, he smoked three packs a day, and this led him to finding hiding places to smoke where it wasn't allowed. One of his favorite places was behind a boiler in the laundry room, where he would go after taking a quick look to see if anyone was watching. Johnny noticed this, keeping an eye out for the homo every moment he was out of his cell.

Two weeks later in the laundry, a guard was sitting on a bench with a Thermos bottle, sipping coffee from home that smelled good. They had been loading and unloading the washers for about two hours, and everyone was hot and tired, especially Barrel Chest, whose lungs were heaving; his nicotine starvation was causing him to sweat bullets. At the other end of the laundry, a machine broke, and the oversized device shook noisily. A couple of men were trying to shut it down and the guard jumped up to see what the matter was. He hesitated for a moment, wanting to stash his precious Thermos, but the ruckus increased and more inmates were getting into it, so he pulled his billy club and walked over to the rattling oversized dryer. Johnny, the closest to the bench, slid over and snatched the Thermos before anyone else could, and then walked quickly behind the boiler. Barrel Chest took a quick look around and followed him.

Johnny crouched down as soon as he got behind the boiler, and when Barrel Chest came behind it, he didn't see Johnny. Johnny grabbed the bigger man at the belt and yanked his pants forward, pouring the hot coffee onto his groin. Then, Johnny stepped back and kicked Barrel Chest in the balls as hard as he could. As the man dropped to his knees in pain, Johnny snatched the predator's cigarettes out of his breast pocket, saying, "Thanks for these, sissy boy."

The dryer was finally shut off, its contents emptied, and a mechanically-inclined convict set to working on it. When the guard came back to get his Thermos bottle, he cursed, and promised himself never to bring something that valuable to work again. Then, he spotted Barrel Chest hanging onto the boiler, cursing and then kicking the Thermos across the floor.

The guard yelled, "What the hell do you think you're doing, you son-of-a-bitch?" He ran over and slammed his club over the man's neck, driving him to the ground. Grabbing the convict by the collar, he dragged him off to solitary confinement for stealing. Other guards came and lined up the other convicts to return them to their cells, not a few of them chuckling at Johnny's maneuver.

That night, while Johnny was lying on his bunk, smoking Barrel Chest's cigarettes, Carmine said, "Hey, Walters, I hear you had a nice little vending operation going in Buffalo . . ."

# CHAPTER 65

## ATTICA CORRECTIONAL FACILITY, 1952

His clothes clean and mended to his size, his cigarette debt paid, and Barrel Chest out of his hair, Johnny found out more about his cellmates. Carmine was a bookmaker out of Niagara Falls who had run horse rooms and set up card games, and crap games around town. Danny had been a lineman for Western Union who had done the wire rigging for Carmine and others on the side, and Barry was a burglar who had got caught when he tried to branch out into hijacking trucks. Danny and Barry had sentences of two years, but Carmine got five because he had run over a guy's legs with a Buick Roadmaster when the guy wouldn't pay up.

The four cellmates talked about what many career criminals do in the endless hours incarcerated—brainstorming how to set up their next score. They all saw a future in pinballs, especially since it was all cash. Johnny's insurance policy of trading the rap for future consideration and locations was a good idea, but the venture could always use some investment capital and other help to make sure the other vendors kept their word when he got out and wanted to set back up.

Carmine said he would have Johnny meet a guy he called Mr. T. He was the one who got all the messages through the guy with the twitch. Johnny found out his name was Tutulomundo, and he was from Niagara Falls. Watching him in the mess hall, the man looked familiar. The black eyes and the cannonball of a head. Where did he know him from?

One day, at lunch, Carmine made eye contact with the Twitch, who nodded, then turned to Mr. T., his shoulder jerking up and his head tilting down. Mr. T nodded, and Twitch turned to Carmine and nodded to him. "You're on for this afternoon in the yard, Johnny," Carmine whispered.

Tutulomundo sat on a bench in the yard with six guys around him, passing messages outside the circle through the Twitch. After about ten minutes, T got up and began to walk around the yard, his men in formation around him.

"When he comes by us," Carmine said, "Fall in with his boys. They'll take it from there."

As they passed by, Johnny stepped into the circle in front of Tutulomundo, and two guys closed ranks right next to him. After about a minute of silence, Tutulomundo began, "So, Johnny, you change your name, eh?"

"Uh, yeah, I got tired of it getting screwed up all the time."

"You've got a bunch of contracts for vending service, all over Buffalo. More than you used to have."

"Yes, sir. A lot of guys were bailing out when they got pinched for gambling."

"Couldn't take the pressure, eh?"

"Uh, huh. I gotta have some way to make a living when I get out."

"Who's running your business while you're in here, Johnny?"

He hesitated, but thought these guys would find out anyway, and answered, "My mechanic, Steve, is running things, and a couple of young guys are helping him."

"You think these can handle it okay?"

"For now, but when I get out, I might need help when I get bigger."

"That's good. Somebody reliable. You always got to have people you can trust."

*Hmmph,* Johnny thought, *This guy wants to get one of his guys inside fast.* "Yeah, but there aren't many people that know these machines well, and they're changing all the time. It takes money to get the machines, and sometimes the bar owners want loans

before they give you the contract."

"Uh, huh. Good. Exercise looks like it's over. Johnny, we'll talk more about this later, in the yard here."

"Okay, Mr. T."

A few days later, out in the yard, Johnny milled around with Carmine and Danny. Carmine, who was facing into the yard, nodded to Twitch, and he nodded back. "Meeting time, Johnny. The man wants to talk to you."

Johnny ambled over to the row of Tutulomundo's board members, nodding to each as he approached their boss and stopping two feet from where T stood, standing at a right angle to him. Several of his men wandered off, while T looked right in Johnny's eyes with eyes that burned like black coals as he crushed out a smoke. Johnny receded a second and realized this was the man behind the tree outside the morgue when he was a kid.

"Johnny, you okay?"

"Sure, damn cheap shoes just hurt my feet sometimes."

"So, you will stay in the vending business?"

"Oh, yeah. I've spent a lot of time learning the business, the machines, drumming up business, and I got deals set up with people when I get out. No, I'm in this business for good."

"That's good, Johnny. Good that you will stay in business. A man in my position is always looking for places to invest. With smart guys who know their business and work hard. We could perhaps invest in your business, Johnny, help you out in other ways, too. But we gotta have some help, some assurances, too, Johnny. Here, I need some exercise, come walk with me, Johnny," T said, and off they went around C Yard, T's men following discreetly behind, ever alert.

That night, he talked with his cellmates and new associates. Danny could help with the moving of the machines and help convince anyone who didn't want to give up his location, as promised, that a deal was a deal. Carmine had the connections in the gambling crowd and Italian parts of town to open up business there, and would be his connection to T. Barry said he was headed back to the city when he got out; there was too much snow upstate.

# CHAPTER 66

## SOUTH BUFFALO, 1952

Gliding along South Park, Lou geared down as the first fat drops of a heavy rain smacked the hood and windshield of the inspector's maroon Hudson. "Listen to that. The way that transmission just slides right in and doesn't miss a beat. What a car, huh?"

Pat looked ahead as they rolled over the bridge at Lee Street. Just on the other side, a salesman pulling out of the forest of pipes at the National Aniline dye plant was trying to reach behind his seat and rearrange his samples. A kid racing down South Park on his bike to get out of the rain didn't see him and veered away from the plant's exit at the last moment. The salesman yanked the steering wheel hard to the right and drove his Dodge hard into a telephone pole. The impact slammed his head into the metal steering wheel, and then bounced him back against the seat. The salesman shook his head and staggered out of the car in a daze. Moments later, Lou drove up and parked diagonally across the street to keep traffic away from the wreck. Pat called in the accident and location.

The detectives got out of the car, pulling their coats around them in the rain.

"I'll get the guy who's walking around," Lou said. "You check out the car."

Pat nodded, and as Lou guided the reeling driver to sit on their bumper, he looked inside the car, where samples were scattered over the seats. *Good, no one else in here.* He opened the door, took the car out of drive, pulled on the brake and turned off the ignition, then, stepped back to look for leaking gasoline. *None, good*, he thought.

Pat checked again, looking under the front of the car, and staggered backward at the sight of the oil pulsing out from underneath the engine. The oil was spreading fast across the wet pavement, *Just like Voessler's skinny neck bleeding out.* His brain screamed, *He's not going to make it and there's nothing you can do.*

Then, Lou came up, "This guy says he was the only one in the car, Pat. I'm gonna check the inspector's trunk for a first aid kit. . . Hey, you okay partner? You look like you seen a ghost." Lou looked inside the car, fearing there might be another victim, but finding none, turned back to Pat. "Hey, Brogan, snap out of it, boy. There's no one else inside. You know if the inspector's got a first aid kit?"

Pat shook his head and finally heard what Lou was saying. "Uh, dunno. . . Maybe in the trunk or somewhere?"

"Keep an eye on this guy," Lou said loudly, nodding at the dazed driver sitting on the bumper. "I'm gonna go check the car for a kit."

Pat nodded and walked over to the injured driver, who had blood from his forehead running down his face and dripping onto his lap. Pulling out his handkerchief, Pat wiped the blood from his chin upward, over his eye until he found the gash. Pressing the blood-soaked, white handkerchief to the leaking incision, he knelt down in front of the man and said, "Hey, buddy, look at me. You okay?"

The driver stared into Pat's eyes for a moment, and then looked around and tried to stand.

Putting his hand on the man's shoulder, Pat kept him sitting down. "It's okay, pal, you had an accident."

Lou came over with an olive drab box with a red cross painted on it. "Here we go. The inspector had some Army surplus stuff." He opened the box and pulled out a bottle of alcohol and some gauze bandages, and handed a roll of adhesive tape to Pat. While Lou was cleaning the wound, the driver jerked about from the stinging liquid, still trying to grasp what had happened.

"He's got a concussion, along with the gash, there," Pat said, taping the gauze that Lou held tightly over the wound.

After they finished, Lou went through the driver's papers and gathered the license and registration from the glove box. When a patrol car arrived, Lou talked to the patrolmen as they got out, handed over the papers, and explained what they had done.

Lou got behind the wheel of the Hudson and they drove off.

After a moment, he glanced over and asked quietly, "What happened there, my friend? I lost you, there, for a minute." He added with a slight chuckle, "You ain't getting scared of the sight of blood, are you?"

Pat waved his hand, "Ahh, I dunno. Nothing, I guess. Sometimes I just remember stuff," he replied, and left it at that.

Lou left it at that, as well, and they drove on to the precinct in silence. It wasn't the first time Pat had faded away on him, but it hadn't happened in a while, and Lou worried what would happen if they had real trouble.

# CHAPTER 67

## NORTH PARK, 1952

Len came around the bar and opened the front door, stepped out onto the sidewalk, and spat. Coming back in, he latched the wooden door open with a hook-and-eye and the spring on the screen door squeaked as it closed.

"Nice day out there," he observed, surprised at shirtsleeve weather in April.

Pat turned on his bar stool, looked out the front window, and watched three children tear down the street in pursuit of a taller kid laughing at them. *That used to be me*, Pat thought. *Nobody could catch me.* He turned back to the bar while Len wiped nicotine and splashed booze from the bottles. Glancing up at the mirror, Pat spotted black curls just coming over the tops of his ears. *Need a haircut*, he thought. He looked at Len, whose hair was starting to turn gray and thought, *Len got out of St. Margaret's, what, five years before I got out of St. Mark's?* Next to him, Mr. Crehan sat silently with the same beer he had ordered when the place had opened an hour before, a few bubbles rising to the dissipated head. Jerry N. was talking about how he had been in basic training with Bob Feller at Great Lakes, and all that time in the service would leave him flat.

"Other than the Van Meter Heater," he explained, "The Yankees got better starters than Cleveland. And—*and*," he repeated, to make sure his audience was paying attention, "I'll bet you that Lopat, Raschi, and Reynolds all win twenty games this year, and—*and*," he repeated again, principally for the benefit of the Irish patrons at the bar, "Maybe even Spec Shea can win twenty . . ."

This was the second time Pat had heard this year's version of

Jerry's "The Yankees Are the Best" speech, and he decided it was really time to get a haircut. Pat stood up.

Len looked up from the bottles and smiled as Pat downed the last of the beer. "Another Iri, pal?"

"Nah, gotta get a haircut, Len," he said, putting on a windbreaker. Pulling some change from the pocketful of coins remaining from last night's venture into the saloons, Pat paid for his beer and left a tip.

"Okay, my friend," Len said, scooping up the coins and wiping down the bar.

Pat went out the door, and Jerry continued his baseball forecast, saying how six of the Yankees would bat over three hundred, and DiMaggio might even hit four hundred. Mr. Crehan stirred as Pat exited, looking at Pat and saying, "Remember me to your father, Pat."

"I sure will, Mr. Crehan," Pat replied, knowing he wouldn't, as it would place him in a bar at midday and raise his father's ire. Out on Hertel, he walked up to Parker and took a right, where he would have the pick of barbershops—Johnny's, where the conversation would be baseball; and Sam's, where the talk would be fishing. He wandered by both of them, daydreaming until he hit Amherst and found himself in front of the stone edifice of St. Mark's. He looked over at the school where he had gone as a child, and walked right into Father Crotty, nearly knocking the glasses off the little red haired man.

"Oh, my, Patrick, excuse me, I'm rushing to get to the church to hear confessions and I ran right into you."

"My fault, Father, you okay?" Pat said, talking down at the sidewalk and stepping away, avoiding breathing beer on the priest.

Planting his feet and looking Pat in the eye, Crotty replied, "I'm fine, lad, just in a bit of a hurry. Yourself? Is all well?"

"Sure, Father, just going to get a haircut . . ."

"Well, if Johnny's can spare you a moment, come with me. I'll need someone to turn on some of the church lights so I can get into the confessional. They're probably waiting for me, now."

Unable to escape, Pat followed the swift, little man into the church, where there were a good fifteen people, either lined up at the confessional door, or in the pews. The Connelly sisters both turned in their pew and looked at him, and Pat knew they would report his presence far and wide by dinnertime that night.

"Patrick, go and turn the number five and eight lights on over the altar," the priest declared, kissing his purple stole, "And then make your examination of conscience," he said, loud enough for the old ladies to hear.

*Trapped,* Pat thought. *The old priest knew I'd remember where the light switches were from being an altar boy, and now, all the old biddies thought I was expecting to go to confession. Good Lord, how long's it been?* he thought, as he walked up the aisle and genuflected in front of the altar. *I guess since just before I left for basic,* he remembered as he went into the sacristy and twisted the light switches. When he came back out, he noticed a few more familiar faces, and he remembered holding the paten under their chins as they received Communion. He settled into a pew far enough away so he couldn't hear the most deaf of the old ones confess their sins, loudly telling of eating meat on Friday or wishing evil upon their neighbor's dog for barking. *Examination of conscience, huh. Go through the Ten Commandments, like the nuns said. I am the Lord thy God, thou shalt, nah, no false gods I can think of,* he chuckled to himself. *Using the Lord's name in vain, yeah, well, I do that, I guess. Keep the Lord's Day holy. Dad flogs me out of bed for that with "as long as you're under this roof," speech. Kind of scares Tim when I don't want to go, poor scared guy, just like Mom, worried I'm going to hell forever. Yeah, maybe, for killing those Krauts . . . Honor thy father and mother. Ah, jeez, mom. She'd a been here, or at some other function with Tim.* He thought for a moment about his mother, dead a little over five years, and then about his brother, Timmy, falling apart. *Ah, shit,* he thought, *ah shit. There, I did it again,* he thought to himself about swearing. What did they say? Is that a near occasion of sin? Thou shalt not kill was next, and the image of the Kraut sergeant came into his head: the body flying backwards, his hair tossing, and blood bursting out his back.

Gripping his hands on the pew before him, he rested his forehead on the wood and could feel his heart start to race when he heard a cough. He looked up. No one was in line on the left side of the confessional and only one person on the right. Pat pushed himself up and went over, opening the door into the darkened cubicle. Closing the door, he knelt down in the tiny chamber, his feet pushing up against the back of the room, and heard the unintelligible mutterings from the other side as the priest spoke to the other penitent. He heard the distant kneeler creak and the door open as the person left, and then the small wooden hatch before his face slid open and he could just make out the aged man's profile through the thick, brass screen. After a moment of awkward silence, Pat blessed himself, as he had in his childhood, and began, "Bless me father, for I have sinned, it has been. . . It has been . . ."

"A considerable number of days?" the priest prompted, using a trick learned from old Father Fitzgerald in the seminary.

Pat exhaled, and then repeated, "A considerable number of days since my last confession. In that time, I have. . . used the Lord's name in vain . . ."

"Often?" Crotty imposed gently.

"A lot. I don't know how many times, Father."

"I see. Go on . . ."

"I missed Mass a lot when I was in the Army . . ."

"Was this because of your own negligence?"

"Sometimes, Father."

"Continue, my boy . . ."

"I . . . I . . . killed people . . ."

In a near whisper, the priest began, "The church tells us that we do not violate the Fifth Commandment if we kill in self-defense, in a just war, or when it is a judicial execution of a criminal. Did you kill under these conditions?"

Leaning his head against the wall above the screen, Pat twisted his neck, grinding his forehead against the wood and said, "Yes, Father, but one time it was different . . ."

The priest waited a moment, and then said, "Say what happened, my boy, and remember, God is always listening to us, and sees what is in our hearts."

"We shot some Kraut prisoners, Father. We were scared and . . ."

"They had already surrendered?"

"Yes, Father."

"Were they unarmed?"

"Yes, Father."

"Were they attacking you?" Crotty said.

"No, Father," Pat said, his voice shrinking.

"Were they trying to escape?"

"No, Father. I was nodding off, and there was some noise, and one of our guys panicked. He started shooting, and then we all started shooting them. I killed at least one of them. . .,"Pat said, remembering the man hitting the ground, his arms flung wide, and the instantaneous knowledge that he had murdered an unarmed man.

"You have done well to confess this to God. Are you heartily sorry for this?"

"Yes, Father. . . I think about it often," Pat replied, remembering he hadn't said any of this before, to anyone.

"Good. Good." He paused a moment, and then said, "We are all men, son, and we all sin. St. Paul persecuted Christians, even participating in the stoning of St. Stephen, the first martyr of the Church. We must remember that if we are truly, heartily sorry for our sins, there is nothing the Lord cannot forgive."

"Yes, Father."

"Do you understand that? God can forgive us any sin, if we are sorry, and promise not to sin again."

"Yes, Father," Pat said in a low voice, hoping for it to end.

"Jesus would even have forgiven Judas Iscariot, had he asked our Lord for it. Do you get that?"

Pat was reminded of an old missal with a picture of Judas in it. There was a black outline of a man with a bent neck hanging from a tree branch on a blood-red background. Underneath, it read "The End of Judas."

Pat replied, "Yes, Father."

The priest waited a few moments and then went on, "Are there any more sins you have to confess? Sins of the flesh? Sins of drunkenness?"

Pat knelt back up straight, quivered a bit, thinking of the endless nights of booze, the whores over in Europe, and recalled the old teenage dodge. "I can't remember all of them, Father."

"Very well. Now, for your penance, I want you to say ten Our Fathers and ten Hail Marys. Now, make a good act of contrition."

As Pat began the prayer, "O my God, I am heartily sorry. . .," the priest began to pray the prayer of absolution.

"Ego absolvo te a peccatis tuis in nomine Patris . . . "

When they both finished, Father Crotty waited a moment and said, "Go, your sins are forgiven. . . And don't forget, son, that when God forgives you, you must learn to forgive yourself, as well."

Pat slowly climbed up off the kneeler and said, "God bless you, Father," the way he had done as a child, as he opened the dark, wooden door.

"God bless you, too, my boy," the priest answered.

Pat went up to the altar rail and knelt down, thinking on what the priest had said about forgiving himself. He blessed himself and started to pray, reciting the Our Fathers and thinking hard on the "and forgive us our trespasses," rocking back and forth slightly. After several minutes, he fell into daydreaming about the other guys and where they were now. *Some of those guys will be scared forever after combat,* he thought, *They'll be just on the edge of panic all the time. Ah, well, time to get out of here,* he thought, crossing himself and going outside.

He walked for a while, and then looked around and thought about going back to the bar. *Nah, enough about the Yankees, already.* Rubbing the back of his neck, he thought, *haircut. That's what I was going to do in the first place,* but looked at his watch and saw it was getting late. Seeing some kids run past him and across the street to a corner store, he thought, *Yeah, what the hell, get a candy bar, or something.* He followed them into the store where the smell of old food permeated the wooden floors, and the plaster walls were jammed with shelves of bread, canned goods, and bottles. The children were pooling pennies on a glass counter before the white-haired woman watching them, as they figured what they could afford. He remembered Snaps as the cheapest. Little, white, hollow licorice cylinders that tasted almost as bad as the red and white cardboard box they came in. Yuck.

"Hey, what do you guys think is the best candy bar?"

"Good and Plenty!"

"Mars Bar!"

"Nooo! Gotta be Three Musketeers!"

"I'm with you, pal," he said to the last kid, who gaped at him with a lazy eye. Reaching into his pocket, Pat pulled out some change and gave each of them a nickel. The last kid jumped up and down as he anticipated the coin. They all slapped their money down and bought their favorites, and then carefully swiped the pennies back off the counter and into their pockets. Picking up his own candy bar, he followed them out onto the corner and watched the kids take their pennies out and line up at the curb to pitch them against the store's brick wall. The kid with the Mars Bar ripped off a big chunk of the candy bar with his teeth and tossed a penny that landed a foot from the wall and then dribbled within four inches of it. The Good and Plenty kid closed the box of the good licorice lozenges and tossed his penny with a high arc, so it bounced off the wall and rolled around in front of the building, finally stopping a good eight inches from the wall, to his disappointment. The kid with the lazy eye put his Three Musketeers bar in his shirt pocket, bent down low, and flicked his penny with his wrist, watching it skim across the pavement and rest less than an inch from the wall. They all hooted as Lazy Eye rushed forward to scoop up all three pennies.

"Hey!" a man shouted from an upstairs window, "You kids knock that off!"

Pat looked up to see the store's owner leaning on the sill, sporting a white undershirt and pulling up his suspenders. The kids took off down the street, and Pat smiled. He walked slowly home, eating the candy bar under the still-bare branches of the elm trees that would make a canopy of their leaves over the residential streets once summer came.

Going in the side door, he hung up his jacket, and then went into the living room where he dropped into a straight, overstuffed chair, and rested his head on a doily that hung over the top. *Huh,* he thought, *Mom probably made this. Uncomfortable all the same,* and he pushed the doily out of the way. Looking up across the room he saw colored lights shining on the yellow pine floor, the light reflecting through the two small, leaded glass windows over the mantelpiece. *I wonder if those windows were ever opened since we moved here*, he thought. Looking down, he stared at the bookcase to the left of the fireplace, and spotted a small brown, covered book. *I know that one*, Mungo Park's Travels and Adventures. *I must have sat next to the fireplace I dunno how many times, looking through that book, reading about the Congo, trying to memorize the different tribes' words for numbers to make up a code.* He pulled it out and opened the cover, glancing at the faded writing in pencil on the inside cover. In a fine hand it read, "Peter Brogan, Christian Brothers School, Cork." The book had belonged to one of his dad's older brothers, a plumber by trade, who had moved out West and hadn't been heard from for years.

"Your Uncle Pete's," his father said quietly, standing in the doorway, watching his son.

Pat looked up and asked, "Anyone ever hear from him?"

"Not since the thirties. The letters we sent started coming back in 1932, and we haven't heard from him since. I was hoping Charley might find him when he was out there in the service, but nothing. . . Hey, Timmy wants to go to the ballgame at Offerman Stadium, so, we're eating early tonight. Mrs. Cleary put a leg of lamb in the oven for us," Joe said, causing Pat to sniff the air for the sweet smell of the meat with garlic and rosemary.

"Mint jelly?"

"You betcha," his dad replied with a quick nod.

Tim came tripping down the stairs, then slowed as he saw Pat, glancing at his dad, who smiled at his youngest son, who gave him a smile of relief in return.

"Hey, Pat, I'm gonna go see the Bisons play tonight. It's their first game up here since they got back from Florida. Wanna go?"

"You know, Timmy, that sounds good," Pat replied, and then the phone rang. It was Lou with more work for them that night.

# CHAPTER 68

## BABCOCK, 1952

"This stag lacks for nothing, and my compliments to Yosh and Emil for another grand function," Jazz proclaimed at his table, observing the half-empty pitchers of beer, plates with crusts of bread, and smears of cake icing, "But, I think, as Christian gentlemen and," he added in a low voice, "Examples of upright public servants, it would be best for us to wish the future groom our best and depart," Jazz said, nodding at the girls in long coats who had just arrived to the hoots and clapping of the drunken men in the hall.

The mayor leading the way, Ocky, Ed Falk, Carl, and Judge Dickerson got up and headed for the door on Baitz Street. They stopped by the groom's table, where piles of change and not a few bills were piled in the center.

"Good night, boys, have fun," Jazz said, shaking hands with the groom, who was having a hard time concentrating on his cards by this time. "Good thing ten percent of every pot goes to him," Ed commented, "He's not going to know which end is up in another hour."

"Oh, I have a feeling the latest visitors will manage to focus his attention, Ed," Jazz added, and his companions chuckled as they got in the car out on Clinton. As Ocky fired up his new Oldsmobile Rocket 98, Jazz said, "However, there's no reason for us to go home just yet," getting his companions' attention, who were thinking of the latest arrivals at the party. "How about some kegling over at the Royal?"

When they entered the bowling alley, Jazz waved to the

bartender and pointed up the stairs. He nodded, and they trotted up the stairs where there were six lanes, took off their coats, and tossed them on the benches by a lane in the center of the place.

Jazz went around shaking hands and greeting the other bowlers like it was his place, while the others gathered a score-sheet, shoes, and balls.

"Sorry, fellas, but the waitress called in sick, tonight," the manager apologized as he handed over a pair of size twelve shoes to Ed, "You'll have to get your own drinks from the bar."

Suitcoats were removed, ties loosened, and sleeves rolled up as the mayor's friends settled in for the first game.

"Hmm," the judge said. "Five of us this evening. Uneven numbers for a team. I guess it's every man for himself, tonight!" he said, to which Ocky rubbed his hands together.

"Carl, Judge, I'll spot you both twenty pins. The rest of you, I'll take on even up for five bucks!" They all assented, with only Carl hesitating, thinking about the cost to his family's budget if he lost.

The first game went by quickly, with a difference of fewer than ten points, thanks to the handicap. In the second game, Carl rolled his best all-time game, and his total pins with the handicap put him in the lead. "Well, young man," the mayor said, "It seems hanging around with us has improved your game considerably.

We'll have to keep an eye on you."

"Between the guys in the office and you fellas, I've been getting plenty of practice at this game, that's for sure. All of you love to bowl."

"Nothing like it for relaxation, my lad. Say, I spoke to the people over in your office, and I understand your position in the Felonies Bureau is becoming permanent next week."

"Yes, it is, and I guess I've got you to thank for some of that decision."

"Well, I did speak to a few people on your behalf, but what's most important is that fine young men like yourself get into positions where they can do the most good and get rewarded for their work."

"Thanks. . . Your Honor," Carl replied, to which Jazz smiled and nodded.

"Lemme get this next round," the young lawyer said, turning towards the bar.

"Don't throw the game, Carl, just 'cause he helped you out," Ocky shouted, "Because I'm still going to beat you anyway."

The mayor got up to bowl, and the judge kept score at the desk while Carl got their drinks.

At the back bench, Ocky told Falk, "The judge wasn't kidding when he said 'It's every man for himself,' Ed. Now that they've stomped on the Vendor's Association, your guys are going to have to collect for themselves. The captains might have to settle for less than the two-fifty a month they've been getting, and you're going to have to scramble to get your five hundred dollars from the bar owners and the rest of the locations."

"What about the money that's already collected?"

"We'll keep an eye on that. Licensing's okay, and our guys in the council've been taken care of. Let's just hope we'll have the rest for the next elections."

"Hey, everybody!" Carl said, bringing over their drinks. "The bartender made all ours doubles," setting the highball glasses down.

"Probably wants a job in City Hall," Ed said, as they raised their glasses to their new friend.

# CHAPTER 69

## ATTICA, N.Y., 1952

Johnny's sentence was for a year, but he kept out of trouble and was let out after ten months. He told Harriet he would get a ride from Attica back into town; he didn't want to embarrass the boy. This went along with everything else that composed their marriage over the last couple of years—ignoring the fact that they were living apart, that he was chasing dames all over town, that she didn't love him, either. Prison meant he was even farther from them, physically and emotionally, and his few letters sought to justify that distance by saying it was better for the kid this way, he wouldn't have to hear about his jailbird dad as much. Her few letters told of what Jimmy was doing in school, and that Steve was delivering the money to her weekly, as promised.

They gave him the cardboard box with his clothes and property that he'd brought into the penitentiary with him. It seemed like he had moved to another planet for the ten months and time stood still. The contents of the box smelled a little musty, but he stripped off his coarse prison garb in a matter of seconds and shoved his nose into the clothes to smell the freedom in the green work pants and flannel shirt he had been taken out of what seemed an eternity ago.

As he was escorted by the guards into the outer rings of the prison, he tingled with excitement. Each time a guard said, "Number 51A6623, coming out," and then the steel bars clanged shut behind him, he breathed deeper and deeper to suck in clean air. When the two-story steel doors creaked behind him at the exit, Johnny never looked back at the thirty-foot, yellow brick walls rising up out of Western New York's flatness, fearing it would somehow drag him back inside that snake pit.

Johnny wasn't the only serpent to have crawled out of the pit recently, though. He smiled as he spotted Danny and Twitch sitting in the front seat of a purple bulbous-nosed Cadillac humming across the road from the penitentiary. There was Carmine sitting in the back, and when Johnny got close, he could see the little bookmaker was smiling, too.

Hopping in the back, Johnny shook hands all around, and then exhaled and flopped back into the deep, leather, cushioned seat. He pulled out his smokes, and then, realizing they were stale from their months in stir, crumpled the pack up. Carmine gave him a smoke, lit it for him, and then waited several seconds.

"Better?" he said. Johnny nodded and inhaled the first smoke where he didn't have to worry about where he was.

Danny turned around, and, laying his big arm on the seat back, said, "How 'bout some food?"

Johnny nodded again. Twitch then looked in the mirror and said, "There's this diner in Batavia. Food's okay. We take all the boys there first for a free meal."

"Mr. T's there, too," Carmine added. "Wants us to get right to work."

"Sounds good to me," Johnny agreed. *A ride home, a meal, and making money. A good start for sure.*

They parked the car in front of a silver-framed diner on West Main Street, and the men went inside, where Mr. T sat quietly in a booth with coffee in a ceramic mug in front of him, unnoticed by the punters at the counter, and the other tables studying their racing forms. He had put on weight, but Johnny saw the serious black eyes were as underlined as ever. Carmine's glossy, pointed shoes squeaked across the floor, announcing their presence, and Twitch sat down at the counter where he could watch both entrances, the dining room, and look into the kitchen through the swinging door in front of him.

Tutulomundo shook Johnny's hand silently, and waved the others to their places. "You have lost weight, Johnny," he began. "Do you feel all right? You are good?"

Johnny chuckled. "I feel like a million bucks, Mr. T," and they all laughed, knowing how he felt.

"That's good, that's good, Johnny. You have a place to stay in town, Johnny? Where we can take you?"

"Yeah, well, I figure I'd stay in the apartment above the shop."

"We went by your house, Johnny, picked up some clothes for you and brought them over," Danny added.

"Steve let us in above the shop. We figured it was okay. Your wife gave us your stuff right off the bat," Carmine continued, and they were all silent.

The waitress came over and took their order. Even though it was past noon, Johnny ordered a huge breakfast, looking forward to food that was fresh cooked—real eggs, butter, and as much orange juice and milk as he could drink. He checked the coffee, smelled it, and rejoiced when it didn't taste like dishwater.

When the food came, the business meeting commenced. "So, Johnny, what is the first thing you are going to do?" Mr. T inquired of his hungry partner.

"Get out on the route with Steve, first thing tomorrow morning, see how things are standing up."

Mr. T nodded in assent.

"Then, if there's any problems, like machines that need to be moved or aren't working, bills that aren't paid, stuff like that, get that taken care of."

"Okay, good."

"Then, when that's squared away, get on the phone and call up all the people that promised me locations when I went away and tell them I'm back in business."

"Very good, Johnny. A good plan, but do not use the phone for this. Danny will have a car, and he will drive you to meet with these people. Any problems, you tell Danny, and we will take care of it. What else?"

"Once I get a handle on what I'm. . . We're gonna need to expand, I'll figure out what machines to buy and where they ought to go. Steve's been sending me the trade papers, and I been trying to keep up on what's popular with jukeboxes, cigarette machines, bowlers, and pins, of course."

"Very good. When you have that figured out, we'll see

how much money you need and get started. We have friends in Cleveland and Chicago that can help get you good prices. Still hungry, or are you ready to go home?" Mr. T hesitated, and then stopped everyone by raising a finger "And remember, any problems, tell Carmine and Danny, and we will see they are taken care of. Okay?"

# CHAPTER 70

## NORTH BUFFALO, 1952

Johnny had dropped Steve off at a bar to cash out the machines and told him that he'd be back in less than an hour. He drove down Hertel and turned left on Delaware until he spotted the simple, square building with the name in neon, Oscar's, written in cursive across the gray and silver art deco front. *Pretty simple, but not bad, I guess. Place does a hell of a business.*

He pulled around back and noticed several Buicks and Pontiacs and even a few Lincolns and big Chryslers in the lot. *Just fine*, he thought. *After the lunch rush and the lot's still got cars in it; expensive ones, too.* When he walked in the back door, he spotted a new Keeney cigarette machine by the men's room, one with push buttons and a match dispenser. He glanced towards the front door. *Have to move that into the foyer, right by the front door*, he thought. *No pool table for this place; white linen tablecloths and men waiters, not even a jukebox. I figure thirty to fifty dollars a week out of this place. They wouldn't have wanted any pins in here, anyway. Ah, well, it's okay*, he figured, spotting Benny Gilbert sitting at a table, talking to the manager.

Benny caught him out of the corner of his eye, but concentrated on the piece of paper before him, tapping it with his pen to emphasize his pitch. "I tell you, Frank, this will make us another twenty dollars a week."

"Split Fifty-Fifty, right?" the manager answered.

"Uh, yeah, we can do it that way. Oh, hello, Johnny, how are you? Just. . . uh, get into town?"

"I'm fine, Benny, I'm fine. I was in the neighborhood, and thought I'd stop in."

"Oh, Johnny, this is Frank Desmond; he's the general manager here. Frank, this is Johnny Walters, he's in the vending business here in town, too."

Desmond stood up and shook hands, finally getting a look, in person, at the guy from the papers.

"Pleased to meet you, Mr. Desmond. Do you suppose I could talk to Mr. Gilbert, here, for a minute?"

"No, no, go right ahead, Mr. Walters, I've got to go check the receipts from lunch, anyway. You want anything, John?"

"No, I'm good," Johnny answered, moving into Desmond's seat. Desmond went forward, towards the register and away from Benny's latest pitch.

Waiting a moment, Johnny watched Benny screw the cap onto his pen.

"So, Johnny, how ya been? Everything okay now?"

"Yeah, Benny, everything's fine. Just getting the business rolling again."

"Ahh, that's good."

The conversation lapsed, and Johnny stared at Benny. Looking around, Benny said, "This is a good layout. Nice place, but just a cigarette machine for right now."

"That's great, Benny. Remember our deal?"

"Sure, Johnny, you saved me a lot of aggravation doing what you did. For me and a lot of other guys, too."

"You're right, I did."

"Hell of a thing you did for us, Johnny," his voice trailing off. His glance went to the spot on the table where he was tapping the pen continuously.

"It's payback time, Benny. You gotta contract with these guys, here?"

"No, no, nothing written, John. Just the cigarette machine. My guy Tom does all the service and cashes them out, fifty-fifty every week."

"Good, my guy, Steve, knows this machine. He can take over next week. What day do you normally cash out?"

"Hey, John, wait a minute. This is my machine, you know."

"Yeah, I know, and now, you don't have any use for it. I'll buy it off you for, oh, eighty-five dollars."

Benny's eyes opened wide. "That's crazy Johnny. Hell, I paid one-fifteen for this one, top of the line. It's practically brand new," he said, turning the pen over and over his fingers.

"Okay, I'll get a new machine in here by Sunday. I was trying to help you out, since you're turning over of some of your locations to me, Benny."

Benny thought for a while, rapping the pen on the tablecloth. *The wife's barely talking to me since I got dragged into court over this. God knows who Johnny's got behind him, now. Some guys from Cleveland or the Falls, they say.*

"How about ninety-five dollars, Johnny?"

"Ninety, Benny, and I'll give you cash."

"Okay, you win, Johnny. This has been taking too much of my time, anyway," Benny said, and stuck out his hand.

Johnny shook it, and added, as he went towards the back exit, "Oh, yeah, Benny, don't have your guy cash the machine out in the meantime."

Most of the rest of the other vendors he had taken the fall for, turned over their locations the same way as Benny did; a reluctant surrender. A couple who didn't found their tires slashed before they wised up, and on one occasion, Danny and another big guy showed up in the lobby of a hotel, picked up the cigarette machine, carried it out the front door, knocking three patrons aside, and pitched it into the street. A sweating hotel manager wiped his forehead with a handkerchief when he saw the damage, and realizing the potential trouble, called Johnny's number from a card politely proffered to him just the day before by Carmine.

After a few weeks, Johnny arranged to meet Tutulomundo in a truck stop on Ohio Street. Again, Twitch sat at the counter while Johnny talked to Mr. T at a table.

"So, Johnny, good to see you," he said, half rising to shake the vendor's hand. "Everything is well?"

"Just fine, Mr. T. Everyone's coming through and holding up their end of the bargain. Too much aggravation for them to keep running these small operations."

"Good, good. How's the money?"

"It's all right, and going to get better."

"How about the new machines? They are okay?"

"Top notch. Fred and Basil have been coming through as fast as possible, and at good prices, too."

"That's fine, Johnny, that's fine. You have plans to expand, still?"

"Oh, yeah. We've got candy machines going into plants along Military Road, and I'm looking at some new places out in Tonawanda that'd be easy to service and cash out."

"Very good, Johnny," Tutulomundo said, smiling slightly, as it was the same report he had gotten earlier from Carmine.

"Danny and Carmine have been helpful?"

"Oh, yeah, Mr. T. All they need are some business cards and some scrap paper and we're in business."

Tutulomundo closed his eyes and waved his hands over the table. He didn't want to know the how.

Johnny sat silent for a moment, thinking his latest tactic clever. Carmine or Johnny would go into several locations along a commercial street, talk to the managers or owners, offer the company's services and give them a card. If they said yes, great. If they didn't, Carmine would leave, and later that night, Danny, or some other friend of theirs, would return, order a drink, and, on the sly, drop a coin covered in paper in all the vending machines in the place, causing a coin jam to the pool tables, jukeboxes, cigarette machines, and pinballs. When several establishments in the same district had to make service calls to get all their machines operating again, they'd get the hint and most would seek out the new big vendor in town to avoid trouble.

"Anything else? Something you need help with, Johnny?"

"We might need some cash later on, but not now. Some of these businesses are having a tough time, and the banks won't loan them money. I figure if we can help them out, strictly cash loans, the better for them, the better for us. If they can't make it anyway, well, then we can run the place ourselves and they work for us."

"Let Carmine handle that, Johnny. He has experience and keeps very good records of such things," he said, tapping the side of his head. "Now. You were saying that the money is not as good as it could be. You have some ideas, how to make more?"

Carmine's been talking to him first, the greedy Guinea bastard, Johnny realized. "Well, we could move some more of the slots we've still got stashed on location, but right now, that'd attract a lot of attention that we don't need; things are going so well."

Tutulomundo nodded.

"I've got another idea, though, and it'd boost our take without any trouble."

"Oh? Tell me about this idea of yours, Johnny."

"Fees. Right now, we split the cash out of all the machines fifty-fifty with all our clients. But I figure, some of these cigarette machines sell two, maybe three hundred packs a week. Just give 'em a penny or two a pack, and they're still makin' money, plus, they'll want other machines to make up the difference. Then, once we've sized up how much a joint can make, we can hit up the high rollers with some fees that we take out before we do the split on the jukes, pool tables, and pins. That way, if we've got a written contract with a place, the split stays the same, just like the papers everybody signed says."

"What sort of fees, Johnny?"

"Oh, all kinds of expenses: chalk for the pool tables, licensing fees, charges for service calls, front money for new machines, stuff like that. That money comes out first then we split fifty-fifty."

"Johnny, you're a good businessman. We'll all do well together," the older man said, half rising and shaking Johnny's hand. Johnny nodded at Twitch at the counter on his way out and thought, *Things are going just fine, and I've got that wisenheimer Carmine out-maneuvered.*

# CHAPTER 71

## POLICE HEADQUARTERS, 1953

Police Commissioner Corcoran looked around his office on the top floor of police headquarters and glanced at the many plaques and certificates he had garnered in his almost forty-year career with the Buffalo Police Department. He then looked out the window into the city. Along the lakefront, he saw the grain ships lined up in the harbor, the giant, crab-like claws unloading them into the twenty-story grain elevators. Looking south, he saw the ribbons of Swan and South Park Avenues stretching into the distance, past the brick and concrete factories with the smoke from their gigantic chimneys rising into the clouds. Beyond that, the neighborhoods of wooden framed houses laid out block after block. *I'm in charge of keeping it all safe,* he thought, *And I've done my job. I worked my ass off to get here. I'd put good people around me and figured I could sail off into retirement without a hitch. Shit, now they tell me the problem is right here on the force, maybe right here in this building, God damn it.*

*It's one thing when a bunch of percentage bulls glom onto a way to make a fast buck with these damned pinball machines. I know how to handle it. Send a boy with strong teeth like Wachter to chew 'em up. Now, I find out my own men, men I brought along on the force, are taking money from these bastards to cover for them, and worse, passing it up the line. Cripes all mighty, this job never gets easy, whether you're wearing your feet out on the beat, keeping a bunch of wild boys on payday drunks in line, or wearing a fine suit of clothes in a top floor office. Ah, well, best to get on with it, find out what the DA has, and get the cudgel out. . . If only it were that simple, for you never knew where these things will lead you.*

"Mary Clare," he said, hitting the intercom button.

"Yes, Commissioner."

"Have Dan get the car; I've a meeting to attend."

"Yes, Commissioner."

Patrolman Daniel Alessi had just under two years to go until his retirement when a drunk driver ran his motorcycle off the road where Delaware Avenue curved through the park, sending him sliding sideways down the street, the big Harley on top of him, the asphalt tearing most of the skin and muscle off his leg, before it came to a stop at the curb. An off-duty fireman stopped, scooped the mauled officer into the back seat of his car and sped to Millard Fillmore Hospital, where they stopped the bleeding and saved most of his leg.

When he got out of the hospital, he was still confined to a wheelchair and looked like hell.

"You get out of that chair," the commissioner had promised, "And you'll stay on the job, as my driver, as long as you want."

Alessi walked in with a slight limp, his uniform neatly pressed as usual, and his hat tucked under his arm, military style.

"Yes, sir. Headed out to the South Park game, Commissioner?"

"Not yet, Dan," he smiled. "Got one more meeting today. At the University Club, no less," to which both non-collegians nodded in appreciation of the club's toney reputation.

They drove down Delaware, once Buffalo's Millionaires' Row, to the dark, brick and white columned University Club. The commissioner let himself out, saying, "This'll be about an hour, Dan."

The policeman nodded and sat back. Corcoran went in through the heavy, wooden front door, wiped his feet, and removed his broad-brimmed, gray fedora.

The coat-check girl looked at the big white-haired man, and said, "May I help you sir?"

"Where's the Men's Grill, lass? I'm here to meet Clifford Stone there."

Recognizing that name, she pointed and said, "Straight ahead, sir. Through those double doors."

He nodded and smiled at her, but kept his hat as he walked through the white hallway with hunt pictures adorning it. At the double doors, he saw a small, brass sign that read *Men's Grill. Members and Their Guests Only.* Corcoran pulled open both doors, causing several aged members to look up from their table, where they were rolling dice from a leather cup to see who would pay for the next round of drinks. He sat himself down in a Windsor chair and dropped his hat on the polished, wooden table, nodding at the old gentlemen who went on with their game more quietly than before. An ancient, bald waiter in a white coat and a bow tie silently approached and asked the big Irishman, "May I help you, sir?"

Smiling at the small man, he said, "Yes, I'm here to meet with Clifford Stone. What have you got for draft beer, my friend?"

"I'm afraid we have no draft beer available, sir."

"Okay, then bring me a bottle of Simon Pure."

The waiter nodded and went away. Corcoran looked around the room, paneled with dark wood and adorned with squash trophies. *The old fellas seemed to be enjoying themselves,* he thought. *Hell, in a little while that'll be me, only I'll be out on the lake with a fishing pole.*

The waiter was pouring the commissioner's beer into a pilsner glass when Stone entered. The attorney waved to the old ones, held up a finger to acknowledge Corcoran, and nodded to the bartender, who immediately set to work putting ice in a shaker cup. He came over to Corcoran's table, and the commissioner rose to shake hands, wondering if the attorney got his hair cut every week.

"Clifford."

"Gerald."

They remained silent until a martini and a small glass of water were set down on napkins before the DA, and the waiter vanished. Corcoran placed his closed fists on the table.

"How bad is it, counselor?"

Stone exhaled, leaned forward and tented his fingers. "Very bad, I'm afraid. It seems the money has been flowing all the way up to several precinct captains and . . . beyond."

"Ed?"

The lawyer nodded.

"Shit. Wachter and his boys dig this out?"

"Some of it. My staff has been investigating this on its own, as well, especially through the grand jury. There's trouble in the License Commission, City Council, other politicians."

*Well, at least it isn't just my boys,* Corcoran thought, relieved to find out, nodding in thought.

"Get me the names. They go right from your mouth to my ear, and nowhere else."

"Will you be using Wachter and his men on this?"

"I may need their help later. This calls for a confidential squad to be formed, like we've used before. I intend to get these right bastards from all sides, Clifford, and have them hog-tied before my fortieth anniversary on the force."

"We believe there's something else about this, Gerry."

"Oh, what's that?" the policeman said, already planning his next move.

"We think there might be some organized crime behind the vendors now. Gangsters from out of town financing some of this."

"Whaddya mean? Some Black Handers from New York or Chicago? Something like that?"

"We're not sure, but we think Tutulomundo up in Niagara Falls may have gotten together with some criminal elements in

Cleveland to take over Monteduro's operations on the West Side."

*Hmmph,* the old policeman thought. *You've got a grand imagination, Counselor, and grander ambitions. The Buffalo gangbuster moves up in Dewey's footsteps, eh?*

"Once we get the rotten apples out of the barrel, counselor, and set things right in the precincts, we'll be ready to get after il Zoppo and whoever is with him.

Closing his eyes and nodding, the DA acknowledged the policeman's limited vision.

"We'll get the politicians, Gerry, and I'll get you the names of those men you want. We should stay in close touch on this matter. If necessary, we can always meet, here, quietly."

"A fine place, indeed, Clifford," he finished, as they both stood up and shook hands.

Outside in the car, Corcoran felt tired and wished it were all over and he was retired, until Dave Alessi asked, "Head out for the game, Commissioner?"

"Certainly! Some hot dogs for dinner and we'll watch the grandson shoot some hoops."

# CHAPTER 72

## LACKAWANNA, 1953

Ed Falk ordered a hamburger while he waited in the booth for the mayor and Ocky to arrive. He had left headquarters after his conference with the commissioner, the four inspectors and the chief of detectives, where they had discussed the enforcement of the pinball licensing laws.

The meeting had begun with the commissioner tossing the morning *Courier Express* before them, the lead story on the front page reading, "Are Gamblers Operating 'On the Sneak' in Buffalo?"

"Did your men see this?" Corcoran demanded.

They all squirmed uneasily in their waxed wooden chairs around the conference table. Driving his index finger into the newspaper, the commissioner tossed his glasses on the table, squinted at his top commanders, and said, "They think we've been bought off, for Christ's sake!" Then, looking right at the newest inspector, continued, "Martin Wachter kept the hammer down on these bums, Quinn, can't you?"

Promoted to inspector, Dave Quinn had gone from the quiet Seventeenth Precinct into a political maelstrom, downtown. When once, he could show up at the station house on Colvin around nine and check with his lieutenants about car accidents on Delaware, and shoplifters on Hertel Avenue, he then supervised squads of plainclothesmen coming and going at all hours, who dealt with gamblers, arsonists, prostitutes, pimps, dope peddlers, and con men. Lawyers from the DA's office were constantly calling and looking for information, and prisoners always getting hauled in for interrogations. Now all this with the pinballs. Were they licensed? Were they rigged to pay off? Were the fees paid? Were they located too close to schools? There were hundreds, maybe thousands of the damn things all over town, and everyone was playing them.

"Commissioner, to tell you the truth, I'm still trying to replace the men that Inspector Wachter took with him to the DA's office before we get back up to full speed on the pinball machines . . ."

"That's only two men, dammit!" the old waterfront patrolman snarled. Looking at the smooth-faced young man, he thought, *College boy. Knows all the answers on the test, but what would he do with a bar full of drunk scoopers on the waterfront going at it, I wonder.* "Look, boyo, if you think you can't handle it, maybe traffic and radios are more in your line." How he wished he could make the appointments without interference from City Hall.

Quinn sat back in his chair, wondering what to say next. Ed Falk cleared his throat, and then said, "Commissioner, even though Dave's still getting his feet wet with his different units, I've got some good reports about raids at newsstands from his gambling squad. They're really pushing the policy boys out of downtown. Also, if I may suggest . . ."

This last line finally got the boss to look his way and not stare at the unwanted college boy.

" . . . I think we need to use some of the men in the precincts and the licensing office on this, as well. After all, there are several hundred of these machines out there, and who knows the locations better than the men on the beat? They can locate them, then, the men we have assigned to the licensing commissioners office can check up on them, and if we need some men for raids, they're right there. This way, Dave's men can stay on top of the horse rooms and numbers guys."

Corcoran liked the idea of the uniformed officers making their presence felt. "All right, Ed, that sounds good. Get on the captains to have their men go into the bars and delis and wherever else they find these damn things, and check them out. That'll put the fear of God into 'em. And get those plainclothes boys off their asses over in the license office to snatch up the ones with no licenses. And get hold of Mike McDougall right away. I want to see him pronto. All right, that's enough. I'll probably be hearing from the mayor on this shortly, and he'll want to get the papers off his back for sure."

Ed was just finishing his lunch when Ocky, and then the mayor, slid quietly into the booth. He pushed the button on the hardwood-paneled wall for service, and they all ordered beers from the waitress.

"Nice spot, Ed," the mayor observed. "Right by the Basilica. We can light some candles for the orphans if anyone asks what we're doing here." He smiled. "And how is one of Father Baker's best boys, Commissioner Corcoran, today?"

"Ready to eat Dave Quinn alive. I calmed him down some, gave him some ideas that he liked about using the bluecoats in the precincts and the guys in Rybeck's office to enforce the licensing regulations. Gerry's never trusted the detectives or any plainclothes men, and he thinks anyone with a college degree is too soft to be in the department. I'll get with the captains we've been working with, and they'll arrange some raids to get the papers off our backs."

"Excellent, excellent. Ocky, you may wish to speak to some of our friends and ask them to take the free plays off their machines for the next two, three weeks, right, Ed?"

"Three weeks means a lot of money lost to these guys, Jazz," Ocky said. "Some of these pinballs are taking in a hundred bucks a day, apiece."

"Ahh, but you must explain this to them in terms of a long-term investment, Ock. Also, I'll speak to Commissioner Rybeck and have him suspend issuing any new pinball licenses for the time being, while the mayor's office is investigating the public good of the pinball industry."

"There is one more thing," Ed put in, while the mayor finished his beer.

"And what would that be, Edju?"

"The commissioner told me to get Mike McDougall and send him to his office ASAP."

Ocky and the mayor looked at each other and shrugged.

"That probably means he wants Mike to form a confidential squad. Him and two or three other guys who'll work directly out of the commissioner's office to look for guys on the take. Jerry's an old locust stick swinger, but he's not stupid. He thinks something's going on, and he's going to get his old partner to look for it."

# CHAPTER 73

## POLICE HEADQUARTERS, 1953

Commissioner Corcoran sat at his gleaming empty desk and drummed his fingers, the meeting with the Republican DA on his mind. *Thirty-nine years on the force, thirty-nine years,* he thought. *Made it all the way to the top. Thought I had good people watching things for me, and could take it easy, just before I retired, and now, this. Rogue cops. I can't ignore it. It'll bring the department down. It'll make me look the fool, especially if I have to let that Ivy League lawyer Stone clean it up. Ah, it was simpler in the old days, back when I was walking a beat—crush the bad guys, stay away from the boodlers, and the politicians would leave you alone. The old days, me and McDougall meeting up where our beats came together on the Ohio Street Bridge. Hell, he bailed me out there one night, the Learys and their gang almost had me there. If we'd run, we'd have lost the neighborhood to them. If we'd gotten thumped, worse, still. Hah. Those boys were all pissed up, and even if there were five of them, we nailed them, but good. When Mac knocked Pat Leary into the river, the heart went right out of them, and by the time the wagon got there, we had 'em all trussed up to the bridge with their eyes swelling up and their teeth in the gutter. Nothing like a taste of locust wood to make a fool see the error of his ways. That won't work here, though. Hmm, that gives me an idea, and Mac's just the man for it, too.*

Corcoran hit the button on his intercom. "Mary Clare, get Detective Sergeant McDougall in the Robbery Squad on the line, will ya? And send Dan Alessi in here, too, when he's doin' nothin."

Patrolman Alessi walked into the Commissioner's office with a smile and asked, "Ready to go home, boss?"

"No, not yet, Dan. I've got some errands to run after work. I'll be taking the car by myself, so why don't you take the rest of the day off and I'll see you here tomorrow."

Alessi nodded, adding, "I'll be here at eight-hundred hours, Mr. Commissioner."

The intercom buzzed, and the secretary came on the line, saying, "Detective Sergeant McDougall for you, sir."

Corcoran picked up the phone, and said, "Well, if it isn't the terror of Louisiana Street. I hope I didn't disturb you, up on your cushioned seat at Robbery, Mac," in reference to the old detective's hemorrhoids.

"Ahh, you old Mick," McDougall said, shifting in his chair, "You'll get old, too, one of these days."

"Well, you cheap Scotchman, how about proving it isn't true what they say and buy me a drink after work?"

"Although I am against the consumption of strong drink, I think I shall today, if only to try and save your soul, you evil old Papist. Where'd you have in mind?"

"How about Dave's, in about an hour?"

"Righto, and a thrifty choice, too," McDougall replied, and they both hung up, laughing.

Corcoran drove up Bailey Avenue slowly, the habits of a long career making him look for signs of trouble all the way up the East Side into North Buffalo on Buffalo's longest street. Remembering Schneider's Fish Market, he stopped in and got some fresh yellow pike for dinner. Returning to the block where the bar was, he carefully locked the big Buick, looked around for shady characters, and then walked down the alley and entered the back room of the bar, through the side door. On the other side of the pool table, Mac sat at a small table with two chairs, sipping straight scotch and watching a couple of autoworkers play eight ball. Settling in, Corcoran shook hands with his old comrade and signaled the barman over.

"What'll you have, Commissioner?" McDougall said.

"I lied, Mac, this one's on me," Corcoran said to McDougall, and then told the bartender, "I'll take a Simon Pure, and another Cutty Sark for my father, here."

Mac waited a moment until the bartender had moved away, and said, "What's doing, Corky?"

"Some of the apples are rotting, and it's beginning to stink."

"I've heard some of the lads have been taken over by temptation. The pinball games?"

"Exactly. What's worse is, they're passing on their ill-gotten gains."

"How high?"

Corcoran closed his eyes and shook his head.

"Ahh, shit. There's been grafters in this job since Red Jacket was a papoose, but this is bad, my friend."

"It is, Mac. And neither one of us wants to go out leaving that load of pommes de rue behind when we leave."

"What are we going to do about it?"

Their drinks arriving, Corcoran sat back while they were served. Holding up his glass, he tapped McDougall's, said, "Cheers," took a sip, and set the glass down carefully.

"I'll need you to set up a confidential squad, answerable only to me. Pick two sharp lads to help you, anyone you want. And, if you need more help, go to Wachter. He and his boys have been working on this from the start. The DA, Stone, is on top of it, too, and as you might guess, is going to try to make some hay out of it for your Republican friends."

McDougall nodded. "How do you want me to go about this?"

"Well, it can't be with the rough stuff these days," he answered. "This ain't exactly the old days in the First Ward anymore. The politicians won't help, hell, they're . . ."

McDougall smiled and nodded again.

"You know what my mother used to use to try and catch rats?"

"Cheese."

"Right. Old cheese that no one would eat, not even the rats. But when I got married, Mary Pat showed me something that worked every time. Peanut butter. Everyone loves peanut butter, and it works quick, too."

"Bait the trap with what they want."

"You betcha. And make the trap a strong one. We'll need witnesses, ones we can trust, who see the money change hands and be ready to testify."

They paused thoughtfully, for a moment, and then McDougall

asked, "Have you heard that Charley Cusimano had another stroke?"

"No, I didn't."

"He's right up here at the VA. When we finish these, we should pay him a visit."

"Good idea.

"Remember the time Charley and Right Hand Snidecker caught those guys sneaking into Buffalo Forge through the vent pipe?"

"That's right," Corcoran replied, starting to laugh, "And when they wouldn't come out, they set off a plumber's smoke bomb in the vents to chase them out . . . "

"And some passerby called the fire department because he thought the place was on fire!"

"Ah, shit, of course! The firemen had to cut the trapped sons of bitches out of the ventilators!" Corcoran laughed.

Mac gasped through the laughter, "And then Cus and Right Hand rapped 'em across the noggins with their sticks as they come out covered in soot, shouting, 'What's this, a minstrel show?'"

# CHAPTER 74

## THE FIRST WARD, 1953

It was just one in the morning. when Ed Falk untucked his bib, wiped the last of the white clam sauce from his lips, finished his beer, and bid good night to the cook at the serving window at the end of the bar. He took his hat from the rack by the door, turned up his collar, and walked across Seneca Street to the lot where half a dozen plainclothes men were waiting for him. They stood up from the bumpers of the cars they were sitting on, crushed out cigarettes, and became silent when he arrived, awaiting his orders.

"Okay, boys, the mayor has promised a crackdown on illegal gambling with these pinballs, and tonight is when it starts." The deputy commissioner pointed to the men at his left and said, "You guys from the Fifteenth Precinct, you're gonna raid the Mahogany. You know where the machine is, right, Tony?" looking at Tony Regan, who smiled at the thought of getting even with the old Donkey.

They all nodded, knowing where the doors that had to be covered were.

Turning to the right, Ed then said, "You men from the Third Precinct. Inspector Wachter's boys checked the Golden Dollar a little while back and didn't find anything, but I'm sure those *Courier* boys and the bartenders got something going with those machines, and you're just the men to find it—am I right?"

They all nodded in silent assent. "Okay, then. You men get out there, find the machines, confiscate them, arrest anyone using them, and the bartenders." Looking over at Regan, he added, "And if the owner is on the premises, arrest them, too. Now, one of the mechanics, there, at the city's garage will be standing by with a truck to pick up the machines when you've got them, so once it's done, call there immediately. You've got the telephone number with you?"

More nods.

"All right, then, let's get going, and don't forget to call as soon as it's done. Good luck."

Ed stood there as the two teams got into their cars and rolled out onto the street. He then went to the city's police garage to await their calls, thinking about the timing. He'd call the respective precincts in about ten minutes and let them know what was going on. Not too soon for some friend to tip off the bars, but soon enough for the cavalry to be ready, in case there was trouble. Then, once he heard from the raiding parties, he'd send out the mechanic to pick up the machines and to call the papers with the details of the Buffalo police's latest crackdown on illegal gambling. He'd call the *Buffalo Evening News* first. They'd love to hear about the Republican mayor's efforts to stifle illegal gambling, found right in the favorite hangout of their Democratic rival newspaper's bar. Then, a less complete call to the *Courier*, who would probably hear what was going on, as the Golden Dollar was right next to them anyway. Finally, phone calls to the commissioner and the mayor, the latter of whom would already be preparing what he was going to say to the public in the morning.

*Hell,* Ed thought, looking at his watch, *I spend as much time working at night now as I ever did as a patrolman. So much for the privileges of rank.*

# CHAPTER 75

## THE WEST SIDE, 1953

The mayor, Ed, and Ocky were at the weekly card game, and after Carl and the judge had left, the three of them discussed the progress that the DA and Inspector Wachter's team were making.

"They're calling in a bunch of bar owners to testify, and recalling some of the vendors, too," Ed said, forgetting how many cards Ocky had called for and misdealing.

"Edward, I wouldn't worry about those guys. The vendors only know the dues money went for mutual good and welfare with some political contributions, like any good business association. The bar owners have too much to lose with their liquor licenses to say anything, and even if they did, they only dealt with Johnny, or one of a few of your lads, whom I'm sure were picked carefully for their discretion."

"Yeah," Ed worried, "But they could offer some of them immunity . . ."

"Well, perhaps it would be good to have some more information on the subject, and perhaps our friend Stormy Snyder might be amenable to help us."

"They aren't giving him much to do over at Wachter's unit, the way I hear it," Ed said.

"Ahh, well, Deputy Commissioner, I wouldn't be too sure of that," the mayor said, arranging his cards and smiling. "A little bird has been telling us that our friend's responsibilities have increased of late."

"Really? Hmmph," Ed said, folding his hand.

"Perhaps, Ocky, it's time to speak to Detective Snyder, and see if he is amenable to rejoining the communion of the faithful."

"Ahh, I'm all in, guys," Ed said, pulling on his coat. "You let me know what you figure out."

When the policeman had left, Ocky and Jazz continued their discussion as Ocky dealt seven-card stud.

"You know how to talk to him, Ock. He won't be mad at you for his transfer, and he's probably gotten over that some time ago, anyway. Let him know that when this unit is disbanded and they return to regular duty in the police department, he will get a choice assignment for services rendered."

Ocky nodded and said, "That would be good, if he goes along. We had a hell of a time getting another bug on Wachter's phone in his new office in County Hall. Two aces. Not much, but can you beat them?"

"Two kings, sandbagger. You got me this time."

Stormy got off the No. 8 bus at Main and Ferry, and not seeing a thirteen car coming, tucked the transfer in his suit coat pocket and walked into Maxl's Brau Steuberl. He liked this place. Hadn't been in there much lately, and no bad nights in the old days came to mind.

He was sipping his third beer and considering the sour beef and dumplings advertised on the chalkboard behind the bar when Ocky sat down on the bar stool next to him.

"Hey, look who it is, the great Stormy Snyder," Ocky began. "Eh, Fritz, get me a Phoenix, back my friend up one, and get something for yourself."

"Huh," Stormy said, "Winning at cards lately, Ocky?"

"Some. Some there, pal. We had some good times when you were working for the mayor, didn't we?"

"Hmmm."

"So, where they got you now there, Detective? Last I heard, you were chasing car thieves in North Buffalo."

"No, not anymore. Special assignment these days. DA's office."

"Ohh, I gotcha. The DA's office with the grand jury I keep reading about in the paper. Sure, sure. Sounds interesting."

"It's okay," Stormy said.

Picking up his beer, Ocky held it before Stormy, and they

clinked glasses. "Cheers, my friend, and here's to more good times coming." Then, stepping closer and lowering his voice, Ocky continued. "I was talking to Jazz just today, Stormy. He's really glad you got your career turned around, now."

"Oh, is that right?"

"Yeah. And he thinks that, when this assignment in the DA's office is over, you'll be able to get your choice of assignments."

Stormy nodded.

Putting his head closer to the policeman's, Ocky went on, "And, any information you could pass on to me about what you guys are doing over there would be greatly appreciated, my friend."

Stormy blew the air in his lungs out. "I always wanted to make Detective Sergeant," he said.

"Hey," Ocky said, glancing behind him and putting his hand on Stormy's shoulder, "I think after a big job like that one in the DA's office, there'll be promotions and rewards handed out, for sure. Say, Fritz," he said, raising his voice, "A couple of schnapps for my friend and me, when you get a chance."

Ocky hung around for a couple more beers, and then left when Stormy's food arrived.

*How do I handle this?* Stormy thought, shoveling in the vinegary meat. *He said he'd meet me here or any place else after work whenever I left a message at his bar.* Pulling the paper with the phone number out of his pocket, his streetcar transfer fell out onto the floor. *Hmm,* he thought, *I'll bet I could afford a car on a detective sergeant's pay.*

# CHAPTER 76

## NORTH PARK, 1953

Pat woke up with his chest pounding, sweating and cold at the same time. He looked out the open window, saw the branches of the elm tree swaying in the breeze, and wondered how he could possibly feel cold. *Yeah,* he thought, *Voessler.* He had dreamt he was in that Belgian field again, but somehow, he was looking up at Voessler from the ground, when he caught the bullets from that automatic that Sarge Dunaway had taken home with him. He saw the bullets strike his chest and neck, powerless to do anything, like he was a mouse, or something running around on the ground. A couple of rounds ripped up his coat and left burn marks where they entered, and the one that hit him in the neck turned on the blood like a faucet. Tall, skinny kid with glasses, wore his helmet all the time for fear of forgetting it. That was him, and suddenly, no more. *Shit, I haven't had that dream before, and just when the ones about Father Kessler had faded away.*

Pat rubbed his face and swung his legs onto the floor. It felt warm, so he left his robe where it was and went to the bathroom, where he urinated and poured himself a glass of water. *Damn, I'm thirsty, just like after combat.* He walked down the stairs and sat down in the wingback chair in the living room, listening to the clock on the mantelpiece tick, letting his eyes adjust to the darkness.

His father awoke when he heard the springs creak in Pat's bed, as his son swung his feet onto the polished wooden floor of his bedroom. Joe lay there awake, and when he heard Pat's feet going down the steps, he put his slippers and robe on. When he got to the bottom of the stairs, there was just enough light from the front windows to tell the boy was sitting in Eileen's chair, no drink in his hands, holding the armrests.

"Are you all right, son?"

"Yeah, Dad, I just couldn't sleep."

Joe asked him, "Bad dreams?"

"Ahh, bad memories."

Joe paused a moment, and then plunged on, asking, "The war?"

"Uh, huh."

Joe grabbed onto the railing and slowly settled himself down onto the bottom step of the staircase where sometimes he had greeted the kids years ago when they would come tumbling in the side door from school, or playing.

"A fella that died come to mind?"

"Yeah, a young guy, seemed like a teenager, never knew what hit him."

"Did you know him well?"

"Hardly at all. Seemed like guys came and went so fast, right then . . ."

Joe paused again, struggling to speak. Finally, he said, "I remember many an empty cot that got filled, just to be emptied again in a day, or two."

"Huh?" Pat asked, for he was pretty sure his dad had never gone overseas during The Great War, as the old Doughboys in the neighborhood called it.

"Influenza. We spent all our time marching around in Georgia, and the great influenza epidemic hit and killed those boys by the score. They didn't have the slightest idea what to do about it, just isolate them when they got sick and bury them when they died."

"Did you know any of those guys well?"

"It seemed like it, at the time, but in the course of a lifetime, those memories get a smaller place in your heart with everything else that happens since. One week, you're all wearing a wool uniform, kicking up the dust in Georgia, and then far, far away, some great fool of a Kaiser quits and the next thing you know, it seems you're on a train crammed with sweating soldiers like yourself, going home. Those days, drilling with those Springfield rifles, doing close order drills with some sergeant screaming at you or the man next to you, it seems those moments will never end. Then, years later, you look back, and there's a life filled with work, bills to pay, a wife. . . Children, sickness, and more deaths, and you have a harder time remembering the face of a boy in line next to you who was only there for a few days. . . Now, the drill sergeants, you never forget them, the right bastards." He thought a moment and chuckled, remembering how he tore the fitting band out of a sergeant's hat on the sly, making it droop onto his face, making the whole platoon explode with laughter while the man stormed about red-faced, looking for the culprit.

"I think the only thing I saved when I got home was my campaign hat and a few badges."

"Yeah, I remember that. We used to wear them when we played army as kids."

"Ahh, that's right. I had the carpenters over on LaSalle cut up some toy guns from scrap wood for you kids."

"Yeah, that's right," Pat remembered. *I wonder where they are now?* he thought, his mind then shifting from the thin pine guns of his childhood to the heavy, thick weapons of polished wood and steel that caused real death and mayhem.

They were silent for a while, and, as their eyes had adjusted to the darkness, looked at one another for a moment.

"Well, I'm back off to bed. You?"

"Yeah, me too, Dad," Pat answered, pushing himself out of the chair. His father nodded in relief as his son followed him up the stairs to get some rest.

# CHAPTER 77

## ERIE COUNTY HALL DOWNTOWN, 1953

Their desks were in sight, but Wachter used the intercom to summon Lou and Pat to his new office, and this time, after a particularly long buzz on the system. They looked at each other as they approached the frosted glass of their superior's door, figuring that it couldn't be something good.

Once inside, the inspector told them to close the door. That done, he practically jumped up from his desk, causing the two detectives to jump back.

"Now, see here, you two," he said, waving his finger at them. "You screwed up part of this job when you got involved with those two women before. I don't want to do this, but I've got to trust you, so don't hash this up again, or I'll have the both of you walking a beat along the tracks on William Street. We know, the redhead, Helen Volker," he said, looking right at Brogan, "Has left town, but we don't know where. I want you two *policemen*, to go over to her house on Schreck Street and see if you can pick up her trail. Got it?"

"Yes, sir," they said in unison.

"Well, get moving. . . Blast it!"

Pat did the driving up into the Kensington neighborhood, and Lou looked out the window as they rode. "Pretty nice neighborhood up here, Pat. Maybe I can get one of those GI loans when I get some more money saved and get a house up here in North Buffalo. Settle down."

"Yeah, it is pretty nice over here. Lots of stores over on Bailey, some on Delevan and Kensington. Quiet on the residential streets."

They pulled into the driveway of Helen's address, two

bands of concrete with a carefully mown grass strip in between. Knocking on the side door, they heard children running down the stairs shouting, "I've got it!" and were greeted by two boys with brush cuts and striped tee shirts, the remnants of peanut butter and jelly smeared about their faces. Looking up at the two men in suits, they went silent.

"Hiya, boys," Lou said cheerfully. "Is your mommy home?" he asked, at which both kids stormed back up the stairs into the kitchen shouting "Mom!"

Their mother, a tiny woman with a big smile, wiped her hands on her apron and came to the screen door.

"Yes? Can I help you?"

"Good morning, ma'am," Lou said, tipping his hat. "I'm Lieutenant Constantino with the police department, and this is Detective Brogan. We're here about Helen Volker."

"My, well the other policemen were here before, and I told them all I know. She hasn't been back to her flat. Is she okay? Have you found her? Such a pretty girl with that red hair. I hope she's not in trouble . . ."

"Yes, ma'am, that's what we're trying to find out. Do you mind if we take a look in her flat?"

"Oh my, you mean look for clues? Oh my. Well, if you think it will help," she said, pushing open the screen door and leading them to the second floor.

It didn't take long for them to figure out that the Volker girl had left for good, and in a hurry. All her clothes and personal effects were gone from the bedroom and bathroom. All the furniture had stayed. Questioning the landlady and the neighbors all got the same story. She went to work in the morning, came home at night, sometimes late, but always by herself. Then, she just disappeared. No car, so time to check the bus, boat and train stations.

At the foot of Main Street, the Hudson bumped across the railroad tracks and stopped in front of a two-story, gray masonry vault on the lakefront. A rusting red and white metal sign between two Doric columns in front advertised the Cleveland and Detroit Navigation Line. Dark green wooden doors creaked as Lou and Pat pushed open the discolored brass handles and Lou noticed an

old sign hung sideways covering a broken window: Remember—
Steamer sails for Detroit at five thirty in the evening, Eastern War
Time.

"My dad used to tell me about taking cruises from here and listening to big bands in the dining room on the *City of Detroit* back
in the twenties," Lou said, taking in the scarred, heavy, timber
floors, and the cracked, white plaster above the dark wainscoting.

Pat looked up at the exposed sprinkler pipes hanging from
the ceiling, and then down the walls and said, "Hey, look, they've
still got some old gas fixtures coming out of the walls," as they
approached the ticket counter.

The clerk was leaning on his hand, reading a magazine, as the
two policemen stepped around two empty baggage wagons. The
clerk looked up, smiling, and asked, "What can I do for you gentlemen? A business trip to Cleveland, perhaps?" His smile faded as
they held up their badges.

"We're looking for a woman who may have taken a boat from
here recently," Lou said. "Her name is Helen Volker. Five-ten, five-
eleven, red hair, pretty blue eyes . . ."

"Wow. I wish I had seen her, fellas. I sure would have remembered a dish like that. It's been pretty quiet here, since the war . . ."

"Okay, well, thanks anyway. We're going to leave our car out
front, here while we walk down the way to the DL&W station."

"Okay, if you need anything else, just gimme a call here, officers. I'm Herb and the number's Cleveland 8500," he said, returning to his magazine.

Farther down the waterfront, they entered the Delaware,
Lackawanna and Western Station through brass doors and had
to dodge rushing passengers, porters pushing freight and baggage carts. White-coated stewards were moving for the boats and
trains as they ascended the marble stairway to the upstairs waiting
room. Entering and departing trains made the brass lamps alongside the oak benches shudder with the thunder of steam engines
and screeching brakes as the detectives approached the brass cage
ticket windows. There, they found a young guy who remembered
their witness when they described the redhead.

"Man-o-shevitz, do I remember her. She came in with big

sunglasses, a scarf on her head, and a long raincoat, see? You could still tell she was a knockout though. It was hot in here, and she sat down right over there," he said, indicating a wooden bench in the waiting room.

"Showed some leg, then, did she?" Lou smiled.

"Yeah, man, all the way up just past her knees. Anyway, it's hot in here, see? Gotta keep it warm for all the doors opening and closing all the time. So, she takes her coat and scarf off before she catches her train. Just made my day, I tell ya."

"So, where'd she catch the train to, my friend?"

"Miami, via Pittsburgh. I thought all night about how she'd look on the beach down there. Man!"

With that information, they returned to the office and called the Miami police, who had no objections to looking for the witness the newspapers would later describe as the "statuesque siren."

# CHAPTER 78

## ERIE COUNTY HALL, 1953

Lou walked into the office, hands in pockets, toothpick in his teeth, white Panama tipped back on his head, topping off a blue pinstripe suit. Pat sat at his desk in his shirtsleeves, typing a report.

"You shoulda come to lunch with me, partner. The scenery in Bowles was great today," Lou said.

"Ahh, I'm gonna leave early today, take my kid brother to see the Bisons this afternoon. Gotta finish this report on what we found out from the Miami PD."

Sitting on the edge of his desk, Lou twisted to see what Pat was writing. "How many pages does it take to say, 'Nothing yet'?"

They both looked up when they heard the intercom buzz through the inspector's open door.

"Inspector Wachter, a long distance call from Canada for you."

Pretending not to listen, the two detectives heard "Ontario Provincial Police? What? I'm on my way," and with that, Wachter snatched up his coat and headed for the door. Looking around at Pat and Lou he said, "Something's come up that I have to take care of right now, men. I probably won't be back this afternoon," and was gone.

"That's the second or third long distance phone he's gotten lately," Pat said.

"He's been acting antsy lately, gotta say that," Lou added.

"He said something before, about his cottage over in Canada. Maybe the roof's caved in or a pipe's broke."

"I wonder if his wife and kids are out there?"

"This time of year? I doubt it."

# CHAPTER 79

## THE EAST SIDE, 1953

Stormy got off the streetcar at Main and Ferry in the pouring rain, holding a newspaper over his head as he dashed into Maxl's. *Shit on this*, he thought as he stuffed the transfer into his pocket and headed directly for the phone booth. He closed the door with difficulty, squeezing his legs inside as he sat down, and pulled out the number to Ocky's Bar. Looking over the customers at the Maxl's bar, he saw Fritz pour him his usual and put it at his spot at the bar.

Ocky's wife answered.

"Ocky's Select Bar and Grill."

"Hi. Is Ocky there?"

"He's upstairs sleeping, now."

"Hmm, that's no good. Can you tell him to call . . . Emerson at Ferry 1125 please? It's important."

"I'll pass it on Mr. Emerson. He should be getting up to get behind the bar in about half an hour."

"Okay, thanks. You got the number right? Ferry 1125?"

"Oh, yeah, I got it, don't worry, Mr. Emerson."

The rain kept coming down, and Stormy put away four beers before the phone in the booth rang. He jumped to answer it before someone else got there.

"Hello?"

"Who's this?" Ocky replied, recognizing a voice, but unable to identify it.

"Ocky?"

"Yeah, who's this?" he replied in a perturbed manner.

"It's me, Snyder."

"Oh," Ocky returned with a smile in his voice, "Why didn't you say so, my friend?"

"Hey look. I'm over at Maxl's. I thought you might want to have a beer with me."

"Yeah, yeah, sure, Stormy, sounds good," Ocky replied, thinking of what he would say to keep his wife behind the bar awhile longer.

Pulling up twenty minutes later, Ocky ran through the puddles into the bar.

"Hey, pal, what's going on?"

"Well, I thought you might just want to have a beer and talk a little, Ock."

Ocky restrained his impatience to find out what Stormy knew and get back to the bar where his wife was fuming. He'd told her he had "important political business to take care of right now." Ocky had two beers with the big policeman before they got around to business, and then Stormy said it'd be better to tell him on the way home.

*This had better be good,* Ocky thought, looking at the clock that said "Time for a Manru," and finished his beer. As they drove down Ferry towards Stormy's house, they were quiet for a while, the detective thinking carefully about what he was going to say.

Finally, Stormy sighed and said, "There's this redhead. Volker. She was the bookkeeper for the Vendor's Association. They think she's in Florida. They want to bring her up north to be a witness. The whole nine yards—first the grand jury, then put her in a hotel someplace, for whatever trial they can use her at."

*Shit, shit, shit,* Ocky thought. *This crap gets deeper all the time. I'm going to have to pass this on, and it's going to get some people real worked up.*

"Well, thanks, Stormy. That's good to know. And I can tell you, your help won't be forgotten when the time comes."

As he got out of the car, Stormy hoped he had done it right. Maybe one step closer to the detective sergeant's badge and there wouldn't be any more wet transfers for the streetcar.

# CHAPTER 80

## DOWNTOWN, 1953

Pat sat in the car, reading the report from the DA's office about their latest raid, when the wind howled so bad it shook the car. He looked up just as the latest gust off the lake subsided and watched the snow resume its steady fall in big, thick flakes. *Gonna be a bad one, according to the radio.* He shivered a little, wishing Lou would hurry and get the car started so they could put the heat on and get moving, before they had to shovel the damned thing off again.

*Ah, there he is, at last,* Pat thought, rubbing his gloved hands together. Lou approached, smiling and waving the keys.

"Had a hard time getting the keys to the Hudson, partner. Had to get the inspector to pull rank on one of the lawyers and get out of there while he went running to the DA."

"Turn the heat on, Lou, or we're gonna freeze, here."

"All right, all right, take it easy, I don't like it, either. Not as bad as the North Atlantic, though."

"North Atlantic, huh?" Pat said as he observed Lou's dress: natty, gray fedora; earmuffs underneath; thick, tweed coat with a black, wool muffler; black fleece-lined gloves; and zipper galoshes.

"Phew, yeah. Standing watch in twenty-foot seas, wind blowing, no way on Earth to keep warm or dry, brother."

"What were you on?"

"A destroyer escort, the *Janssen*, DE 396. Escorting convoys. One of the things that would get you out of the rack and on deck for watch was a U-Boat, which could put you in the drink permanently."

"Huh," Pat thought, thinking of his brother Charley shuffling paper and hustling supplies in New Caledonia in the Pacific. "Ever sink any subs?"

"Dunno, really. They'd pick them up on sonar, or some liberty ship would explode and sink like that," he said, snapping his fingers, "And we'd go hunting for the sneaky SOBS, dropping depth charges, firing hedgehogs, and hoping there wasn't a torpedo with our name on it. They traveled in packs and always seemed to attack in bad weather, when the planes couldn't find them. Couldn't find debris in the rough seas, either, to see if you'd nailed them. Scary."

Pat nodded, thinking about ambushes and luck.

"How about you? Army, right?"

"Yeah, Patton's Third Army. Got up to the front right towards the end of the Battle of the Bulge. They say it was the coldest winter on record."

"Where would you guys sleep? In tents?"

"Houses, if there were any around. Sometimes tents. Holes. Ditches. . . alongside roads. . ."

After a long pause, Lou took his eyes from the road to look at Pat and asked, "You okay, pal?"

"Yeah, okay. Just remembering some bad places."

"Lose some friends?"

"Yeah, but mostly guys I barely knew."

"Huh," Lou reflected. "We picked up guys who had been sunk. Bad. The cold gets 'em in no time at all, out there. Frozen. Shrapnel from explosions. Burns. . . They were the worst. . ."

"Whoa! Look where you're going, Lou," Pat said as the Hudson skidded across the street.

"Wah hoo! I got it, partner," he replied, turning into the skid and regaining control. He straightened the car out and waved to an oncoming car that wasn't sure they were going to make it. They both laughed, and Lou said, "Maybe we should stop talking about what we already got through and make sure we get through this mess, eh?"

"Yeah, good idea, Lou. The place we're gonna check out should be coming up on our right."

# CHAPTER 81

## LACKAWANNA, 1953

At twenty past ten, Joe gave up on Charley arriving and gave Pat the keys to his Studebaker, shaking his head.

"C'mon, Tim," he shouted up the stairs, which brought his youngest son down, his hair slicked into place for the visit to his mother's grave.

"Is Charley here?" Tim said, looking around. Joe shook his head silently as Pat guided him out the side door to the car.

"Maybe he'll meet us there, Tim," Pat said, at which the boy dropped his head. "Mary Agnes and Pete'll be there, for sure."

The long drive through Buffalo was mostly silent that Saturday morning as they went all the way down Main, through a quiet downtown, past the DL&W Station where a few engines were building up steam, and then down South Park through the First Ward past Eileen's old street, Hamburg.

*Nah, don't even stop to look,* Joe thought. *I haven't heard from Bridy and the rest of them since she died.* Leave well enough alone. They continued on through industrial South Buffalo, where some of the residents were washing the soot off their wooden houses, and finally arrived in the steel city of Lackawanna.

"Look, Pop, there's the Basilica," Tim said, brightening. People were coming and going up the steps of the copper-domed Basilica, making Pat wonder what sort of troubles drove people into church on Saturday morning. *Probably praying for the rest of their family, who are still sleeping one off.*

"Hah, there it is, Tim. Father Baker's," Pat said, referring to the orphanage beyond the Basilica. "Where mom and dad used to say they would send us if we were bad."

"I don't remember that."

"Well, Charley and me, anyway."

Parking alongside the iron fence by the gate, Joe picked up the lilies wrapped in green paper he had bought, and led the way. Mary Agnes and Peter were already there, he in a suit, she in a veiled hat. She smiled when she saw them coming, but Pat could see from her reddened eyes she'd been crying.

"The flowers are beautiful, Daddy," she said.

"What's that you've got there Agnes?" Joe said, pointing to the brown grocery bag she carried.

"Oh, I got a vase from Murphy's, see," she said, pulling it out of the bag. "It's tin, so it'll keep, and it's got a spike at the bottom, so we can put it in the ground."

"Why, that's wonderful Agnes," Joe said.

"And Pete's got a bottle full of water so they'll last, too."

They arranged the flowers in the vase and gave it to Tim to put before the gravestone, and then stood silently before the polished limestone that read *Eileen Brogan, Born 1888, Clare, Ireland. Died 1945, Buffalo. Beloved Wife and Mother.*

Joe looked up into the misting, cool sky and commented to the clouds, "A fine, soft day, like in Ireland. Not bad, at all, for this time of year."

"It'll help the flowers keep longer, Pop," Tim said.

"That, it will, my boy," he answered, putting his hand on Tim's shoulder.

With that, Tim turned and put his head on his father's chest and began to cry. His father patted him on the back, and Mary Agnes came over and turned him to her, putting her arms around her brother. After a few more minutes, Pete suggested getting something to eat, and Mary Agnes said maybe they'd take Tim to the botanical gardens afterwards.

"You go on ahead, kids," Joe said. I want to stay a few more minutes with your mother."

"C'mon with us, Tim," Pete said, and he and Mary Agnes led him away, sobbing.

Pat stood next to his father for several minutes, and finally Joe said, "She was the most kind and open woman who ever lived, your mother. There wasn't anything she wouldn't do for us. I . . . I didn't think I was going to make it when she died."

Pat nodded and looked around. There were four other gravestones marked Brogan: Michael Brogan, 1896-1898; Catherine Brogan, 1897-1903; Dierdre Brogan, 1856-1910; James Brogan, 1852-1914.

Taking off his rimless glasses and wiping his eyes with a handkerchief, Joe said, "Time goes by, boy, before you know it. Everything changes. Cat and Michael, they were just babies."

"What happened to them, Pop?"

"Consumption. Ate their little lungs up and there was nothing anyone could do. There's two more, buried in Cork. Your uncles Terence and Timmy."

"You ever go back there?"

"Nothing but death and misery there," he said, shaking his head. "No, we're much better here." Then, turning to Pat, he said, "We've got to grieve, son, but you've got to go on living, and work and hope and pray to God things'll get better, or you'll fall apart entirely and be no good to anyone. Heaven knows there's those who've got it much worse than we'll ever know." The older man then stood and looked at the grave silently, remembering it all, for a good fifteen minutes, and Pat with him, thinking about the dead, and how their lives must have been so different. Finally, Joe shook his head and said, "When people die. . . You've got to hang on to the living all the stronger. . . It's why I worry so, about. . . " He went silent again, and then added, "Let's go over and see what the Macedonians at this diner have to eat."

# CHAPTER 82

## THE EAST SIDE, 1953

Ocky thought the better part of the night shift, about what to do with the information that had come from the tap on Wachter's phone line. What, with Johnny working with Tutulomundo, the cops hunting around in their own department, and the DA whipping up a storm in the holdover grand jury, you couldn't be too careful.

"You're awful quiet tonight, Ocky," said one of his regulars, Stash, who had been prattling about the Bills being revived and getting into the NFL. "Hell, we used to close up this joint, catch a cab down to Central Station and ride down to the city to see them play when the All-American Conference was going. If Buffalo got an NFL franchise, we wouldn't have to go out of town to see the Giants, or the Browns, or any of the big league teams play."

"Got a lot on my mind, Stashu. Dunno if I could afford the same season tickets in the big league. Another drink?" he asked, pouring another shot of rail whiskey into the empty shot glass and picking up two dimes from the man's cash before he could reply. All but the newest patrons understood, if you didn't say no but quick when Ocky was working, you must mean you'll have one. Stash threw down the whiskey and scooped up his money, and then washed it down with the last of his beer. "Gotta go. I'll check and see what the Browns are charging and let you know."

Ocky picked up the phone and called the mayor's home.

"Good evening, the mayor's residence, who may I say is calling?" a teenaged voice answered.

"Hello, Chet, Mr. Owczarczak here. Let me talk to your dad, please."

"Sure, Mr. Owczarczak. Dad! Mr. Ocky's on the phone for you!"

A few moments later, Ocky heard the metal receiver tap against the table, a muted, "Thanks, Chetcha," and then Jazz cleared his throat like he was readying a speech. *The guy never stops*, Ocky thought.

"Ocky, my boy, what can I do for you?"

"I was wondering if you needed some coffee? There's a few campaign plans we should go over."

"Tonight, eh? Very well, I'll meet you at the Deco in say, an hour. Can you get the wife to cover the bar for you?"

"Yeah, I'll get it covered. See you then."

When his wife came down to watch the bar, Ocky walked down Broadway and turned into the blue and white Deco coffee shop at the corner of Wilson where he found Jazz already waiting, telling the white-hatted guy behind the counter about a math teacher they'd both had in high school.

"I tell you, I don't know how I got through geometry, but I did it. If I got a problem at the board right, Mr. Cohn would raise his eyes up to heaven and say, 'Jerzerowski, you got it right! Mirabile dictu!'" the mayor said, at which both men laughed.

"Ahh, Ocky. Good to see you," he greeted Ocky. "You know George, don't you? A few years ahead of us, over at East?" Then, as they shook hands, he said, "George, get Ocky a cup of your freshest coffee, would you? He's been burning the midnight oil at his saloon and could use some refreshment."

As George went to get the coffee, Jazz smiled, spread his hands and said, "I'm all ears, my boy."

"A little bird gave me a message. And another bird, not so little."

"Oh?"

"The little bird has wires, the big one flies around in a storm all the time."

"I see; pray, continue."

"They're going to be calling some of the people who used to work for the coin operators. And some of the people in the city council. And probably you, too."

Jazz took a sip of coffee and concentrated. "I think our contributors would definitely want to know this." He then turned back to George. "So, tell us, George, if you had Mr. Cohn for geometry, did you have Mr. Bork for algebra? Ha, hah! He was another one that stood for no nonsense, wasn't he?"

# CHAPTER 83

## NIAGARA FALLS, 1953

The meeting between Johnny and Tutulomundo was held out in the open air on Goat Island by Niagara Falls, on a day with wind that could rip the trees out of the ground. Carmine smiled when he told Johnny to be there and don't be late. Johnny parked his truck by a souvenir stand on the American side and walked the narrow path, through the wooded park to the footbridge, listening to the rushing water that cascaded around the small island. The wind was whipping the leaves in the trees, and bending the branches when Johnny saw the big car pull up over by the stand. Three men got out, not just T and Twitch, this time. The third guy was a moose, with a furrowed brow and hands like suitcases. They weren't taking their time like usual, either. He couldn't remember T walking that fast in the yard, or that far on the outside, ever. It felt like the temperature dropped ten degrees as the three men came across the narrow bridge to the island, with the swift waters of the Niagara rushing over the rocks around the island, just a few yards before going over the Falls. The two guys with T stopped just this side of the bridge, and T kept on for Johnny. When he got to him, he said, "Come," and cocked his head along the path towards the Falls that goes along the rapids. Johnny followed.

"Johnny, Carmine told me of a problem. It seems some people know about our friends we help in the city."

Johnny's teeth clenched, and he nodded.

"You did some talking, yes?"

He nodded again.

"Tell me to who. All of it."

Now, Johnny was sweating despite the cold breeze. "This was

before, when we had the association collecting."

"Yes. What else?"

"I was. . . sick," he said, remembering a boozy afternoon, when he had been playing liar's poker at Deubell's with Bukowski and Hayes. He had been winning and didn't want to quit.

"Steve! You got the cigarette machine filled? Three sixes, you phonies," he said.

"Four sixes," Bukowski countered. Steve came up and gave Johnny the huge ring of keys to their machines. "All done," he smiled and nodded.

"Four sevens," Hayes said hesitantly.

"Call!" Johnny shouted, dropping his folded dollar. "I ain't got any, fool!"

"I just got one," Bukowski said.

"Shit, just two here," Hayes said.

"Pay up suckers!" Johnny demanded, deciding to stay in the game. "Steve, c'mere a minute, "he said, standing up. "Don't you guys go anywhere, I'll be right back." Stopping Steve by the door, where he was getting ready to exit with cartons of extra smokes, he put an envelope under the big Ukrainian's arm. "Hey. I need you to take this envelope to a guy down the street in Klavoon's. His name's Regan, you've seen him before . . ."

Johnny winced at the memory of one of the stupidest things he had ever done, toning down the story for T.

"And the girls? Tell me everything!"

Johnny clenched his eyes at this one, shook his head, exhaled, and said, "I was in the association's office . . ."

Standing behind her chair, Johnny said, "You know, Helen, we've got the mayor, everybody working with us," stroking the redhead's shoulder while she typed. She twisted slightly, getting out from under his fingers.

"Maybe," Johnny said, tugging on the lapels to his new, gray-worsted, wool suit, "The three of us could go have drinks with his campaign manager and the deputy police commissioner tonight at the Peter Stuyvesant Room."

"Oh, that sounds nice," Betty said, but Helen gave her a quick look that said no.

Johnny pulled the envelope out from his coat pocket and let the cash peek out. "Yeah, we've got some campaign contributions to make, but there's no reason we couldn't spend some of it on dinner."

"Uhh, Johnny," Helen said, "We already promised our boy-friends we'd go to dinner with them, tonight."

"Well, girls, it's your loss," Johnny said, slapping the thick envelope against his hand. "Maybe another time."

"This is all, Johnny? You're sure? That's everything?" T demanded.

He nodded, again and again. "Yes, I'm sure. It was way before I even went to jail. It never came up . . ."

"Johnny, that was very foolish of you." A hard finger jabbed against Johnny's eyelid, pushing it up against his brow, forcing Johnny to look up at his face. "Never again, Johnny. You cannot succeed in business with a big mouth. And," jabbing him again, T said, "You must always tell us everything." He waited a moment, and then clapped his hands on Johnny's shoulders. "We will take care of this. Go home, now, and do what Carmine tells you," T ordered, and then he put his hands in his coat pockets. After a few seconds, he said, "You know this business, Johnny. All the machines. We need you, but you cannot be a fool anymore."

Tutulomundo abruptly walked off, back to the footbridge. Johnny stood there in the middle of the small island until the two men by the bridge followed T back to the car and drove off. Then, he exhaled and went home like he was told and waited for Carmine's instructions.

# CHAPTER 84

## THE WEST SIDE, 1953

Torreo looked at the clock on the stove, finished his coffee, and figured it was time to leave. Looking out the door from his kitchen, he saw the sun was shining. *No scarf or hat today*, he thought as he put the cup and saucer in the sink. "Mama, I'm going out for a walk," he announced, and heard, "Okay, Papa," from down in the basement, where his wife was doing laundry for their son, the college boy. *He has an easy life*, Torreo thought as he stepped out onto the back porch, looking one way, and then the other across the backyards. *I hope it was worth it*, he thought.

A quick look at his watch, and then down the steps, through the back gate, across the neighbor's backyard, down the driveway, and a quick look again up and down 16th Street, and he began his brisk pace of a daily walk to try to keep what strength he had in his atrophied leg. The neighbors who were out shoveling snow nodded and said hello to him on his way. *No one throwing shit at me anymore*, he thought, as he turned down York Street, towards the park.

He slowed his walk as he entered the park, observing the kids playing football in the snow and others walking their dogs. He stopped by a bench where a young man sat feeding the squirrels.

"Good morning, Felix, how are the squirrels today?"

"Calm, Mr. M., calm. Very nice, here, today."

"Is that our friends in the purple car over there?" Torreo said, gesturing with his chin to the Cadillac parked along a park path leading to the waterfront.

"That's them, Mr. M. Been here about twenty minutes. Drove around a little, first, and then settled there."

"Okay, good. Keep an eye on the squirrels while I take a walk with my friend, huh?"

Felix nodded and threw a little stale bread to the animals.

Approaching the car, Torreo spotted Tutulomundo tossing a cigarette out the window, and noticed Carmine in the back, and Twitch in the driver's seat. He scraped his foot along the pavement when he was about fifteen feet from the car, and Twitch had already tapped T on the shoulder to let him know of Monteduro's approach. The boss heaved himself out of the car and embraced Torreo twice, and then shook hands, clasping his right in both of his.

"A nice day to walk in the park, Mr. M., a wonderful day.

"It is, Mr. T., a good day to fill our lungs with fresh air."

"So, my old friend, how do you feel? Strong?"

"If you had told me fifty years ago I would be walking in the park today, I would not have believed you," Torreo said, and they both chuckled.

"That's good, my friend, that's good."

"You didn't come here today just to get away from the bad air around Niagara Falls, though. Carmine says there is a problem."

"Yes, Torreo, there is, and it could be a big one."

"Tell me what it is, Vincente, and that the both of us need to discuss it. Carmine sometimes worries too much over little shit."

T frowned and said, "The grand jury has found witnesses that involve the police."

"Ahh," Torreo said, waving his hand as if to shoo a fly. "The district attorney always has witnesses that blab in front of grand juries. There is a lot of noise, a few indictments, a trial or two, and what happens? He gets re-elected, a few people pay fines, maybe one goes to jail for a little while. What happened the last time? A few fines, our friend Johnny does his time and keeps his mouth shut, and then we are back in business. Such things happen."

T stiffened at Monteduro's mention of people going to jail, and remembered all the things he had done with Torreo over the years. He stopped walking, turned, and looked up at the eyes of the broad-shouldered man before him, causing Felix on his bench, and the men in the car, to take notice.

"Our machine man, Johnny, got drunk and blabbed to some girls and his helper, the Russian, about where the money was going. He even had the Russian deliver once to a policeman. I talked to Johnny and straightened him out, but the two girls and the Russian . . ."

"Women? This is not right, Vincente."

"This is our business, sir. It leads them to the police, our other friends, it can lead to many bad things. This Wachter and the DA, they are not fools. They think one of the women is in Florida. They will not give up and go away like the others."

"We cannot hurt women, Vincente. And this foreigner, this Russian, what can he say that can hurt us?"

T turned to the eastern end of the park, away from the water, and nodded. "Over there, Torreo. Remember? It was many years ago, and we had a problem with that man on Busti Avenue, right there. I took care of it that night, and I have taken care of many things since. And," he said raising a finger, causing the men in the car and on the bench to sit up straight, "I have paid the price, more than once, for some of the things we have done."

Monteduro looked down and shook his head.

T clapped him on the shoulder, and they began walking again. "So, Torreo, how is the boy, and how is our Donna?"

"They're fine, Vicente, just fine. The boy does well in college, and she is happy, cleaning up after him when he is at home, like he was still a child."

"My friend, maybe you should take a vacation after this business is taken care of. Bring the wife down to Florida for a while. I'll take care of things while you're gone, don't worry. Maybe think about retiring down there. Get away from these Buffalo winters, like we talked about so many years ago. You've worked hard for what you've got, you deserve it."

They walked around the park, Torreo, with his head down, and Tutulomundo doing most of the talking, about anything but what was on their minds, and everyone watching them relaxed. When they got back to the car, they embraced again and shook hands. Torreo watched the car drive away, then nodded to Felix, and walked east out of the park towards Busti. *The pharmacist,* he thought. *He was going to talk after he bandaged me. He was the first one.*

They all watched Monteduro in the mirrors as they drove north out of the park. When he was out of sight, Tutulomundo lit a cigarette, cleared his throat, and spat out the window while the others waited. "The Russian. Get the man in Lovejoy for this.

Find the other woman, too."

# CHAPTER 85

## DEPEW, 1953

Johnny was behind the wheel, puffing on a Chesterfield, and Steve was chattering away about how the buds on the trees were coming out in the spring weather as they drove out to the Grove with a new pool table. Steve had his hand out the window, palm up, as he described the mechanics of the season. "Here, it doesn't take as long for the ground to get warm. The snow melts, giving the trees and plants plenty of water just as the, the. . . How do you say?" He hit his head with the heel of his hand with his eyes closed then, raising both palms, "What comes up from the roots. . .?"

"Sap, like you, Steve."

"What? Yes, sap. The insects, the bugs, you call them, they come up, too. Everything changes, you see. The colors, from the leaves and flowers, all new. The insects start to buzz, buzz, buzz in the heat, and the plants and flowers smell like nice perfume. I love spring. I like to go out to the country like this," he said, hoping Johnny would take him out there for a picnic with his family again, sometime. Johnny's wife would fix terribly cheap sandwiches on awful white bread like she always did, but that was okay, he guessed. He could listen to the boy talk about what he learned from school and tell him about science. Johnny would bring lots of beer, cheap beer, but that was okay, too, and he could ride in the car and enjoy the country.

They pulled up to the Grove, a roadhouse far east of the city, where Germans and Poles held big picnics in the summer. As Johnny screwed the pool table's frame together, Steve saw flyers on the bar's wall, advertising outings for churches and fraternal groups, and saw framed pictures of such outings from years past; black and white photographs fading to shades of yellow and brown; of smiling people satiated on wurst, potato salad, and beer; with hand-written, white lettering on them announcing the group and the date. One group particularly caught his eye—the Harugari Frohsinn and Bickelman's Band, 1926, a bunch of men in white shirts, some with tubas, trombones and trumpets, instruments in one hand, beer in the other. Steve nodded, thinking music, too; what joy it must have been to have many friends like that. Raising his index finger, he proclaimed, "Very good for working people to come out in the country, Johnny. Get out in the fresh air," hoping this idea would germinate and blossom with a reward for himself. "Breathe country air and get the soot out of the chest."

"Yeah, well, suck in a few more breaths of fresh air and let's go out to the truck and haul that slate in here," Johnny replied, flipping the butt of his cigarette into the gravel parking lot. "You drop this baby and you'll be cutting the grass for these Krauts all summer, paying for it."

While they carefully lifted the heavy slate for the pool table, Johnny braced his face up against its flat, cool surface and thought about what Tutulomundo had said. Listening to the Uke wheeze as they slowly walked the slate back into the bar, he, too, saw the notices of outings when it hit him. *Perfect. Get him out in the country with a bunch of people he hardly knows. He rolls back into town at a set time with a bag on and has to walk home at night.*

As they drove back to town, Johnny spoke little, even less than usual. "That pool table's on the only sorta flat surface on the floor in the room. Took me a while to get the legs adjusted so it'd be flat."

"Stupid game, this pool," Steve spat, reflecting on the only occasion he'd tried playing it. Three young guys with leather jackets had been looking for a fourth to play partners, and Steve had jumped in, hoping to make friends with some of the barroom regulars. His first shot, he had sent the cue ball twirling off the side of the stick, knocking one of the opposition's balls into a pocket.

"Oh, Christ, whaddid I get for a partner?" his teammate asked, as the others laughed.

Embarrassed, Steve silently kept playing, never sinking a shot, and often setting up the opposition for a long run of the balls.

"Hell, man," his partner complained, "At least don't give them a leave."

Steve looked blankly around the table, wondering what a leave was. When the game was over, Steve put the stick down and went back to the bar. He had never even learned their names, those rude boys, and when other friends of theirs arrived, they never even noticed he was gone.

*Jesus*, Johnny thought, *Why do I bother trying to teach this guy stuff? Hmmph, won't matter now, anyway, I guess.*

"I gotta stop by the house on the way back, make a phone call."

"Are Harriet and Jimmy going to be home?" Steve said, smiling at the thought of seeing the family.

"Dunno, maybe," Johnny replied, wondering for just a second what the kid might be doing that day.

When they pulled up in front of his house, Jimmy was playing with a model airplane, zooming it around the tiny patch of a front yard in a great air battle. Steve smiled and nodded, then got out to watch, bouncing on his toes.

"Hiya, Mr. Tovsenko," the boy greeted him. "Did you see my new plane? It's a P-51 Mustang!"

"Oh, yes, let's see that, Jimmy," Steve said as Johnny went around them, up the steps, into the house, and into the kitchen. He looked around. She must be in the basement. Quickly dialing the number of the lounge, he cupped his hand around the receiver and looked around again.

"Yeah, lemme talk to Twitch."

"Who wants him?"

"Johnny."

"Yeah, Johnny."

"It's gonna be all set for this Saturday. I'll let you know where and when tonight."

"I'll see you at the joint."

"Right. Bye."

As he hung up, his wife came up the steps from the basement with a basket of laundry. She stopped when she saw him, her lower lip tightening.

"Just came to use the phone. Gotta go back to work," and, brushing by her, he went out the front door.

"C'mon, Steve, we got work to do."

"Aw, dad," Jimmy said as Steve handed the silver plane back to the boy, their smiles fading.

When they drove away, Jimmy watching them, Johnny pulled out the last cigarette from the pack, crushed the paper package and tossed it out the window. Snapping open the Zippo lighter he'd lifted from a drunk guy at the Legion Hall, he took a puff, spat a strand of tobacco out and asked Steve, "You like the country, huh?"

Jerking his shoulders slightly in surprise, Steve looked at Johnny, wide-eyed with surprise, and answered, "Yes. I grew up on wheat farm. My family lived near Valky. That is near Kharkov. For generations before the war . . ."

"Well, here, pal," Johnny interrupted, pulling an orange ticket out of his shirt pocket. "They're having this shindig out at the Grove this Saturday. Thought you might like it."

Reading the ticket, Steve said, "St. Mary Magdalene Church. That is near my house. . . Can I go to this? I am Orthodox, not Catholic."

"Sure, you can, they don't care. Go and have a ball, Uke."

Reaching for his wallet, Steve continued, "How much. . ."

Smiling through the smoke, Johnny waved it away. "Nuthin. You been working hard, the business is doing good, go and have some fun. I'll take the service calls that night."

"Oh," Steve said with disappointment, "So, you will not be going?" Then, brightening again, Steve asked, "Will Harriet and Jimmy be going?"

"Nah, they got stuff to do. There's lots of people going, it'll be fun."

"But," he said, staring at the ticket, "I don't have a car, how will I get there?"

"Not to worry. Just show up at the church when the ticket says. They'll have a bus to get you there and back. Practically door-to-door, you can drink all you want."

Remembering the blonde-haired Polish girls coming and

going from the church, Steve spent the rest of the afternoon boring Johnny with the history of Ukranian-Polish conflicts over the centuries, right down to the foods they prepared, how they didn't seem to matter here, and how he spoke a little Polish himself. While he prattled on, Johnny concentrated on how he would drop Steve off after they were done, what route he would take from Steve's neighborhood to the bar in Lovejoy, and where there might be cheap gas to buy for the truck.

# CHAPTER 86

## ERIE COUNTY HALL DOWNTOWN, 1953

Assistant District Attorney Roth had dry-cleaned his gray suit and gotten his hair cut the day before, anticipating today's hearing, but he was disappointed when he opened the door into the waiting room and didn't see his prize witness.

"Tovsenko. Stepan Tovsenko," he said, looking around the room at the other scheduled witnesses and their blank looks. "Any of you see Mr. Tovsenko? Heavy set, beard, glasses, foreign accent? No?" He then went out into the hallway and looked up and down, but the only one there was the janitor swinging a mop.

"Hey Kaz," he called, smelling the ammonia floor wash, "You see a fat guy with a beard anywhere around here?"

The janitor shook his head and continued swinging the mop to and fro on the linoleum floor.

"Shit," the lawyer said softly, and then cleared his throat and went back through the waiting room, avoiding the stares of the witnesses. In the grand jury room, the jurymen watched him slowly walk over to the table where Mr. Stone and another lawyer were bent over some papers.

"He's not here, Mr. Stone," he said in a whisper.

Stone's head jerked up in surprise, and then he thought for a second. "Ken, go find one of Wachter's cops and tell them to go get him. Tim, go get the next witness."

Roth quietly exited the jury room, went through the waiting room, and dashed down the hall over the wet floor, into the investigator's office. There, he found Stormy, by himself, at his desk, hat tilted on the back of his head, steaming coffee before him, reading the sports page. Roth hesitated, knowing Stormy's reputation, but seeing he was the only one available, Roth went forward.

"Detective Snyder," he began.

Stormy smiling at the unaccustomed respect.

"There's a witness who seems to be late. Mr. Stone needs you to go and pick him up."

Pulling on his suit coat, Stormy moved quickly, grateful at the opportunity. "Sure," he said, buttoning his coat and adjusting his hat forward. "Who is it?"

"It's the Ukrainian guy, Stepan Tovsenko." Looking at the papers in his hand, Roth said, "He lives at 166 Woeppel Street. He's got a phone, too, Fillmore 4319. Make sure he knows how serious this is, and get him here." Roth then walked out of the office and back to the Jury Room as Kaz thought, *Nobody gives a shit about what I do here*, mopping that section of the floor for the third time.

No one answered the phone at Tovsenko's number, and Stormy was glad for that. Now, he could get out of the office and take one of the DA's cars and go get this guy. Getting into the elevator, he heard the janitor mutter something in Polish, and wondered what that guy's problem was. In the basement parking lot, he admired the sturdy Ford and settled into the front seat, feeling like a detective again. As he drove out to the East Side neighborhood to Tovsenko's address, he started thinking like a detective again. *Let's see, two-story houses there, probably lives upstairs. Check the front door, see if it's locked, and then go around the side; the tenant always uses the stairs on that side. Go right upstairs and surprise him, and then check with the owners downstairs to see where he's been if he ain't home.*

Pulling slowly past the house, he saw the front door closed tight, a few grocery store flyers scattered on the porch. *Good, they don't use the front door*, he thought. He looked down the driveway as he approached. No one in the backyard, just the laundry fluttering in the breeze, hanging out to dry. Stormy let himself in through the side door, which was unlocked. He trotted up the steps to the second floor and tried the flat's entrance, which was locked. Somebody on the first floor called out, "Who's that?"

Knocking on Steve's wooden door until it shook, Stormy announced, "Police. Mr. Tovsenko?"

At this, the housewife downstairs came out in the hallway and looked up at all six-feet-two of him. "What's this, the police?"

"Yes ma'am. Detective Snyder, district attorney's office." He pulled his badge out. "Is Mr. Stepan Tovsenko here?" Stormy figured they always knew when someone was home upstairs from the creaking wooden floors between the flats.

"No, he hasn't been home for a couple of days."

"Is this your house, ma'am?" He checked out her slender build. *Hmm, around thirty, not bad*, he thought.

"It most certainly is," she said.

"Do you have keys to his door, ma'am? He was supposed to be downtown today, and they were worried about him."

"Of course I got 'em. Why, did he do something wrong?"

"No, ma'am. He's okay with us. He was expected for a hearing this morning."

At ease now, the landlady pulled her keys out of her apron pocket and started sorting through them as she came up the stairs.

"Let's see, this one here should do it. I *never* come into his flat, you see. I give him his privacy. What was the hearing for? Is he getting his citizenship papers or something?"

"Yeah, something like that, I guess. They didn't tell me, just sent me to check on him."

"Oh, good, for a second there, I was afraid he might have been hooked up with some Commies or something. He says he's Ukrainian, and I hear that short wave radio of his speaking Russian, or something. I was born here, you know. My parents came from Poland, so I know it wasn't Polish."

She opened the door and twisted on the light to reveal the kitchen. A linoleum-topped table with steel legs and matching chairs were in the center. There was one place setting at one end, and two identical Zenith radios at the other, most of the guts out of one. The other appeared to be mostly assembled. Parts and tools were scattered on the table.

"He fixes radios for people sometimes. Takes him a while, but he does a good job. Fixed our floor model Admiral right away when it was on the fritz."

Mop and broom in the corner, glass-windowed cupboards,

pretty sparse with mismatched cups and plates. Coffee cup and plate in the sink. *Not a slob, must have left in the morning,* Stormy thought.

"Ma'am, could you stay here a moment while I look around in the other rooms? He might've fallen or something and . . ."

Grabbing the cross at her neck, she stepped back and said, "Sure, sure. Take a look round, see if he's okay."

He found more radios stacked around the dining room, boxes with parts from several models and a desk with manuals piled on it, a stack of correspondences, mostly bills and receipts, and a cup with pens and pencils. Down a narrow hallway, there was a bedroom to the left with nothing in it but cheap, cotton curtains on the windows facing the driveway. Across the hall was a bathroom, white, tiled floor, claw-foot tub, threadbare towels and face cloths. Standard stuff in the medicine chest—straight razor, toothpowder, toothbrush (worn). *Hmm, no pills, not even Aspirin.* Then, quickly into the back room. A bedroom with a big, double bed, rumpled sheets and blankets. *Just man-sweat, hmm, no girlfriend.* Open the closet, nothing but work clothes. Out the back door, a porch, one chair on it. As he walked by the kitchen the other way, he asked, "Mr. Tovsenko have many friends come over, ma'am?"

"No, not many at all. Mostly people come by to get their radios he fixed."

"Anybody stop by since Saturday, looking for him?"

"No, nobody I saw."

In the front living room were a sagging couch and an easy chair, a big RCA floor model radio and a short wave set on top of it. Across from the radios, a brick fireplace with cold ashes, probably from this past winter. On the mantle, a few framed pictures. One of a house with a thatched roof, an old man with a beard and a cane out front. Another with a much thinner Tovsenko with his arms around an even skinnier version of himself and a girl with the same smile and dark hair. Family. Another picture, this more recent, showed a beaming Steve standing over a new pinball machine with Johnny Walters. Must have been taken at a trade show. A quick glance in the coat closet—overcoat, jacket, raincoat, sweater. Stormy snatched the picture from the trade show, tucked it under his coat, and went back into the kitchen.

"Well, he's not here, ma'am."

She exhaled with relief.

"When

did you last see him?"

"Well, let's see. Saturday morning. He left kind of around ten. Had a new plaid summer shirt on, like he was going out somewhere."

"Does he have a girlfriend?"

"No, I don't think so. He watches the Pozluzny girls across the back fence from his porch when they're hanging out the laundry, but he's too shy to talk to them. He works for that machine company during the day, sometimes goes out on service calls at night. That and his radios, that's Steve."

"I see. Well, when he comes back, have him call our office." He fished a card out of his pocket, and took a pencil out, and wrote the DA's office number on the back. "My name's Snyder, Detective Snyder."

"Well, okay, then," she said, following him to the door. "I hope he's all right. We'll give you a call when he comes in, detective."

With a slight tip of his hat, Stormy left, wishing he'd gotten a chance to take a quick look in the refrigerator without her noticing him snooping. Some guys told their whole lives with what's in the refrigerator. *This guy's was probably empty*, he'd bet.

Driving back, he tossed the picture on the seat next to him and got two ideas. One was that the Dom Gabryszak was around the corner on Fillmore, and they were quiet this time of day. The other was the phone number of Walters Vending he'd gotten off a calendar in the kitchen. As he rolled up to the curb by the bar, he thought about how he'd yanked a drunk off the stool with one hand and tossed him through the screen door there, years ago, when he was in uniform. The old lady was in the bar by herself and the guy was a real loud drunk, telling her how he wasn't going to pay. Stormy showed up, and the guy looked around, and then bent over and spat on the floor, just in front of his shoes. One hand on the scruff of his neck, a good yank, and the bum was face-first on the concrete. A foot on his neck convinced him to come up with his wallet, and rather than arrest him, Stormy had left him with a dollar from about eight, paid the bartender and stowed the rest.

Glancing through the big glass window of the bar, Stormy saw the same old lady behind the bar. You'd have to put dynamite under this one to get her away from the business, he thought as he strode through the screen door.

"Hello, Mrs. Gabryszak." He beamed as she adjusted her glasses to focus on him.

Slowly taking the cigarette out of her mouth and putting it carefully in an ashtray, she looked the big man over and nodded.

"Remember me?" he said with a smile, sure that she did.

"Yes," she replied, nodding slightly.

"Snyder. I helped you get a nasty rumball out of here a few years ago."

"I remember. Are you still on the force?"

He pulled out his badge, chuckled, and said, "Oh, yes, I'm a detective now." Ignoring the payphone on the wall, he pointed to the phone behind the bar and inquired cheerfully, "May I use the phone? Official business."

Stepping back, but keeping an eye on the freeloading cop, she waved him towards it. Stormy stepped behind the bar and picked up the receiver. In the spotless mirror, he noticed two old guys down the bar reading the paper and silently drinking short drafts of beer. The old lady watched him like a hawk. The old guys he figured for retirees, and the old lady probably had a bat behind the bar to hit him with if he tried as much as swiping a quick shot of her cheapest whiskey. No one answered at the Walters Vending office. As he dialed the number to the DA's office, he noticed the old lady fidgeting. *Yeah, that's right, you old bat, I'm making another phone call on city business.*

"Assistant State's Attorney Roth, please," he said in his most officious voice. Then, "Detective Snyder calling."

When the lawyer came on the line, Stormy turned away so the old lady couldn't hear. "Mr. Roth, Snyder here. I checked Tovsenko's house. Hasn't been there for a coupla days. He went out on Saturday like he was going to a party, or something, and never came back. Nothing hinky in his flat, either. I called his work, the vending company, but no one answers. Probably out on business. You want me to go check over there?"

"Yes," Roth replied, "Find out when they saw him last, and then get back here."

Stormy barely got out, "Right," before he heard the click from the other end. Strutting out from behind the bar, he said "Thank you," and went out the door. Out of the corner of his eye he saw the old lady looking around the phone to see if he'd taken anything.

Stormy parked across Allen Street from Walters' vending shop and observed the place for a few minutes. He didn't see anyone moving around inside, and the storefront was pretty nondescript—no signs hanging out over the sidewalk or painted on the storefront window. He crossed the street, tried the door and found it locked. Above the door in the recessed entrance was the street address, 69 Elmwood, so he knew he had the right place. Through the window, Stormy could see a desk with nothing on it, and a chair. That small room was separated from the back by a cheaply made wall that extended up about six feet with a curtain over the doorway. He walked down a driveway to the back of the place where a very solid garage door facing the alley was secured with a big padlock. He was walking back up the driveway when a pickup truck with a jukebox in the back squeezed past him and into the alley. Stormy waited a minute, and then followed the truck. The driver, a little guy with brown hair, was bent over, unlocking the padlock when Stormy suddenly stood over him and said, "Is this Walters Vending?"

Johnny jumped up and looked around for which way to run.

"I said," Stormy repeated, recognizing Johnny from the picture, "Is this Walters' Vending?"

Trapped, Johnny squared his shoulders and dropped his chin. "Who wants to know?"

Pulling out his badge, Stormy stepped closer to the little man and said, "Snyder. District attorney's office. Do you work here?"

After a quick glance to see what was behind him, Johnny said, "Yeah, I work here."

"What's your name?"

Staring at a brick in the wall over Stormy's shoulder, Johnny answered, "John Walters."

"Do you know Stepan Tovsenko?"

"Yeah, he works here."

"Where is he?"

"Dunno," Johnny said, steadily looking at the brickwork. "He didn't show up for work today."

"Did you call him, check on him?"

"Yeah, yeah, called his house, rode over there, he ain't home. Must have a broad or something. All I know is, now I gotta find somebody to help me get this juke off the truck and into the shop."

Nodding at the garage door, Stormy said, "Is it possible he's inside?"

"No, nobody's inside, it's locked. Look, officer, I got a lot of work to do, and I gotta go find somebody to get this juke inside. I been in and out of this shop a couple of times today already. He ain't around. . . Did he do something wrong?"

"No, we just want to talk to him about citizenship papers he put in a while back."

"Oh."

Writing his name and office phone number on paper from his notebook, Stormy said, "Well, Mr. Walters, give us a call when his girlfriend tosses him back, or he sobers up, will you?"

"Oh, yeah, sure," Johnny answered, saluting the policeman with the paper. "I'll have him call you as soon as he shows back up."

Stormy walked back down the driveway to his car, hands in his pockets, whistling to himself. Johnny stared after him and took a deep breath, thinking, *I'm between the cops and Mr. T's guys, now. I gotta stay cool as a cucumber, whatever happens.*

Back at his desk, Stormy tilted his hat back and thought, *The guy, Walters, is a lying son of a bitch. He never checked on this Tovsenko guy, the landlady would've known. He knows something.*

# CHAPTER 87

## SOUTH BUFFALO, 1953

As Probationary Patrolman Leo Dunleavy walked down a deserted southside parkway, he caught the first rays of the sun rising over the buildings on his right. Checking his Timex, he thought, *Less than two hours until the end of the shift and I don't feel tired at all.* Coming down the street, he practiced twirling his nightstick, bouncing the wooden tip on the pavement and sending it up into the air at the end of the long, leather thong. At a hardware store, he took the stick in his right hand, stepped into the building's open foyer and shook the door handle, making sure it was locked. Shining his flashlight into the store, he looked "for signs of burglary, fire, or vandalism" like the training manual said. *Nothing.* Stepping back out onto the sidewalk, he glanced up where Abbott met Southside and spotted the green light lit above the police call box. Rushing up to it, he wondered, *What could it be? Burglary? Robbery? I didn't hear any gunshots.* He pulled out his keys and fumbled for the one that would open the cast-iron box, picked up the phone, and heard it buzz. When the operator picked it up, Leo said, "Patrolman Dunleavy, Three Platoon, Fifteenth Precinct."

"Investigate the report of a body found along Cazenovia Creek. See a boy named McCarthy at the Stevenson Street Bridge."

Hearing sirens in the distance, Dunleavy ran as fast as he could to Stevenson. *Gotta be first on the scene for this one*, he thought.

# CHAPTER 88

## ERIE COUNTY HALL, 1953

The inspector was checking over the assignments as the three detectives waited outside his office. Lou sat on the edge of Pat's desk, describing the Bisons' prospects in the AHL next season, how many games he figured on attending, and would Pat want to go in for two season tickets with him?

"I figure it this way," Lou said. "They play thirty-five home games, and I figure on making twenty of them. Okay, you figure you'll make maybe fifteen? They made the playoffs last season, and they're stronger this year with Don Marshal and Eddie Slowinski, so it'll be a lot of good games to see. That means there's thirty-five tickets to take care of. Sometimes you take a date, maybe that nurse from the accident room, huh? Sometimes I'll bring a date. That'll take care of at least ten tickets. Your dad, your brother, Tim, your sister and her husband, my brother and," he added, *sotto voce*, "My Uncle George will use most of the rest. Anything left over, maybe we sell them."

Stormy sat at his desk silently, drinking coffee, wondering if he was going to be invited in on the deal. He stared straight ahead, thinking that these guys would never trust him when the inspector tapped papers on his desk to straighten them, and cleared his throat—his signal for them to come in and get their assignments. They all approached his office and waited for him to wave them in.

"C'mon in boys, we've got some witnesses to interview and some. . . other details to take care of."

The three walked in and stood before his desk, careful not to put their hands in their pockets, which the inspector said "made them look like some farmer waiting for the hay to ripen."

"Okay, Lou and Pat, I want you lads to head down over to the morgue and see if you can identify a body they have over there. From its description, it may be our missing witness Tovsenko. Then, I want you to go down and talk to the homicide detectives who caught this case and see what you can dig up about it, and talk to the patrolman, uhh," he hesitated, looking over his glasses at the paperwork, "A rookie patrolman named Dunleavy down there in the Fifteenth Precinct who found the body."

Stormy slowly raised his hand at the elbow and coughed. Wachter looked up at him.

"Uh, Inspector? If it'd help, I've got a picture of Tovsenko to help identify the body."

"A picture of the witness we're looking for?"

"Yessir."

"Where'd you get it?" he said with mild surprise.

"I lifted it from his flat when Roth sent me to pick him up for the grand jury hearing, the day he disappeared. I've been showing it around at places he hung out, trying to get a lead on him when I got a chance. It's a picture of him and his boss, the Walters guy from a trade show."

Pat and Lou glanced at each other and the inspector looked at Stormy with a new eye, placing his hands on the armrests of his desk chair. "That's very diligent work, Detective. That being the case," he said slowly, "Let's rearrange the details. Pat and Lou, go talk to the men in Homicide and young Patrolman Dunleavy down in South Buffalo, and Snyder, you go to the morgue and see if you can identify the body—and get his landlady or somebody to make a positive identification if you think it's him. You take the squad car, and you, Lieutenant, you and Patrick walk over to the homicide office and talk to the men there. When you're ready to go down to the Fifteenth Precinct and see Donovan, take my car." Wachter stood up, again tapped the papers straight on his desk, and the three detectives took their leave.

Pat and Lou stopped to get their raincoats from the office rack, but Stormy went out after just grabbing his hat. On their way over to police headquarters on Franklin Street, Pat asked Lou, "Do you think that guy can be trusted?"

Lou shook his head, "I dunno. I heard that he used to do a hell of a job when he had a mind to in the old days, but after the shakedowns, the whores, and the booze got to him, he had to trade doing favors for politicians to keep his job. I'm guessing the boss wants to see if he's still in somebody's pocket or not."

Going past the spit-shined and starched lieutenant at the First Precinct's front desk at the entrance to headquarters, they went to the fourth floor of the building where the murder detectives met behind a frosted glass door that read *Homicide Squad* in curved Algerian script above *Lieutenant Pasquale Tedesco, Chief.*

They knocked at the door. On hearing a brusque military, "Come in," they walked into an office similar to their own. A couple of the desks were occupied, and Pat noticed the men favored shoulder harnesses for their weapons, either military automatics or long-barreled revolvers. A dark-skinned man with a black flat top stood up and said, "You're the guys from Inspector Wachter?"

"That's us," Lou answered with a smile.

"I'm Lieutenant Tedesco. Detective Sergeant Hourihan has the case you're interested in." He pointed to a desk where a curly-headed detective stared hard at a hatchet held between his hands. After they approached the desk, Hourihan took a couple of seconds to notice them.

"Yes, gentlemen," Hourihan said, coming out of his study and putting the hatchet down on his desk. He stood up, waved to a couple of chairs and shook their hands. "Pat Hourihan," he said as they sat down, curious about the heavy blood-stained object between them.

Hourihan picked up the hatchet and said, "Trying to figure out how an eighty-five-pound woman, barely five feet tall, could damn near split a five-foot, ten-inch man's skull almost in two . . . Well, you guys are here about the body that was found along Caz Creek." He picked up a report from an in basket and read. "The body was found by a kid who was walking his dog along the water. He called the police and the first to respond was the beat officer on duty, a new guy named Dunleavy. He protected the scene until the precinct detectives got there, and they called us. Looks like the body had been there about two, maybe three days. Checking out the scene, we didn't find much. It's pretty marshy right there, and any footprints were gone. We talked to the kid, he didn't know anything. We canvassed the neighborhood, and so far, it doesn't look like anyone saw anything. The body had one bullet hole right in the back of the neck. Small caliber. His head had a big lump in the back, too, and he had ligature marks on his wrists. Looks like the killers snatched this guy from someplace else, tied him up, whacked him on the noggin, shot him, and dumped him nice and quiet in the bushes. No tire marks around there, either."

"Anyone missing from the neighborhood?" Lou asked. "They're pretty tight around there in Saint Theresa's," Lou asked.

Giving Lou a "What, do you think we're dopes here?" look, Houlihan continued. "We checked around for missing locals, bad guys, shifty guys, and good guys, and it doesn't look like anyone's missing and no one's coughing up anything to us, yet. Police surgeon's report says the guy was a white male; about thirty years old; six feet; about two-eighty-five; brown, straight hair; beard; and blue eyes. Dressed in green work pants; scuffed, brown shoes; and a new plaid shirt. The doc said he had a pretty good package on board when he died. Nothing found in his pockets—no wallet, no keys, no change, not even a handkerchief. Somebody was being real careful when they bumped off this guy. They left him where we'd eventually find him, long after they were gone—and maybe send a message to someone else."

"Any ideas about who did this?" Lou asked.

"We've been hearing some noise about local gamblers getting squeezed out by some guys from Cleveland lately, so, at first we thought it might be some local bookie. One guy, named Ferraro, disappeared last year and we hear he's in Lake Erie for not giving up the franchise. We've been checking out rumors in South Buffalo, but nothing's come up yet, and that's when we heard you guys are missing a witness in your pinball investigation, a Russian guy or something, who vanished a little before this guy turned up."

"Anything else?" Lou said to the sergeant.

"Not much, yet. The young fella on the beat who found him, Dunleavy, he seems pretty squared away. He's been helping us and following up on stuff down there in South Buffalo. I'd go talk to him, and if you guys can ID this body, it'd help a lot. We sent the fingerprints out, but that'll take time to come back, if they can get a match at all."

Firing up the inspector's big car, Lou finally said, "If this is our guy, and I think it is—height, weight, hair, and eyes match Tovsenko's, he gets found a few days after our guy goes missing— it means we're dealing with a whole different animal here, partner. Not just some guys trying to make a fast buck on a bunch of suckers with pinball machines, but someone who's willing to kill, and a government witness, too, to cover it up. Not good. Let's face it, there's also some guys in the department looking the other way about gambling on these machines, and if this leads back to some people on the force, it's going to get real ugly around here."

They pulled up in front of the Fifteenth Precinct on South Park Avenue, with its red brick walls and sandstone pillars. Trotting up to the double door entrance, both plainclothesmen hoped all the patrolmen noticed the late model Hudson with the white walls they drove. Inside, Lou shook the rain off his hat and Pat wiped his face with his hand. They approached the front desk, and Lou and the desk lieutenant both smiled and shook hands.

"Well, as I live and breathe," the desk lieutenant said. "If it isn't the mighty Lou Constantino."

"Hah! Fatboy Meegan, how are ya?" Lou said. "Marty, this is my partner, Pat Brogan. Pat, this is Marty Meegan. He used to try to crack my head open when he played linebacker for South Park."

"Lieutenant," Pat said as he shook hands, reaching over the tall desk.

"It helped him later on, when we were wrestling hop heads, drunks, and perverts out of the bars on Allen Street."

Lou shook his head at the memories of his days on a beat.

"Hey, Marty, we're here to see a patrolman, guy named Dunleavy."

The lieutenant nodded over to his right, where a tall, young man with curly, fair hair sat straight on a wooden bench. He wore a new, uniform tunic with a highly-polished belt and shoes. Pat noticed the patrolman had his black slicker raincoat folded neatly beside him with his hat atop it, regulation rain cover in place. He stood up as they approached and shook their hands. "Patrolman Leo Dunleavy, Fifteenth Precinct, Number Three Platoon," he introduced himself.

Lou asked, "Someplace we can talk, Dunleavy?"

As if giving directions, the young policeman pointed to the reserve room, and followed them in through the swinging doors.

Lou smiled, "Have a seat, kid, this is your station house."

When they were all seated and at ease, Lou asked the blue suit about finding Tovsenko's body. Pulling out his notebook, Dunleavy spoke, glancing occasionally at his notes.

"Let's see, April Twelfth. Okay. Midnight shift, six-hundred forty-five hours. Thomas McCarthy, age twelve, address 71 Mumford Street. He tells me he found a body along Caz Creek when he was walking his dog Punchie. He leads me over there, through the bushes, just off of Melrose Street, where I find a heavyset, white male, on his face, partially submerged. There's a lot of water there in the bushes by the creek, swallows up any footprints as soon as they're made. I check the body first. He's cold as a mackerel. Except for where we came through, none of the bushes are pushed down out of place. Then, I ask this McCarthy kid his address and if he called the police from his house. He says his family doesn't have a phone; he called from a neighbor's house on Stevenson. From that, the time it took me to get the call and get over there, I figure he found the body right around six-hundred thirty.

"I step back, away from the scene, the way I came in. While I was waiting for the detectives, I keep everybody away from the scene, check the ground and street for tire tracks, but I don't find any. I look around, and I try to see where this spot's visible from the houses nearby. Then, when the detectives get there, I help them canvass the neighborhood. I gave them all the notes from that." He stopped, blinking, trying to remember if he'd left anything out.

Lou waited a second or two to see if the young man would remember anything else, and then said, "That's good, Dunleavy, that's a good report. Sergeant Hourihan up in Homicide says you've been looking around since then, too."

Dunleavy collected his thoughts a moment. "I didn't find any-one who saw anything, yet, but there's this old lady, Miss Murphy, who lives on Stevenson by the bridge, who's kind of a busybody. Lives there with her sister and brother-in-law, doesn't work any-more. If anyone saw anything, she would've. Kinda shy, though. I stop by their house when I'm walking the beat and talk to her from time to time, getting to know her. Turns out I was an altar boy with a nephew of hers named Pete McGowan over at St. Brigid's when I was a kid. Anyway, I'll keep talking to her and to some of the other neighborhood people and see what I can turn up for you."

They all stood up, and Lou tapped the patrolman on the shoul-der with his notebook. "Keep up the good work, kid, and keep your eyes and ears open, eh?"

Dunleavy beamed with pride.

Lou handed Dunleavy a card with their DA office phone num-ber on it. "And if you come up with anything else about this case, anything at all— like about pinball games, give us a call directly."

Dunleavy looked down at the card, and, knitting his brows, nodded. He slipped the card in a pocket and answered, "Yes, sir."

As they went out to the car, Lou asked, "Whaddya think?"

"I think the kid's sharp, like Houlihan said. He did the right stuff and he's following up well. He's a go-getter, all right."

"Yeah," Lou said. "You think he's on the pad with any of these guys down here?"

"No," Pat answered firmly. "The way he answered when you gave him our card tells me he knows something about it, though."

"That's the way I got it figured too," Lou said as they got into the Hudson. "We should stay in touch with young Mr. Dunleavy there." As they drove off, he added, "Hey, I wonder how Stormy's doing at the morgue?"

Pat nodded, thinking that Dunleavy was a few years younger than they were, and how he reminded him of himself before he went off to war.

Stormy hustled down the steps towards the garage and then

remembered the picture. He was breathing hard when he got back to the office and rummaged through the drawers in his desk until he found the picture of Tovsenko and Walters at the trade show. Going quickly back down to the garage, he thought out his moves. *Let's see, got the picture of the witness, next, go pick up the landlady on Woeppel Street, make sure she gets a good look at the picture first, and then show her the body.* As he drove, he twisted his neck around in anticipation. Pulling into the driveway, he noticed the landlady through the screen door, pulling newly-delivered bottles out of the milk box. He nodded and smiled at her, then tucked the photo into the glove box. She stood there, cradling the milk bottles in her arms as she watched him get out of the car. He walked slowly around the car, and then asked, "May I come in?"

She nodded, and he followed her up the short staircase to the first floor flat.

*Nice ass*, he thought, but quelled his thoughts about trying to make her, and concentrated on what he should say.

When they got into her kitchen, he began by taking off his hat. Indicating to her with the fedora, he began, "Mrs. Zelinski, we need your assistance."

"Oh?" she said, arms across her chest.

Forcing his eyes upwards to hers, Stormy continued. "Yes, ma'am. We found someone we believe may be your tenant, Mr. Tovsenko."

"Oh, where is he? I mean is he . . ."

"The man we found is dead, ma'am, and we think it might be him. We need you to come and see, for sure, if it is him."

"Well, I . . ."

"It'll take less than an hour. I'll drive you there and back before lunchtime," he said, wondering if she had kids in school that might come home for lunch.

"Well, I suppose . . ."

"If you'll just get a coat," he smiled, "It's raining pretty hard out. I don't want you to get all wet."

After she got her coat, he followed her out to the car. She stood by the passenger side door, but he gently directed her towards the back of the car and opened the rear door.

"Oh, my. Just like a taxi," she smiled.

"Everything nice and clean back there?"

"Oh, yes. Is this your car, detective?"

"This is one of the district attorney's cars that we use."

They drove off, and Stormy noticed her in the rearview mirror, looking out the windows as they went through the neighborhood. *Her phone will be buzzing this afternoon,* he thought, *With the neighbors asking all about where she went. I wonder what her husband will think?* After a few minutes, he reached into the glove box and pulled out the photo.

"Do you think you could look at this picture for me?" he asked, handing it to her.

"Sure," she answered. "Yeah, that's Steve. I know the other guy, too. That's Johnny Walters, his boss." Shifting in her seat, she added, "He thinks he's quite the ladies man, that guy."

"Have you seen him lately?" he asked, watching her in the mirror.

"The last time I saw him was the last night before Steve disappeared. He dropped him off after work and gave me a look and drove off."

Stormy digested that for a second. "Any idea where Steve went out that Saturday?"

"No, I think it might've been a party or a picnic, or something. He had a nice shirt on."

As they drove up to Myer Memorial Hospital, Mrs. Zelinski pulled her raincoat around herself a little tighter and said, "Is that where he is?"

"Yes," Stormy answered, pulling the car around back. He, again, opened the door for her, and led her past smoking orderlies and nurses to a rear entrance. Mrs. Zelinski took his arm as they went down a yellow terra-cotta-tiled hallway to the morgue. He left her in the hallway, saying, "You stay here. It'll only take a minute."

Inside, two of the morgue attendants were eating sandwiches on a table to his left, and a desiccated skeleton, jaw agape and a few wisps of gray hair attached to the shriveled head, was laid out to his right.

Stormy winced, pulled out his badge and announced to the attendants, "I'm Detective Snyder with the DA's office. I have a witness outside who has to identify a body. Male John Doe; heavy-set, white guy; found along Caz Creek a few days ago."

Continuing to chew, the one attendant said to the other, "Gotta be the big boy in drawer eight. Take care of that, will ya Stew?"

Stew, putting down the sandwich on the butcher's paper, nod-ded and got up, heading for the far wall where there was a row of oversized drawers. As he walked across the hex-tiled floor, Stormy stopped him, grabbing him by the arm, and said, "Hey, do me a favor, pal, cover the old stiff up, will ya?"

"Oh, yeah, sure, no problem," Stew pulled a sheet across the deteriorated remains, and then went over and opened drawer eight, where the blue gray body of a big man with a beard was laying naked on the tray.

"Stew," Stormy commanded, "Get a sheet to cover most of this guy. It's a lady, and she only needs to look at his face."

"Oh, yeah, sure, detective."

As Stormy went past the other attendant who was finishing his sandwich and reading the paper, he shook his head.

Taking her arm again, he led the landlady into the morgue, hoping there wasn't anything still exposed that would make her puke and not go through with it. She held on tightly while he led her over where Stew stood by the drawer, waiting to get back to his sandwich. He pulled it open, and she stared in with curiosity.

"Is that him? Stepan Tovsenko?"

"Yes, I'd say it's him, all right. Beard and everything."

"Okay, that's fine. You can close it up again, Stew. Do you have his personal possessions?"

"Yeah, you want a look at that, too?" "Yeah, now," Stormy ordered.

Stew sighed and went and got the big bag with his clothes. Stormy rooted through it until he found the shirt. He showed the checked shirt to Mrs. Zelinski.

"Do you think this is the shirt he was wearing the last time you saw him?"

"Yeah, it sure looks like it, I guess."

"Fine," the policeman said, stuffing the shirt back in the bag. Looking at Stew, he said, "I'm gonna need you to sign the witness papers that she," indicating the landlady, "Positively identified the body of Stepan Tovsenko and the shirt listed as being on him when found."

"Yeah, yeah, yeah, I'll take care of it, detective, don't worry," Stew said, returning the property bag to its file cabinet.

Driving her back to her house, both were silent. Just a couple of tears, he noticed.

"You know," she finally said as they approached her street, "It reminds me of when my Uncle Gregor died. He looked a lot like that guy in the morgue, but not as big." When he let her out of the car, he thanked her for her service and noticed the tears starting.

Sniffling, she said, "When they get done with him. There. Give us a call. I don't know if he's got any family to bury him," and, with that, she turned away, crying, and went into the house. Stormy rushed back to the office with the news.

Back at County Hall, Stormy saw the elevator would take a while and rushed up the stairs. He stopped just outside their door, took a deep breath, and walked into the bullpen where Lou and Pat were talking to the inspector. Wachter looked at him and asked, "Well?"

"It's him, all right. The landlady identified him and his shirt. She says he went out Saturday morning to a party or a picnic, but she doesn't know where. Not only that, she ID'd Johnny Walters as dropping him off the night before at his house after work."

The three other detectives looked at each other, and then the boss spoke carefully.

"All right, then. Patrick, call over to Detective Sergeant Hourihan at Homicide and give him the news. We'll want to work this together with those guys. Tedesco keeps a good shop, we can trust them. Lou, you sit on Walters, so we can get him when we want him. Storm. . . Snyder, good job. Make sure you cross all the Ts and dot all the Is with the paperwork for the identification. When you're done with that, a lawyer from the DA's office and I want to see you in my office. We've got another assignment for you. Boys, we're going to build a little sweatbox for Mister

Walters with the men from Homicide, and we're going to do it right."

Pat got Hourihan on the phone and gave him the update on Stepan's death. "Uh, huh, uh, huh," he said. "Good. We'll set up Interview Room Number Two for our friend Walters. You, me, Constantino, and my man Palezewski, will work it. Before we get him in here, we'll all sit down and talk about how to get the facts from Mr. Walters there." Before he hung up, Pat asked Hourihan if he'd figured out the axe murder. The sergeant chuckled, and then sang the Ethel Merman line, "Some get a kick from cocaine. . ."

# CHAPTER 89

## DOWNTOWN, 1953

Sam Dunaway got off the bus at the art deco Greyhound station on Main Street and lit a cigarette. Exhaling, he grabbed his suitcase when the driver tossed it out of the baggage compartment. He went into the busy waiting room, where the loudspeaker was announcing a bus boarding for Cleveland. A dozen or so travelers got up from the wooden benches and headed for the gate. Looking at his watch and the clicking schedule board, he saw he had a good two and a half hours before catching the connecting bus to Albany, where the gun show was being held, so he walked over to the bank of phone booths and shut himself into one, and then propped the thick phone book on his knee. *Hopefully*, he thought, *The page with Brogan's number on it won't be torn out of it.* Finding the Bs, his index finger tracked down Brogan. *Hell, there's gotta be twenty of them. Must be a lot of Irish in this town. Hmm, two Patricks and two more P. Brogans. What's a few nickels*, he thought as he dialed the first Patrick Brogan. Four phone calls later, between a cousin, a girl that sounded like a dish, and a guy who had gotten a lot of phone calls "for some cop named Pat Brogan," he connected with the number for Brogan, Joseph; 429 Woodward, and didn't the surly SOB answer the phone himself!

"Corporal Brogan! This is Sergeant Dunaway, 60th Infantry. Time for you to fall in and buy me a drink, son!"

There was silence while Pat processed the voice, the message, and the memories.

"Sarge?" he finally answered.

"Yeah, you dumb Yankee. How many Sergeant Dunaways you work for in the Infantry?"

"Uh, jeez. It took me a second, there. Where are you, Sarge?" he asked.

"At the Greyhound station with the bus exhaust and the cold wind blowin' in every time some fool opens the door. Is it always this cold and smoky in this town?"

"Uh, well it's nice in the summertime," Pat said.

"Shit, it's May now, going on June. When's that gonna happen?" he chuckled.

"It's not so bad, Sarge, you get used to it."

"Well, hell, boy, I ain't hangin' around long enough for that. Everything's been blooming in Kentucky for about two months, now."

Pat asked, "What are you doing in Buffalo, Sarge?"

"Changin' buses, Paddy boy. On my way to a gun show in Albany. Got a layover here and thought I'd call up an ol' Army buddy, see how he's doing. Maybe he'd show me a good place to eat and we could wash down some dinner with what passes for bourbon in these parts."

"Uh, okay, Sarge," Pat answered. "I'll come on down to the station and we'll get some chow. I'll be there in about thirty minutes. You like spaghetti and meatballs?"

"As long as it ain't C-rats, I'll try it."

Pat caught the cars downtown, and when he walked through the revolving doors on Main Street into the station, Dunaway jumped up from his seat on the bench and rushed forward to shake hands.

"Brogan, boy, it's good to see you. My," he said, continuing to shake his hand with his right and holding his elbow with his left, "You're lookin' good, soldier, skinny as ever."

"Good to see you too, Sarge."

"Hey, son, forget that 'Sarge' stuff; we're civilians now, remember? I'm Sam and you're Pat with our ruptured duck pins," the Kentuckian said, fingering the honorable discharge pin on the lapel of his jacket. "Hey, I been having a whale of a time just watching the people come and go from this place waiting for you. Some hot numbers passin' through here. Hitched yet? Kids?"

As they walked across Main Street, Pat wondered how much

"sippin' whiskey," as he called it, Dunaway had tipped from his flask in the waiting room. When they got to the Town Casino, a red-faced Dunaway looked around the brightly-lit dining room, smelled the fresh bread on the red checkerboard, linen-covered tables and said, "Yessir, this is my kinda' place, Mr. Patrick. Good job, soldier!" as they sat down at a table against the pressed tin wall.

Sam started to tear into the Italian bread and asked what his sharp-shooting corporal had done since the war. Pat briefly told Sam about the return to home—dropping out of college, going on the force, working as a detective. Sam asked about girls and family as they had drinks and then wanted to check out "his sidearm," which Pat was wise enough to leave under his coat, promising to show it to him later.

"See, one of the reasons I'm so interested in weapons is I sell them now. I run a hardware store back home, sell some hunting rifles and shotguns, but pistols, too, along with everything else. Always been interested in firearms, way before Uncle Sam got hold of me. Remember that automatic rifle we snatched from the Krauts near Monschau? Turns out the Russkies got some of them, too, and are making a weapon like them by the thousands. They call it a Kalashnikov. Before long, all their infantrymen will have them."

"Yeah, I remember Monschau," Pat said, looking down at his plate, and for the first time since leaving Kentucky, Sam Dunaway slid into melancholy as he remembered the three boys in his squad bleeding in the snow.

"Yeah, Monschau," he said, seeing Sweeny's shattered face, Voessler's blood pooling, and Thomas' silent death. They had another round, and although Pat had a late start, he was catching up to Dunaway's inebriated state.

Pat stared at the table for a few moments and then said, "Do you remember the prisoner detail you sent us on, Sarge?"

"Yeah, you brought those SS guys back to the POW depot in a bad snowstorm, sure."

"Well, all of them didn't make it back there," Pat said quietly.

"I don't get it, what do you mean?" Dunaway said, knowing

exactly what he meant.

"We were resting by the road. The prisoners were in a ditch. I fell asleep. The next thing I know, my guys are panicking, there's shooting, and the unarmed prisoners are getting killed by my men. I even bayoneted one of them and shot him, too, a young kid who was yelling 'don't shoot' with his hands up."

Swallowing some whiskey, Dunaway said, "Pat, an hour before that, those Nazi sombitches were trying to kill us. Remember Voessler, Thomas, and Sweeny? There were plenty of other good men I could name they killed, too. Heard of Malmedy? They shot our boys down, POWs, and didn't think twice about it. To hell with those Nazi bastards, son. Don't give them a second thought. They got it and we didn't. That's war."

"I lost control, Sarge. A simple easy detail, and I screwed it up."

"Now, listen to me, boy. Who knows what those sombitches had coming? Did I ever tell you about the concentration camps we liberated after you got transferred? You smelled the bodies two miles away. Never smelled anything like it, never saw anything like it in my life. Run by the SS. They killed thousands and thousands of innocent people. I tell you every damn thing they say happened in those camps is true. I was there, I saw it. Now, you forget about those Kraut SS assholes in Belgium. Shit, the two of us are lucky to be alive today." He paused, and Pat remained silent. Looking at the clock behind the bar, Sam said, "Say, what time is it getting to be? Holy shit, I got a bus to catch."

The two of them walked back quietly to the bus station, their somber mood finally broken by the people hustling around the waiting room, the clicking of the arrival/departure board, and the dispatcher announcing the buses. They shook hands and said goodbye.

Sam clapped Pat on the shoulder. "Stop worrying, Pat, you're a good man. Get a girl, start a family; you got your whole life in front of you." Sam got on the bus and sat down in the back, shaking his head at Pat's confession, and his reaction to what Sam saw as a desperate battle for survival, a time of madness to be lived through, a pit they were thrown into with guns and grenades that they had climbed out of alive by wits and luck. He stifled a gag, as tomato sauce and pasta came up into his throat, and then took a pull at the flask as the bus thumped down the curb onto the street, hoping his own demons, visions, and smells of fly-covered corpses, and walking skeletons dressed in ragged stripes would stay away.

# CHAPTER 90

## DOWNTOWN, 1953

The homicide detectives had been dragging everybody and his brother in for questioning, and Constantino and Brogan were running back and forth from the DA's office to police headquarters on Franklin Street to assist. Wachter had a long conference behind closed doors with the homicide detectives before they brought Johnny Walters in, figuring he could tell them about the murder, the grafting, and the connections to the politicians and the hoods.

The inspector put Stormy to work, bringing witnesses to and from the grand jury. Most of them had been nailed before for owning the pinball machines, and they didn't know much about where the Vendor's Association dues money went, or so they said.

"Dunno," they would say, "I just paid the dues, Johnny ran the association. Figured it was good and welfare for the members. Backing politicians? Dunno, have to ask Johnny that one. Gangsters? Ahh, Johnny always liked to pretend he knew all these tough guys. Knew some bad hombres in jail, that sort of crap."

*The funny thing was,* Stormy thought, *Three main witnesses had disappeared. They were looking for the redhead in Florida, Tovsenko turned up dead, and the blonde had vanished off the face of the earth, no one knew where. Clothes, everything, were gone from her apartment in North Buffalo. Funny, hell, this whole thing was getting real deep, and I'm treading water in the deepest end of it.*

Today, the other guys in the unit were getting ready to interrogate Walters, and Stormy had just dropped off a vendor named Gilbert to the grand jury. This guy was nervous as hell, kept asking Stormy on the way there if anyone had found the killers of the Ukrainian guy the papers were talking about.

"I gotta family. Two girls and a boy, and he's sickly. I can't get mixed up in this again. I got a job selling washing machines, appliances, since I sold the vending business."

"Uh, huh," was all Stormy said. *Yeah,* Stormy figured, *Don't say nothing. Let this guy stew all the way up there, and he'd spill his guts. Probably didn't know anything, though. These crooks were pretty careful about what they told who.*

Walters, though. He was different. He collected the money from the vendors and spread it around. Politicians who kept the pinballs legal as long as possible. They werere looking for cops who looked the other way, and with Tovsenko murdered, there's some real bad actors behind that. *Walters connects them all. I wonder what Ocky knows about Tovsenko getting bumped off. Nah, couldn't be. Him and Jazz wouldn't have anything to do with something like that.*

Driving back, Stormy looked at his watch and saw it was past lunchtime. Wachter and the others would be all tied up with Walters the rest of the day. *I wonder what they'll get out of that Polack,* he wondered. *I never saw him around Jazz or Ocky, but you never know. Shit, I might as well take a break this afternoon, they haven't got anything for me.* He pulled over at the Central Park Grill, where he used to have a couple of pops after he'd visit Big Gray if the mayor was playing cards late.

After two beers, Stormy switched to Black Velvet and soda. *It's Friday, what the hell,* he thought. *I wonder what Ocky does know about this murder. Shit, I've got one of the DA's cars for the rest of the day, I might as well put it to good use.* He finished his second BV and soda, got in the car, and started heading downtown again. Thinking about Ocky, he cut down Fillmore and rolled the window down so he could smell the bread from the big bakery there. *Hmm, still haven't had lunch yet. Get a sandwich over at Ocky's.* He bumped the curb as he parked the car on Broadway by the bar with the red neon sign.

Setting his fedora slightly over one eye, he entered the saloon, which was mostly empty, this time of day. Ocky's wife was wrapping up a sandwich for an old lady who was yammering in Polish to her. When she finished, she looked at the big policeman whose hands were jammed into the pockets of his double-breasted, brown suit.

"Yes?"

"Is Ocky here?" he said, glancing around.

"He's asleep now. He'll be coming on tonight if you want to come back."

"I'm Detective Snyder. I need to speak to him."

"Uh, okay, lemme get him," she said, wondering what scam of Ocky's brought this bruiser around. She went to the far end of the bar, opened a door to the back stairs and called, "Billy! Wake your father up, there's someone here to see him."

A teenage voice called back "Okay," and five minutes later, Ocky came down, tucking in his shirt.

"Shit. Stormy. Whadder you doin' here?"

"Gotta talk," the big man said, waving Ocky to come over to a quiet table in the back. When they had sat down, Ocky recognized a guy more than halfway to drunk.

Stormy exhaled and said, "Whadda you know about this dead guy they found down in Caz Creek?"

"The vending mechanic? Nothing. Never met him. What's going on, Stormy?"

"Don' worry about it." Leaning forward, Stormy said, "The murdered guy worked for Walters."

"Okay, so what? Say, you had lunch yet? We still got some breaded haddock from lunch left." Looking at his wife with a practiced, "This guy's trouble" look, he added, "Hey, babe, see if you can rustle up some of the fish fry special for our friend, here, with the coleslaw and fries," his nod telling her, *So we can get this drunk cop out of here ASAP.*

Lowering his voice to a whisper, Ocky said, "I haven't talked to Walters since before he went to Attica. I don't know what he's up to, these days, and I don't want to know."

"How about Jazz? They used to be big buddies, I remember. Specially 'round election time."

Looking around to see if anyone heard, Ocky said, "Nope, Jazz hasn't heard from him, either. Way too busy these days. Hey, look, here's lunch," he said as his wife set down a steaming platter and some silverware. "Hey, babe," he added, looking at the plate, "Get our friend, here, some extra tartar sauce, huh? Here, pal," Ocky said, "Lemme go get you a beer to wash this down with," and the two bar operators moved away.

Back a few minutes later with a tall lager, Ocky watched the detective wallop into the food like a starving man and said nothing. Stormy looked up at Ocky and said, "This is good. Best fish fry I've had in a long time."

Ocky smiled and clapped Stormy on the shoulder. "I'll be back in a couple of minutes," he said, and nodded to his wife, who went upstairs while he went behind the bar. When Stormy finished, Ocky was still behind the bar, chatting with a couple of pensioners whiling away the afternoon. Stormy started to get up, and Ocky said, "Don't worry about that stuff on the table, pal, I'll take care of it," and came out from behind the bar.

As Stormy approached, Ocky got between him and the bar, and very gently led him by the elbow towards the front door. Out of earshot, he whispered to the belching policeman, "You got nothing to worry about with us and Walters, or us and that guy they found in South Buffalo."

As they went out the front door, Ocky looked up and down Broadway to see if anyone was watching as he escorted Stormy to his car. Looking in the driver's window, he said, "Good seeing you, pal. Make sure you call, next time, though. Just to make sure I'm in," and gave a sigh of relief as Stormy drove down Broadway towards downtown.

Driving down the wide avenue, Stormy hung his arm out the window and belched again. *Shit, Ocky wanted to get rid of me quick. Didn't even ask for money for the lunch. Didn't want to even hear about the murdered guy or Walters.* Rubbing his chin and figuring he'd known Ocky for a long time, Stormy figured he was probably telling the truth. *They'll probably haul him up before the grand jury, before long. Him and Jazz both, especially if Johnny cracks. Hmm, Johnny Walters, big shot vendor. The man with the cash. I wonder what he's telling the boys over in Homicide. Didn't he used to sit in on some of those card games in the old days?* Stormy started to sweat when he thought of that. He knows a lot of these guys in City Hall. *Johnny'd sell his own mother out if it'd get him off the hook. I wonder what he's telling them?*

As he pulled into the parking lot, Stormy felt himself getting mad. *Go pick up the witnesses, Snyder. Shit, I could interrogate these guys, have them talking in fifteen minutes. No, nowadays it's all by the book. Hell, I never had to smack them around. Squeeze the muscle at the top of the shoulder first, then, after you let up on that, push down on the pressure point, nailing the nerve right on the collarbone. Let up there and squeeze them just behind the kneecap. Get them comfortable, talking about anything. Then, distract them with the pressure points, then, ask them what you want to know. They'll give it up, pronto, scared of what might happen to them.*

Walking away from the car, Stormy started for the DA's office, and then turned and headed for Franklin Street. *Let me just see how these college boys are doing with that Polack. Hells bells, I got the landlady to do the ID. I got the picture of the guy. With all my experience, they ought to trust me with the interrogations.* Stormy waved his badge at the front desk and went up the back stairs to the third floor where the interrogation rooms were. *Probably in Number Two, the real small one with the acoustic tiles all over.*

Pat Brogan loosened his tie as he walked down the hall. *Damn,* he thought, *forty-five minutes with the guy, and all he did was stare at the wall and shrug.*

"Hi, Stormy," he said as he passed the big man in the hallway, breathing hard from his march up the stairs. *I wonder what he's doing here? Oh, well.* Brogan shrugged, headed for the coffee pot in Houlihan's office.

*College boy, hmmph,* Stormy thought as he approached Interrogation Room Number Two. *Pissant.* When he looked in the small, wired, glass window, he saw Lou Constantino leaning on the desk and shaking his finger in the smaller man's face, who stared at him blankly. He turned around quickly when a red-faced Stormy threw the door open so hard, it bounced off the wall. Before Lou could do anything, Stormy skewered his index fingers and thumbs under Johnny's deltoid muscles and pulled him out of his chair. The vendor shrieked in pain as the policeman spun him around and slammed an uppercut into his solar plexus, and then backhanded him against the wall. Grabbing him by the neck with both hands, Stormy picked him up off the floor and ran him against the wall while Lou came around the desk yelling, "Stormy, stop!"

As Stormy squeezed Johnny's neck tighter, Johnny could smell the booze on his breath and choked out, "Pops, no . . ." Then, Lou got an arm in the crook of Stormy's arm, wrenched one hand away from Johnny's neck, and, leveraging his weight downward, pulled the bulkier cop away from the prisoner. Still trying to reach Johnny with his free hand, Stormy roared, "You son of a bitch! You got that poor slob Ukie killed, you bastard. He worked for you and you got him killed, you no good cocksucker!"

Hearing the uproar, Pat ran back down the hall and helped Lou drag the enraged Stormy to the stairwell while Johnny gasped for breath on the floor of the interrogation room.

"I'm a fucking detective! Gimme five minutes with that bastard! I'll get him to talk!"

Holding Stormy by the arms, the two younger men forced him backwards down the stairs.

"You lost your mind, Stormy?" Lou shouted. "What the hell's the matter with you?"

On the first floor, they pushed Stormy away from the front desk, down another hallway, and outside into a parking lot. Exhausted, Stormy waved his hands downward at Lou, who kept shouting, "You're outta your mind! Get the hell outta here! Whatta you, drunk? Just get the hell outta here, we're handling this, Snyder! Get the hell outta here before the inspector hears about this!"

Purple-faced, Stormy pulled down his tie and told them to go to hell and walked off, cursing. When he'd left, Lou rapped Pat on the chest and said, "Quick! Let's get up there and get to work. That crazy bastard might just have scared him enough to talk."

They dashed up the stairs, where Johnny was back, sitting in his chair, telling them his lawyer would have all their badges.

# CHAPTER 91

## THE EAST SIDE, 1953

When Pat got to the office the next day, he found Lou, Stormy, and young Dunleavy waiting for him.

"What's up, Lieutenant?"

"We got another tip. Seems the boys have been pulling some of their machines out of locations and stashing them."

"Oh, yeah, where?"

"Well, you know how a bunch of them have shops and offices on Main Street up past North?"

"Sure, the Operator's Association was up there, Seneca, Freeberg. Distributors, a bunch of them are around there. We've been checking all of them. Nothing much there, lately."

"Yeah, and now we know why. It seems they made a deal with this colored guy over on Northhampton to store a bunch of their pinballs until the heat's off."

"Have we got a warrant yet?"

"Certainly. I was showing young Dunleavy here the way to schmooze a judge for just such an occasion this morning."

"The four of us are going to handle this?"

"After the job on Pearl Street, the boss insisted."

"Gotcha."

The four policemen drove up Main Street in the oldest Ford in the inventory, and turned right on Northhampton, past two-and-a-half story wood frame houses, and brick-built stores with witches hats on the corners. Lou slowed the car slightly when they went past their objective, number 265.

"There it is, fellas. One-and-a-half-story in front, telescopes out to two-and-a-half-stories in the back. Business in front, residence out back. There's a church behind it on Southhampton. I figure the machines are in front, but you can't be sure until we check. Pat, you and Stormy take the rear, me and the kid go in the front."

Parking the car around the corner on Jefferson, the four split up, Pat and Stormy going up Southhampton and slipping through the Braswell AME Church property and into the backyard of number 265. Lou and Dunleavy went right to the front door. Lou gestured with an open palm to the young patrolman, who pounded on the door and shouted, "Buffalo Police! Open up!"

Lou nodded in appreciation, and when no one answered, kicked the wood-,frame door so hard, the glass broke and shattered loudly. The two of them entered with guns drawn, and Lou said, "Ahhh!" when he spotted five pinball machines lined up just inside the door. Leaving Dunleavy there, Lou went to the rear and opened up the back door, letting the two other raiders inside. Searching the front, the rear, the attics, the cellar, the closets, and every space capable of holding a pinball machine, the policemen found only the five machines in the front shop, and a cheaply furnished residence in the back that didn't seem to be lived in, lately.

"Dammit!" Lou shouted, as uniformed police carried the rigged devices to a truck out front. "I know the snitch was good. He said they were hauling a lot of pins, and slot machines in here over the last few weeks."

"Huh," replied Pat, noticing scratches on the floors leading to the rear. "Stormy and Dunleavy went out back to canvass the neighbors. I wonder if they turned up anything?"

"I doubt it, Pat. Folks around here are pretty closed-mouthed about what the crooks, black or white, do in this neighborhood."

Pat walked out back where Dunleavy was taking notes while talking to a bespectacled, black man in a dark suit in the church lot. A few doors down, Stormy was sitting on the back porch with an elderly woman in a rocking chair waving her arm and pointing her finger. "I dunno, Lou," Pat said, "These two guys seem to have a knack for getting people to talk to them."

When the machines were all hauled away and sealed in the police garage, the detectives returned to the office to report to the inspector. Lou stated the facts about what he believed to be a good tip and the disappointing results of the raid, but then, smiled and said, "However, some of the junior members of our raiding party discovered some interesting information. Go ahead, kid, tell him."

Dunleavy cleared his throat and read from his spiral notebook. "I interviewed the Reverend Milton from the Braswell AME Church on Southhampton Street, behind the house we raided. He said that several white men had been carrying a lot of machines into the house, but that several colored men had been taking them out at night after dark through the backyard and loading them into cars and trucks."

"Go on," the inspector said, raising an eyebrow.

"He also complained that several of his congregation had been led astray by these gambling devices, and they were used in several locations around William Street, Michigan, and one particularly evil establishment that was open all night on East Utica. I have the addresses here, sir. The Reverend Milton said that he hoped that the police would close these places that were ruining the lives of people in the neighborhood."

Wachter looked at Lou, who nodded with approval. He then looked over at Stormy, who was sitting on the edge of a desk with his hat on the back of his head. "What have you got for us, Snyder?"

"I talked to a couple of the old folks in the neighborhood. They're kinda lonely, they like to talk. Anyway, it seems the house is kind of a safe house. Been used by guys on the run since Prohibition, also stashed bootleg booze there back then. The vendors found out about it and made a deal with the locals to hide their stash, but the colored guys swiped 'em and sold them to the nigger clubs around here."

"Then," Lou added, "We get a tip and raid the place, and no one's the wiser, they been had."

Everyone laughed, and then the inspector rubbed his chin. "Well, it seems our darker brethren have got one over on the smart boys this time, lads. We'll just tell the press that a raid was conducted and a number of illegal gambling devices have been seized. Alright, good job, men. Dunleavy, I think you can expect to hear from Detective Sergeant McDougall in the near future for some confidential work, so keep yourself sharp." Then, as the crew dispersed, he added quietly to Lou, "Word will get out about this scam, Lieutenant, and I have a feeling it will cause mayhem. In the meantime, we've got a public service to perform, helping the Reverend Milton reform some colored citizens over on the East Side."

# CHAPTER 92

## THE EAST SIDE, 1953

McDougall pulled his car around the corner from the church on Michigan Street about ten minutes before he figured services would end and kept his eye in the rearview mirror for his man. *Best time to catch him is Sunday morning. All the good people around here are in church, and all the bad ones are in jail, or sleeping one off.*

Even at a distance, he could hear the organ playing and the congregation's voices singing "Wade in the Water." When the final note ended, a parade of black worshipers began leaving the church, smiling and dressed to the nines, away from their usual workingman's dungarees and domestic uniforms.

When he spotted Calvin, dressed in a blue pinstripe suit and white fedora, walking with his family, he tooted the horn briefly. Calvin caught him out of the corner of his eye, nodded, and kept on walking. McDougall then fired up the DeSoto and drove home, waiting for the young black man's call, which came three hours later, when he had found a little privacy.

"McDougall, here."

"It's me, Sergeant Mac."

"Special Officer Garrett. How are you?'"

"I'm okay, you?"

"Fine. How's the family?"

"They're fine, too. What's up?"

"I got a job for you. It'll just take a couple of hours, early in the morning."

"Hmm, what's the task?"

"How about some crooked, white men?"

"Gangsters?"

"Nope, policemen gone bad."

"Now, you're talkin'. Any colored folk gonna get hurt?"

"Nope, just the white boys, and you'll testify against them."

"Include me in, Sergeant."

When Lou got to work on Monday morning, the inspector was in his office behind closed doors with an old guy he recognized as the legendary Sergeant McDougall. *That guy's a pipeline to the commissioner. I wonder what this is about?* He sat down at his desk, and when Pat came in, Wachter signaled them both inside.

Closing the door behind them, Wachter introduced the young detectives to the man who had shut down racketeers, shot bank robbers, and ferreted out fugitives from every corner of the city, but who seemed to be quasi-retired in his office with the robbery squad those days, and no one disturbed him, thanks to his connections with the commissioner. Pat noticed his blue drape suit with wide lapels that reminded him of one of his father's, and the tightly-laced high-top black shoes that a lot of the older policemen wore.

"Boys, Sergeant McDougall is helping us out here. He's running a confidential squad for the commissioner and he's got a job that needs your assistance."

Lou thought for a second about the fact that he outranked the old Sergeant, but kept it to himself. Pat wondered where this was going, but figured the inspector knew what he was doing.

McDougall leaned forward just a bit, his fingers clasped before him in his lap. "Boys, there is a notorious after-hours nightclub on East Utica Street that caters to the coloreds and white people alike, and it's run by a one Micah Thornton. I understand they have a number of pinball and slot machines in the house, which are of interest to you people." He nodded to Wachter. "A tip I received informs me that some of our own have been shaking down Mr. Thornton to ignore his activities."

# CHAPTER 93

## THE EAST SIDE, 1953

Lou was behind the wheel of the DeSoto; McDougall sat next to him quietly as they drove; and Pat and Calvin Garrett sat in the back. Pat was wearing one of his work suits, but Calvin wore a gray, plaid suit with a bright, red bow tie on. In what little light came from the streetlights, the polish on his shoes showed. Eyes forward, the veteran policeman went over their plan.

"All right, lads, you all know what to do. We'll park on the street behind the house, and when the coast is clear, you'll walk through the backyards and enter through the basement door, just like the gas man does. You two," he looked at Pat and Lou, "Will go and wait in the coal bin," a circumstance that Pat knew would cause his lieutenant to grimace. "When the damned weasels come in the same way, stay put. They'll knock on the door at the top of the steps, and Calvin will answer it. Remember, Calvin, crack open the door so you can recognize them, and nod to Michah. He'll come over, take a quick look down the stairs, give you the envelope, and you slide it through the door to them. Then, you two guys in the basement nab these scum and bring them out quickly and quietly the same way you came in."

Lou cleared his throat, "Are we gonna close up this shop afterwards, or is someone else going to?"

McDougall and Calvin exchanged glances. "Not tonight, boys. Mr. Thornton is doing the city a favor this morning, and I'm certain will be made to see the error of his ways in the future."

The three younger detectives walked carefully and quietly through the backyards, hopping a chain link fence into the yard of the double-decker house. The two white men entered a door in the back that led down the basement steps. They closed the door behind them while Garrett tugged on his lapels, straightened out his boutonniere, and went up wooden steps to the first floor.

Pulling a flashlight from his suit coat pocket, Lou carefully looked around the cellar. "Looks like any saloon's basement," he whispered, taking in the barrels of beer and cases of liquor stored there. Finding the coal bin, Pat led, kicking some coal out of the way so the two of them could make room for themselves in the small room as Lou sighed.

Listening to the cheers and groans of the crapshooters upstairs, they hadn't long to wait when the basement door to the outside opened again. Pat and Lou held their breath as they heard two voices, familiar white ones, and caught a whiff of whiskey. Two men chuckled as they walked through the basement. "Hey," said one, "You go get the moolah, I'm gonna see what else we can snatch down here."

Standing in the coal bin, the raiders froze, motionless as the cop came closer, snickering as he examined the cases of booze.

"These jigaboos all love their gin," he commented as he broke open a case of House of Lords. "Ahh, the good stuff." He pulled out a bottle.

Lou tilted his head, listening for the door upstairs. He could hear the crowd noises coming down through the open door for a few moments, then, that went away and he heard footsteps on the stairs. He heard Calvin's signal as the black detective stamped his foot twice, right above them. When the creaking on the steps stopped, Lou stepped out of the coal bin, causing the two grafters to turn as he shined his flashlight on them. Blinking, the one with the bottle held his hand up to the glare and said, "What the. . . "

The other, thinking fast, pulled open the outside door and tried to run out the back, where McDougall jabbed him hard in the gut with a short locust, wood nightstick.

"Stop," he ordered, raising the club under the doubled-over man's chin and guiding him to upright. "You're caught. Come quietly and you might not spend the night sitting in puke with the drunks and the lungers."

Pat recognized him and stared while Kevin McDermott, who

graduated first in his 1946 Recruit Class, stared back and burped, half in the bag.

"Pat, what's this about?" he said, rallying a smile for his old classmate.

Lou, all business, took the bottle from him, got a grip on his forearm, and twisted him around, handcuffing him quickly.

"What's this about, Pat?" he pleaded, as Lou pushed him out the door and out into the yard.

"Shut up, stronzo, before you wake up every colored in the neighborhood," Lou told McDermott. Finally quiet, the policemen hauled their quarry across the yards, followed by Calvin, who came down from the back porch, wishing the crap shooters a good morning as he closed the door behind him.

Taken quickly into empty offices in the county hall by the DA's office, the two crooked cops were separated and sat down, one closeted by the scowling McDougall, the other by the freshly-shaved and pressed inspector.

"Now," the sergeant began, putting one foot up on a chair and his face inches from McDermott's reddened countenance, "How many years do you want to do with the queers in Dannemora?"

Inspector Wachter stood rock-rigid and silent behind a wooden chair with his arms folded across his chest while Lou took the handcuffs off and sat the other policeman down on a hard wooden stool with legs that rose just eight inches above the floor. Lou nodded at his commander and silently left the room as the rogue cop rubbed his wrists and looked anywhere but at Wachter, who remained silent for a good two minutes before addressing his prisoner with an unblinking stare.

"Thomas John Albertson, assigned to the Sixth Precinct, Number Two Platoon."

Albertson looked back at him, his neck and head slightly quivering. He was shocked that the inspector, a man he had hardly seen and had never spoken to, recognized him.

"You are suspended forthwith from this department and under arrest for soliciting bribes, neglect of duty, conspiracy, failure to enforce the law, and extortion." Then, leaning forward and looking into Albertson's blinking eyes, "You are a disgrace to everything we stand for as policemen and will suffer years in jail for this."

Within an hour's time, Lou reported both men were "spilling their guts," while he and Pat remained outside, fetching whatever the interrogators requested. After an hour and a half, they brought small, paper cups of water; after two hours, coffee; and after three, two of the DA's stenographers, who had slipped quietly into the building. When the sun was up, texts of the crooked cops confessions had been prepared by the DA's staff, checked by Stone, and were ready for the grand jury.

# CHAPTER 94

## SOUTH BUFFALO, 1953

Leo hopped on the bus at Seneca and checked the address on the ticket—1953 Seneca, Rose's Inn, where they were having a benefit for his cousin Austin who'd got his leg torn up in the railroad yard. When he got off at Keppel, he spotted the bar across the street and saw Patrolman Regan talking to a guy at the garage next door. He started to cross then recognized the guy with Regan. *Holy shit, that's Johnny Walters, the vendor.* Leo stopped and ducked around the corner and watched as Johnny gestured towards the garage and Regan nodded. They shook hands and Johnny got in a pickup and drove away. Leo waited while Regan headed towards Bailey. When Regan was well away, Leo walked over to the garage, glancing quickly through the window on the big roll-up door. Inside, was a truck and two guys were unloading chrome boxes— *those are slot machines!* He stepped away, then, walked around the building and gave a quick look in another window. A third guy was in there, holding a rifle on his hip talking to the truck driver. *Damn! I hope I kept the card they gave me*, he thought, pulling out his wallet and heading for the pay phone in the bar.

Pat leaned back in his chair and stretched, answering his old partner Ray Zeoli's questions about being a detective. He had been just about finished with the last report when Ray had knocked on the door. Ray was asking about the hours they worked as the phone rang. *Should I answer that?* Pat thought, looking at his watch, *five-fifteen, time to be gone.* It rang again and he picked it up.

"Investigations, Detective Brogan."

"Detective Brogan, this is Patrolman Dunleavy from the

Fifteenth Precinct."

"Hi Dunleavy, what is it?" *Another kid who never thinks about anything but police work.*

"Well, you said to call if I ever picked up anything about pin-balls, and this is kinda like that."

"What is?"

"There's guys unloading slot machines in a garage, and another guy guarding them with a rifle. I think it's one of those army carbines with a long clip."

Pat shot straight up in his chair, thinking, *Holds thirty rounds, Dunaway said,* while Leo gave him the location. "Don't do any-thing, kid, just watch the place. I'm coming right over."

*A car, I need a car to get to South Buffalo. Shit, the inspector's got the keys all locked up in his office. Wachter, Lou, and the D & D boys are all gone for the night.* He pulled on his suit coat and asked Ray, "Have you got your weapon with you?"

"Yeah, sure, why?"

"C'mon with me. I got a hot tip, but we gotta move fast."

They ran out the door, headed for the garage under police headquarters, across Church Street. They ran into the entrance of the garage as Dan Alessi slowly walked up the ramp towards them, putting the keys to the commissioner's car in his pocket.

"Hey, young bucks, where's the fire?"

"Patrolman Alessi! Is the attendant here? We gotta get a car, right now!"

Alessi's eyes narrowed. "What's this about, boys?"

Two minutes later, Alessi was driving them in the commis-sioner's car, feeling twenty years old again. They slid down Seneca, past the garage, scanning the scene and spotting Leo in front of the bar.

"Get in Dunleavy!" Pat said. He jumped in and they drove around the corner. Pat turned around to Leo in the back seat.

"Anything happen in there?"

"Nobody came or went, detective."

"Okay, here's the plan. Leo, you go around back and cover the door, there. Ray and I are going to go in the front door. Patrolman Alessi, you turn the car around and pull it out front and block the garage door. When we get these guys in cuffs, Patrolman Alessi will call for the wagon. Everybody got it?"

They all nodded. Pat and the two young officers hopped out and headed to their positions, and Alessi pulled the car into a driveway to turn it around as they headed off. Pat put his hand on Ray's arm to slow him down.

"Give Dunleavy a few seconds to get there. Then, follow me."

When they got to the front, Pat pulled his revolver and tested the door handle. Locked. Just then, the garage door started rolling up. As it went up past his waist, Pat ducked under and aimed his pistol to the left where Leo said the guard was.

"Stop! Police!" he shouted, aiming his weapon at no one.

The guard, talking to the two helpers at the back of the truck, leveled his carbine at Pat. Ray fired at the same time as the guard and both missed. Pat spun to his right and fired twice. The first bullet chipped the concrete floor and ricocheted between the guard's legs; the second one hit him in the thigh. He collapsed, dropping the carbine. The two helpers ran for the garage door as the truck kicked into gear and roared out. Leo ran past Pat and tackled one of the helpers. Ray fired a warning shot, stopping the second one in his tracks. Alessi stood aside the commissioner's car, pistol ready, but was knocked into the street as the truck smashed the sedan out of its way. Pat scooped up the carbine, ran to the front of the building, and fired six rounds, blowing the rear tires out and sending the truck careening into a parked car. Alessi hobbled up and pulled the driver out of the cab, shouting, "Smash up my commissioner's car, will ya?"

The commissioner called all four men to his office to give commendations for what the papers referred to as a "Dramatic Raid in South Buffalo," congratulating them all for their courage, and Pat, in particular, for his leadership and quick thinking. Wachter stood to the side, hands behind his back, and nodded with pride. The commissioner finished the ceremony saying, "Hell lads, this is a confidential squad even I didn't know about!" to which they all laughed.

# CHAPTER 95

## SOUTH BUFFALO, 1953

Agnes Murphy had gathered all her quarters and left the house at one o'clock on a Saturday afternoon, walking up Stevenson and down Legion Drive along the creek towards the park. When she got to the park, she smiled as she spotted the children playing, and stood on Cazenovia to watch them. About quarter of two, kids started hopping off swings and slides and heading across the street to the Shea's Seneca Theater, where the marquee promised a matinee of twenty-five cartoons. When the kids lined up to get in the theater, Agnes watched the others hanging back in the park and approached them, asking them if they'd like to see the show that afternoon. With faces alight and nodding, she would hand them a quarter for admission, and another for candy and popcorn until her change purse was empty. As she stood there and watched them swarm around the theater entrance, she saw Leo Dunleavy there, laughing while some kids jumped up and down in front of him. When the doors opened, the kids pushed and shoved to get in, and Leo went in himself, half out of nostalgia and half to try and keep the disorder of scores of kids running wild to a minimum.

When he came out, there was Agnes in front of the place, holding her purse in front of her. "Hi, Ms. Murphy, you going in to watch the cartoons?"

She shook her head and smiled. "Noooo, far too loud in there for an old lady like me." She remembered her own childhood and not always having enough pennies to get in herself. "I just like to see the children having fun. When we lived in the Ward we used to go to the Red Jacket Theater, way up Seneca, that way," she said, slowly pointing a blue, veined finger towards downtown. "It was a nickel then, and they still had silent movies, like Charlie Chaplin, and Laurel and Hardy."

"Yeah, I think I remember—it was still around when I was a kid. Up past Smith Street, right?"

"Yes, that's it, right at the corner of Hydraulic," she said, taking his arm and walking back across the street. They walked quietly for a while, then, she said, thinking back, "It's too bad all the children can't go to the show."

"Uh, huh."

"There's one boy, his name's Ricky. I didn't see him there today, but he can't get a quarter to go because his father spends all their money on those pinball games, you know."

"Really? That's too bad, Ms. Murphy."

"Yes, his father works in a store up on Bailey and spends most of what he makes in a saloon on Lovejoy, right by where he works, I hear, playing those pinball machines. What do they see in those games, anyway, Leo?"

"Dunno, Ms. Murphy, but it's a problem, that's for sure." He put Lovejoy and Bailey into his head.

"I hear he runs into the place on his lunch hour, even. Goes in there after work and sometimes has to walk home because he spent his last nickel in there to play those games. Why would a father do that, Leo?"

"I dunno, Ms. Murphy. It's not right."

"Well, I'm headed over to the store to get some cat food for Thomas. He's our cat, you know. We gave him the name because he always seems to doubt we'll come back when we get ready to leave for somewhere. Mews and mews. He knows when we're leaving, you know. Do you like cats, Leo?"

# CHAPTER 96

## LOVEJOY, 1953

Dunleavy sat quietly in the backseat of Sergeant McDougall's car, his hands on his knees. Dressed in work pants and a flannel shirt, he listened to what the three detectives were saying as the car drove slowly up Bailey Avenue towards Lovejoy.

McDougall turned around from the passenger side and put his arm on top of the seat. "You're sure that neither Schmidt nor Battaglia will recognize you as a policeman, now, right lad?"

"No, sir, it's like you said. They've been in the Eleventh Precinct, and I've been on my beat in South Buffalo since I got out of the Academy, Sergeant. I never knew them from sports, church, or school, or the neighborhood."

McDougall nodded, having shown the young patrolman pictures of the police he was going to witness accepting a payoff.

Lou looked in the rearview mirror and grinned. "You'll do fine, kid. You did a hell of a job following up on that Tovsenko, even if we don't have the killers, yet."

Dunleavy reflected on all the people whom he questioned on his beat about the dead vending mechanic found by the creek. He was starting to realize that a lot of crime goes unsolved.

"You keep talking to people on the beat, Dunleavy, whether it's about a crime or not," Lou said. "All that information comes in handy, sooner or later. Look at this—the old lady tells you about a guy losing his shirt on pins in Lovejoy, that leads us here to the bar owner paying off; we squeeze him, and now we're gonna get two bad cops off the street."

"All right, here's where you get out," McDougall said, having pulled past the Ideal Bar.

"Your first undercover assignment, kid. Go get 'em," Lou encouraged as the young policeman got out at the curb. The car then drove on, pulling around the corner onto Moreland Street where they could see the front of the bar. Ten minutes later, a patrol car pulled up, and Schmidt and Battaglia got out, put on their hats, slid their nightsticks into their belt holders, looked around, and entered the bar.

Leo, with a handful of nickels and a bottle of Pabst on the table next to him, was playing the Sphinx game in the back of the bar. The two uniformed men came in, ordered Cokes, and nodded to the owner, who was behind the bar. Battaglia looked around and didn't see anyone unusual at the bar, but turned his wide back between Leo and where his partner stood. Schmidt took the envelope the owner passed under the hinged opening in the bar and tucked it under his uniform blouse coat.

"Getting warm out there, Sam. Won't need these coats, soon," Battaglia commented.

A bleary-eyed autoworker who had been downing whiskey since the end of the midnight shift looked up from his glass, and, spotting the policemen, waved the barman over.

"Another shot, John?" the owner inquired.

"Hey," John slurred, pointing at the patrolmen. "Don' give them cops nuttin', Sam. I know theesh guys. Alla time, freebees. They're alla bunch of crooks." Pointing to his head and winking, "I know all about it. The games, everthin'."

The two patrolmen stiffened, and Schmidt picked up his quarter from the bar so the drunk could see it. "Huh. Five cent Cokes. Fifteen cent tip enough, my friend?"

"Just fine, Steve," Sam said. He hesitated, then forced out, "I wished all my customers tipped like you boys do," nodding at John, who waved his hand and sat back on his stool.

The patrolmen gulped their Cokes, put the glasses down on the bar, nodded to Sam, and took a last look around as they left. *That young guy in the back, playing pinball,* Battaglia thought. *He looks like a cop. Nah, just getting crazy with this stuff. He couldn't have seen anything, anyway. I haven't seen him in here, before, though.* As they went out the door, he said to his partner, "Let's get the hell out of here, Steve, something ain't right."

"Ahh, we're okay," his partner said, getting into the prowl car. However, as they pulled away, he spotted the green DeSoto pulling out in front of them and the young guy hurrying out of the bar behind them. Rolling down the window, he pulled the envelope out from under his coat and with a twist of his wrist, tossed it along the pavement towards the gutter. Dunleavy spotted it, too, and rushed across the street to dive and grab it as it slid halfway over the iron grating to the storm drain.

The two uniforms jumped out of the car, and Battaglia shouted, "What the hell do you think you're doing?" He clammed up when he recognized the detectives.

"Schmidt. Battaglia. Shut the hell up," McDougall ordered under his breath. "We're going to keep this as quiet as possible out on the street, here. You guys get back in the car with me and give me your gun belts where nobody can see it. Pat, you drive the car. Leo, park their patrol car, and then get in the back with these guys and keep an eye on them."

"I did like you said, Sergeant," Dunleavy said quietly as they piled into the car, eager to get out of the middle of the street. "I waited five seconds when they left, and then came out and signaled. I had to rush to catch this." He held out the envelope, which McDougall took from him.

"You did fine, lad. Now just hang onto their weapons and make sure these 'officers' don't try anything stupid."

Like dominoes, the network of corrupt police began to fall. Moving rapidly, the confidential squad of McDougall, Garrett, and Dunleavy hauled in bad police in different parts of the city, each set up by squeezing bar and club owners in fear for their freedom and liquor licenses. Stone, Wachter, and McDougall all agreed it had to be done fast, as word would get out and the grafting police would shut down operations. The first policemen brought in panicked and gave up, at least, some names of higher ups, and how the payoffs worked. Within forty-eight hours, the payoffs had stopped being collected and several of the bad cops, warned of what was coming, took the fifth and hired lawyers.

# CHAPTER 97

## SOUTH BUFFALO, 1953

Dan Finnegan sat back after finishing his breakfast of black sausage, eggs, and toast and admired the way the sun came in through the front door of his tavern. The light was glinting first off the freshly scrubbed floor and just then, was reflecting on the polished mahogany bar. *Clean as a whistle*, he thought to himself. He liked having breakfast sometimes in his saloon, drinking his coffee with the deliverymen and salesmen that came in at the early hour. Sopping up the last of the egg yolk with bread, he heard the screen door squeak and saw a large gray-haired figure opening it.

Squinting to make the visitor out, he heard the big man growl, "Have you any coffee left, you Fenian bastard?"

"Well, as I live and breathe, if it isn't the terror of the First Ward, Patrolman McDougall, back from the dead! Tom!" he called out to the dishwasher. "Fetch another cup of coffee for this highlander." He stood up to heartily shake hands with the old policeman, and then both sat down at the little table by the bar.

"The place looks good, Finnegan. Not covered with broken bottles and blood, like I remember it."

"Ahh," the barkeeper waved his hand. "It's not like the old days much, anymore. We keep the damage down to concussions and bruises, mostly, these days. No need to disturb the lads in blue."

"I have heard," McDougall continued in a lower voice, "That perhaps some of the lads might be disturbing you."

Sitting back in his chair, Finnegan paused, looked hard at McDougall, and clenched his fists on the table before him. "They snatched up the pinball machine I'd bought. That is a matter of record. Cost me a hundred-dollar fine, as well."

"That's not what I'm talking about, my friend. I have heard that some of them tried to shake you down."

Finnegan clenched his teeth and shook his head. "I told Falk about it when I threw that little bollocks Regan out, and all it did was get me raided."

"Falk?" McDougall whispered.

"Yes, Deputy Commissioner Edward V. Falk. Used to walk a beat around here, God, how many years ago? I couldn't get hold of your friend, the high and mighty Corcoran after I pitched Regan's arse out onto Abbott Road. I got some rubbish about 'night watch commander,' so I called Ed Falk and figured he'd crush the little bastard, good and proper. And what do I get? Raided. Arrested. Convicted. Fined. My license under review, of all things. Look at this place! You could eat off the floor! Cleanest saloon in the city of Buffalo!"

When Finnegan stopped, the policeman rubbed his chin and said with a glint in his eye, "Turnabout is fair play, there, Belfast. How would you like to get even with the son of a bitch?"

Finnegan ground his teeth and shook his finger at the detective. "I'll not turn informer on anyone, even that damned peeler!"

"Of course not," McDougall said, sitting back and drumming his fingers on the table while Finnegan fumed. "Of course not."

# CHAPTER 98

## THE VALLEY, 1953

Finnegan loaded the box of lettuce into the trunk of his car when he spotted Terry Lucenti pulling up in the parking lot. *Just like clockwork*, the Irishman thought, *Gets some produce Tuesdays at eight, after the trains are done unloading*. Terry got out of his car and waved at Finnegan, who left the trunk open so Lucenti could look over the lettuce. A short, portly man with wavy, dark hair, Lucenti wasn't smiling as he usually did when he walked over.

"Morning, Terence," Finnegan said and stuck out his hand. Lucenti switched his car keys over to his left to shake it. "Hi Dan, how's the lettuce?" he said, indicating the box in the trunk.

"Good, today, Terry," he said as a steam whistle shrieked and the Erie produce train began to chug away from the food terminal. "Beans look good, too, but some of the tomatoes look like they got bounced around a lot."

"Yeah, I'll have to look them over careful." There was a moment of silence, and then Finnegan asked, "How's business?" and with a smile, "Still getting out of the kitchen to play the drums once in a while?"

Lucenti jingled his car keys, smiled for just a moment, and said, "Business is okay. Real good, as a matter of fact. Don't get to sit in with the band as much as I'd like to," and looked down, scraping his foot on the pavement.

"Well, guess I'll get the vegetables back to the joint," Lucenti said. "We're going to be having pork chops as a special, today," Finnegan said, shutting the trunk. As he stepped toward the driver's door, Lucenti tapped him on the arm with the keys.

"Say, Dan, I heard all about your trouble with the cops."

"Oh, yeah, a real pain in the arse. But the money I was making from the machine, I tell you, it was worth it."

"Yeah?"

"Yeah, but looking back, I should've just dealt with the boys in the precinct right off."

"You mean they'll lay off you?"

"Aye, if you take care of them. Awful shites, but what are you going to do?"

"Huh. A couple of those guys from down at the Ninth Precinct have been hanging around, looking my machines over, but they

didn't say anything until just the other day."

"Well, he's an utter arsehole if you ask me, but Tony Regan's the man to talk to, Terry."

"Tony, huh?"

"Yeah, he's the one takes care of it for all the cops in South Buffalo. It felt good heaving him out when I did it, but it cost me in the end."

"Yeah, well, maybe I'll see what he's got to say, you know?"

"Well, if you do, Terry, I'd be sure to leave me out of it. Mention me and he and the rest of those pirates might just wreck your place for the hell of it."

Terry reached over and shook hands with Finnegan, and then saluted the him with his car keys.

"Thanks, Dan, I'll check into it."

He walked toward the yellow, brick terminal along the Erie Railroad tracks to see if he could talk down the price of the damaged tomatoes to use for sauce.

# CHAPTER 99

## LITTLE HOLLYWOOD, 1953

A little before he opened for lunch, Lucenti heard someone rapping on the back door to the kitchen. He stepped away from the chopping block, wiped the tomato juice off his hands, and said "Yes?" through the screen door, not recognizing the two big men in suits he figured for salesmen. McDougall and Lou glanced around and held their badges against the screen.

"Come in, officers," Terry said with a confused look as he pushed open the door. "Is anything wrong?"

Seeing a woman he figured was the wife washing chickens in the sink, McDougall said, "Can we talk out there?" indicating the barroom.

"Sure, sure, c'mon out here," Terry said.

Lou tipped his hat to a frowning Mrs. Lucenti as they went out.

Once out in the barroom, Lou pulled out a screwdriver and went directly to the Big Parlay game in the corner, opening the back of the machine to check if the free-play device was activated while McDougall sat heavily on a bar stool.

"Hey, what's going on here?" Lucenti asked.

"Relax, Mr. Lucenti, you're not in trouble, at least, not yet," McDougall said calmly.

"Yup, it's rigged, Mac," Lou said from behind the flashing pinball.

"Is this a raid or something?"

"I'd say, 'or something' for the moment. You see, my boss here, Lieutenant Constantino, knows all about these pinball machines, and it seems he's found one that's rigged illegally to give free games."

"Oh, shit, I . . ."

"Now, don't get in a tizzy, we're not interested in arresting the drummer who makes the best sauce in town, right, Lieutenant?"

"Not unless we have to," Lou growled from the corner.

"Uh, so, what do you guys want?" Lucenti asked.

"I take it you're familiar with a fella named Tony Regan. . .," and, as he explained the plan, Terry Lucenti was thinking what a devious old Mick Dan Finnegan was.

# CHAPTER 100

## LITTLE HOLLYWOOD, 1953

Tony Regan rarely left South Buffalo and walked everywhere in that part of town. There wasn't any nook or cranny a book-maker or stick-up guy could hide south of Eagle Street where he couldn't find you if he set his mind to it—and it was worth his while, which was why he chuckled when Terry Lucenti first came to him and offered him a part time job guarding his restaurant on paydays when he cashed checks for the local workers.

"Naw, actually I got something else in mind," Tony said, nodding over at the clattering pinball game, which was just then ringing up a housewife's free game.

*Well, the dope finally caught on,* Tony thought as he walked down Exchange Street to make his first pickup. He stopped about twenty feet from the front and lit a cigarette, tossed the wooden match into the gutter, and looked over the two-story white-framed house. A neon sign that read *Lucenti's Little Hollywood Lounge* had just lit up, flashing in the dimming, evening light as a couple went up the steps into the barroom on the street side. Along the white clapboard side where the parking lot was, a banner proclaimed, "Music and Dancing Nightly—Best Spaghetti in Town— Fish Fry Fridays." *No, no strange-looking cars there,* he thought. A dish-washer was having a smoke on the back steps as a bird chirped in the maple tree overhead while the leaves fluttered in the breeze. When the dishwasher went back inside, Tony went up and rapped on the screen door to the kitchen. Lucenti, at the stove, nodded at the man outside, and rinsed his hands in the sink. He stepped outside, and pulling an envelope out of his back pocket, handed it to Tony, who slid it into his inside coat pocket. Regan was just touching the brim of his hat to the silent Lucenti when he heard a chain link fence shaking, and turned to spy a young guy in tennis shoes and a baseball hat, hopping a fence at the back of the lot and charging towards him.

Grabbing Lucenti by the belt, Tony swung him down the steps between himself and the on-rushing Leo Dunleavy and ran through the kitchen, knocking pots and pans of cooking food everywhere, to the yells of the staff. Entering the barroom, he spotted Pat Brogan coming through the side door. Picking up Terry's snare drums from the bandstand, he threw them at Pat and rushed to the front of the dining room and out the front door. Once outside, he spotted Lou coming across the street.

*Oh shit,* Tony thought, *I can't let that big, frigging Guinea catch me.* He turned an abrupt right and began sprinting up Exchange Street. A car horn blared from behind, and McDougall shouted out the driver's window, "Surrender, you bastard!" and rolled towards him.

Tony juked left to avoid the diving Lou, who lost his hat as Regan's feet danced out of his grasp. Tony kept on running down the sidewalk and pulled his black fedora on tighter. Racing under the Hamburg Street Bridge, he spotted it—a freight train rolling slowly through the neighborhood, but picking up speed. McDougall was keeping pace with him in the unmarked car. Lou was cursing him as he lost ground to the faster man, and Tony leapt into the open door of a maroon Canadian National freight car. Lou watched as the train pulled away and bent over, hands on knees to catch his breath. Once inside the freight car, Tony rolled over and inhaled deeply. *Shit,* he thought, *I betcha this train goes all the way over the International Bridge to Canada. Maybe I can make it over there and get a good head start before they get the law up there to look for me.*

Two hands slapped on the wooden floor of the freight car and Leo Dunleavy pulled himself into the accelerating boxcar. Tony jumped up and threw a right at his head, which Leo blocked with his left, then grabbed Tony by the shoulders.

Tony kneed him in the groin as hard as he could. Leo moaned, but tightened his grip on Tony's shoulders and then pulled the two of them out the car door, tumbling down the gravel roadbed into the bushes alongside the tracks.

Lou, who had been jogging alongside the tracks, went into a sprint. When he caught up with the pair, Leo was rolling on the ground, holding his groin, and Tony had finally shaken loose of his grasp. Grabbing Tony by the hair as he tried to scramble to his feet, Lou slammed the man's head onto his knee and tossed him backwards into the weeds. Looking over at Leo, Lou shook his head. "I thought you were from South Buffalo, kid. I gotta teach this rookie how to fight dirty, now?"

Tony Regan settled his fedora on his knee, which was bent almost as high as his face because of the low stool, and shook his head at Wachter's questions. "Inspector, I don't care what that old Mick or anybody else tells you. I never asked anybody for money to look the other way at illegal pinballs, slot machines, or any gambling. Hell, I was part of the raiding teams that grabbed up some of those machines and arrested the crooks runnin' 'em."

"Deputy Commissioner Falk was in charge of those raids, was he not?"

"Uhh, yeah, yeeah, he was running the show."

"Did he choose the places to be raided?"

Tilting his head back, Regan answered, "Oh jeez, I dunno how they picked the places to be raided, Inspector. Patrol cops' information, Vice, Gambling Squad tips, I dunno. I worked some of those raids on my own time, ya know."

Switching interrogators, McDougall went inside to follow up with Regan, and Wachter came out in the hallway where he loosened his tie and Stone handed him a cup of black coffee.

"How goes it?"

"Not good with this one. He knows where we're leading, and even though we've got him cold, he keeps denying everything and won't snitch on the other ones."

The DA shook his head. "We've got enough evidence to get the grand jury to indict Falk. Some of these cops of yours," he said, causing the inspector to wince, "Folded up like a house of cards, named everybody they could to stay out of jail. Now, though, they've all been talking to one another, and some of them even think they can beat the charge."

"We'll keep at it, counselor, as long as it takes. Every little piece of evidence, every slip of the tongue gives us more to go on. I'll flush these crooks out of the department if it's the last thing I do."

"I'll give you through the end of the week. The leads are drying up, and if I keep the grand jury in session too long, they'll just stop listening to me and want to go home, no matter what."

Wachter took a last sip of the black coffee, put down the cup, straightened his tie and looked into the interrogation room where McDougall walked around Tony Regan, who turned his palms up and shrugged again.

# CHAPTER 101

## MIAMI, FLORIDA, 1953

"Welcome to Florida," the blonde stewardess greeted the arriving passengers. "Did you enjoy the flight?" Monteduro nodded and walked down the stairway, working his index finger in his ear, trying to make the incessant hum of the aircraft engine go away.

"Mr. Monteduro?" the young man in sunglasses asked at the gate.

He nodded again.

"I'll get your bag and take you to the hotel."

On the ride there, Torreo described her—tall, red hair, pale skin. Torreo gave the young man a picture, taken with Betty, Johnny, and others at a restaurant.

Monteduro was in Miami five days when the young man called. "Meet me out front with a car," Torreo told him. The young man drove him past the apartment building where she was living. "She lives on the top floor, back. Calls herself Nellie Walker, now." He drove them by the bank where she worked. "She walks home this way," he said, pointing down Brickell Avenue. "Comes home a little after five."

"You have canals here, no?" Torreo asked.

The young man smiled. "With alligators, too."

"It's Saturday, now. We'll get her on the side street by her apartment Monday evening when she comes home from work. Find a canal out in the country."

Monday morning, Torreo finished his breakfast in the coffee shop and went into the phone booth there. He dialed the bank where Helen worked.

"I wish to speak to Nellie Walker."

"Just a moment, please."

"This is Miss Walker. . . Hello? Who is this?"

"Helen Volker," Torreo whispered, and then heard the line go dead. He exhaled, then went back to his room and called home, telling his wife Donna he'd arranged for a train ticket for her to come down; the airplane flight was too noisy, there were too many changes in the airports and the food was terrible. He would be looking for a house in the meantime.

Torreo and the young man waited well past five outside the bank until all the lights were turned off inside.

"Drive by her apartment," Torreo ordered. When they arrived, Torreo said, "Go in and check her apartment." The young man nodded, and got out of the car, looking around. He came back ten minutes later.

"Well? Is it done?"

The young man took off his sunglasses and shook his head. "She's gone, Mr. Monteduro. Furniture's there, but all her clothes are gone."

Torreo slammed his fist on the dashboard. "Take me back to the hotel. Have someone watch her apartment. You start looking for her."

# CHAPTER 102

## EAGLE STREET, THE HYDRAULICS, 1953

Stormy decided to do a little splurging after he got off work that payday, and stopped at Emhof's for the turkey dinner special. *What the hell,* he thought, *If this works out, I'll get promoted. The extra one-hundred twenty dollars a detective sergeant gets a year will buy me a lot of good dinners.* He ordered a VO and soda at the bar, picked up a nickel from his change, and went to the wooden phone booth, closing the door tightly. He dialed the bar's number and Ocky answered.

Checking his watch, Ocky figured Stormy had just gotten off, so, he was probably still sober when he cheerily said, "Hello, Detective Snyder, how are you? What can I do for you?"

"Hey," Stormy said, lowering his voice, "They brought in the last witness for the grand jury, today. They're going to send the jurors home tomorrow. The DA was mad as hell and went home."

"Any sign of the girls?"

"I never saw 'em, and I been in and out of there every day. They're still looking for the redhead in Florida and the blonde's disappeared, too."

Ocky gave a sigh of relief. That matched what the wiretaps said. "Thanks, Storm—I mean, Detective Sergeant Snyder," and they both laughed.

# CHAPTER 103

## SOUTH BUFFALO, 1953

After he got the word on the grand jury finishing up at the end of the week, Johnny thought it was time. He remembered how Charley Brogan's mouthpiece tied Judge Worth in knots, and got him off with a fine, so, Johnny gave him a call at his office on South Park.

"Jim Nolan, here."

"Counselor, this is John Walters. I hear you did great things for our boy Charley Brogan in front of Judge Worth a while back."

"What can I do for you, Mr. Walters?"

"The city's got a bunch of my pinball machines tied up in a warehouse. I want 'em back."

"I see. Are you saying you want me to seek recovery of the pinball machines?"

"You got it. And, if I get mine back, there's several other guys who will hire you to get theirs back, as well."

"Uh, huh," he said, thinking. *I've got a will to do for the Keefe's, the Ryan kid's assault and battery case to prep for, Kinal's hearing is coming up. . . This will probably require a trip to the law library,* he considered, looking at his small, but expanding collection of law books. "How about Monday, next week, ten o'clock, at my office?"

"I'll be there. You're over at South Park and Boone, right?"

"That's where my office is," he answered.

"Okay, see you then."

The librarian at the University of Buffalo Law School was amazed at the guy's concentration. He kept reading, even after the light bulb on the small desk lamp he was using burned out. When he was finally finished, he slapped the last book shut and shook his head, brought the books back to the desk, and left muttering to himself.

Jim Nolan was standing in his office, hands in his pockets, when he spotted Johnny coming up to the door of his office, recognizing him from the pictures in the newspaper articles he had dug up. He pushed his hair back off his forehead, opened the door and put his hand out.

"Mr. Walters, or do you prefer Walenty?"

"No," Johnny said slowly, "Walters. Johnny Walters."

"Fine, fine. Have a seat, Mr. Walters."

When they were seated, Jim folded his hands on the desk between them and began. "I don't think I can take your money, Mr. Walters."

"Oh, why's that?"

"I don't think this is a winnable case."

"Huh. I want my property back, Nolan."

"Well, the problem is that the property, in this case, are devices that have been, for the most part, converted for use, and used as gambling devices. Further, the other machines that have been seized that have not been converted for use as gambling devices can be readily adapted for purposes of gambling. The law is quite specific on the subject, stating 'devices used for gambling purposes, or readily converted to gambling purposes.' I believe, the best I could do is recover the machines which had not been converted already for gambling purposes, and even that will be difficult, as they had been seized in a place where gambling with said machines had occurred."

"What about my private property rights?"

"I am sure you are already aware from your own past experience, Mr. Walters, possession of gambling devices is a crime which abrogates an individual's right to possess them."

"Those machines are worth a lot of money to me, especially out on the street. How about the judges?"

Pretending he didn't hear that, Jim went on. "If I may suggest a more long-term strategy, Mr. Walters, you may wish to delay this hearing for the time being, that way the State will have no immediate reason to order the machines destroyed. They will remain in limbo, as it were, until perhaps the city council might see fit to enhance the liberties of local. . . Amusement interests, shall we say, and then, you might seek recovery more successfully. My advice would be to delay seeking redress in the courts, concentrate your efforts politically, and perhaps, your machines, and those of the others, might be returned to you at some time in the future."

Johnny drummed his fingers on the desk. "You know which judge will be getting this case?"

"Not at this time, no."

"Okay, look. You get ready to go to court, and let me know as soon as you know when the hearing is. How much I owe you for today?"

"For today's, and any other consultations we may require, I charge seven-hundred and fifty dollars," he said, watching Johnny carefully for a response. "To engage me for a hearing will be an additional seven-hundred and fifty dollars when we conclude. . . I also must tell you, Mr. Walters, that tampering with jurists, or even attempting to tamper with them, is a serious crime, and I cannot advise you against it too strongly."

Johnny took money from his billfold and flipped fifteen-hundred dollars in hundreds onto the desk between them. "Lemme know if there are any more expenses; gimme notice when the hearing is, and I'll see you in court."

When Johnny left, Jim stared at the money and thought to himself, *That's the most money I've ever made in one shot*, but this is also why lawyers hire secretaries, to keep trouble like that guy on the other side of the door.

Judge Harold Worth folded his arms under his robe behind the high bench and felt comfortable. His robe was dry-cleaned, the bailiff had polished the bench to a gleaming shine, his pince-nez was spotless, and he had read every local and state statute and decision he could find about gambling. When this latest pinball case came up, he had swapped cases to get it, pleading previously made Park Club duties to arrange it. It wasn't those Brogan rascals, but it was close enough, with that night-school-Johnny, James Nolan, again.

Jim Nolan kept his eyes on the papers before him until Johnny came in and sat down in a conservative blue suit; white shirt; and an orange and blue striped tie for the occasion.

He looked over his glasses at his client and whispered, "You can still cancel this hearing if you want."

"What the. . . I figured this was Dickinson's case," Johnny replied, spotting Judge Worth on the bench. Jim shrugged while rearranging papers. "Happens all the time, especially when the weather's good for golfing."

"Nah, I ain't backing down, now. You do your stuff, Counselor." Judge Worth and Johnny sat motionless as the hearing began.

The state's attorney cited *New York State Consolidated Law*, the fact that the machines had been seized in police raids, and had been, or could be, readily adaptable for gambling purposes, and that Mr. Walters had been convicted previously for violations of the gambling laws.

"Objection!" Nolan shouted. "Your Honor, Mr. Walters's previous record has nothing to do with this hearing, and is prejudicial to my client's case, which is about a citizen's property rights."

"Overruled, Mr. Nolan," the judge said quietly.

When the state's attorney finished his arguments, the judge smiled and nodded, and then called on the defense. Nolan presented his case citing property rights of citizens, previous cases concerning pinball machines that hadn't upheld such seizures, a citizen's rights to do business without harassment from government, the lack of clarity with regard to what is and is not a gambling device, and added that Mr. Walters was a long-established, small businessman in the community and a good family man who needed the tools of his trade to make a living. He concluded by saying that the legality of these machines was already established by the facts that the city of Buffalo and other jurisdictions issued licenses for these devices and, he said slowly for emphasis, "Collects fees for such licenses and taxes on the income from them."

That completed, the judge checked the time and dismissed the court for lunch, stating he would render his judgment upon his return in the afternoon. Nolan reminded Johnny that it still wasn't too late to withdraw his petition. "Nah. You sounded good up there, Nolan. I'm rolling the dice on this one. I got a feeling they'll turn up seven."

Judge Harold Worth had a cup of tea after his lunch at the Saturn Club, not seeing any reason to rush back to the courthouse. When he did enter his chambers, he checked his messages and made a brief call to the house to see if the gardeners were finished putting in the new rose bushes. As he donned his robe, his secretary heard him whistling and thought, *That's a new one for him.*

He opened the door to the courtroom and hesitated, making sure those present were on their feet and the bailiff was finished announcing him before he entered. Striding to the bench, he sat down for a moment as everyone sat in silence. Looking out over the courtroom, he nodded to the bailiff, who said, "The petitioner and counsel will stand."

Judge Worth began. "I have given this case a great deal of consideration before arriving at a decision. I have listened to the erudite arguments of counsel, and studied the statutes and previous decisions concerning this matter. I have further contemplated the effect of what any decision made here today will have on, not only the litigants involved, but on our community as a whole, before coming to any conclusions.

"The statute, which is most relevant to this case is, without a doubt, Section nine-eighty-two of *the Penal Law of the State of New York*, which states that 'possession of gambling devices. . . or devices that can be readily adapted for gambling purposes, shall be illegal.' These devices were seized by the police and were being used for gambling purposes. The owners, who include Mr. Walters, had adapted these pinball machines for gambling purposes, or knew very well that they had been adapted for gambling purposes. They also profited, along with the establishments where they were located, from gambling done with these devices. That has already been determined by other court cases, including Mr. Walter's previous conviction for owning machines used for gambling purposes."

Jim whispered out of the corner of his mouth, "Here it comes . . ."

"Until this time, my learned colleagues of the judiciary have hesitated to proclaim these pinball machines, which have been adapted for gambling purposes, 'gambling devices.' The manufacturers of these pinball machines allegedly did not build them to give free games or payoff the user; because of the disclaimers that these devices were 'for amusement only,' and because local jurisdictions license and tax these machines.

"However, as these pinball machines, which have been seized are quite readily adapted, and used for gambling purposes, it is obvious that they are precisely what Section nine-eighty-two of *the Penal Law* is referring to as gambling devices or devices readily adapted for purposes of gambling.

"Further, when we consider the damage that these pinball machines wreak upon our city, it is incumbent upon this court to take action to protect society. Every day, we hear of wages lost and grocery money frittered away on these pinball machines by workingmen, housewives and even children. This is not the time to stand by while the legislators debate.

"It is my decision, then, that these machines should not be returned to Mr. Walters, and further, that they shall be destroyed forthwith by the law enforcement agency that has seized and sealed them. It is also my decision that when such devices are seized in the future and found to be adapted and used for gambling purposes by a court of law, they should be destroyed by the law enforcement agency having jurisdiction.

Johnny gasped. "What? Destroyed? He can't do that!"

Judge Worth aimed the gavel at the sound block carefully, and slammed it down as hard as he could. Jim said, "I tried to tell you," as he stuffed papers into his used, leather briefcase.

"This case is concluded," Judge Worth said, holding back a smile until he got into his chambers.

"What the hell is going on here?" Johnny fumed.

"They're going to keep your machines and destroy them, Mr. Walters," Jim said, adjusting his glasses. "I warned you this might happen."

"The court is adjourned," said the bailiff, and Assitstant DA Roth scrambled from his seat in the rear of the courtroom to tell his boss the news.

# CHAPTER 104

## ERIE COUNTY HALL DOWNTOWN, 1953

District Attorney Stone hung up the phone and took a breath. *I've got to make sure all the bases are covered on this one before I let Corcoran and Wachter off the leash.* He carefully tapped his pipe out in the ashtray, buzzed his secretary, and told her to hold all calls. He stood up, put his hands on his hips, and looked out his office window on the third floor of the County Hall, at the steam coming out of the chimney on police headquarters, and the clouds forming over the lake. *No, it's not quite time to plan a move to Albany, yet. I've got to lock up the ward heelers and the crooked cops, along with the gamblers. I've got to see this mayor and his friends flushed down the toilet. That will put me one better than Governor Dewey, who still can't stop the O'Connells from operating right outside the State Capitol building.*

*All right. Draft an order to Corcoran and the sheriff to seize all the pinball machines in Erie County. Call them and Wachter in, and give them the word. Find out how much time they'll need before I make an announcement to the press. Let's see. As a result of a decision made in New York Supreme Court, and after a careful legal review, the possession and use of all pinball machines has been declared illegal under Section nine-eighty-two dash two of the* State Penal Law, *and are hereby banne . . . I, therefore, have directed all the law enforcement agencies in Erie County to seize every and all such devices. . . While the police tear around town seizing them all for the press to see. Okay, now, what else? Just as the excitement dies down about the raids, get Roth and Lauria to bring the last witnesses before the grand jury. Hang that license commissioner out to dry, and wrap up those dummies in the city council that the vendors have been paying off. See what shakes out from them, maybe the mayor himself will get caught up in this. Can't say Pfeiffer didn't warn him. Finally, they've gotten about all the information out of the bad cops that Corcoran's confidential squad had scooped up, so make the arrests on the lieutenant, two captains, and the deputy we know we can convict. Sorry, old man, your number two's going to get hammered just before you retire. Stupid politicians and crooked cops locked up, pinball machines smashed and banned, all over the course of a few weeks in the spring, and the state Republican convention in the summer.* Lifting himself on his toes, he thought, *Who knows, the Stone family might be doing some skiing on the slopes near Albany this winter, or. . . I might be getting fitted for a black robe.*

# CHAPTER 105

## THE WEST SIDE, 1953

When Police Commissioner Corcoran met the district attorney at the University Club, Stone was wearing a three-piece suit and his hair shined with hair oil. He was checking his watch when the commissioner got to the quiet, corner table, and gave him a rapid handshake.

"I heard Judge Worth gave the go-ahead to smash that weasel's machines today, Clifford."

"He certainly did. Do you know what this means?"

"Well, I'm no lawyer, but I'm guessing that the State Supreme Court says we can crush them all now."

The district attorney raised a finger. "Seize and seal them, Commissioner. Destroy all the machines that you already have and put all the rest you seize under lock and key for inventory, and later destruction. How much time will it take you to set up this campaign?"

"Not long. With the bad actors the confidential squad have already scooped up, it'll put the fear of God into anyone else who might want to let these maggots slip away. I have a list of good men in every precinct that I'll tell the captains to put in charge of the raids, in case they have second thoughts. I'll have to get hold of someone with trucks to carry all the machines away to the police garage, though."

"I'll contact County Public Works and have them report to some lot in the city to await assignment. They'll never suspect what the purpose is and won't be able to get word out."

"Good. What about the people in City Hall?"

"Let's just say that the district attorney's fffice has taken steps to lull them into a false sense of security, for the time being. When do you think you can begin the raids?"

"Tonight. I'll call the precinct captains in as soon as I leave here and give them their orders in the next two hours. I take it," the old policeman said, nodding at the DA's appearance, "You have an announcement planned?"

Looking at his watch again and rising, Stone said, "I'll call the papers in four hours. That should be enough time to start the seizures, don't you think?"

"Certainly, your grace," Corcoran replied, rising for the exit.

Outside, Corcoran exhaled deeply, got into his car and told Dan Alessi to head back to headquarters; they were going to be up late that night. Back in his office, he called all the precinct commanders and told them to meet him in the Louisiana Street Precinct's reserve room forthwith, in uniform. When they were all assembled, he paced before them like he had as a shift commander years ago, before sending the patrolmen out onto the streets, and in a stentorian voice announced, "The district attorney has informed me tonight that all pinball machines are hereby illegal. Dan," he nodded to his driver, who began handing out lists to the assembled captains. "You are to use the men listed and begin seizing all the pinball machines in the area under your command immediately, if not sooner. Trucks will be provided by the county's public works to collect the machines. They are to be seized, sealed, and delivered to the police garage on East Ferry Street. A complete inventory of them is to be made and matched against a list of those machines licensed later. Include any unlicensed machines and any other gambling devices you find on your inventory. There's almost two-thousand of these damn things out there that we know of, so, let's get cracking, lads. Any questions?"

Stunned, the commanders didn't react.

"Very well. . . Oh, Captain Pronobis," he said to the captain of the Eighth Precinct that covered Broadway. "Inspector Wachter and a couple of his boyos will be assisting you with one particular raid tonight."

# CHAPTER 106

## ERIE COUNTY HALL, 1953

Lou looked at the clock on the wall and over at Brogan, who was feverishly typing. He almost felt bad about reminding his partner they still had to go over to the police garage on East Ferry Street to do the inventory of the seized pinball machines that they referred to as "the haul."

"Pat," he asked, "How much more do you have to do on that?"

"Ah, shit! I screwed up the damn thing again," Pat said as he slapped the carriage across the machine. He, too, looked up at the clock and saw it was after four. "Shit. It's going to take me another good half an hour to finish up this chicken shit paperwork."

"Well, partner, we still gotta go do the machine count today, too, don't forget," Lou said, still feeling guilty, but mostly grateful, that he could detail the report writing to Brogan, the former college student.

Brogan yanked the three pages and two pieces of carbon paper out of the typewriter and threw them over his shoulder, growling. Lou wagged his finger at Brogan and said in an Alan Ladd voice, "A typewriter is a tool; no better or worse than any other tool, an axe, a shovel or anything. It's as good or as bad as the man using it. Remember that." Pat dropped his head down onto the Remington's heavy rubber feed roller and rolled his noggin slowly back and forth. Lou chuckled and walked over to pick up the paper scattered on the floor by the windows.

Glancing out the window, Lou heard, and then saw, two police motorcycles roaring up the street. "Hey, Pat, take a look at this," he beckoned the frustrated detective to the window.

"Cripes almighty, what now?" Pat pushed himself out of his

chair.

"See for yourself. Looks like the boss is gathering a convoy."

When Pat got to the window, the two of them looked down upon two police motorcycles followed by their inspector's maroon Hudson, a shiny black Buick, two City of Buffalo dump trucks, three other city cars used by the police department brass, and a black and white patrol car with its light flashing.

"C'mon, Pat, get your coat," Lou said, snatching up his suit coat with one hand and slamming his fedora on with the other. Pat followed, leaving the office door open. Running down the steps, Lou shouted behind him, "The judge musta given the order!"

"The boss probably was in the courtroom!"

"Hell, yeah," Lou shouted as they burst into the lobby. "He probably wrote it up just to get him off his back for the weekend."

When they got outside, Wachter was standing on the sidewalk beaming, and, sure enough, there was Judge Worth, sitting in the black Buick, his clerk behind the wheel. The assistant commissioner was in another car and the captains from the South Park and Colvin Precincts in theirs.

"I was just coming to get you boys," the inspector greeted them.

"C'mon, let's go over to the garage and pick up the machines."

"Whadda we gonna do with 'em. boss? Dump 'em in the lake?"

"No, Lieutenant, we're going to do this right and proper after you inventory them for the last time. We're going to take them out to the dump and destroy them so they can't be salvaged, ever."

The three of them smiled as they looked at the men grousing in their cars behind. *You're next, you crooked bums,* Wachter thought as they piled into the inspector's car. Pat got behind the wheel, and the inspector waved the motorcycles forward as he got in the back seat. The motorcycle cops adjusted their sunglasses, revved their engines, turned the sirens back on, and roared down Court Street. As they went around McKinley Square in front of City Hall, Wachter hoped the mayor heard them and was watching from the second floor.

"Looks like Wachter's putting on a big enough show, Jazz," Licensing Commissioner Rybeck said, as he looked down on the vehicles noisily going around the circle.

"As well he should."

The mayor thought for a moment, smiled, and then said, "Let's get the car and meet them. We should show them that the mayor and City Hall are a hundred percent behind their crime fighting efforts."

Wachter had told the motormen to take Broadway out to Bailey on their way to the East Ferry Street garage, with the sirens wide open all the way. *Let those saloon keepers on the East Side see it*, he thought.

When they pulled up to the garage, the garage supervisor was just getting in his car out front and talking to the coverall clad night man. "What the hell is this?" he said, as the night man threw away his cigarette. The motorcycles pulled past, finally silencing the sirens, and the inspector's car pulled up front.

"Ah, Mr. Banas, just the man I want to see." Wachter brandished Judge Worth's court order. "We've come for the one-hundred-and-fifty-six pinball machines you have in custody here. This order from the Supreme Court of the State of New York, issued by Judge Harold Worth, calls for their removal and destruction, forthwith."

Banas held the order and looked at it, and then at the convoy on the street. The other cars looked like they were full of big shots, and the supervisor shrugged, wondering when this would be over and he could go home. He nodded to the night man, who opened up the two overhead doors to the garage and turned on the lights. Wachter led his two detectives into the garage, pointing to the machines carefully stacked and sealed with tape.

"Inventory them boys, count every last one owned by Superior, K Squared, and JRS," and as they walked over to the pinball machines, the inspector spun around, waving the dump trucks to back into the garage.

Falk and the captains stood outside the garage. The precinct commanders waited there with their hands clasped behind their backs, looking to Falk.

"Well, guys, it'll take them a while to load up the machines, so, what do you say we go across the street, here," Falk said, indicating a store called Schoetz's Market, "And get some coffee?"

"I could use something stronger than that, right now," the Colvin Precinct commander said.

"How far do think this thing will go, boss?" a downtown commander asked as they walked across the street.

"Don't panic, men. Let's go out there to the dump and congratulate Inspector Wachter and his men on a fine piece of police work. Just get your coffee and keep your mouths shut."

When the dump trucks were in place and the machines counted, Inspector Wachter stood back with his hands on his hips and said to the night man from the garage and his assistant, "All right, let's load them onto the trucks, men."

Lou and Pat stood to the side, watching as the two garage mechanics carefully picked up one of the polished wood, chrome, and glass machines and, cradling it, walked to the back of one of the trucks. They put the pinball on the tail board and slid it forward slowly.

"No, not that way, guys," Lou said, a smile spreading across his face. "It'll take all night that way." He walked over to the stacked machines. Grabbing one of the smaller, table top models, he carried it to the back of one of the trucks and launched it the length of the truck bed where it smashed against the compartment's forward steel bulkhead with the sound of shattering glass, crunching wood, and crumpling metal. "That's the way you do it, boys. Now, let's get these goddamned things loaded pronto!"

Pat went over to the stack and bowed to Lou, who bowed back. Then the two of them picked up a large floor model and took it over to the truck where they gleefully heaved it into the back, the machine's tilt sensor frantically setting off the bells and the steel ball rolling across the field for the last time. Hearing the noise, two patrolmen came to the front of the garage to check it out. Watching the two detectives' performance, they looked at each other and wondered what to do. The inspector waved them in, saying, "Help these men get this contraband loaded, officers." Then, to the two mechanics, "Well, what are you waiting for?"

For about an hour, the six men went on a joyous destructive rampage, oblivious to the flying glass and rolling cogs and wheels.

When all the machines were aboard the trucks, the only sound was the men breathing heavily. His feet crunching in the shattered glass on the floor, Wachter went up to the silent men who stood at the front of the garage finishing their coffee. Addressing Falk, he restrained himself from saluting, as he was not in uniform, and said, "DC Falk, the contraband is loaded."

"Good job, Inspector," Falk replied. "I know you've been waiting a long time to get this done. All right, let's get going out to the dump and get rid of these . . . gambling devices."

When the trucks backed out onto the street, they formed up in the middle of the cortège that drove, again, through downtown Buffalo on Wachter's orders, this time down Pearl Street, past more of the nightclubs and bars, and then out of downtown, down Furhmann Boulevard by the lakefront, to the city dump.

At the entrance to dump's main road, they discovered the mayor, councilman Merriweather, Licensing Commissioner Rybeck, and a number of reporters already on the scene. To avoid blocking the road, the vehicles parked along the side of it, with the motorcycles, Wachter's car, and the patrol car parked on one side, and the deputy commissioner's and the captains' cars on the other. The men all got out of their autos to the pervasive smell of rotting garbage and smoldering debris from incinerators and picked their way carefully along the muddy road. They walked single file on their respective sides of the road towards the pile, where the dump trucks were depositing the machines in a metallic cacophony, along with the sound of hundreds of screeching seagulls. Even that noise, though, couldn't drown out the mayor as he told the reporters, "This is result of the tireless work of your police department, which will continue until the last gambler realizes it's time to clear out of the city of Buffalo. I especially want to thank Inspector Wachter and his men, and the captains and men of each precinct, whose vigilance makes our city a place where families are safe from vice."

A bulldozer coughed to life and pushed all the wrecked machines into one pile, and then ran back and forth over the heap, its steel treads crunching them like dying, metallic insects. In another act of stage play, Wachter had requested a fire department unit to stand by, with the black-coated firemen from Engine 8 standing upwind of the heap with a charged hose line for the final act. The superintendent of the streets department, eager to get in on the act, stepped up and waved to a couple of his trash men, who proceeded to dump several cans of gasoline onto the pile. When they backed off, the superintendent looked to the inspector, who nodded back, and with that, he lit an old broom on fire and swung it dramatically onto the petroleum-soaked machines. The pile lit up with a loud whoosh, and the observers jumped away from the blaze.

After a few moments, the mayor said loudly, "Well, that's that!" and walked briskly back to his car with the licensing commissioner and councilman, telling Merriweather, "Step lively, or the stench of garbage and burning gasoline will get into your clothes."

The others trudged back the way they had come, Wachter and his men smiling and chuckling, Falk and his men walking carefully to keep the mud off their shoes.

Once the Councilman was seated in his car, the mayor hesitated a moment until Falk walked close by, and said quietly, "Ed, remember what Mr. Grotski used to say, 'Sic transit gloriam mundi,'" and then, with a final wave and a smile to the others, got in the car and drove back downtown.

Getting into his car, Ed remembered the phrase: "Brief is the glory of this world."

Ocky was relaxing with one foot resting on the sink board as he watched the Friday Night Fights on the new DuMont television.

Carmine Basilio had just slammed a hook into Gaby Ferland's ribs when he heard approaching sirens.

"Ooooh, he got him a good one there, Ocky. The parrot's gonna be selling razor blades any second, now," Stash said.

When the siren stopped wailing in front of the bar, Ocky looked over the crowd for possible troublemakers wanted by the law. *Nah*, he thought, *No axe murderers, just working stiffs tonight*, while the two pinballs rang away in the corner. Then, Wachter threw the front door open, two bluecoats following.

"What the . . ."

"Mr. Owczarczak, those machines," the inspector said, pointing at the pinballs, "Are illegal in the state of New York, and we are seizing them by orders of the district attorney."

Ocky had barely got out "That son of a bitch Stormy," when he noticed something sticking out of the buttonhole in the inspector's topcoat. "Hell," he exclaimed, shaking his head as he recognized the microphone attached to the wires. Just like the ones they had planted in the bastard's office phones.

# CHAPTER 107

## ERIE COUNTY HALL, 1953

Stormy had left, and Lou sat on the edge of Pat's desk. "So, you got a date with the nurse, at last, huh?"

"Yeah, I think my good deed for the old lady turned the trick," Pat said, wondering where the old lady's son was pissing away his nickels these days.

"So, where you gonna take her?"

"Chez Ami. Johnny Ray's appearing there, tonight."

"Yeah, man. Girls love that sentimental sound," and playfully punched Pat's shoulder.

"Brogan!" the inspector said through his open office door. "Come on in here."

Lou and Pat looked at each other.

"You need me, too, Inspector?" Lou asked.

"No, just Brogan. You can go home, Lieutenant."

Lou shrugged and picked up his hat. As he headed for the door, he whispered, "Good luck," to Pat and vanished.

"Yes, sir?" Pat said presenting himself before Wachter's desk.

"Has Lieutenant Constantino left?"

"Uh, yes, sir."

"Brogan, I've got a job for you, and I expect you to do it right."

"Sir?"

"They're having a special night session of the grand jury tonight, and I need you to bring a witness there and back."

"Tonight, sir?"

"Yes, tonight. You'll be leaving right away and taking my car. This session of the grand jury should last quite a while, so stay alert while you're waiting," he said, looking Pat right in the eyes.

"Where is this witness, Inspector?"

"At my cottage up in Canada, Brogan. It's Betty Ann Harper. That's why I want you to handle it, not Lieutenant Constantino." Brogan stood there blinking.

"Whatever you had planned tonight, Brogan, cancel it, and don't tell anyone where you're going, or what you're doing. Got it?"

"Yes, sir."

"Here's the keys to my car, and here's directions to the cottage. This is important, Brogan, don't foul it up."

Going across the Peace Bridge and through the Ontario countryside to Bertie Bay, Pat tried to figure out Rita's reaction when he had told her he had to cancel their date. She didn't get mad or tell him to get lost. She didn't say much of anything when he told her he had to work tonight, just "Okay." He tried to read her voice. Disappointment, but, with him? Or, the fact she couldn't see him tonight? Did she really want to see him, or did she figure he was lying and made up an excuse? *Dammit, I hope this doesn't blow the whole thing with her.*

He got to the cottage just around sunset. It was tucked away from the roadside, and partially hidden by big oak trees. Small, but with nice flower beds laid out, and the grass neatly trimmed. He and Lou had wondered what happened to Betty, figuring the inspector had got someone else to bring her in after he dressed them down for fooling around with the witnesses. He wondered where that knockout redhead Helen was. They'd heard nothing since they put the police in Florida after her.

Pat heard the radio playing when he knocked on the door.

"Who is it?" came a happy, feminine voice from inside as he remembered the blonde's curvaceous body.

"Detective Brogan, Buffalo Police."

"I'll be right ther-rrre," she said. Her perfume, her tits under a tight sweater, and her smile all hit him at once when she opened the door. "Oh, it's you, Pat. Just give me a minute, Officer," she said with a smile, "And I'll be ready to go." She turned, her backside swinging, picked her purse up off the coffee table, and then bent forward to shut off the radio.

"Okay, let's go," she said, sweeping past him to the car. He noticed her hair was a lot longer and tied up in the back, but a blonde curl still escaped and dangled in front of her eye.

They had gone about a quarter of a mile when she ran her hands next to her along the car seat and said, "These leather seats are nice."

"It's the inspector's car," Pat said.

"I know," she said, "He comes out and visits me. With those lawyers, usually, but sometimes he brings me groceries and other stuff I need."

"How long have you been out here?"

"Oh, I dunno. Inspector Wachter had a couple of other policemen bring me out here a few days after Helen and I went out with you and Lou that night."

"Oh."

"Did you guys get in trouble?"

"No, not really."

"Yeah, I figured that. Martin's bark is worse than his bite."

"Have . . . have you heard from Helen, at all?"

"Not a word. The lawyers asked me that, too. Just dropped off the face of the earth, like. She's seen trouble before, though. I figure she can take care of herself."

The rest of the trip, Betty talked about Helen's past—growing up in Syracuse, dangerous boyfriends in New York, and her plans to move where it's warm.

After both declared their citizenship to Buffalo at the Peace Bridge, they were waved back into the United States and drove downtown to County Hall. He escorted her to the grand jury room, where she was met by a phalanx of assistant DAs and swept to her place. Pat waited outside, reading the papers and scaring up coffee from the maintenance people. When Betty came out two hours later, everyone was smiling and talking happily.

"Okay, see ya," she said to the lawyers, and strutted off with Pat.

"Well, that was kind of exciting," she told Pat on their way back to Canada in the darkness. Pat kept quiet. He couldn't see her face, but he could still smell her Chanel No. Five.

"It gets pretty boring out there in the country after a while. Listening to the radio, reading magazines, going out in the backyard. They say it's dangerous for me to go out, but a couple of times I snuck out and nothing happened. The inspector got mad once when he caught me, but he calms down quick. I guess it'll be over soon, huh, and I can go back home again."

"Dunno. I hope so, though."

"Yeah, I got a lot of catching up to do after a few weeks in the country. What's Lou been doing lately?"

"Ahh, we been working a lot on this stuff, you know. Job like this keeps us pretty busy."

"He's got a girlfriend, doesn't he?"

"Nah, not that I know about. He's been spending a lot of time studying for the captain's test, lately.

"How about you, Pat? You got a girlfriend?"

"Uhh, yeah, there's a girl I been seeing for a little while."

"Do you like Helen?"

"Yeah. . . But she's gone . . . "

When they pulled up in front of the cottage, Pat shut off the engine and watched the house for a few moments. Betty turned to him and smiled.

"Did you leave a light on in the house before we left?" Pat said. "Gee, I dunno. Probably."

Pat watched and listened for a minute. He went around the car as she got out, and she took his arm as they walked up the gravel path, the crickets going silent at their approach. Another light came on in the cottage, and Pat spotted a big shadow moving towards the door.

"Gedown!" He grabbed her shoulder and pushed her away.

"Oh!" she said, surprised and wrapped her arms around his leg to keep from falling into the bushes. He pulled out his revolver, thinking, *Damn, I wish I had my M-1 and a couple of grenades.* The door to the cottage opened, and McDougall appeared, filling up the doorway.

"Brogan. Miss Harper," the older detective said, his nod at the pistol enough for Pat to quietly put it back.

"Everything go okay?" his Scottish burr resonating in the silence.

"Just fine, Sarge," Pat said as they all went into the living room.

"The commissioner thinks we should keep a closer eye on the lady until the trial, so I or someone else will be here looking after you, Miss Harper."

"Oh," she said, inspecting the gray-haired man in the wrinkled, brown suit. "It's nice to have some company out here."

"That's good," Pat said. "You're sure to be safe with Sergeant McDougall, Betty. Well, it's a long ride back to town, and I've got to get the inspector's car back."

"Good night, lad."

"Yeah, good night, Pat. See you soon, I hope," she said.

Pat was relieved when he was on his way back to Buffalo. *That girl's dynamite,* he thought. *Secret witness, the association's bookkeeper. She might be able to hang all of them. Hiding in the inspector's cottage. That's what all the phone calls to and from Canada were about. The boss was pretty upset about some of them.*

He pulled the car up into Wachter's driveway and knocked on the side door softly around midnight. There was one light on, from the kitchen in the back. The inspector answered instantly, in his shirtsleeves, and it was the first time Pat had seen him without a tie.

"Everything go okay?" he said standing in the unlit doorway.

Pat nodded.

"Remember, don't tell anyone anything. Got it?"

"Yes, sir," he said, handing over the keys to the Hudson Commodore. A patrol car waited at the curb to take Pat home, the two patrolmen talking about how it must be nice to work in plainclothes.

# CHAPTER 108

## THE HYDRAULICS, 1953

Johnny walked into Wally's Grill and tossed the big bundle of keys to the kid, and then sat down at the bar. Lighting a Chesterfield, Johnny cleared his throat and said, "Oay, Kevin, let's see if you can fix it. Gimme a BV and plain water, there, Mr. W." With that, the dark- haired teenager walked over to the cigarette machine and examined the lock. He adjusted his glasses and sifted through the dozens of keys, looking for the ring that held the ones that opened the cigarette machines. Finding that ring amongst the half a dozen others, all of them attached together, he pulled off the *Out of Order* sign taped over the coin slot and began trying one after another to open the machine.

"New guy?" the bartender said, nodding at the youth.

"Yeah. Business is still growin' even without the pins. Hired two new guys, help us move the machines around. Now, we'll see if he can remember what I showed him."

"That was bad, what happened to Steve. The cops got a line on who killed him yet?"

Johnny shook his head and spat a flake of tobacco. "Nah, nothing yet. I been down there a bunch of times, telling them every little thing I knew about the guy, but I don't think they got anything, yet. Sad, really sad. Guy gets killed after goin' to a church picnic. Makes you wonder . . ."

"Yeah, makes you wonder what the world's comin' to."

Finding the right key, Kevin opened the machine, placed the cover to one side, and then looked the slotted coin mechanism over. Smiling, he turned the coin slots outward and tapped a stuck nickel loose. "Easy one, Johnny, just a coin jam," he said as he grabbed a bunch of coins out of the bucket at the bottom of the machine, replaced the cover, and fed them into the mechanism to test if it would work. Pulling the Chesterfield lever, the pack fell into the dispensing tray and Kevin tossed the pack up onto the bar in front of Johnny.

"Open it back up, kid. Let's cash 'em out while we're here. I'll have another one, Wally. After all, you can't fly on one wing, can ya?" Wally smiled while he poured the whiskey into the same glass, dropped one more ice cube into it, and replaced the swizzle stick from the bar. He waited in front of Johnny with the bottle in his hand until Johnny got the hint, pulling out some change for the second drink.

Kevin jingled the keys, searching for the right ones to open the pool table and the jukebox. He picked up all the cash boxes, and then they went to a back table with the bartender to split up the money and write out the receipts away from the eyes of the Penn railroad workers at the bar. Johnny was into his third BV and water when they were finished and ready to leave.

"Hey, Johnny, how about letting me drive," Kevin said, "It'll help me learn the route."

"Good idea, kid, here's some more keys for you." Johnny let his eyes adjust to the sunlight outside.

Driving down Seneca, Kevin said. "Next stop is Stengel's, right?"

"Yeah, yeah." As they approached Bailey, Johnny said, "Hey, hang on. Before we go down there, there's a guy I wanna see over on South Park. Head over there, first."

They rumbled over the bridge across the Buffalo River, driving through the smoke belching from a black-hulled ore ship below, with the fore and aft deck houses. Kevin wished he and Jack had switched places today because Jack was riding with Danny, cashing out locations up in North Buffalo. Lately Johnny was spending a lot of time "stopping by to see a guy," which usually meant knocking back a few, bitching to bartenders about the cops smashing his machines and harassing him, keeping them out on the route late.

Jim Nolan sat in his office humming "Yankee Doodle" to himself while reading the statute on juvenile assault. Finally, he slapped the book closed and, as he put it back on one of his new shelves, he heard Mary Alice in the outer office.

"No," the retired schoolteacher said, "You can't see him. I don't know who you think you are, but . . ."

"Ohhh, big shot lawyer, now," Johnny slurred. "Too good to see me, huh?"

Mary Alice tried to step between Johnny and the door, but the vendor's hand grabbed the knob and twisted it, then pushed it open, shoving her out of the way.

"Hey! Get outta there!" she shouted.

Jim stepped forward, right arm extended, and put the point of a captured Japanese bayonet against the center of Johnny's chest.

"What the. . .," Johnny sputtered.

"Out," Jim said, pushing steadily forward, the steel pushing through Johnny's shirt against his skin.

"I . . ."

"Out," he repeated, as Johnny stumbled backwards onto South Park Avenue, through the door Mary Alice had opened. Kevin's eyes went wide when he spotted this, and he jumped out of the driver's seat to guide Johnny back to the truck as Jim watched them, stepping back through the door into his office.

Inside, Mary Alice stared at the bayonet in Jim's hand. Jim said, "Uh, I've been meaning to hang this up someplace."

She cleared her throat, and then said. "I've heard of beating them away with a stick, but . . ." and they both laughed.

# CHAPTER 109

## ERIE COUNTY HALL DOWNTOWN, 1953

Betty was surrounded by lawyers when she entered the grand jury room that night. She smiled, they smiled, and the jurors smiled, or at least the men did. Assistant DA Roth and Lauria had prepared well, and when asked, "Did you ever see Mr. Owczarczak talking to Mr. Walters?" she looked out into space and said, "Yes."

"Can you tell the jury where?"

"It was at the Checkerboard Lounge."

"When was that, Miss Harper?"

"The day after Columbus Day, a year ago. It was right after they had a Vendors Association meeting."

"Did you ever see Mr. Walters give anything to Mr. Owczarczak that night?"

"Yes."

"What was it?"

"It was an envelope with four-hundred dollars in it."

"How do you know that it had four-hundred dollars in it?"

"Because Johnny, Mr. Walters, that is, gave me the money and told me to put it in that envelope at the office, just before we went to the Checkerboard."

"How do you know it was the same envelope, Miss Harper?"

"Because I saw the letter O written on it."

"What did that O mean to you, Miss Harper?"

"I dunno. I just know Johnny told me to put four-hundred dollars in the envelope, mark it 'O,' and then he put it in his coat pocket."

"Where did the four-hundred dollars come from, Miss Harper?"

"It was from a green, tin box that Johnny had at the vendors meeting every month."

"You were a bookkeeper, at the time, for the Vendors Association, were you not, Miss Harper?"

"Yes."

"Was this money ever recorded in the books for the Vendors Association, Miss Harper?"

"No."

"Where were you when you saw Mr. Walters give this envelope to Mr. Owczarczak?"

"Coming back from the ladies' room."

"Did Mr. Owczarczak know you saw this?"

"I don't think so."

"Did Mr. Walters?"

"Yes."

"Did he say anything later to you about it?"

"Yes. He said to keep quiet about our friends."

"Why do you think he did that?"

"I don't know, he was kind of funny about that. He was always showing off how he knew all these important people, taking Helen and me out when he saw them sometimes, but then he'd tell us it was all hush-hush, top secret stuff."

Even the women were nodding by the time she finished, being acquainted with more than a few men known to show off for cuties like her.

# CHAPTER 110

## ERIE COUNTY HALL DOWNTOWN, 1953

"I remember Red Carr telling his boys before they got into the ring," Steve Barry said to Lou Villardo outside the grand jury room, "'Never let 'em see you sweat,' but this guy's got 'em all beat."

"He acts exactly like he did the night he won the election," Villardo said to his fellow reporter. "Amazing."

Jazz swept down the hall, nodding greetings to some, a word to others, pointing his hat and smiling to those further away. He pulled off a long, white scarf and shrugged a brown overcoat with padded shoulders to an aide and waited outside the grand jury room "without a substantive answer to any of the press' questions," as Villardo would later write. When the door opened, the reporters stopped questioning the mayor, as a sweating License Commissioner Rybeck came out. The pressmen immediately switched their focus and the mayor entered the chamber without acknowledging his friend.

When called to the witness stand, Jazz stood up, shot his cuffs, tugged his lapels, and sat down, crossing his feet and folding his hands on his stomach after being sworn in. Roth waited a moment, and then began.

"Mr. Jezerowski, are you familiar with the Niagara Coin Operated Vendors' Association?"

"I am."

"Are you friends with that organization's President, Mr. John Walenty, also known as John Walters?"

"I am acquainted with Mr. Walters."

"Have you ever socialized with Mr. Walters?"

"Well, I've been to various functions where Mr. Walters has been present, certainly."

"Have you ever had drinks with Mr. Walters?"

A big smile crossed Jazz's face as he replied, "Counselor, in my job, I've had drinks with just about everybody in the city of Buffalo."

When the jurors stopped laughing, Roth continued his questions as Lauria fed him the papers documenting the money trail they'd established.

After watching the mayor leave the grand jury room and exchange trivialities for questions with the reporters, Steve Barry wrote, "If the mayor's demeanor is any indication, the DA's office is going to have a hard time connecting anything to City Hall."

# CHAPTER 111

## COURIER EXPRESS BUILDING
## DOWNTOWN, 1953

"Wait," the city editor said, holding up a finger to his chief, who was standing over his desk, grinding a cigarette into the rug. They both listened as Steve Barry, in the next room, banged incessantly on the steel keys. The clattering stopped, and the chief started to move. Again, the city editor held up a finger, and a moment later, the typewriter, again, rattled at a furious pace.

"Two three-second breaks means he's almost finished, but not quite," the city editor said. The chief pulled down his tie and looked at his watch. *If it isn't done in five minutes, we won't make the baseball edition,* he thought. Another pause, followed by the screech of paper being pulled out of the roller, and both men ran into the newsroom and scooped up the sweating reporter's copy. Steve Barry kicked his chair back across the linoleum floor and put his hands behind his head in relief.

The city editor read quickly and passed the copy to the chief. "The holdover grand jury investigating rackets in the city today named nine policemen, four city officials, and two others, today, in indictments of accepting payoffs to protect pinball operators in Buffalo." He continued reading, scratching his own rewrite with a pencil, as the two of them strode down the corridors onto the block wooden floor of the typesetters room.

"Headlines!" the chief shouted. "One inch print: 'Two Thousand Monthly Payoffs' at the top. 'Fifteen Indicted in Pinball Inquiry' underneath!"

"The Ivy League sonofabitch DA waited until the last minute

to announce this, just to make my life miserable," the chief reflected.

"If he really wanted to be a prick, boss, he would've waited until we'd gone to press tomorrow and let his Republican backers at the *News* get first crack at it."

"You're right. He's probably holding back something juicy for the *Evening* boys to get. Call over to The Golden Dollar and tell Cleary to get off the friggin' barstool and find out what it is!

Immediately, if not sooner!

"Lemme look at this," the city editor said. "Four high-ranking cops: Deputy Commish Falk; three captains, one in North Buffalo;. . . One plainclothesman; that hot dog Regan, down in South Buffalo; and four patrolmen. Licensing commissioner, that figures, city councilmen, two Republicans, one Democrat. One vendor, Walters, he's up to his neck in this; and Cornelius 'Ocky' Owczarczak, East Side tavern keeper and the mayor's campaign manager. Shit, Ocky's the money man. Get Villardo outta the city council meeting and get him shaking the bushes around the Broadway Market and Dom Polski. One of those Polacks over there's gotta have a grudge or two against Jazz and Ocky . . . Who's ratting out these cops? Bray's on the police beat, dammit, he's gotta find out, now."

# CHAPTER 112

## CITY HALL DOWNTOWN, 1953

Joe Jezerowski hung up the telephone and put his hands palms down on the big, wooden desk before him and wondered how bad it would get. The last phone call from his cousin, Tad, in County Hall made it sound pretty bad. Ed, Rollek, Siefert, and the rest of the captains were all indicted. The girl had come out of nowhere to testify, and several of the vendors were rolling over. *Well, let's see. No one saw me with any of those vending guys, unless it was at a big function, and they just happened to be there. The gamblers had all kept clear. I never touched any of the cash. Looks like Pfeiffer and the boys in Albany are doing this just in time for maximum exposure, figuring the trials will be in the papers for months, right up through the November elections, at least. Stone, looks like you got me.* The phone rang again.

"Mr. Ocky on the line for you, Mr. Mayor," his secretary said.

*Ahh, we're all gonna miss your strut through the offices sweetheart,* he thought, and answered, "Well, put the gentleman on, my dear, by all means."

"Hey, you hear?" Ocky said.

"I have. We should get together this evening, Ocky, and survey the current situation, take an accounting of our resources and liabilities."

Ocky knew how much money they had in his head, down to the nickel. "You want to go kegling?"

"No, I think a few private hands of cards might be in order, though. We should get there earlier than usual, I think, and talk to Ed later on, after we've discussed matters. I'll meet you there after *Family Theater* goes off the air. The wife likes when we listen to that together."

After he had hung up, Jazz looked around his office and felt his confidence ebb away for a few moments. *Hmm,* he thought, *Souvenirs for the law office on Broadway.* He picked up the heavy, brass plate that read "Mayor Joseph Jezerowski," and wondered if it would be too much to have on his desk as an attorney. *Nah,* he thought, *I'll always be the mayor to my people on Broadway. Not too showy at all. Hmm,* he wondered, *If we can hang on to most of the money Ocky's got stashed, a run for the county legislature in a few years is always a possibility.*

# CHAPTER 113

## DOWNTOWN, 1953

Martin Wachter had given specific instructions to his men that, unless they were testifying, they were not to be hanging around the courthouse as the trials progressed, for, as he said, "Gambling is alive and well in this town."

Wire rooms, numbers runners, and private clubs that tried to hide their slot machines and pinballs were the new targets while the district attorney methodically hauled three city councilmen; the licensing commissioner; and then the policemen, Johnny, and the other vendors; and Ocky before Judge Worth in a steady cascade of falling dominoes winding around City Hall.

Councilman Merriweather, after proclaiming, "This indictment is something you'd find in Stalin's Russia, a show trial of innocent people by party bosses," pleaded guilty to lesser charges, when he found out his aide, Patrick Hruska, was a witness prepared to testify about cash received from vendors, with names, dates, and times carefully recorded.

When Jazz heard about it, even he was speechless for a few moments.

Jerry Hallinan told everyone in his office "he was as prepared as Clarence Darrow ever was." He had studied the indictment of his client, Cornelius Owczarczak, examined the witness list, read the case law, and weeded out the potential jurors who might not like Polacks, saloon keepers, or have a hidden grudge against anyone in Ocky's family.

When he made his opening remarks to the jury, the tall, wavy-haired advocate took off his glasses, and a couple of the women jurors were sure they saw his eyes turn from green to blue and back again. When the court clerk mispronounced Ocky's last name, Hallinan corrected him. "It's pronounced, Off-char-zak, Mr. Clerk,"he said, which got silent nods from jurors Kajencki, Brodnicki, and Millemaci, whose mother's name was Procyk. Ready to argue anything. The night before the examination of witnesses began, Hallinan even got into a dispute with his girlfriend, Vanessa, wondering out loud how she could think they were going to the Old Spain for dinner when they were driving in the other direction, a discussion which got him an early night.

When Assistant DA Roth called Carl Verrone to the stand, Hallinan thought on what Ocky had told him.

"He doesn't know much, just played cards, and went bowling with us sometimes. Hell, Jazz helped him get his spot in the Felonies Bureau in the DA's office."

After Carl was sworn in, Roth remained seated for a moment, straightened the papers in front of him, and then stood up and tugged his suit coat straight.

"Is your name Carl Verrone?

"Yes."

"Do you live at 344 Virginia Street, Buffalo, New York?"

"Yes."

"Are you employed by Erie County in the State of New York as an assistant district attorney?"

"Yes."

"Were you present at the Royal Bowling Alleys on the night of February 6, 1952?"

"Yes."

"Who were you there with?"

"Mr. Edward Falk, Mr. Joseph Jezerowski, Mr. Herbert Dickenson, and Mr. Cornelius Owczarczak."

"By Mr. Dickenson, do you mean Judge Dickenson?"

"Yes."

"By Mr. Jezerowski, do you mean Mayor Jezerowski?

"Yes."

"By Mr. Falk, do you mean Deputy Commissioner Falk of the Buffalo Police Department?"

"Yes."

"By Mr. Owczarczak, do you mean the defendant, here, today?"

"Yes."

"Did you hear a conversation between the defendant and Deputy Commissioner Falk concerning policemen collecting money from tavern owners in exchange for not enforcing the laws against gambling?"

"I did," he replied, at which the bulbs from the newspaper cameras began to pop in rapid succession.

"What did they say?"

"Mr. Owczarczak said, 'Now that they've stomped the Vendors Association, your guys are going to have to collect the dough for yourselves. The captains might have to settle for less than the two-fifty a month they've been getting, and you're going to have to scramble to get your five hundred dollars from the bar owners and the rest of the locations.' Then, Mr. Falk said, 'What about the money that's already collected?' and Mr. Owczarczak answered, 'We'll keep an eye on that. Licensing's okay, and our guys in the Council've been taken care of.'"

"Those were his exact words?"

"Yes."

"I have no further questions."

Jerry Hallinan gripped the table and swung around it like he had wrestling opponents on the mats at the University of Buffalo. "Mr. Verrone, where were you standing when you say you heard this conversation between Mr. Falk and Mr. Owczarczak?"

"Directly behind the bench where they were sitting on lane number six."

"What were you doing when you supposedly overheard this conversation?"

"I was holding our drinks."

"Drinks? You had been drinking when you say you heard Mr. Falk and Mr. Owczarczak exchange these words? How much had you had to drink that evening, Mr. Verrone, if you can remember?"

"One eight-ounce draft beer, about two hours before I heard that conversation. The rest of the night, I was drinking pop."

"Mr. Verrone, how could you possibly understand the exact words that Mr. Owczarczak and Mr. Falk were saying in a loud, crowded bowling alley?"

"I could hear their exact words because, as I said before, I was standing directly behind them."

"Did they know you were there?"

"I don't believe so," Verrone answered, which drew murmurs from the observers in the courtroom.

Hallinan kept hammering away at Verrone like that for another half an hour, but the young lawyer stood fast, and DA Stone nodded in approval from the back of the courtroom.

The next morning before court, Ocky waited for Hallinan at the defense table. When he finally arrived, he pulled up a chair next to his client, leaned in close and said, "Along with the girl's testimony, that guy, Verrone, is hurting us bad. I just talked to Stone and he's willing to make a deal. Plead guilty now, tell him what you know about. . . City Hall's involvement, and you'll get a year and a fine."

Ocky just shook his head. Hallinan nodded and started pulling papers out of his briefcase.

# CHAPTER 114

## ERIE COUNTY HALL, 1953

"I want her dressed like a nun, or as close as you can fix it that way, anyhow," the inspector told the policewoman, who promptly left to prepare her charge for tomorrow's hearing. That drew a smile from both Lou and Pat, who didn't see how it was possible. "And you guys," he continued, pointing at the two detectives, "Especially you, Lieutenant Constantino, stay the hell away from the courtroom when she testifies. Nobody knows about you hound dogs chasing after the witnesses, and I don't want the defense attorneys getting any ideas. Got it?"

The two men nodded and withdrew.

The policewoman had chosen a long, gray, wool dress that was oversized and fairly shapeless. Her makeup and rouge were minimal, and her curly blonde locks had grown and were tied up with a ribbon at the back of her neck. The press, which had been speculating about "the missing redhead" and "the blonde bookkeeper's testimony" were quiet, but flashbulbs began to pop when Betty was called to the stand, and a few whispers were exchanged when her chest came into profile as she swiveled her hips in front of the judge's bench. After being sworn in, she sat down, tugging the gray wool as far down as she could, affording a minimal sighting of her shanks as she had been instructed.

"Miss Harper, were you employed by the Niagara Coin Operated Vendors Association?" "Yes," she nodded.

"Did you work there between July of 1949 and August of 1951?"

"Yes."

"Did Mr. John Walters, also known as John Walenty, ever give you cash money and tell you to put money in various denominations in plain, white envelopes?"

"Yes."

"How often did you do this?"

"Pretty much every month, unless Helen was doing it."

"And how much money did you put into these envelopes?"

"Three hundred dollars in two of the envelopes, and one hundred dollars in the others."

"How many others were there?"

"Six, sometimes seven."

"Were these envelopes ever marked?"

"Yeah, Johnny told Helen and me to mark them with one letter each."

"By Johnny, do you mean Mr. Walters?"

"Yes."

"Was this cash that was put into these envelopes ever entered into the books of the association?"

"No. Johnny, I mean, Mr. Walters, would bring out the money and tell us to put it in the envelopes."

"When would this happen?"

"Usually right after the association had a meeting." "Did you ever see where these envelopes went?" "Yes," she said in a whisper.

"Can you repeat that, Miss Harper? I don't think all of us could hear you."

"Yes," she repeated.

"Where did the envelopes go, Miss Harper?"

"Well, one time, Johnny picked up an envelope with three hundred dollars in it and went down the back stairs."

"And then?"

"Well, Helen got up and then was looking out the back window and said, 'There he goes, paying off the cops.'"

"And what did you do?"

"Well, I got up and looked out the window, too."

"And what did you see?"

"I saw Johnny, out in the parking lot, talking to a man."

"Anything else?"

"He gave the man the envelope."

"Do you see the man he gave the envelope to, here in this courtroom?"

"Yes."

"Can you point him out please?"

The bracelets clinked on her arm as she pointed to Falk. "That man there, in the brown suit."

"Let the record show the witness indicated the defendant Falk."

"Did you see Mr. Falk, the man you just pointed to, at any other time?"

"Yes."

"And when was that?"

"Well, another time, Johnny, I mean, Mr. Walters, snatched up one of the envelopes with the money in it and went down the back stairs again, so I looked out the window like we did before, and he gave the envelope to the same man."

"Did you see him any other times?"

"Yeah, one time we were in a restaurant."

"Which restaurant, Miss Harper?"

"The Checkerboard Lounge. Johnny bought us dinner there sometimes after work."

"I see. Continue, Miss Harper."

"Well, Johnny got up from our table and went up to the bar and talked to this man. The same man I saw him give the envelopes to."

"Thank you, Miss Harper. I have no further questions, Your Honor."

Betty gave a little smile.

The defense lawyer watched her eyes. *Hmm*, he thought, *Always on the prosecutor's table or looking down to remember something. Trained this dame well.* He rose, flexing his hands outward. He slowly walked before the bench, and then slid in front of the witness box, his hands gliding on the polished wood. Her eyes followed.

"Miss Harper, where have you been the past several weeks?"

Betty pulled her dress down her hips a little further and said, "Up in Canada."

"Why were you up in Canada, Miss Harper?"

"Well, Mr. Roth says there were some guys who might try to hurt me, so they had me stay up in a cottage there."

"Where 'up in Canada,' were you Miss Harper?"

"In Bertie Bay," she answered, and smiled, looking at the prosecutor's table.

"Were you in a hotel, Miss Harper?"

"No, sir."

"Well, where were you staying, then?'

"In a cottage," she answered, tucking a loose curl behind her ear.

"Do you know who owns the cottage, Miss Harper?" "Inspector Wachter's family," she said, nodding.

"Were you alone in the cottage all this time, Miss Harper?"

"No, sir."

"Who was there with you, Miss Harper?"

"Some policemen."

"Men or women policemen, Miss Harper?"

"Both. They kept changing."

"Which policemen, Miss Harper?"

"Uhh, well, there was Policewoman McGuire, and Sergeant McDougall . . ."

"Miss Harper, do you know why Mr. Walters had you put cash in the envelopes?"

Betty blinked a few times, and then answered, "I dunno why."

"Miss Harper, did Inspector Wachter ever spend the night up in the cottage in Bertie Bay with you?"

"Huh?"

"Were you ever alone, at night, with Inspector Wachter, in his cottage in Canada?"

"Wha? No, he never spent the night there with me alone."

"Miss Harper, did you see Mr. Walters give any of those envelopes, the envelopes with the cash, to any of the other men at the same table as Mr. Falk?"

"Uhhh, no, I don't think so."

There was a collective sigh amongst the captains on trial with Falk when Betty left the stand. The defense attorney chewed on a pencil eraser and asked the court for the right to recall the witness.

# CHAPTER 115

## DOWNTOWN, 1953

Johnny parked his car on Washington Street at the beginning of rush hour. He sat in the car for a good five minutes, looking around before he got out and walked through the brass revolving door onto the mosaic-floored lobby of the Rand Building. Ever since that broad, Harper, had testified, he felt as jittery as he did that day on Goat Island. He waited until there was a bunch of people going up before he got on an elevator up to the lawyer's office on the twenty-fifth floor.

The day before, Carmine was still answering the phones in the office when Johnny and Kevin had come back late. Before Carmine could say a word, Johnny shouted across the room, "Danny and Jack make the deposits before they went home?"

Carmine nodded.

"Good. How much was it?" he asked loudly.

"The receipts are here on the desk," Carmine answered quietly.

When Johnny strutted over and picked them up. Carmine said in a whisper, "I was talking to Mr. Tutulomundo today." Johnny nodded.

Through his teeth, Carmine said, "He wants you to see this lawyer, Sturges, downtown. He's in the Rand Building."

"Didja write his number down?"

Carmine whispered, "Suite twenty-five ten," while Kevin was finishing soldering wires on a jukebox. When he finished, Kevin closed up the machine, slapped it on the cover, and said, "Done! Need anything else?"

"Nah, kid, here, take an extra pound today," Johnny said, giving the youth a five-dollar bill. "For your overtime," he said, winkinh.

Kevin touched his forehead with the bill and left. Johnny turned and faced Carmine straight on, leaning forward on the desk. "The girl's lying, I never did any of that bullshit."

"He knows. That's why he wants you to quit screwing around with that other lawyer in South Buffalo and see this guy," he said, handing him a business card. Carmine stood up and put his coat on. "He says say we gotta protect you, Johnny. You're the one that knows this business," Carmine said and walked out.

Johnny called the number and made an appointment for the next afternoon.

Glancing up and down the hallway, Johnny stepped out of the elevator and went to the office of Geoffrey K. Sturges, Attorney at Law. Real office, and oh, yeah, a real receptionist with one of the tightest business suits he'd ever seen. Sturges, a tall man with blonde hair and a long face, met him at the door of his personal office, smiled, shook his hand, and beckoned Johnny to a big, leather chair. He offered Johnny some coffee, put an ashtray in front of him, and sat down. He put a match to his pipe, puffed the tobacco to life, dropped the extinguished match in the ashtray, and began.

"My services, Mr. Walters, have been retained by a client in Niagara Falls to represent you. I have known him for a great number of years, and he tells me that he will be responsible for any and all the fees that will accrue from your case. This case of yours, as you no doubt understand, presents certain challenges to any counsel, but challenges which my office is particularly well qualified to handle."

Johnny nodded.

"First, however," Sturges said, "There are certain formalities to be taken care of. For example, do you wish to engage me as your legal representative?"

"Well, yeah, sure."

"Excellent, then let us begin. I took the liberty to examine your indictment, and . . ."

Stepping out onto Layfayette Square, Johnny exhaled and went straight to his car, which had a ticket on the windshield. *Hah,* he thought, *Just add this to the "accrued fees," as those lawyer assholes call them. This calls for a cocktail, maybe a stop at the Checkerboard. Let everybody know I'm still in business. Nobody knows this business like I do, and everybody knows it, including that bum, Carmine.*

When Johnny left the Checkerboard, it was snowing hard. *Damn*, he thought, wrapping his collar close, *Better make my next stop close to home. I got half a bag on now, don't need to crash the car*, and went straight down Main to Allen. He couldn't find a parking spot on Allen, so, he took a left on Mariner and found a spot there. He walked back up to Allen and thought about going back to the apartment above the shop. *Nah, go see the Tapper*, and he walked to a bar with a green, brick front and the snow piling up on a striped awning. Shaking the snow off his coat, he greeted a rotund, little bartender inside. "Colder than a witch's tit out there, Tapper."

"Damn late in the season for it. Radio says there's a blizzard comin' off the lake, Johnny. What'll it be?"

Sitting down and adjusting his key ring to hang off the side he answered, "This kinda weather calls for whiskey, Tapper, my man. Gimme a Wilson's and water."

"That's all!" Tapper said, quoting the whiskey ad.

"You betcha that's all!" Johnny said, "Until I want another."

They both chuckled as another man came into the bar, shaking the snow off his hat. He sat at the bar a few stools from Johnny.

"Hey, buddy, I wouldn't sit there if I was you," Johnny said, gesturing at a piece of pipe jammed into the ceiling above him.

The man, his dark overcoat saturated with snow, looked up and jumped aside. "Jeez, what the hell is that?"

Tapper shook his head and Johnny laughed. "That's how Tapper, here, got his name, friend. Seems the deliverymen were playin' basketball with some of the kegs one day, and the ace bartender, here, went to tap one of them. Jams the rod down through the cork on the keg, but it goes right back up like a rocket to where you see it now."

Tapper tossed a rag on the bar and, touching his nose, said, "If my schnozz had been a millimeter longer, it woulda got me."

With that, the man moved a couple of stools closer to Johnny. "Oh, shit, don't want that coming back down on me."

"Tapper, get our new friend a drink on me," Johnny said, and putting out his hand, added, "John Walters, Walters Vending. If it's coin operated, we got it. If it'll fit in a machine, we'll sell it, brother."

"Thanks, John. Make mine the same."

The two new pals then proceeded to kill the bottle of Wilson's while Johnny talked about the vending business. "My luck runs hot an' cold, see. I bought my first machines after a good day at the track, see? Learned right there always to play it right out to the end, no matter wha'. Right now, I ain' quite sure how it's runnin', but I think it's gonna be okay," he said, holding up his index finger. "Hey Tapper, les' get a look at Mr. Wilson, there. Watch this, pal, my, it looks like the last two shots in the bottle. Tha' means me an' this guy get 'em on the house, right?"

Tapper shook his head and sighed.

"Don' worry, my man, you know I always take care of ya. 'Sides, we'll leave after this one." Tapper poured the last of the whiskey and rapped his knuckles on the bar.

"Tapper's a good man, my friend; we gotta make sure we leave him a good tip."

"No problem, Johnny, then I gotta go," his new friend said.

"Sure, sure, but les' finish this one, firs'."

When they finished, Johnny's new drinking buddy steadied the vendor as they walked down Allen Street. "Friggin snow, gotta be a foot of it out here too-nigh!" Johnny hiccuped. "Hell, I may not even go out in this tomorrow, it gets bad enough."

"The damn wind is a killer," his partner said.

"Well, shit, since I ain' goin' to work tomorra, let's stop up the street and get one more. I know this joint where the hooey girls hang out when it's too cold outdoors. Whaddya say?"

"Yeah, all right, but I gotta take a piss, first."

"Me, too, now that I think of it. We'll jes' go over in this alley here, take care of business."

As the streams of urine steamed off the red, brick wall, Johnny said, "Say, pal, how far you gotta go to get home tonight, anyway?"

"I live over in Lovejoy, Johnny," which was the last thing Johnny ever heard.

Some kids off of school tripped over him the next day, stiff as a board with his pants down, under several inches of snow in the alley. The coroner said he must have slipped, or been pushed and rapped his head on the wall, knocking him out. The cold did the rest. With the heavy snow that fell throughout the night and following morning, there were no footprints, a bruise on his forehead where he hit the wall, and a bloodstream full of antifreeze, the pathologist reported with a laugh. Tapper, the bartender, had gotten trapped in the bar during the storm, drank all night, and couldn't remember anything about the guy Johnny was drinking with the night he died.

# CHAPTER 116

## HUMBOLDT PARK, 1953

The inspector pulled the Hudson into his driveway, loosened his tie, and exhaled. *Almost over*, he thought, as he stepped out of the car and quickly walked to his side door. He opened the screen and walked in, hearing the radio playing in the kitchen. Up the stairs he went, taking off his coat, thinking it unusual there was no one greeting him. He opened the kitchen door, and saw the newspaper spread all over the polished wooden table. His wife, Jo, looked up at him, tear in her eyes, handkerchief clutched in her lap.

"What is it? What's happened? Are the girls all right?"

"They're. . . fine," she got out, "But what about this?" she cried, spinning the evening newspaper towards her husband. He read "Defense Attorney questions witness about relationship with police hiding place in Canada."

There were two pictures, one of Betty in the witness chair and the other of the Wachter's cottage in Canada. Betty's curly hair looked just like Jo's in the picture, he thought. The caption read, "Where Buffalo Police Hid Surprise Witness."

"You don't think . . ."

"I don't know what to think . . . It's on the radio, too," she said, waving the handkerchief towards the radio on the counter.

He looked to where he could hang up his coat, hesitated, then tossed it on a chair and knelt before his wife, now doubled over and weeping.

"Jo, she was a witness, you knew that. We had to hide her from those gangsters. They would've killed her . . . We couldn't trust some of the other policemen. I told you that."

Jo kept crying.

He took her by the shoulders and said, "It's all over now. She'll get her stuff out of there and we'll be able to spend time out there ourselves, now. "

"Those times you went out late . . ."

"Jo, I'm your husband, you and the girls are the only ones I've ever cared about . . . You've got to believe me."

She kept crying, sat up, and looked at him through her tears, "It's all over the place, what will people think?"

He stood up and said, "I can't help what people think. I did the job properly."

She looked up, and then bowed her head again and cried, "It's always the job. Now, it's in our cottage and all over the streets."

He turned sideways and put his hands in his pockets. "It'll be okay. I'll go up there after work nights and repaint the whole place."

Her crying muted, she sat up straight, and hoped he would hold her. He picked up his coat and went to hang it up in the closet. When he came back she had wiped her eyes and was calling out the back door for their two daughters to come in for supper.

# CHAPTER 117

## ALLENTOWN, 1953

When Kevin got to work, Jack was already out front shoveling snow. "Get yourself a shovel, palsy, we got money to make today," Jack said.

Inside, Danny was reading the paper and Carmine was behind the desk, rolling his gold lighter over and over on the blotter. "We got a lot of catching up to do, kid," Carmine greeted him. "People been trapped in saloons for a couple of days, putting money in the jukes, shooting pool, smoking cigarettes. Streets are getting clear, now, so we got to get 'em cashed out and filled up, pronto. Here's the keys," he finished, dropping Johnny's key ring on the desk.

"What happened to Johnny?" the younger man asked. "The paper said they found him dead, covered with snow."

"Dumb son of a bitch got all pissed up, fell down drunk in the alley, and froze to death. Now, listen, Jack and Danny will be riding together doing cash outs and moves, you take care of the service. I'll be taking care of things here. There's a shovel in the corner. Help Jack get the place shoveled out, kid, we got work to do."

# CHAPTER 118

## ERIE COUNTY HALL DOWNTOWN, 1953

Lou looked at the brass nameplate on his desk and, taking out a handkerchief, began polishing it before putting it into the cardboard box before him. The inspector, standing in his office doorway, said, "I was looking at the captain's list, Lou, and it looks like you'll need a new one of those soon."

Lou smiled and said, "Wow. Captain. It doesn't seem possible."

"You worked hard for it, son. Here, all your assignments. Scored what, a ninety-three on the test?"

Lou nodded.

"That puts you second on the list. It's sad to say, but since those guys that we nabbed got convicted, that makes several openings."

"Huh. Never planned it that way, though."

Pat came in from the office carrying the city edition of the *Evening News*.

"I dropped off all those files over at the D.A's office, Inspector. You guys hear about DC Falk?"

"No, what happened, Pat?"

"The paper says," as he laid it out on Lou's desk, "He can remain out on bail until his appeal is heard, but his suspension stays in effect. The three captains are scheduled to be sentenced next week."

Wachter came over to Lou's desk and looked at the picture of the ex-deputy commissioner, flanked by his lawyer leaving the courthouse.

"Well, I guess that's it, lads," Wachter said. "Just finish cleaning out your desks. By the way, where's Stormy?" He glanced over at Snyder's desk, still littered with coffee-stained newspapers, crunched up butcher paper sandwich wrappers, and paper bags. Pat jerked a thumb over his shoulder. "He was taking a last ride in one of the DA's cars. Said he was heading over to his new assignment in the Sixteenth Precinct 'to report in.' Had his new detective sergeant's badge hanging on the outside of his coat pocket."

"Well, that's one guy who turned himself around ... For now, anyway," the inspector said, shaking his head. "He's a hell of a policeman when he wants to be ... ," Chuckling he added, "But I'm glad I don't have to ride herd on him, anymore." Pointing at Lou, he continued, "You'll find out, 'Captain' Constantino. Wherever you get assigned, you'll find guys you practically have to dress in the morning and watch every minute to keep them on the straight and narrow." With that, he went back into his office and returned with a flask of schnapps and three metal shot glasses. Pat and Lou gave each other a surprised look but took their oversized thimbles as the inspector carefully poured the hot sweet liquor.

"Day's done, boys. Assignment completed. Here's to a job well done. Cheers," he said as they raised their shot glasses.

Lou sat back, looking at the paper. "Hey, boss, for all that work, did we really do all that much good? I mean, we know the mayor was behind a lot of this, but we didn't touch him. He's still in office, drawing a paycheck from the city."

Before he could answer, there was a knock at the hallway door. They all turned, and Leo Dunleavy stood there in a plaid shirt and khakis.

"Am I interrupting anything?" the young patrolman asked.

"No, we're just cleaning up after work," the inspector assured him, waving him over to the desk.

"Hey, Balls, how ya feelin'?" Lou asked, getting a laugh.

"You can't hurt steel, Lieutenant," he answered, getting a chortle from them all.

"To answer your question Lou," the inspector said, putting down his shot glass. "The Gambling Squad's not going out of business. We stopped something bad that was happening, and kept it from getting worse. People are always going to gamble, and there's always going to be weasels to take their money any way they can in rackets, bribes, political contributions, or whatever else they can call it. We stopped the pinball racket, but people will spend that money on numbers, lotteries, whatever they can think of next." He shook his head, and then added, "Seems like ever since the war ended, a lot more people are going for the easy money.

"Anyway, Jazz's future in politics is pretty much done. Dewey and the Republican bosses in Albany will cut him loose. He's damaged goods, whether we nailed him or not. The councilmen, the license commissioner, some of the others, they may not go to jail, but they're done politically, too, and won't be getting into the taxpayer's pockets anymore." He hesitated, and then shook his index finger and said, "But the most important thing is, we cleaned up our own department. We got those bums out of our profession—top to bottom. I hope all of you were paying attention working with McDougall. That man has forgotten more about police work than we'll ever know."

"I just came from the homicide office," Dunleavy said. "Lieutenant Hourihan says that they've come to a dead end with the Ukrainian guy's murder, pretty much when that Walters guy died, or got killed. What happens there, now? Do we just give up?"

"You're learning an unfortunate lesson about police work there, young Patrolman Dunleavy," the inspector said. "Sometimes, we don't even get all the murderers." Lou nodded, and Pat thought about McAvoy and Vicigliano. "When some of these bad actors keep their mouth shut or get killed off, the trail goes cold. But," he continued, "You keep your ear to the ground, and sometimes, eventually, somebody in a jail cell or a bar says something to somebody, and if you're paying attention and know which doors to knock on, things open up again."

They all paused, Dunleavy gritting his teeth. "What about you, boss," Lou asked. "Where are you going to wind up now that this is done? They gonna make you the deputy commissioner? I heard Commissioner Corcoran wanted to promote you there before he retired."

"Not as long as Jezerowski . . . Well, never mind that. No, my next assignment is to the First Inspection District—I'll be supervising the north side precincts, operating out of number thirteen."

"Huh, long commute," Pat mumbled, causing more silence, as they all knew the inspector was living by himself most of the time at his cottage in Canada.

"Well, boys, it's time to go," Wachter said, "Time to move back into the police department." Lou put his box under his arm and shook the inspector's hand. "Good luck, boss."

Dunleavy stepped forward and shook hands with Wachter like he was getting a medal.

"Remember, Dunleavy, keep your ears and eyes open. You've had a good beginning, young bloodhound, keep it up." Finally, turning to Brogan and taking his hand firmly, he said, "You've made a good record for yourself here, Patrick; time for you to think about promotion. The lieutenants test. They'll be needing some leadership in this department, lad; time to step up to the plate.

Pat nodded, and said, "Yes, sir," quietly.

They all took their gear and went out to the elevator in silence. Going down, the inspector cracked, "Oh, and, Brogan, make sure you tell the nurse the number at your new assignment. The D.A's office won't forward the messages." Pat flushed, and the others laughed, for he had been calling Rita daily.

Outside on Franklin, Lou turned to Pat. "Well, partner, time to ride off into the sunset. They say I might be getting the Seventeenth Precinct, so I might be up your way. Stop in and gimme a scream, hot shot."

Pat answered, "I'll try not to embarrass you there, Cap-ee-tan," as they shook hands. Pat stood there as Lou walked off, cocking his white panama hat forward. Then he stopped, turned, and said, "And get a decent hat, will ya?" touching his brim, and then he went off down the street.

As Pat walked up Church Street to Main to catch the bus, people were streaming out of the office buildings and he heard a woman's high heels clicking behind him in long strides. He turned and spotted a redhead marching the other way towards Franklin. He watched as she stopped for the light, and turned her face to look at the traffic. *No, not her,* he sighed, and he went off home to see if Rita was available that night.

# CHAPTER 119

## THE WEST SIDE, 1953

When the Cadillac pulled up right in front of the cafe on Jersey, Tutulomundo smiled and told the driver to wait, and then got out of the car without first looking around. *All this is mine, now,* he thought, as he crossed the street. He opened the door, went inside, and stood silently in the doorway until the white-shirted manager acknowledged him, and then sat at the table where he had met il Zoppo all those years ago.

The manager brought him a cup of coffee, the cup and saucer rattling slightly as he placed it on the small table with two chairs. "Will Mr. Monteduro be coming in today, Mr. T?"

Leaning back against the wooden chair, he said, "No, he is down in Florida, now. He will be moving there, year around. He wants to be close to his boy who is going to college down south there."

The manager wiped his hands on his apron and nodded.

# CHAPTER 120

## UNIVERSITY HEIGHTS, 1953

Pat was assigned a cake job that day, up in North Buffalo checking garages for stolen cars. He didn't expect to find much, and the detail put him in a car on his own, on a nice day. After about five stops, where he found all the cars properly registered, he went out to the call box at Highgate and Cordova, checked in, and put himself on lunch break. Going by the Seventeenth Precinct on Colvin, he decided to pull in and see if Lou was around. Presenting himself to the lieutenant at the front desk, he asked if the captain were on duty and available.

"I'll ring upstairs, Pat, see if he's busy," the lieutenant said. After a moment, he hung up and said, "The precinct commander will be right down." Pat looked around the big room for a moment at the people waiting to be interviewed. A crying old woman who had lost her dog, a muttering lunatic waiting to be taken back to the hospital, and a couple of fidgety scared kids playing hooky being left to worry while their parents were called. *They'll get it now*, Pat thought. *Their dads will have to leave work and will come down here and kick their asses, but good.*

"Hey! Detective Sergeant Brogan! Good to see you, pal."

Lou shook Pat's hand with both of his.

"You look great, boss," Pat said as he admired Lou's double-breasted tunic with the gold buttons running down both sides of the flap. Lou beamed and rose on his toes with pride at his new position. Then, affecting a Spencer Tracy fisherman accent, Lou said, "Very nifty suit, with shoes to match and. . . Bright, brass buttons, eh?"

Quietly, Pat leaned a little forward and said to him, "Hey,

can the captain get away for lunch?"

"Well," Lou said, looking around at the desperadoes sitting in front of the desk, "Despite the obvious crime wave," he said, lightly swinging the top of his fist into Pat's arm, "I think I might just be able to get away, especially considering the urgent business I'm sure we'll discuss," he finished with a wink and a smile.

"You remember where my dad lives right?"

"Sure, sure. Over on Woodward."

"Why don't we go over there and see what's in the refrigerator? He'd get a kick out of seeing you with your captain's bars, too."

"Great!" Then, quietly to Pat, "Watch this." Clearing his throat, he spoke to the deskman, "Uh, Lieutenant, get Patrolman Keating to bring the car around, I'll be going with Detective Sergeant Brogan to a meeting, if anyone asks."

"Yes, sir," he replied, as he picked up the phone.

Pat nodded in admiration as Lou said *sotto voce*, "Not bad, huh?"

"Pretty good, indeed, Captain Constantino. I'll meet you over there."

"Fine," Lou nodded, "I'll see you in ten minutes, as soon as they get Tom Keating out of the basement. He's got six months
to retire and spends most of his time filing papers."

Pat went out the front and hopped into the Ford, and after the V-8 engine roared to life, slipped it into gear and drove the few blocks to his dad's house, which is how he referred to it since he had moved out on his own. He pulled into the driveway and scooped the mail off the floor beneath the mail slot. Going into the dining room, he called out to his father and flipped through the envelopes, dropping the bills and the cards on the table, checking a return address on a letter for Tim (*Hey, something from that Alice girl in college*) and then he focused on an envelope for himself, marked from the U.S. Government, official business. *What the hell is this?* he thought, tearing it open. "Greetings" it read, and when his father came into the room, Pat turned to him, blinking in disbelief, and said, "They're recalling me. The Army. Friggin' Korea."

# ACKNOWLEDGMENTS

No story that occurred before the author was born can be written without help, and I needed a lot of it. Special thanks for all their help go out to:

Lt. Mike Kaska, Buffalo Police Department; Sgt. Charles Morgan, Baltimore City Police Dept. (Ret.); Ptl. Ernest Gaspari, N.Y.P.D. (Ret.); Sara Ogden, Erie County District Atty's. Office; David Pfalzgraf, Pfalzgraf, Beinhauer and Menzies; Kevin Kinal, Julune Enterprises; Jack Siracuse, the Maroon Grill Group, Ltd.; Fr. Michael Roach; Douglas Turner; Terence Hannon; the South Buffalo Boyos—William Keenan, Mary Clare Keenan, Vincent Lonergan, Tom Grinder, and Michael "Pieface" Maloney; Jim D., June B. and the rest of the crew at Ulrich's Tavern; Don Williams, Mel Pawlak, Roxanne Bennett, Teri Evansanko, Spencer Morgan, and Michael Malyak of the Steel Plant Museum; Tim Wendel; Michael D. Langan; the editors reining in my verbosity— Elizabeth Leik and Ric Cottom; 1st Lt. Mark W. Hannon, 65th Infantry Division, Third Army; Ernie Imoff, Editor in Chief, the *Baltimore Evening Sun*; Manny Dare; Pete Barone; Sam Voltolino; Jeffrey Lawton; David Silverman of the National Pinball Museum; Daniel Dilandro, Peggy Hatfield and Mary Ruth Glogowski at the E.H. Butler Library at Buffalo State College; Jack Messner & the other great people at the Lower Lakes Marine Museum; the Staff in the Grosvenor Room of the Buffalo and Erie County Public Library; Erik Brady; George Sicherman; James Dierks; The DC Wildcats—Chase Hieneman, Linda Maxwell, Jason Nehmer, and David Hubbard; Cynthia Van Ness and the Buffalo and Erie County Historical Society, and Joel Silverstein.

These people were most generous with their time and knowledge. Any historical inaccuracies and other blunders are all my own.

And finally, thanks to Mary Del Plato and Alexandra Chouinard from Apprentice House for their design, editing and marketing expertise along the way.

—M.H.

# ABOUT THE AUTHOR

Mark Hannon is a retired firefighter who grew up in Buffalo. This is his first novel.

Apprentice House is the country's only campus-based, student-staffed book publishing company. Directed by professors and industry professionals, it is a nonprofit activity of the Communication Department at Loyola University Maryland.

Using state-of-the-art technology and an experiential learning model of education, Apprentice House publishes books in untraditional ways. This dual responsibility as publishers and educators creates an unprecedented collaborative environment among faculty and students, while teaching tomorrow's editors, designers, and marketers.

Outside of class, progress on book projects is carried forth by the AH Book Publishing Club, a co-curricular campus organization supported by Loyola University Maryland's Office of Student Activities.

Eclectic and provocative, Apprentice House titles intend to entertain as well as spark dialogue on a variety of topics. Financial contributions to sustain the press's work are welcomed. Contributions are tax deductible to the fullest extent allowed by the IRS.

To learn more about Apprentice House books or to obtain submission guidelines, please visit www.apprenticehouse.com.

Apprentice House
Communication Department
Loyola University Maryland
4501 N. Charles Street
Baltimore, MD 21210
Ph: 410-617-5265 • Fax: 410-617-2198
info@apprenticehouse.com • www.apprenticehouse.com